Praise for Harold Coyle and *They Are Soldiers*

"Harold Coyle is a superbly talented storyteller . . . the Tom Clancy of ground warfare." —W.E.B. Griffin

"Nobody knows war like Harold Coyle, and nobody writes it better." —Stephen Coonts

"Coyle is a master at high-tech suspense. He spins his story with such power that you're swept along to the climatic finish." —Clive Cussler

"Harold Coyle has been dubbed the Tom Clancy of ground warfare and it's easy to see why. He focuses on the grunts because no matter how fancy the weapons are, eventually the military has to send in men to take and hold new territory." —*The New York Post*

"Coyle's attention to detail, and his intimate knowledge of small-unit fighting is remarkable. On top of that, his story is told with an implied, 'we'll soon be there' quality, like an ominous echo of today's headlines." —Thomas Fleming

"Disturbingly plausible. . . . Describes in excessive detail the heroic patriotism of the military men and the complexities of the U.S. Military situation. . . . A solid read." —*Publishers Weekly*

"[A] shatteringly suspenseful tale of near-future military engagement." —*Kirkus Reviews*

ALSO BY HAROLD COYLE

THEY ARE SOLDIERS

HAROLD COYLE

TOR®

A TOM DOHERTY ASSOCIATES BOOK
NEW YORK

This is a work of fiction. All the characters and events portrayed in this book are either products of the author's imagination or are used fictitiously.

THEY ARE SOLDIERS

A Tor Book
Published by Tom Doherty Associates, LLC
175 Fifth Avenue
New York, NY 10010

www.tor.com

Tor® is a registered trademark of Tom Doherty Associates, LLC.

ISBN 0-765-34460-2
EAN 978-0765-34460-1
Library of Congress Catalog Card Number: 2003071107

First edition: August 2004
First mass market edition: March 2005

Printed in the United States of America

0 9 8 7 6 5 4 3 2 1

THEY ARE
SOLDIERS

PROLOGUE

Normandy, France, 6 June 1944

The transformation that had taken place in the span of a few hours startled Jonathan Faucher. Standing upon the same cliffs that the German defenders had fought so hard to hold, the young Virginian looked down at the strip of gravel and sand he and his companions had stormed across that morning. It was difficult for him to fully comprehend the magnitude of what he was looking at. The beach that had been swept by machine-gun fire was now teeming with American soldiers and equipment. Everywhere he looked were tanks, half tracks, jeeps, trucks, and prime movers hauling guns and howitzers of every caliber and description. Mixed in among this wild assortment of tracked and wheeled vehicles were bulldozers laboring to cut roads leading from the gapping mauls of the monstrous Landing Ship Tanks and up along the winding defile that sliced through the very cliffs Faucher stood upon. Even as he watched, men and machines filled a newly cut stretch of road. Anxious to leave the chaos of the beach behind them, they began their journey inland to join the battle that Faucher was now leaving.

The sprawling display of armed might before him so mesmerized Faucher that he almost managed to forget his left arm. Shattered by a German grenade, it now hung limply across his chest supported by little more than a sleeve that a harried battalion medic had pinned to his fatigue shirt. The wound had earned Faucher the right to retrace his steps back to the beach. Since transportation at the front was still sparse, those wounded who could do so were patched up as best as conditions allowed and sent on their way to seek out the makeshift field hospitals in the rear. From his perch on the cliff, it was not hard to spot the conspicuous red cross on white background blazoned upon the OD green tents below. After determining how best to get from where he stood to the field hospital, the young Virginian carefully secured his wounded limb with his good arm and braced himself to make his way against the oncoming tide of fresh troops.

During this solitary trek, Faucher became aware of the hushed silence that greeted him as he passed the endless files of fresh soldiers going in the opposite direction. At first he had no idea as to what was causing them to cease their cheerful if nervous babble, the same sort of chatter that he and his own friends had engaged in that morning before climbing down a rope ladder and into the waiting landing craft. Looking from face to face he tried to discern what it was that was striking mute men who were ostensibly no different from himself as he approached. It never dawned upon him that he no longer was like them. The bloody sleeve that he gingerly cradled with his good hand was more than a harbinger of the physical destruction that awaited them. It was a chasm, a great psychological divide. The men who had just stepped off the landing craft and marched across the beach without giving that act a second thought had yet to taste battle. Despite proud boasts and the manufactured self-confidence that their training had instilled in them, none knew for sure how they would respond when they came face-to-face with the enemy. Even to the dullest among them, it was clear that the bloodied and bedraggled Virginian making his way past them, had not only faced and mastered that greatest of all challenges, but was coming away from it with what a writer of another age dubbed a red badge of courage.

The gulf that separated the lone Virginian and the troops bound inland cut far deeper than either party could have imagined, for the damage inflicted to Faucher's arm was trivial in comparison to the loss which his mind had yet to come to terms with. Just how devastating his brief flirtation with battle had been struck him as he approached the temporary field hospital that had been set up to deal with those who had fallen that morning.

With an eye toward shielding the freshly arriving troops from the horrors of war for as long as possible, the day's harvest of dead had been gathered up from the surf line and tucked away behind the hastily erected hospital tents. The follow-on forces would have to wait until after they were locked in their own battles to be introduced to this aspect of war. Faucher, on the other hand, was going against the planned flow. Approaching the field hospital from the land side, the young Virginian found that he had little choice but to pass the open-air mortuary. Nothing hid from his unblinking eyes the rows of pale white corpses, dressed in fatigues soaked in seawater and their own blood. In a day when he had faced one stunning new experience after another, the sight of these shattered remains neatly stretched out and left unattended, proved to be the most devastating to Jonathan Faucher.

Coming to a dead stop, he gazed down upon the bodies of men who had been as alive as he was mere hours before. Against his better judgment Faucher began to search the faces of the dead in an ill-advised effort to see if any of his companions were among them. The first he recognized was Tommy Jarrick, a lad he had gone to school with. He and Tommy had played together on the very same fields where their grandfathers had fought the Yankees during the War of Northern Aggression. Since none of the boys wanted to be the Union, they had been forced to wage war against an imaginary foe. Of course, Tommy and Jonathan Faucher had always won, just as they had that morning. But the foe that had been waiting for them on the cliffs that loomed above the beaches had not been imaginary. Even before

Tommy Jarrick was able to step foot off of the landing craft and into the swirling surf, he was struck down dead by an enemy who was all too real.

Slowly, as if in a trance, Faucher made his way along the rows looking at each and every man who wore the blue and gray patch of the 29th Infantry Division. He paused when he came upon Francis White. Both he and Francis had joined the National Guard together in 1939. When the 176th Infantry Regiment had been federalized in 1940, every member of their two families who could manage to do so had gathered at the train station to see them off. It had been an exciting time, one charged with all sorts of emotions. Now as he looked down about the shattered remains of his friend, Faucher found himself overwhelmed for the first time with what he had been compelled to do that day merely to survive. In the scramble to get out of the landing craft and make it to shore where he hoped to find cover to hide behind, Jonathan Faucher had stepped on the body of a man who had become something more than just a good friend and companion. How, he found himself wondering as he turned his back once more on his friend, do you explain to someone's mother that you trampled across her son as he was drawing his last breath.

The next face he recognized belonged to Ed Frazier. Ed had been a deputy sheriff. Though he was but a few years older than Faucher, Frazier's peacetime duties and his broad shoulders had instilled a degree of maturity and strength in him that made Ed a natural squad leader. Even after four years everyone still referred to him as the Deputy as much out of respect as habit. Along the surf line that morning it had been Ed who had managed to rally those who had survived the slaughter that had occurred when the ramp of the landing craft had been dropped right in the line of fire of a German machine gun. With the same calm demeanor that he had used time after time to defuse many a barroom fight back home, Ed led his diminished gaggle of Guardsmen ashore and through the killing zone. Just when he had gone down was hard to tell. Like everyone else that morning, Faucher's full attention had been riveted upon assaulting the cliffs that bristled with enemy positions. Only after they had scaled those cliffs and metered out upon the Germans the same cruel punishment that they had inflicted upon the Virginians did anyone notice that their Deputy was no longer with them.

Farther along Faucher came across Brian McIntire. Someone had thoughtfully covered what was left of his face with a scrape of discarded canvas. Yet even with that Faucher was able to recognize the lanky frame of the man who was arguably the oldest and most ill-starred member of the National Guard unit that hailed from Bedlow, Virginia. McIntire had once been the proud owner of a men's clothing store before the Depression. Its loss and the hard times that followed did nothing to diminish a cheerful disposition that knew no season. Whether he was picking apples in the fall at a local orchard or doing odd jobs about town in an effort to support his fledgling family, Brian always had the time to greet all comers with a ready smile and a warm hello. Even during their run in to the beach that morning Brian had somehow managed to find the strength to push aside his own fears and flash a warm smile Faucher's way. As the young Virginian looked down at the faceless body at his feet, he wondered if Brian was still smiling when he jumped in front of him and took a burst of German small-arms fire that had been meant for him.

Unable to go on, Faucher just stood there. Slowly he turned this way, then that like a lost child. The bodies at his feet belonged to men no different than me, he found himself thinking. Most had been born and raised on small farms that barely sustained the families that lived upon them. To a man they had survived a grueling depression that spanned an entire decade and all but squeezed every bit of hope and joy from their lives. Yet when their nation had called none of the men he knew had hesitated. As one they took up arms to save a world that they knew precious little about.

Now, as the wounded young man stood rooted to the bloody ground they had fought over that morning he realized for the first time that they were gone, gone forever. None of them had given their lives. None of them had come to this place to die. They had been killed. Struck down in midstride in a manner that was as random and capricious as it was awful. Yet somehow he had lived. He had survived the butchery that had taken so many of his friends. As terrible as it was for Faucher to see their lifeless bodies all about, even worse was the realization that was only now beginning to slowly worm its way into his exhausted and stunned mind. He was on his own, alone in a foreign land where madness and death were the order of the day.

Pushing his way out of the hastily thrown-up tent that served his unit as an aid station, Carl Baxter staggered into the fresh sea air for the first time in hours. Overwhelmed by the horror that he had been helping to sort, the young medic needed a moment alone, a few seconds to clear his head. With shaking hands he nervously fished through his pockets in search of a cigarette. Finding one, he pulled it from his pocket and raised it to his lips. He paused, however, when he saw that it and his hands were coated with blood, the blood of countless young men he had been struggling to save. They had saved many of them, but not all. Angered by this and his inability to escape his grim duty, Baxter threw the tainted cigarette aside.

Lifting his eyes, he stared into the leaden gray skies above. Today was his nineteenth birthday, a fact that he somehow managed to forget. How many of them, he wondered as he lowered his eyes and gazed upon the silent rows of those who never again would celebrate another birthday, were nineteen?

He was pondering this question when he saw Faucher standing there alone and forlorn among the dead. Though he needed a break himself in order to regain his own emotional balance, Baxter could not turn away from a situation that he suspected was unhealthy. Stepping carefully between the corpses, he came up behind Faucher. Reaching out he took Faucher by his good arm and gently pulled him away. "We need to have that wound looked at, my friend," he stated in a calm, low voice filled with true concern. "I know just the doctor who can help you."

Like a child being led away by a parent, Faucher made no effort to resist. Only when they were about to enter the tent did he pause. Turning, he looked back at the silent rows of men who bore the patch of the 29th Infantry Division. "They were all good men, you know. Each and every one."

Baxter nodded. "They still are. I guess they always will be." Then, with his own vision becoming obscured by tears welling up in his eyes, the medic tugged at Faucher. "Come on. We need to get that arm taken care of."

CHAPTER 1

West Bank

For the Israeli soldiers belonging to Isaac Mofaz's squad, the drudgery and monotonous repetition that manning a checkpoint entailed often proved to be nothing short of maddening. It was far worse than normal guard duty. With the exception of casting a leery eye upon the odd character who lingered too long in close proximity to one's post, an armed sentinel standing watch had little to do. Checkpoints were a different matter all together. From the moment one assumed his tour until the next relief showed up, a soldier at a checkpoint had to be on his toes as he dealt with endless lines of impatient and sullen civilians anxious to get on with their daily chores.

The company to which Mofaz's squad belonged was responsible for a stretch of road in the West Bank that lay between an ancient Palestinian town and a refugee camp. In an effort to block the flow of arms and explosives between the two a wide antivehicle ditch had been dug right in the middle of the road forcing anyone who desired to go from one site to the other to do so on foot. While militarily sound, the obstacle came to be hated by both sides. To the residents of the refugee camp who relied upon the shops and marketplace in the town and the businessmen in the town who depended upon the cheap labor that came from the camp, the antivehicle ditch was more than an inconvenience. It was an open wound, another painful reminder that they were little more than victims of an age-old conflict that defied all logic and resolution. For the soldiers charged with manning the checkpoint at the footbridge that straddled the ditch, it meant dealing with people who made little effort to conceal their seething contempt and hatred for them.

Mofaz and the men in his squad had no sympathy for the Palestinians. To a man each and every one of them knew someone who had suffered the loss of a friend or family member to a terrorist attack. Mofaz himself was an uncle to a girl who had lost both legs before she was even old enough to walk on them. It was the memories of such horrors that spurred him and his squad to carry out their dreary and irksome duties with a greater degree of vigor and thoroughness than circumstances called for.

This routine never varied. Over time the faces of the people coming and going assumed a sameness that dulled the senses, made the long hours longer, and engendered an air of indifference within the Israelis when dealing with the Palestinians who had no choice but to endure whatever treatment the soldiers were in the mood to serve up. Civilian foot traffic coming from the refugee camp wishing to cross the bridge queued up along the road behind a white "call forward" line painted on the pavement thirty meters away from where the checkpoint was located at midspan. The actual checkpoint itself was a sandbag bunker. Standing a little over three meters high, it had assumed an air of permanence, just like the Israeli soldiers who occupied it. At the base of the bunker, a trio of soldiers inspected all ID cards and searched every parcel, package and bag carried by each and every Palestinian going from the refugee camp to the town.

The procedure was the same regardless of age or gender. While one Israeli soldier took the ID card being offered by the Palestinian and compared the photo on it to the face, a second patted the civilian down and riffled through any bags or packages they might be carrying. The third member of this party stood with his back against the sandbag wall of the bunker, cradling his weapon in his arms with the thumb of his right hand resting on the weapon's safety as he watched both his comrades and the Palestinian before them. Within the sandbag bunker two more members of the duty squad provided backup for the soldiers who were in continuous contact with the Palestinians. This was where Sergeant Isaac Mofaz normally stood his watch. When standing on the firing step within the bunker he could look out over the heads of his own men and see what was going on at the checkpoint as well as beyond the call forward line. If something happened, which never had during any of his tours of duty here, there was a radio within the emplacement that he could use to call for assistance that would come in the form of a platoon-sized ready reaction force located in a fortified compound little more than five kilometers away. Until that help arrived Mofaz's squad would be on its own.

This by no means meant that they were helpless. On the contrary, Mofaz's squad was armed to the teeth. In addition to their own individual weapons, there was a 7.62mm machine gun mounted on the parapet. From there it had a clear field of fire that swept an area well beyond the call forward line. At the foot of the bridge on the near side of the ditch facing the town was the squad's armored personnel carrier or APC. Like their comrades in the bunker on the bridge the driver and a junior NCO stood ready with their American built M-113 armored personnel carrier throughout the entire tour of duty watching over a second trio of soldiers as they checked IDs and searched packages of the Palestinians approaching the bridge from that direction. To provide covering fire for them the two soldiers manning the APC relied upon the M-2 Heavy Barrels .50-caliber machine gun mounted on their vehicle. In addition to laying down suppressive fire using a weapon capable of spewing out slugs measuring half an inch in width at a rate of up to 450 per minute, the crew of the M-113 also had to be ready to rush forward onto the narrow bridge itself if the situation really got out of hand and it proved necessary to retrieve their comrades.

Day in, day out, the Israelis were there, executing their assigned duties while bearing up as best they could under the blistering afternoon sun or bitter cold of night. Like the demeanor of the people passing back and forth over the bridge, their presence assumed an irritating sameness that was almost painful to endure. As noisome as these mindless and routine duties were for the Israeli soldiers who performed them, in the eyes of some they paled in comparison to what the people who had to pass through the checkpoint suffered. They were the ones who experienced the degradation of being hassled and harassed in this manner on a daily basis by soldiers as they tried to go about their business in the town or return to their homes in the refugee camp. Few of the residents of the camp had a refrigerator that could hold more than a day or two's perishables. This meant that someone in every family living there had to cross the bridge that separated them from the marketplace in the town almost on a daily basis. One very vocal resident compared the experience of living like this to trying to breathe with an Israeli boot planted squarely on their throats.

Heaped upon inconvenience was humiliation. To the Palestinians the checkpoint was more than another nuisance imposed upon them by a people they saw as an enemy. It was a physical reminder that they were little more than hostages within their own homeland. To them the soldiers were an alien presence in their midst, a harsh reminder that they had no control over their own lives or futures.

All of this contributed to the atmosphere that was both tense and volatile. The Israeli soldiers didn't want to be in the West Bank and the Palestinians didn't want them there. As so often happens when a situation such as this exists there were some who were eager to do more than simply bemoan their fate. And just as there always seemed to be men and women ready and willing to take action, there were those ready to provide them with the means of doing so.

One such man was Syed Amama. It hadn't taken much to convince the young Palestinian student to act. Like most of his young companions he could recite without hesitation a litany of grievances that had become little more than a fixture of the rhetoric that passed for political discourse between Muslims and Jews. He could lay out in detail the chronology of events that led to the current sad state of affairs and explain why all blame belonged to the Jews.

Just as the driving force behind the willingness of Mofaz and his men kept them at their duty, Syed's uncompromising hatred of the Jews sprang from the sort of truth that no one outside the region dared to admit. It was simply the way things were. Syed was a Palestinian. From birth he had been taught to hate the Jews. Throughout his childhood the notion that they were evil incarnate was hammered home to him and his compatriots every time the Israelis launched a foray into the Palestinian areas of the West Bank to bulldoze the homes of suspected terrorists. The lingering stench of death that freely mixed with the pungent odor of diesel fumes thrown off by Israeli tanks created a terrible resolve within Syed and others like him that could only be assuaged by the total eradication of his hereditary foe. Though his education had prepared him for entry into a university in Egypt, the circumstances of his people lured him to follow another path, one that promised to be a more violent, far less enlightened future, and incredibly short. Rather than becoming a teacher, a wellspring of knowledge, Syed had chosen martyrdom.

The path to this glorious end was easily found. In Syed's case, it led him to the doorstep of a shadowy organization known as the Palestinian Liberation Army. Like the al-Aqsa Brigade, Hezbollah, and Hamas, the PLA had but one goal: the destruction of Israel. And like its sister organizations, its main weapon was terror. The PLA cell or squad that Syed became a part of was made up entirely of impatient young men such as himself, Palestinians who saw themselves as patriots. To a man they believed they had both a political mandate and a sacred duty to use direct action to liberate their land and redress the wrongs that the Jews had visited upon their people. That this action might entail his own death as well as those of other Palestinians who did not share his ardent convictions did not matter to Syed. After suffering under the daily humiliations that the Israelis inflicted upon his people, Syed had come to view such a death as a form of liberation. "Is it not better," he queried friends and family alike without telling them of his secret life, "to live one day as a lion than one hundred years as a sheep?"

Convinced of the righteousness of his cause and his ability to view his assignment with the same cold analytical technique he used to solve math problems, the young Palestinian was surprisingly calm as he stood in the queue behind the call forward line. One by one he watched his fellow citizens advance when the Israeli inspecting the ID cards beckoned to them. Syed didn't feel any need to cast a leery eye behind him where a pair of his companions lay in wait with a Russian-made RPK-74 machine gun. Ironically this weapon was a relic of another ideological conflict that had once commanded the same unquestioning dedication to diametrically opposed views of the nature of things that the current Israeli-Palestinian conflict demanded of its participants. This cynical little twist was not lost on any of the half-dozen Palestinians who were part of this action. Syed had no trouble picturing the smiles on the faces of his two companions as they watched and waited to open fire with the gun they had named "Justice."

The idea that they might fail to strike a telling blow never entered Syed's mind. They were after all but half of the equation. On the opposite side of the footbridge was another trio of equally determined young Palestinians waiting to mimic every action Syed and the pair with the machine gun were about to play out. Though he hoped that he would have the privilege of striking first, it did not matter. In the end the results would be the same. Israelis would die, Palestinians would be revenged, and the teachings of the Koran would be met.

One by one the people waiting made their way to the sandbag bunker where the Israelis stood, doing little to hide their boredom as they checked ID cards and searched bundles. It wasn't until there were but two people left between Syed and the Israeli that he began to brace himself for the attack. It had been decided that his companions manning the machine gun would break their concealment and open fire when there was still one person between Syed and the call forward line. The response of the unsuspecting and wholly innocent person in front of Syed would be a natural reaction to the sudden mayhem that would break out as soon as gunfire erupted. This, it was hoped, would draw any attention away from the foot traffic as the Israelis scattered in search of cover and sized up the situation before they began to exchange fire with the Palestinian machine-gun emplacement. If nothing else, the unwilling Palestinian would provide Syed with a shield that he could hide behind as he prepared to dash forward with his bundle of explosives.

The only aspect of the entire plan that troubled Syed was the question of whether it would truly be better if the action was initiated by the machine gun supporting him or by the team on the opposite bank. On the one hand he rather cherished the heroic imagery of charging forward into the teeth of enemy fire that would be directed against his comrades once they opened fire. Like so many young men who had never experienced war firsthand, Syed's view of combat was untainted by the harsh realities of combat. The images and notions concerning the events that he was about to participate in contained far more Hollywood and none of the horror.

The outbreak of automatic fire from the near side of the river where the squad's APC sat startled everyone on the bridge. Mofaz's response would have been comical under any other circumstances. While the man who was with him did his best to pull his head in between his shoulders as he threw himself against the sandbag walls of their emplacement, Mofaz fought his own urge to seek cover. Instead he exposed himself as he tried to sort out what was going on around him. Because he had not been on the firing step of the sandbag emplacement and hadn't yet thought to leap up onto it, the Israeli NCO stood on his tippy toes, craning his neck out as far as he could in order to see over the parapet. Like a giant bird startled by an unexpected threat, his eyes darted this way then that in an effort to identify the source of the gunfire and the effect it was having. By the time he was facing the proper direction, the three men who had been on the checkpoint leading out of the town were on the ground.

As if he were totally divorced from what was going on around him, Mofaz took in the unfolding situation. One of his men lay on his back, sprawled out on the pavement and thrashing about. Though Mofaz had never been in combat before, it was clear that the man had been hit. As he watched, he caught sight of another member of his squad crawling forward to where his stricken comrade lay while the third had managed to bring his assault rifle up to his shoulder and began to return fire. The soldier manning the APC's machine gun wasted no time in supporting him in this effort. Though the first rounds fired by that weapon were wild and no doubt were wide of the mark, Mofaz saw that the gunner was quick to adjust his aim point and delivered an effective second burst that succeeded in silencing the Palestinian machine gun.

With everyone's attention focused on the concealed position from which the Palestinian fire had come from, no one was paying much attention to the cluster of Palestinian civilians who had gone to ground at either end of the bridge. By the time Mofaz saw him, the young man clutching a nondescript backpack was already on his feet and sprinting toward the squad's APC. It took but a second for the Israeli NCO to realize what was going on. In desperation, he finally jumped up onto the firing step and began to yell out a warning for all he was worth.

It was already too late. Once the crew of the APC had managed to bring their machine gun into play, the soldier at the checkpoint who had been returning fire ceased doing so, turning his attention instead to helping his mate retrieve their wounded comrade. In stunned disbelief both the unwounded soldier and the Israeli on the ground watched the Palestinian fly past them. An effort to reach out and grab the man by the leg as he went by, came up short. So too did Mofaz's feeble attempt to bring his own weapon into play though he continued to struggle unslinging it even as he turned in desperation to the three men who had been standing before the sandbag emplacement. None of those soldiers had needed to be told what to do. To a man they turned their backs on Syed and his still silent comrades, stepped out into the middle of the bridge, raised their weapons, and made ready to fire on the lone Palestinian making for their APC. None realized that by doing so they had set themselves up.

The failure of the men manning the machine gun nicknamed "Justice" to open up angered Syed. Impatiently, he lay on the ground among his fellow Palestinians, wondering if his companions were ever going to fire. He had no way of knowing that his companions were frantically trying to coax, cajole, or beat their antiquated weapon into functioning properly. After cycling the gun by hand several times, the senior member of the pair ignored the pleas from his partner to cease his efforts and strip down the weapon and replace the bolt. Instead, he lashed out at the mindless mass of steel and plastic, bringing his fist down upon the receiver. To his surprise, the gun began to function, erupting in a hail of fire and bullets.

Because of the crew's efforts these first rounds were wide off their mark, missing the Israelis, their bunker, and even the bridge. Not even Syed, who had been waiting for the report of the machine gun, took note of where those first rounds spiraled off to. This was not entirely bad, for the resolution of the machine gun's malfunction occurred just as the three Israelis who had been facing Syed were making ready to fire on the Palestinians attacking the APC. Thrilled by the fact that "Justice" was now operational, the Palestinian gunner took a deep breath, tucked the weapon's butt firmly into his shoulder, and drew a bead on the exposed Israeli on the span below. The effects of his first aimed burst was devastating.

Even before the last of the Israelis before him toppled over onto the ground, Syed was on his feet and running for all he was worth. Everything around him began to take on an unreal feel to it. Images no longer flowed seamlessly together into a single coherent picture. The best he was able to manage were quick, blurry snapshots of seemingly random events as they flashed before his eyes. Shouts and screams in Hebrew and Arabic alike mingled with the rattle of small-arms fire. Everything, even his own thoughts, was a jumble. What was never in doubt was Syed's goal or, if the truth be known, his ability to achieve it.

Having committed himself, the fanatic young man abandoned all caution as he concentrated on charging home. In the process of doing so he reached into the backpack clutched to his chest, seized the ring on the side of the satchel charge tucked inside, and gave it a quick tug. Ignoring everything but the sandbag emplacement before him, Syed pressed on. When he was but a step or two away, he hoisted the backpack up over his head until it was level with the lip of the emplacement's parapet. Only when he was sure that it would be impossible to miss did he fling the explosive package up and over the sandbag wall.

* * *

Overwhelmed by events that were spinning out of control all about him, Isaac Mofaz found himself stunned into inactivity. In horror he watched as his APC was shattered under the force of the explosives delivered by the first Palestinian attack. He was all but numb to the sight of his own men staggering under a hail of hostile gunfire that pelted them from both sides of the river. Not sure which way to turn or how best to respond, Mofaz did nothing even when he was hit in the side of the head by a bundle that came flying over the bunker's parapet. Like a sleepwalker the Israeli NCO gazed down at Syed's backpack before closing his eyes and whispering, "Dear God!" for the last time.

CHAPTER 2

Bedlow, Virginia

Postal routes tend to take on a character all their own. It is a strange chemistry that is based as much upon an area's geology as its demographics. Equally important to this indescribable brew is the personality of the letter carrier. How he or she interacts with his or her surroundings and the people they serve is crucial in determining just how much a postal worker enjoys his duties. As in all things, the sense of accomplishment and purpose a postal worker derives from his duties is reflected back via the quality of the service they render to their assigned communities. As with any relationship, a bad match makes for a miserable existence, which in turn yields poor performance. Brian McIntire came to appreciate this unwritten truth shortly after he began working for the Postal Service. He stumbled upon it while working a rural route linking numerous small farms and scattered homes that surrounded the town of Bedlow.

McIntire was a quiet man, one who cherished the semi-independence that being a letter carrier gave him. Yet he enjoyed being around people. He was, as one friend liked to say, the best listener in the county. Disarmed by his quick smile and honest face, everyone who knew him felt compelled to bend his ear whenever the opportunity arose. Even casual acquaintances were quick to engage the sandy-haired native of Bedlow in conversations that included intimate details that at times caused McIntire to blush. On his part, it made no difference how hectic his day had been or heavy the load, he would set aside whatever personal or professional concerns he might have and bestow a service that was not found in any job description. Like the motto of the Postal Service, "neither rain, nor shine, nor heat of day" could dampen his willingness to take the time to stop, listen, and when it seemed appropriate, share his views on whatever subject was thrown his way. By giving his full and undivided attention to an elderly retiree starved for companionship or a small child just home from school dying to share a secret with someone, Brian McIntire delivered something to the people of Bedlow that no envelop or wrapping could hold.

This relationship was not a one-way street. Like most of the people he had grown up with McIntire had no burning desire to leave the sleepy rural community that was nestled in the southern portion of the Valley. A tour of duty with the Navy had allowed him to see the world beyond Bedlow, a world he was more than happy to leave to others. By the time he had finished his first enlistment, he had come to the conclusion that he was destined to pass his remaining days in the same quiet manner that the town that was a part of him had through the ages. This, by no means, meant that he lacked personal desires or ambitions. Like every young American male, he possessed an innate need to be an individual, to somehow stand out within the pack to which he belonged without abandoning its code of ethics or changing its character. While some of his buds made their marks by driving the biggest, baddest pickups that they could afford and others settled for simple tattoos, McIntire was able to capitalize upon his God-given ability to deliver both the mail and companionship to the people of his community. The twenty-six-year-old postal worker relished his role as mutual friend, father confessor, and all-round good guy to people who had never understood what all the fuss over school prayer had been about and still believed that tradition was a virtue. It made him something special and allowed him to stand out in a community that often seemed to be as changeless and steadfast as the silent mountains that flanked the Valley of Virginia.

That was why he didn't much care for those routes that connected the outlying farms and isolated homesteads with the rest of the world. The long drives between stops, the forlorn mailboxes set along roads far from houses, and the dearth of people with whom he could interact during the day accentuated the loneliness McIntire felt when working such routes. Only a volley of complaints leveled at a fellow postal employee saved him from languishing in this social purgatory for very long. When the opportunity to work the business district of Bedlow presented itself, he did not hesitate. Before he had completed his first week along his new route, he confessed to his wife that he felt "as if I've died and gone to heaven."

While their fellow Americans on the East and West Coasts were going about the serious business of dealing with the turbulent twists and turns of the twenty-first century's first decade Brian McIntire and the people of Bedlow were content to stay where they were, living the sort of lives that suited them just fine. In short order the quiet letter carrier fell into a daily rhythm and routine that the store and shop owners along his route enjoyed as much as he did. It didn't seem to bother any of them that their mail was being delivered a little later in the day. To people who measured time in terms of generations rather than nanoseconds this inconvenience was hardly noticed. Far more important to them was a visit, no matter how short, by their good friend Brian who delivered a quick smile along with their mail. His willingness to listen to Ellen May's gossip at the card shop or laugh at the latest joke that Ed Rielly had heard on the radio while enjoying his morning coffee at the diner more than made up for any delay.

One of McIntire's favorite stops was at the firehouse, located across the town square from the "new" city hall. "New" was a relative term as applied to the municipal building since it was built in 1922 to replace the "old" city hall that had burned down the year before. That disaster had led to the creation of a volunteer fire company and the construction of a firehouse on the spot where the "old" city hall had stood. Like the people of Bedlow, the firehouse was designed with an eye toward simplicity and utility, built to house a single fire truck and its associated equipment. From the very beginning, however, the firehouse had become something more. Even before it was finished it became a gathering place where the volunteers who manned the engine and anyone who had a mind to drop by to socialize did so without hesitation. Within the walls of that structure, in the shadow of the silent red pumper or gathered about in the streets when weather permitted, generations of Bedlow men took a break from their labors to discuss the hot topic of the day or share stories about their jobs, their families, and their fellow citizens.

In so many ways the members of the Bedlow Volunteer Fire Company were the guardians of their community. To a man they were hardworking individuals and family men. Even the young bucks who were not quite ready to settle down knew that the day would come when they too would marry, sire children, and live out a life that would be as predictable and constant as the seasons of the year. Most of the men who manned and cared for the town's lone fire engine could trace their ancestral ties to the county of Bedlow all the way back to the War of Northern Aggression and beyond. If one took the time to compare the engine company's roster with the list of names engraved on the monument to those who had taken up arms in 1861 to defend their native state, they would have found little difference between the two. Were it not for the nature of his job, a very pregnant wife, and the time he already spent with the National Guard that he had joined after leaving the Navy, the McIntire name would also have shown up in both places.

On this particular lazy fall afternoon the door of the firehouse had been flung wide open, permitting the clutch of volunteers and passersby to spill out into the street and circle their folding chairs in front of the fire engine. Most sipped coffee from foam cups taken from an inverted stack located next to the ever-filled coffeepot just inside the front door and munched on powdered donuts someone had brought along with them as someone always seemed to do from the bakery that was but two doors down. On this day seated at the unofficial place of honor reserved for the senior member of the company present was Alex Faucher. Since he was one of three men authorized to drive the engine, Faucher tended to spend a good deal of his free time at the firehouse, a fact that his wife had little issue with.

Leaning his chair back until it almost touched the highly polished chrome bumper of the engine, Faucher was patiently listening to Ronald Weir as he described his recent interview with one of the candidates for lieutenant governor. As a talk-show host at a small local radio station, Weir often had an opportunity to spend time with county and state politicians. Like most of those gathered about, Faucher wasn't interested in hearing Weir regurgitate what the candidate was promising to do during his interview. Instead, he wanted to hear Weir's personal opinion on what the politician was really like as well as any anecdotes that he might have as a result of the time he spent with him. More than a few members of the Bedlow Volunteer Fire Company cast their ballots for this candidate or that based on what they heard from Ron Weir during these informal gatherings.

As was his usual style, McIntire made his way toward the circle of men taking care not to disturb whoever was speaking. When he was at the edge of the conclave he paused and waited until he was recognized and invited to join in. Usually the person speaking or the volunteer fireman holding court made this offer when there was a pause in the conversation. On this day Faucher interrupted Weir as soon as he caught sight of the postal worker. Turning away from the speaker and straightening up in his folding chair while taking care not to spill his coffee, Faucher called out to the new arrival. "Well?"

McIntire knew what Faucher was looking for. With a smile, he held up an official-looking envelope. "It's pay-day, boys."

Like McIntire, Alex Faucher and several of the other men gathered about in front of the fire truck were members of Company A, 3rd Battalion, 176th Infantry, Virginia National Guard. Faucher, in fact, was their first sergeant. Though pleased by McIntire's announcement, he restrained his joy. "It's about time," he snorted. "How long has it been since summer camp? Two months?"

Twisting about in his seat, Weir made a face as he reached around with one hand and began to message his shoulder. "Not long enough, First Sergeant. Not long enough."

This response brought on a chorus of chuckles from those who were in on the joke. Weir, a man who spent most of the year sitting in a nice comfy chair at the radio station and lifted nothing heavier than that day's schedule, was always being tagged by their C.O. to hump the company radio whenever they were in the field. Though the talk-show host tried repeatedly to explain to his captain that his working in the broadcasting industry in no way made him any more capable of handling a tactical radio than any other man in his company, Captain Richard Melloy would not relent. Melloy was a nice enough fellow who pretty much left the running of the company to Faucher, an arrangement most everybody prescribed to. "What's the point of wasting the time to train someone new when you do this so well," Melloy countered every time Weir protested. Well liked by his men, few bothered to argue with him. "He's got a mind like a steel trap," they all quipped behind his back. "Once it's shut there isn't a power in heaven or on earth that can pry the darn thing open."

While he was making his way around to where Faucher sat, Weir settled back into his seat and followed McIntire with his eyes. "Where's mine?"

Winking at Faucher, the letter carrier glanced back at the

talk-show host. "Well, I had yours until I ran into your wife while I was making my rounds. Since I wasn't sure you'd be here, I gave it to her with the rest of your mail."

In an instant, Weir's face was twisted in utter disgust. Pounding his knee with a clenched fist, he struggled to contain his anger. "Oh, jeez! What did you go and do that for, Brian? Now she'll know exactly how much the check is for and I won't be able to take my usual cut."

After accepting the envelope from McIntire, Faucher shook his head. "Now don't you go whining to me, boy. I told you when you joined the company that the first thing you needed to make clear to your family is that while your regular paycheck is fair game, this"—he indicated by waving his envelope at Weir—"belongs to you and you alone."

Amid a chorus of laughter, Weir tucked his head in and began to mumble to himself under his breath. When McIntire had decided that the dejected talk-show host had suffered enough, he fished out another official-looking envelope and dangled it before him. Weir immediately ceased his rumblings as he glared up at McIntire and snatched the paycheck from him. "That was cold," he snorted as he carefully ripped the letter open, "and not the least bit funny."

With the exception of Weir, everyone was still laughing over this innocent prank when the phone in the office rang. As the senior fireman present, Faucher stood up and strolled over to answer it. In his absence, while Ron Weir studied his check and made some calculations, another member of the group took it upon himself to start up a new conversation. They were just getting into it when Faucher, finished with the phone call, slowly made his way back toward the gathering. When he reached it, he didn't bother to take his place at its head. Pausing, the speaker and the others assembled fell silent when they noted the solemn expression Faucher wore.

Ignoring everyone else, the volunteer fireman and part-time company first sergeant looked over at McIntire, then

Weir. "That was Dave Erickson over at the armory," he announced, trying hard not to betray any discernible emotion.

The mention of the company's full-time training NCO and Faucher's demeanor caused a few of the men gathered about to twist nervously in their seats.

"It seems," Faucher blurted out, "the battalion's in receipt of orders. We're being mobilized."

Stunned, McIntire and Weir exchanged glances before looking back at Faucher. Both men made a point of taking the time required each day to stay abreast of both local and worldwide current events. They prided themselves in their ability to forecast what would and would not have an impact upon Bedlow. For Weir this was an important job skill, one that allowed him to maintain a solid radio audience. In McIntire's case, it provided him with a wealth of knowledge and information he could share as he made his rounds. Never at a loss with a question, Weir broke the silence and asked the question that was on everyone's mind. "Why? Is there something going on that we've missed?"

With a sigh Faucher looked down at the floor as he kicked aside an imaginary pebble with the toe of his work boot. "It seems the regular Army has run out of people. They can't fill the troop list that's going to be needed to man the peace-keeping force the President is sending to Israel."

"And we're being called up to augment them?" Weir ventured.

Faucher responded with a sigh and a nod before looking up into the man's eyes. "That's about the size of it."

"Did Dave happen to say how long this tour of duty would be?" Weir asked cautiously.

Faucher swirled his cup of coffee in a vague gesture. "Don't know. Usually these things last six months or so. But at the moment, that's an open question."

"Open, as in?" McIntire enjoined.

"As in," Faucher replied as he glanced over at the befuddled postal worker, "I haven't the slightest." Sensing that this had unsettled his friend, Faucher was quick to play down this aspect of his unexpected announcement. "I wouldn't worry too much about that right now," he stated with an air of confidence that belied his own concerns. "With all the processing and post-mobilization training we'll need to prepare us, it'll be several months before we're ready for overseas deployment if they even decided to send us. Hell, they may even keep us here in the States as a reserve and send a regular Army unit over. Either way, Brian, I'm sure you'll be here to hold your wife's hand when it comes time to deliver that son of yours."

Doing his best to pretend that Faucher's words were comforting, McIntire smiled. "That's good. That's good." Then looking about the circle of friends, he struggled to collect himself. "I can't imagine Sarah going through all that on her own."

"I'm sure," Faucher stated without even the slightest hint of conviction, "that even if we do move out before that, we'll find a way to get you home for it."

Sensing that the mood needed to be lightened a bit, Weir cleared his throat. "Say, Brian, I've watched Ann give birth to my two. Are you sure you want to be here when Dr. Sarah turns into Mrs. Hyde right before your very eyes?"

Though shaken by the news, McIntire managed to chuckle. "Oh, yeah, I'm sure. 'Cause if I'm not, I'll never hear the end of it from her mother."

McIntire's pronouncement was greeted with a round of halfhearted laughter. When it had died away, the rattled postal worker looked about the circle of men. "Well, I guess I'd better get going. I've a route to finish." He was about to add "And a wife to tell," but let that be since it was something that was both obvious and something that was not going to be pleasant or easy for him or anyone else that was faced with that prospect.

CHAPTER 3

Arlington, Virginia

On the day he had been commissioned in the artillery, Henry Jones had no idea what the Chief of Staff of the Army did. He knew his name. He understood where that high-ranking officer fit in the overall chain of command. But Second Lieutenant Jones didn't have the faintest idea of how the most senior general in the Army went about running the massive organization that he was about to become a part of. If the truth were known, West Point's newest alumni really didn't give a hoot what the chief of staff of anything thought or did. With his wedding but hours away and no idea where he would find himself once he had completed his officer's basic, his interest in such matters was somewhere between nil and zip. Like the picture that hung in a gallery delineating a chain of command that ended with the President, the exalted title Chief of Staff of the Army meant nothing to him back when he stood on the edge of a career destined to span more than thirty years.

From the window of his office Jones looked past the vast parking lots that surrounded the Pentagon and out beyond the Potomac. He chuckled as he recalled how he once felt about the office he now occupied. In his wildest dreams he never imagined that his lone gold bar would slowly morph into the four large silver stars that now graced his uniform. In those early days his goal had been quite simple. He wanted to be with the guns. He loved those guns, all of them. From the British-designed 105mm light howitzer to the big 155mm self-propelled guns that were capable of lobbing high explosive rounds weighing more than a hundred pounds twenty miles or more there wasn't a cannon he had met that he didn't take a fancy to. The ultra-sophisticated and very lethal MLRS rocket launchers held no charm for him. The weak, wimpy "whoosh" of their chemical fuel engines did not quicken his pulse like the roar of a good old-fashioned field piece. Even to this day Jones found himself overcome by those same old feelings he had come to know so well as a junior officer. A whiff of burnt cordite and the rumble of the earth under his feet that accompanied each and every volley unloosed by a firing battery was for him the greatest thrill a man could experience with his pants on.

Unfortunately, as he ascended the chain of command he once had given little thought to, the occasions when he could indulge that particular guilty pleasure became fewer and farther between. As Chief of Staff of the Army his opportunities to escape the gilded square cage that was his office and visit a unit in the field were about as rare as meeting a senator with common sense.

Rather than a thunderous roar of howitzers, Jones now spent his days enduring a steady bombardment of subordinates as they unleashed verbal barrages aimed at defending a pet project, targeting one being promoted by a professional rival, or unleashing volleys of excuses as to why this or that could not be done. The meeting he was about to chair was a case in point.

Sitting in a small conference room down the hall from his suite of offices were three senior generals. Each man was a member of the Army's General Staff, charged with overseeing a portion of that organization and assisted by a vast bureaucracy of their own made up of people reputed to be some of the Army's best and brightest. The senior of the trio was Lieutenant General Scott Dixon, Deputy Chief of Staff for Operations and Plans, or DESOPS for short. His slice of the Army's General Staff was responsible for developing operational plans, drafting the orders required to translate those plans into action, and overseeing their execution. There was much to the claim that some of his more obnoxious colonels bantered about that they were the people who gave the Army its marching orders.

While equal in rank, the second general was viewed by some as being decidedly less influential. Russell Owens, the Deputy Chief of Staff for Personnel, or DESPER, didn't exactly see things that way. His people were charged with dealing with all issues related to manning the Army as well as managing the careers of both officers and enlisted personnel in the active and reserve force. How the Army dealt with its soldiers and what they did from the time they were recruited to the day they retired as well as where each and every one of them went all fell within Owens's purview. This gave him a degree of importance a professional soldier ignored at his own risk. It could safely be said that anyone who crossed his path exposed himself to the danger of becoming the next officer in charge of the Barrows Point, Alaska, Swim Club.

The last man who belonged to this select clutch of three-star generals held a unique position. While officially listed as part of the Army staff, appointed by the commander in chief and approved by the Senate like the others, he enjoyed a degree of autonomy that neither of the other two men could lay claim to. As the head of the Army's National Guard Bureau, Frederick Smart did not hesitate to exploit his unique sovereignty, the nature of the National Guard, or the background he shared with it and not the professional soldiers of the active side of the Army. Of the three, he was the only man who could truly be called a warlord in its truest medieval meaning.

Normally Dixon, Owens, and Smart stood shoulder to shoulder on issues. When there was a battle fought within the curious world defined by the capital Beltway, it was usually against congressmen seeking to use the Armed

Forces or its budget for their own political purposes or a sister service attempting to infringe on the Army's turf. When that occurred Jones managed the Army's staff like a coach, calling the plays and selecting the players best able to execute them. But there were times when problems the Army was confronted with created internal dissension and discord. Because the people he was dealing with were all very senior and accomplished professionals within their own right, Jones could not dictate a solution in the same manner a father would do when dealing with unruly children. Instead, mediation, diplomacy, and rhetoric became the tools of choice.

Like most problems the American military faced in its struggle to prepare itself to deal with threats that even Tom Clancy would find implausible, the one that generated the current rift between the Army's senior officers was not of their making and all but unexpected. Henry Jones had the Secretary of State to thank for that. No one had bothered to consult him when the idea of using troops to patrol and enforce the buffer zone between Israel and the Palestinian state was being discussed. That little gem didn't come to light until a final agreement had been brokered between those two antagonists. When someone in the executive branch finally did get around to informing the Department of Defense of the particulars of the agreement and the Army became the official "Stuckie" responsible for providing the troops to man the security zone, Henry Jones had but five working days to come up with both the plan and the troops to execute it.

Drafting the plans for this new mission was the easy part. This chore fell to Scott Dixon and his covey of highly trained plans officers. Within forty-eight hours they had conjured up a number of options. The presentation of these options to Jones and selected members of the Army staff took place on day three. One by one Dixon's ambitious and hardworking officers briefed their plans, whipping through the details without flinching until they got to the part where the troops list should have been. Without fail, each and every briefer hesitated before launching into that part of their presentation, casting a nervous eye toward Dixon. When they did press on, there was a noticeable change in their voices as they made it clear that the dearth of available troops to meet this requirement was one glitch that even the best and brightest of them could not work around. In the end, when all of his trusty minions had finished, Scott Dixon stood up and addressed the issue head-on. "The bottom line is that at present the active Army does not have sufficient combat units to meet all of its requirements. No matter how many times we shuffle the deck, we're unable to crack that nut without tapping into our strategic reserve or scaling back on other ongoing operations."

In short order the requirement to find the force necessary to keep the warring parties in the Middle East apart turned into a football being madly tossed from one player to another during a rugby game. Since this was a mission that concerned the entire international community, Jones immediately went back to the State Department with the problem. Two entire days were wasted as one international agency tossed the request about to each other. One by one representatives of the United Nations, the European Union, and NATO made it clear that they would not or could not contribute troops to the effort. In the end, that left the United States no choice but to accept full responsibility for enforcing a plan that it had worked so hard to pull together. In short order the mission was dumped once more onto Jones who, as the proverbial low man on the Beltway totem pole, now had no choice but to salute smartly and execute with élan.

Day four was dedicated to nothing else but tackling the issue of manpower. Never much of a fan of the situation in the Balkans, Jones seized upon this new mission as an excuse to shed America's commitment in that disputed region. There was no lack of people, including Scott Dixon, urging him to do so. Like most professional soldiers both men chaffed under the rules of engagement American troops in the Balkans were forced to operate under. Drawn up in Brussels by a committee of bureaucrats and Europeans who had forgotten what armies are used for, the rules of engagement and the mandate given the troops there did not fit the reality of the situation on the ground. The results were predictable. Despite their best efforts, those NATO troops assigned the task of maintaining peace in Bosnia, Kosovo, and Macedonia were failing and failing miserably. After ten years even the dimmest bulb in the President's cabinet had come to appreciate that this sad state of affairs would continue to fester like a wound that refused to heal until the people living there grew tired of killing each other or NATO got serious, abandoned keeping the peace, and got down to the business of rooting out those who opposed their effort to do so. National prestige, however, coupled with America's unique role as the leader of NATO made any course of action that relied on pulling U.S. troops out of the Balkans a nonstarter. Like Brer Rabbit and Tar-Baby, the U.S. Army was stuck fast in that sad part of the world.

The second option available to Jones to overcome the shortfall in personnel wasn't taken seriously by anyone, even by those who mentioned it. The idea of scaling down the Army's contribution to forces deployed in Iraq in order to shift the troops thus saved to the new mission was pronounced dead on arrival. The tenuous situation on the ground in Iraq and their commander in chief's commitment to hold the line there until a viable Iraqi government was able to fend for itself had become the cornerstone of his presidency. Any proposal to alter or delay that effort was viewed as nothing less than heresy, akin to messing with the primeval forces of nature.

Equally off-limits were the handful of combat units scattered about the Pacific theater of operations and the diminished ready reaction force held back within the continental United States. Many feared with ample justification that a further reduction of America's commitment to the defense of the Pacific Rim would encourage and accelerate Communist China's drive to seize Taiwan or lead North Korea's Supreme Ruler to conclude that he was free to do something even dumber. This theater of operations, held as the scene for the most likely war-after-next, could not be ignored. Nor could the possibility that something else might crop up elsewhere in the world, something totally unexpected and unforeseen. This Scenario "X" and the looming "Yellow" menace necessitated the need to maintain a viable and readily deployable strategic reserve. "I fully agree that the idea of dropping the 82nd Airborne or any part of it en masse into the middle of a war might be an anachronism to twenty-first-century warfare," Jones pointed out to Dixon when he suggested using it as part of what was becoming known as the Palestinian Peacekeeping Force. "Fortunately for us, most of the world's troublemakers in waiting don't appreciate that, making it a force to be reckoned with. So the 82nd is off the table, along with those portions of the 101st that have not already been deployed."

Having summarily shot down every proposal that Dixon threw his way, Jones gave him another twenty-four hours to come up with some new ideas. When it came time for this second round of briefings, Dixon himself once more did all the talking.

In military planning it is the duty of a professional soldier to put forth all viable courses of actions, even those that the staff officer knows his superior will most likely reject. Stymied and desperate, Dixon's people came up with two radical suggestions that they themselves had previously dismissed out of hand. The least likely to be bought into and most extreme was for Jones to formerly decline the mission altogether. At first blush the idea of doing so was seen as little more than fanciful, wishful thinking that was a pure waste of time. Knowing that such a suggestion was tantamount to professional suicide, Scott Dixon took his time explaining why this made sense.

During the formal presentation Jones listened in silence, conceding when Scott was finished that the proposal actually had merit. "Your analysis of the overall political, racial, and religious aspects of the region and its people was impeccable, as is your conclusion that the commitment of American ground forces in the Middle East is little more than a prescription to disaster. But . . ."

Knowing what was coming, Scott didn't give Jones a chance to finish his thought. "If we go down this road we had better do so with our eyes wide open and prepared for all the worst possible scenarios we are likely to encounter," he carefully explained to his incredulous superior. "I cannot imagine a worse military situation than this. On the one hand you have a nation who will do whatever it takes to ensure the survival of its people, including using some or all of the two hundred nukes that everyone likes to pretend they don't have. Opposing them is a disenfranchised populace that has the spiritual and financial backing of powerful countries and known terrorist groups determined to wipe that nation off the face of the earth. The word 'compromise' does not exist in either of their lexicons. Radicals on both sides freely speak of a final solution with the same reverence that the men who met at Wannsee, in 1942, used. If the truth be known," Dixon stated grimly, "with each passing day I am becoming more and more convinced that the only way this whole mess will finally be resolved is to let them go at the other until there is but one group left standing." He concluded as Jones listened without commenting, "Given this sad state of affairs, I cannot see how we, as professional soldiers, can do anything but go back to our President and tell him that placing our people between the Israelis and the Palestinians would be worse than a mistake. In my opinion, it will make Johnson's decision to place ground troops in Vietnam look sane and wise. At least there our troops had the right to shoot back."

As soon as Dixon was finished making his case, Jones formerly dismissed the idea without having to give it another thought, for he had already gone over the same ground in his own mind and had come to the conclusion that he had no choice. The decision to send in American troops had already been made, one based on political considerations and not military reality. He did not have the luxury of declining this mission. All he could do was to carry out his orders, just as his counterparts had done during the darkest days of the war in Vietnam. "There is much truth in what you say, Scott. Let there be no doubt that I agree with everything you have said. This is one hole that we shouldn't be running down. It is one place in this world we have no business getting involved in militarily, not like this and not now. Unfortunately the commander in chief has other theaters of operations that he cannot ignore, those of domestic politics and world opinion. To turn his back on a peace accord that his own Secretary of State has hammered out would be political suicide for him here at home. It would throw away what's left of our credibility as a world leader in the eyes of our allies at a time when those allies are few and badly needed. We are in the midst of a worldwide war on terrorism, a war we cannot lose. If winning that war requires that we place troops in the buffer zone between the Jews and the Palestinians to quell that spat so that we can get on with the business of hunting down al Qaeda and all of its offshoots, so be it. The only option open to us is finding a way to make it happen."

Having lost out on the one option he most favored, Scott had no choice but to turn to the one that would solve the problem, but please no one. "Well," he stated glumly as he turned to his notes, "that leaves us but one choice and one choice only. We will need to call out the National Guard and send them. Unlike Iraq where we need to be prepared to go into Iran or Syria in force, the Palestinian Peace-keeping Force will be operating from fixed installations and will face, at the most, lightly armed terrorists and provocateurs."

Sighing, Jones slumped down in his chair. After giving the matter a moment's thought, he turned to Scott. "So be it. Cobble together the details. I'll notify Fred Smart that we have a zinger coming his way."

With less than twenty-four hours to hammer out those details, Owens's flesh peddlers, Frederick Smart's National Guard Bureau, and Scott's planners became embroiled in disputes and squabbled about how best to meet this new demand. When it became clear that his subordinates could not do so without direct and decisive intervention by Jones himself, he arranged a small, closed-door meeting that would not be adjourned until a viable solution had been developed that all parties could sign onto.

A soft rap on the door brought Henry Jones's reflections to an abrupt end. Turning his head he caught sight of his aide-de-camp standing at the threshold. "Sir, Generals Dixon, Owens, and Smart are waiting."

After a slow, almost hesitant nod by Jones, the aide quickly withdrew. Without having to be told, he knew his boss was not looking forward to the maelstrom that he was about to sally into. Like all good aide-de-camps, Lieutenant Colonel James Wokowitiz did more than hold the general's horse. He served as an extra set of eyes and ears for the Chief of Staff, a low-key, almost innocuous figure who could blend into the background where he was privy to comments and discussions his general was not. Of course "almost" was an important caveat, for the gold cord that he wore on his shoulder and his role as the Chief of Staff's second shadow marked him as a man apart of other, more mortal souls that populated the Army's wing of the Pentagon. Because of his proximity to the Chief he was an invaluable source of information, one often tapped when a meeting such as the one that was about to commence was called.

A gathering of four senior officers in private is an occasion that tends to arouse all sorts of speculation and chatter. The participants want to know more than who will be in attendance and what topics will be discussed during the course of the meeting. In order to be properly prepared, they need to be forewarned as to what positions and attitudes each participant entertained regarding those issues. This is no easy feat in a place like the Pentagon. A general officer does not simply pick up the phone and call another general and inquire about such matters. That is bad form. Rather, they dispatch trusted agents, members of their personal staff or selected subordinates to gather in every morsel of information concerning the pending assembly. Traditionally the single best source of this sort of knowledge is the aide-de-camp. In the course of yielding insider information about his own superior, an aide expects a quid pro quo from his counterpart. This courtesy is more often than not honored lest the individual who is disinclined to reciprocate be denied access to the loop in the future. Through the means of this twisted and less than secret exchange of information, Jones was well aware of what he was about to encounter. Not being the sort of man who believed in delaying the inevitable, he took one long last look at the calm, quiet river out there beyond his window before pivoting about and marching off to face the sort of close-in combat that no one at West Point ever discusses.

The conference room was a small one, barely big enough for the smooth, well-polished solid wood table and the eight chairs that were placed about it. Upon entering the room Jones took note that the three lieutenant generals had arranged themselves about it in such a manner as to leave the maximum distance between themselves and their fellow officers. Scott Dixon was seated at the far end of the table, more likely than not because he had been the first to arrive and had his choice. Never one to waste time while on duty, Dixon was leafing through a document that one of his staff had drafted for him and was anxiously awaiting a response. Smart was leaning back in the center chair on the right side of the table, utterly engrossed in a paperback book entitled *The Western Way of War*. Jealous of his time off, the former Texas Guardsman used slivers of idle time like this to catch up on his professional reading. Owens on the other hand was busily scribbling notes on a legal pad. Whether they had anything to do with the issues at hand didn't much matter. It was a mechanism he employed to pass the time before meetings while allowing him to avoid having to socialize or even make eye contact with anyone else who happened to arrive early.

The moment Jones walked into the room all three men stopped what they were doing and looked up to confirm that it was the Chief of Staff before laying aside their busy-work and girding for the main event. For his part Jones imagined that this was how Wyatt Earp must have felt when he walked into the O.K. Corral. Doing his best to maintain his customary poker-faced demeanor, the Chief of Staff of the Army took his seat, planted his elbows on the table, and brought his two hands together just below his chin. After giving each man a quick yet searching glance, Jones began.

"Gentlemen," Jones said, determined to lighten the grim mood that was palpable by making light of the briefing he had left little more than an hour ago, "I have spent a good part of the morning in a meeting where I heard my counterparts from our sister services explain to the Sec Def why they could not do what we have been ordered to do. In doing so their stories of woe reminded me of "the little piggies in the ditty" I play when my grandchildren are visiting. We have airplanes that drop big bombs with unerring accuracy said the Air Force Chief. We will gladly fly the Army to the Middle East and support them if they really and truly need our help, but we can be of little use to them on the ground. The Chief of Naval Operations was next. Our ships patrol the oceans of the world, not land. We'll be just over the western horizon, ready to come to the Army's aid if called upon to do so. Not to be left out the Commandant of the Marine Corps added his two cents. My boys are trained to be elite shock troops, lightly armed and fleet of foot. But they do not possess the logistical tail or the heavy weapons needed to hold ground indefinitely. If there's a beach to be stormed or photo spread to be shot, we're your men. Otherwise, don't call us."

The three officers seated about the table listened politely but made no effort to reward their chief with even the hint of a smile. Deciding there was no alternative but to plow ahead and deal with the issue at hand, Jones sighed. "I have read and considered all aspects of the arguments set forth in the papers your staffs have submitted to me regarding the accelerated use of National Guard units to occupy the Israeli-Palestinian buffer zone. While I concur with some of the points each of you have made and freely admit that this operation will ruffle many a feather, let none of you have any doubt that it will be done."

Jones paused as he looked at each man in turn. "You all know the score, both regarding our other commitments and this new one that has been hoisted upon us. There is no getting out of it, no finessing it. We have been given our marching orders. What we are here to discuss today is how we are going to resolve those problems that remain."

Never shy when it came to a good fight, Smart spoke first without making any effort to abandon the relaxed position he had been in when Jones had entered the room. "I've read the operational summaries that Scott has provided and appreciate the need to get my Guard units over there before the Jews pull pitch and abandon the buffer zone. Like everyone else I would much rather walk in there and take over those posts from them than be faced with the need to eject groups like Hamas or Hezbollah who will surely fill the vacuum left behind if given the chance. Nor can I ignore the inability of the active component to meet this tasking while pursuing other, operational requirements that are far sexier than manning checkpoints and keeping two populations from eradicating each other. The math involved given the Army's current manpower is indisputable. I understand the need to use some of my boys to hold down the fort in that shit hole while your folks go forth and make the world safe for Democrats. Where I take issue with Scott's scheme is with the pace of deployment called for. Even the best Guard unit is incapable of mobilizing and reaching the level of readiness that this mission requires in the time Scott's plan has allotted."

The use of "yours" when speaking of active duty units and "mine" whenever Smart referred to Guard units always annoyed Jones almost as much as his blunt and sometimes colorful language. Both, however, were deliberate foibles that Jones chose to ignore for the sake of maintaining tranquility within the ranks. "I understand that, Fred," Jones responded in a calm, even tone. "And were I going to place those units into an active theater of operations, I would be just as hesitant as you about doing so."

Leaning forward, Smart gave Jones a down-home Texas grin, the sort a gunfighter flashes before drawing his pistol and blazing away. "Well, General, that's the rub. You see, there's a problem with how one defines an active theater of operations. While it is true that there's nothing much brewing over there at the moment, the entire Palestinian state is little more than a loose confederation of hyperactive terrorists in serious need of a lethal dose of Ritalin. They've killed more people than Saddam's Republican Guard and won't hesitate to add our boys to that tally whenever they get a hankering to do so."

Jones gestured with his hands as he spoke. "I'll grant you that. The recent activities of the radical Palestinian groups have been more than enough to provide the Israeli Defense Force just the excuse they needed to get their people out of that snake pit. But the threat your people will face, in my opinion, is neither daunting nor overwhelming. The greatest danger units deployed over there will have to deal with is complacency. In each and every attack initiated by Hamas, Hezbollah, the al-Aqsa Brigade, and the Palestinian Liberation Army over the last six months IDF units targeted were ones that had let their guard down."

"And you think," Smart shot back, "that a handful of regular Army officers liberally sprinkled throughout my Guard units will cure the sort of laxness and inattention to detail that inevitably occurs within a unit when it executes the sort of routine and repetitive duties this mission calls for?"

"That recommendation," Dixon intoned as he sat up and joined the conversation, "is only one of several solutions to the abbreviated post-mobilization training schedule that your units have to deal with. But it is, I believe, a key element. No one can argue that your officers are good when dealing with the sort of missions that they handle on a recurring basis. Where we plan on sending them, however, bares no resemblance to their home state. And the tasks they will be expected to carry out once there are nothing like anything they have had to deal with before. Even those men you consider to be your best and your brightest will be needing additional training to bring them up to spin for this deployment. Besides, the proposal concerning the augmentation of your officers corps with active component officers is not a permanent arrangement or one that is all inclusive. It will be left to your own chain of command to select the officers who would, in their opinion, benefit from the refresher and specialized training. Once those people have achieved an acceptable level of proficiency, they will return to their own units and the regular officers will be withdrawn and reassigned."

Smart flashed a humorless smile. "That's a nice touch, Scott, having my battalion commanders serve as both judge and executioner."

"They are not executing anyone, Fred," Dixon countered. "I repeat. It's only temporary."

"Well, I'm here to tell you that's not how my folks see it," Smart insisted as he dropped all pretense of courteousness. "To them it's 1940 all over again, when Guard unit after Guard unit was decapitated in an effort to provide West Pointers and regular Army officers with commands."

Suppressing his urge to groan at hearing this tired old excuse dredged up yet again, Jones tried to steer the conversation back to where he wanted it to go. "There's very little that I can do about that perception at the moment other than to deny it and hope that you will do your best to convince your fellow Guard officers that it just isn't true."

"That's a pretty tall order," Smart grumbled as he twisted about in his seat to face the Chief of Staff once more.

"But you will try."

"Yes, I'll do my best. Just don't expect anyone in the Guard to be smiling when it comes time for them to bend over and—"

"Yes, well," Jones intoned as he cut Smart short. "Be that as it may, the issues that have yet to be sorted out concern how best to carry this out. Specifically, when will those Guard officers selected for retraining be withdrawn from their units and when and where will the active Army officers marry up with the Guard units."

"There are other concerns that we need to address," Owens stated sharply before Jones could continue. "We have yet to make a decision as to the criteria that will be used in selecting what some folks around here are already calling 'The Temps.' Nor has anyone addressed where they will come from. The last time I checked we were woefully short of fully qualified active duty officers sitting around on the shelf with nothing to do."

Jones did not appreciate the snide manner Owens tended to employ when commenting on a subject that he was not particularly keen on. Making no effort to hide his displeasure, the Chief of Staff turned his attention to him after pulling a sheet of paper from the folder that his aide had placed on the table prior to the meeting. "I've read your recommendations and find that neither solution submitted by your staff is acceptable. To send out an Army-wide tasking to units in the States requesting that they provide the required officers is a nonstarter. You know as well as I do that unit commanders will use this opportunity to rid their own commands of marginal performers." Pausing, he looked up at Owens. "That is precisely the sort of people I *don't* want to send to the Guard. The men tagged to replace popular hometown officers are already going to have a tough row to hoe as it is. There's no need to add professional incompetence to the mix."

Turning his attention back to the paper before him, Jones went on. "Nor do I like the idea of standing down an entire brigade and swapping officers back and forth between the active duty unit and the Guard brigade, man for man. As Scott has pointed out there are no active duty brigades that are currently uncommitted, that are not preparing for deployment or returning from one, or that are not part of our strategic reserve. If such a brigade did exist, we wouldn't need to bother the Guard with this tasking in the first place."

Undeterred by Jones's tone, Owens countered. "If that is the case, sir, we are left with only two viable options. Either we play Go Fish and seek out those officers who just happen to be between assignments or we rape the training base. I do not believe we have the time for the first. And if *you* opt for the second, I fear we will find ourselves mortgaging our ability to correct this problem in the long term as well as prepare the Army to meet future contingencies."

Lacing his fingers together as he rested his elbows and forearms on the table, Jones glared at Owens. It was no secret that Owens had been against this proposal from the start. In his view disrupting an officer's normal career track in this manner would be, professionally speaking, a kiss of death. No matter how the current chain of command justified the need for doing so or how creative the raters spoke of an officer's performance on evaluation reports resulting from a tour with the Guard, Owens believed that future promotion boards would hold it against the unfortunate soul. In a memo he had sent to Jones before the meeting Owens had tried to point out that promotion boards would be left to wonder what unrecorded offense each officer sent to the Guard had committed to deserve such an exile from the mother ship. Remaining steadfast, he returned the Chief's stare as if defying him to tell him that he was wrong. Jones of course knew that his deputy was right. He knew that if he had received orders assigning him to a National Guard unit when he had been a captain, the first thought that would have gone through his mind would have been, "What did I do to deserve this?"

Sensing that they had reached something of an impasse, Dixon took the initiative in an effort to pull the discussion back onto track. "Of all the options we have," he stated crisply, "the only one that promises the least disruption to both the Army as a whole and the officers in question is to raid the training base. Such a move would mean that class sizes would need to be increased in some cases as instructors and cadre departed, but the solution would not be without its benefits. I can't think of anyone better to send to a unit that faces deployment after an abbreviated post-mobilization train-up period than officers currently serving at or attending a branch school. Not only will they be up to speed in regards to both doctrine and hardware, they will have the ability to continue their new unit's training even after arriving in theater. As an added bonus, when their tour with the Guard unit is over they'll return to their previous postings with a better appreciation of the Army's reserve component."

For several long seconds Smart scrutinized Dixon. Without altering his expression, Scott returned the Guard officer's gaze. Finally, the Guard officer smiled. "You expect me to believe that you believe all that hooey?"

Like a poker player whose bluff was being called, Dixon stared back. He knew Owens was right. And he knew Smart was right. No matter how they packaged this, junior officers were going to be screwed. Yet as unfortunate as all of that was, in the overall scheme of things such concerns were petty. The active duty units that would have gone to Israel if it weren't for the Guard would, in all likelihood, find themselves in combat within six months, perhaps less as the next phase of the war on terror kicked in. For the moment Dixon set aside this grim reality and, as was his habit, did what he could to put the best face on an otherwise unsavory arrangement. With a twinkle in his eye and a hint of a smile, he met Smart's challenge. "That's my story and I'm stickin' to it."

Annoyed that his counterparts seemed to be making light of a matter that he considered to be deadly serious, Owens turned back to Jones. "You know there'll be hell to pay if we go through with this."

Like Dixon, Jones knew Owens was right. He also knew he had little choice. Having already fought and lost the good battle with the Chairman of the Joint Chiefs and the Secretary of Defense in an effort to reduce the Army's worldwide commitment, he was fresh out of good options. The need to commit American troops to the Middle East wasn't going to go away. Nor was the war on terrorism.

Suspecting nothing more would be accomplished by discussing the matter any further, Jones slapped his hands on the table and looked at each of his fellow general officers as he announced his decision. "The officers will come from the service schools. Whether they are instructors or students is immaterial. What is important is that each and every one of them is fully qualified for the position they are selected to fill."

Though he made this last point in the guise of a general statement, Owens understood that it was being directed at him. Though peeved that he had not been afforded a greater opportunity to dissuade his superior from what he considered to be an ill-advised course, he knew an order when he heard it. In time he trusted that the wisdom that he tried to impart would be shown to have been right. Until that day came, however, he and his staff had the unenviable task of going forth and translating paper requirements into real flesh and blood officers who were, as of yet, unaware that their professional and personal lives were about to make an unexpected and unwelcome deviation.

CHAPTER 4

Fort Benning, Georgia

With all the finesse of a salmon swimming upstream during mating season, Nathan Dixon nudged his way through the crowded cafeteria. Instinctively, he balanced his nutritionally challenged tray of food while searching for the seat that was being saved for him. This was no easy task given that ninety-five percent of the people in the place were wearing the exact same uniform. His only hope of finding his lunch mate was catching a glimpse of the tightly weaved French braid she sported. This of course was easier said than done amid the riot of mottle green, brown, and black that dominated the room packed wall to wall with hordes of students and faculty who were all attempting to grab a quick bite before their afternoon classes began.

When he finally did catch sight of the striking auburn tress that stood out in stark contrast to the buzz cuts that infantry officers tended to favor, Nathan discovered that he had accidentally achieved a tactical advantage. The female officer not only had her back to him, her attention was completely focused on a newspaper that she was reading while absentmindedly poking her fork in the salad. Taking great care to make his approach without drawing attention to himself Nathan waited until he was all but towering over the distracted redhead before announcing his presence. Holding his tray of food off to one side lest she make a sudden move, bump it, and add a variety of new colors to the drab camouflage pattern of her BDUs, he leaned over and whispered in the ear of his unsuspecting prey. "Hey, there, sweet thing, lookin' for a little company?"

Rather than responding with surprise or anger, the female Chemical Corps officer smiled as she slowly cast her green eyes away from the article she had been reading and up to meet Nathan's. "Why, yes, as a matter of fact, I am," she replied in a low husky voice. "I'm hoping to command a decon company in Germany. What about yourself? What sort of company do you want?"

Before he could respond to this witty retort, a major who had overheard Nathan's question interrupted. "Captain!" he called brusquely to Nathan. "Do you realize that your comments constituted a serious breech in conduct, i.e. sexual harassment?"

Without batting an eye Nathan straightened up, balanced his tray in one hand, and placed his free hand on the female officer's shoulder. "Oh, my wife doesn't mind. Do ya, *hon*."

His nonchalant reply and the redhead's demure smile threw the major. Only then did he notice the name tapes on their uniforms both read "Dixon." Undeterred by this fact, he struggled to regain his balance. "Well, that doesn't matter. Regulations concerning that subject are quite clear. Even the appearance of harassment will not be tolerated."

Doing his best to keep his tongue in check, Nathan nodded. "I will endeavor, sir, to keep that in mind."

Ignoring the manner in which Nathan slurred the word "sir," the major feigned satisfaction before turning away to resume his search for a table, one that was as far away from Captain and Captain Dixon as possible. Reaching up, Christina Dixon laid her hand on Nathan's and gave it a gentle squeeze. "I'm so proud of you," in a tone a mother would use to congratulate a small child who had just done something good. "You're finally learning to be tactful."

Without taking his eyes off the now departed major, Nathan moved around and took his seat. "Tact," he murmured in a menacing tone, "is like political correctness. An artificial set of rules invented by whinnies who are bereft of the required testicular fortitude to say what they really would like to say."

Realizing that her husband had the bit between his teeth with no intention of letting it go, Christina decided that she needed to distract him. Ignoring the glare in his eye, she turned her attention to her salad. After bringing her fork midway between her bowl and mouth she looked back at Nathan, who was still tracking the major like the acquisition radar unit of a surface-to-air missile battery. "Your father called me this morning."

Caught off guard, Nathan turned and faced his wife for the first time since taking his seat. "Excuse me?"

Pausing to chew the mouthful of lettuce she had shoveled in during the interim, Christina watched as Nathan's expression changed from one of unconcealed rage to bewilderment. Only when she was ready and was sure that she had his full attention did she choose to answer. "Your father called me this morning. You know the one, he who is also known as *The General.*"

"My father called you during duty hours?"

Assuming an innocent expression, Christina looked up at Nathan as she waved her fork full of salad about. "Why yes, of course. Just before I came down here. We had a very delightful chat."

Bewilderment now turned to frustration since Nathan knew that his wife must have been just as surprised as he was that "The General" had made a personal long-distance phone call during duty hours. "Okay, what's the deal?" he stated in the tone of voice he used when trying to convey that he was in no mood for sport.

Unfazed by the attitude that her husband was assuming, Christina took a mouthful of salad and slowly chewed, staring into his eyes as she did so. Only when she had swallowed and had dug her fork in her salad again did she bother to respond. "Oh, he asked me if you were behaving in class and how I was enjoying my assignment here."

"And?"

"And what?"

Seeing that he wasn't going to break her via the direct approach, Nathan gave in.

"Okay, you win."

Feigning bewilderment, Christina cocked her head as she looked at her husband. "What ever do you mean, dear?"

"You know very well what I mean. My father never makes a call during duty hours just to exchange pleasantries."

"Well, maybe that's because he's never had anyone as pleasant as me to talk to."

"Can we please dispense with toss cow chips, Chris. What does The General want?"

Sensing that she had gone as far as she dared, Christina Dixon's expression became more somber. "He wants you to call him ASAP."

"Subject?"

"He didn't say. But I don't think it's going to be good news. After pretending to be interested in how we were doing down here your father simply stated that it was important that you call him back, this afternoon if possible."

"Mom?"

"Nate, if there was something wrong in that department he would have told me. No, I think this concerns either your dad or . . ."

As her words trailed off into silence Nathan took note of the concern she was unable to hide. Reaching across the table, he took her hand. "Don't worry. I'm sure that it's nothing."

Knowing his father almost as well as Nathan himself, as well as the way the military mind tended to work, Christina squeezed his hand and looked into his eyes. "You know very well that I do not believe that for a moment. Remember, dear sir, this military spouse also holds the King's commission. I know when the runes have been cast and can read them just as clearly as you, perhaps better."

Realizing that there wasn't anything he could say at the moment that would ease her growing apprehension, Nathan sought to lighten the mood. Setting aside his own misgivings he flashed an impish grin, the sort that had won her heart. "Please, spare me the lecture on feminine intuition. Now please, eat your salad. It's getting cold."

Seeing an opportunity to turn away from the chill that had settled upon them, Christina looked up at Nathan. "Maybe if you had one every now and then instead of a double cheeseburger and fries you'd realize that salads are supposed to be cold."

"See. I knew there was a good reason why I avoided them. Cold foods, like MREs, are capable of sustaining life but little more. Both are to be avoided when there is a clear and decidedly more tasty alternative."

With each satisfied with their own efforts to calm the fears of the other, the pair settled down to enjoying their lunch as best they could. This effort, of course, was all but impossible for neither could escape the fear that there was something lurking out there, something beyond their control that would soon unhinge the precious status quo that they had managed to create for themselves over the past few months.

Bedlow, Virginia

One by one the good citizens of Bedlow and the surrounding communities who dedicated so much of their free time to Company A, 3rd Battalion, 176th Infantry, of the Virginia National Guard began to assemble. There was none of the lively chatter and warm greetings that normally accompanied such a gathering. The demeanor that prevailed throughout the armory and in the parking lot surrounding it on this day was somber, bordering on funereal. No one intended for things to be that way. Quite the opposite. Everyone had set out from their separate and far-flung homes scattered around the county intent on putting up a brave front, of being as casual and lighthearted over the pending departure of their loved ones as the circumstances permitted. Some of the relatives of the soldiers belonging to Company A had even discussed doing something special in an effort to attenuate the oppressive mood that had settled over the town of Bedlow when word spread that their husbands, their sons, and their brothers were being called to the colors. But like the Guardsmen themselves, these well-meaning souls could not find the strength necessary to overcome the sense of melancholy that swept through Bedlow with all the suddenness and force of a spring storm.

No one felt this any more keenly than Alex Faucher, the unit's first sergeant. In addition to tending to all the administrative issues that had to be sorted in order to pass Company A from state control into federal service, an additional burden had been hoisted on him by his commanding officer. Rather than stand on the sidelines and watch his company depart while he reported for what the Army was calling advanced professional training, Captain Jim Preston had opted to resign his commission. During a meeting in which he had announced this to Faucher and the company executive officer, First Lieutenant Gordon Grello, Preston attempted to justify his decision. "I am not quite sure what tipped the scales," he stated in a low, wistful voice as he struggled to explain his reasons for doing so. "Perhaps it was the thought of staying behind, waving a wet hankie while you guys marched away. Or maybe it was the idea that someone in the chain of command didn't think I was good enough to lead the company. Whether that concern came from within state headquarters or the regular Army doesn't much matter. What is important to me is that people I have come to think of as my family are being taken away from me at the very moment when we need to draw upon the sense of unity and cohesion that I have tried so hard to create and foster."

Pausing, Preston looked up from the floor at which he had been staring as he pondered his fate, turned first to Grello, then over to where Faucher sat in silence watching, listening, and doing his best to keep from betraying his own thoughts. "In your hearts you both know I am right. I'm sure neither of you can fault me for not wishing to go to Benning with the company only to pass the unit guidon over to a regular Army officer who has no interest in this unit other than getting his career ticket punched. No," Preston continued as he turned away and gazed at the blue and white swallow-tailed standard emblazoned with the crossed muskets of the infantry and Company A, 3/176th Infantry, "I'll quietly step aside and let that sorry sack of shit have his shot at fame and glory."

Now, with the moment of their departure at hand, First Sergeant Faucher sat alone in the company orderly room looking over at the door of Preston's vacant office. In many ways the senior NCO saw that officer's departure as something of a blessing. While it was true that Preston was a jolly good fellow who got along with just about everyone in the unit and the community, the fact of the matter was that his former commanding officer couldn't organize a pizza party. Even the simplest and most routine military maneuver was a major undertaking for him. To compensate for this he had learned to rely on his platoon leaders and selected NCOs, a technique that worked well during weekend drills and their annual summer camp but would, Faucher suspected, fall short of the mark if push ever came to shove.

As reasonable and necessary as replacing Preston was, the fireman turned soldier could not ignore the fact that the announcement their commander was being replaced by a regular Army officer had a chilling effect on the company, one that only served to make their departure more difficult.

At a time when unit cohesion and esprit would be needed the most, the one person who was expected to personify and promote those attributes was gone. In his place would be a stranger, a man who had no idea of who they, the men of Bedlow, were. The prospect of having to deal with an outsider, an officer bereft of the special knowledge and background needed to handle and care for the citizen soldiers of Company A, 3rd of the 176th Infantry, would be, in Faucher's opinion, daunting. Such skills could not be gleaned from field manuals and Army regulations. They were inbred in the very men who commanded the National Guard units. In all his years with the Guard Faucher had come to appreciate that the key to understanding a unit such as Company A and the men who belonged was the fact that units always saw themselves as citizens first and soldiers second. Whether or not a regular Army officer would be able to grasp this truism was an open question, one that Faucher feared would make or break that officer and the unit as a whole.

What he could do to blend this oil-and-water-like combination into an effective relationship that would maintain unit cohesion while preparing his fellow citizens for the challenges they would face in the Middle East was, in Faucher's mind, the greatest challenge he would have to deal with. Without having to be told, he knew that as the unit's first sergeant, he would play a pivotal role. He was the senior enlisted soldier in the company, a person who represented the needs and interests of the junior enlisted men to the company commander. At the same time Faucher would have to be the right hand of that very same officer, passing on and enforcing his orders and policies. Much of how well he accomplished these seemingly conflicting tasks depended upon the personalities of the new company commander and his own.

Thus the melancholy surrounding his imminent departure was compounded by the challenges of command that he would soon be confronting. Of the two, shipping out would be the easiest, for it would be quick and over soon. The other matter, he suspected, would linger and fester until time and circumstances once more conspired to see them safely back in the sleepy little town that he called home.

The appearance of Dave Erickson scattered these dark thoughts for the moment. In addition to being a staff sergeant and squad leader, Erickson was the unit's full-time training NCO, a position that made him almost as important as the company commander himself. Upon his shoulders rested many of the administrative details that the part-time leadership of Company A could not or did not wish to deal with. Among his duties on this occasion was arranging for and the marshaling of supplemental transportation that would be needed to take the company from Bedlow, Virginia, to Fort Benning, Georgia, where the unit would undergo thirty days of post-mobilization training. Popping his head into the near deserted office, Erickson cleared his voice. With a shake of his head the first sergeant cast aside the gloomy thoughts he had been entertaining and turned toward the waiting NCO. "Alex, the buses are here and have been integrated into the convoy. The company is ready to fall in and start loading."

Glancing up at the clock on the wall, Faucher noted the time. "It's only quarter of. There's no need to rush. Israel has been there for thousands of years. I dare say it won't be going anywhere in the next fifteen minutes. Let the guys spend them with their families."

Understanding his statement completely, Erickson nodded as he closed the door behind him and headed off to where he had left his wife and daughter.

Alone once more, Faucher looked up at the clock again before reaching over for the phone. Both he and his wife had agreed that it would be best if she went to work that day. Yet there was still time for one last phone call, a local one. By making it from surroundings that were as familiar to him as they were comfortable, he could pretend for a few precious minutes more that this was nothing more than another weekend drill during which he had little to do but wait until it was time to go home. On days like that, when he had the orderly room all to himself, he often called his wife of twenty-two years and chatted with her to pass the time. She would, Faucher figured, enjoy doing so one more time.

CHAPTER 5

Fort Benning, Georgia

Somehow the news that he was being pulled from the Infantry Officers Advanced Course for the purpose of being reassigned to a National Guard unit tagged for deployment to the Middle East came as no great surprise to either Nathan or Christina. Both had already learned in the course of their relatively short careers that the only thing a serving officer could be certain of was that his or her professional future, like the weather, was predictable but not guaranteed. The newly married couple had reported to Fort Benning, home of the Infantry School, with the understanding that Christina would serve on the faculty while Nathan attended the six-month course as a student. Upon graduation he was slated to remain at Benning where he would turn overnight from being a student to being part of the Infantry School's staff. That this posting was a major and potentially catastrophic deviation from the recommended gilded path that an officer of his rank and time in service should have been following didn't much bother Nathan. He and Christina were more in love with each other at the moment than the Army, a state of affairs that made them willing to risk their military futures for any opportunity that permitted them to be together.

Strangely, Scott Dixon made no effort to dissuade his son from following a course of action that others considered to be nothing short of professional suicide. Nor did Nathan harbor any regrets over his decision not to return to a troop unit as conventional, career-oriented wisdom dictated. Somehow, in their own way, both father and son knew that somewhere along the long and twisting road that professional soldiers follow, all would turn out well. Long before his son received his commission Scott had made a pledge to himself. Nathan, he told his wife, would have to make it on his own. Scott would do nothing to further his son's career or influence assignments by officers responsible for managing Nathan's career. This did not mean he was not interested in what became of his oldest son. Scott saw no problem with passing on information about what those assignments were after the decisions had been made at the Department of the Army. During the phone call in which he informed Nathan of his pending orders assigning him to a tour of duty with the National Guard, the conversation between the two had been brief and to the point.

In an effort to cast the best possible light on the matter, Scott reminded his son that any assignment well executed was, from a career standpoint, beneficial to an officer. For his part Nathan feigned that he understood this premise and agreed. Both men, of course, knew better. For all the hype and hoopla about how the active Army, the National Guard, and the Army Reserve were all one Army, the men and women belonging to each of these three components entertained a view and philosophy that was more often than not at odds with the party line.

Those who belonged to the active Army, erroneously called the regular Army by some, quite naturally viewed themselves as being the top of the heap. As the nation's international first responders, the units that made up the Army's active component were the best trained, best equipped, and most fully manned. They had to be. Some units such as the alert battalion of the 82nd Airborne Division were expected to be locked, loaded, wheels up and en route to any trouble spot in the world within eighteen hours of being alerted. The sense of superiority that this technical and tactical proficiency bred occasionally made working with them difficult and on occasion down-right insufferable for those who were mere "Weekend Warriors."

The Army Reserve and National Guards, of course, each had their own worldviews based upon the nature of their missions and crafted to provide themselves with their own sense of self-worth. For their part the Army Reserve could rightly claim that the active Army could not go very far or stay there for very long without them since many of the support units such as transportation, engineering, medical, and ordnance came from that command. This made the Reserves important, but definitely an augmenting force welded to the active component. The Guard was a different matter.

The Englishmen who came to America in the early 1600s brought with them the tradition of local militia units, a concept that was an outgrowth of the feudal levy and Saxon Fryd upon which medieval armies were based. The same sense of community that was a source of strength for the militia and later National Guard also influenced and limited their perspective. Men and women of the Guard could not and did not shed their political, social, or cultural values and views when they put on the uniform. While modern Guard units were organized, equipped, and trained in the same manner as a comparable active Army unit, the mission statement of each and every Guard unit committed it to serving the state and community from which it came above all else. Belonging to an organization whose chain of command ended for all practical purposes in the capital of its parent state put a definite spin on the Guard's way of thinking and allowed them a degree of independence that active Army unit commanders could not possibly imagine.

The differences did not end there. An equally important distinction concerned the level of individual and unit proficiency and readiness. No one, Guard or active component, had any illusion that thirty-nine days of training per year allowed Guard units to attain the same level of combat readiness as their active Army counterparts. This included those units designated to round-out active Army units tagged for rapid deployment. Like their brethren, even these Guard units required additional training before taking their place on the front line. Yet despite the odds, year in and year out the Guard somehow always managed to achieve a degree of proficiency in enough critical individual and small unit skills to make them a viable part of the Army's force structure. This feat was accomplished despite the fact that each and every member of those units held down a full-time civilian job and supported the needs of his or her family. It was this dual identity, one that required an astute degree of maturity and balancing that gave the Guard its distinct character and allowed them the right to proudly proclaim that they were twice the citizen; productive members of their community in peace and its guardians when trouble threatened.

The culture of the National Guard is one not easily understood by professional soldiers. Young officers like Nathan Dixon and the soldiers they lead have had the concept "Mission above all else" pounded into their heads until it is accepted with the same reverence as a holy writ. This sort of indoctrination is necessary, for the modern American military finds itself in the unenviable position of having to draw upon a manpower pool in which political correctness and social engineering designed to create a kinder, gentler multicultural society trumps reality. In training its personnel to be less concerned about feeling another's pain and more interested and skilled in inflicting it, the Army has created a professional culture that sets itself apart from their fellow countrymen. In much the same manner that the heritage and habits of the Guard define and limited those who belong to it, Nathan was a prisoner of ideas and concepts he had accepted as gospel. That he would now have to modify and even abandon some of the tenets that had become cornerstones of his professional philosophy was slow to dawn upon him.

This process began during a thrown-together orientation program on the National Guard given by Guard officers hastily dispatched to Fort Benning. Together with the other officers reassigned to the 176th Brigade from the faculty and student body of the Infantry School, Nathan found himself subjected to a series of lectures and briefings designed to prepare them for the clash of cultures that all expected when professional Army officers took over from the hometown boys. "The 'U.S. Army' tape that we all wear over our left breast pocket does not make us equal," a major belonging to the Georgia Guard explained during his portion of this orientation. "When you arrive in your units you cannot expect a sergeant E-5 who has spent his entire military career in the Guard to respond to you in the same manner as a regular Army sergeant E-5 would. For one thing the Guardsman is without exception older than his regular Army counterpart. As such he has a degree of maturity, personal pride, and wealth of real-world experiences that are decidedly more diverse, developed, and deeply rooted. I'm not saying the Guardsman is better," the major added quickly as he halted his lecture in midstride to make this point, "I'm simply alerting you to the fact that he is different and he knows it."

Walking away from the podium the major from Athens, Georgia, began to wander about the room as he spoke. "It is not unknown for an officer in the Guard to be an employee or social junior to an enlisted man within his unit. There are even cases of sons commanding companies in which their own fathers are NCOs. For the Guard this is no big deal. For you people, however, this will create problems," the major stated sharply as he stopped his meandering and stared at the joyless faces of the officers looking up at him. "Just as it will take the Guardsmen time to adjust to the twenty-four/seven military environment that he has suddenly been thrown into, each of you will undergo a period in which you will find yourself adjusting your style of leadership and personal behavior to accommodate our little idiosyncrasies."

Presented in a rather casual, almost offhanded manner this statement threw Nathan. He found himself wondering whether the major meant this to be sage advice or a warning. Up to that point he had not given his personal or professional conduct a second thought. How he would go about accomplishing his assigned duties once he had joined his unit had never entered his mind. He was after all an accomplished leader, an officer who was already well on his way to making his own mark in his chosen profession. The need to modify or moderate proven methods simply to accommodate his subordinates gave him pause. In fact, the more he pondered this concept, the more he realized that doing so meant going against many of the tenets that had served as the core of military leadership as he understood them.

Thrown off onto this tangent and no longer able to pay attention to what the Guard major was saying Nathan spent the rest of the lecture absorbed in an internal debate.

As a commissioned officer with several diverse and challenging postings already behind him, he understood both his priorities and responsibilities. First and foremost it was his duty to prepare those entrusted to him to carry out their assigned mission. To achieve this he had conditioned his people to be ready to deal with any contingency they might encounter in the execution of their assigned duties, to include the worst possible imaginable, by insisting upon realistic and demanding training aimed at attaining the highest standards time and resources available permitted.

Because the 3rd Battalion, 176th Infantry, was going into a potentially hostile environment, this meant preparing the units for combat. To be successful in battle soldiers had to be skilled, disciplined, and hardened to the suffering they inflicted and that which was inflicted upon them. Only tough, realistic training and an uncompromising determination to accept nothing less than superior performance could ensure success on the battlefield. The more decisive the victory was, the more likely it would be that most, if not all, of his people would return home safe. For Nathan and many of his fellow infantry officers this goal could be achieved only through grueling, sometimes brutal training under realistic conditions designed to push their soldiers to the limit and beyond. To him the ancient Chinese proverb that stated, "The more you sweat in peace, the less you bleed in war," was an undisputed fact of life.

Yet here he was, Nathan found himself thinking, being told that the methods that proved so effective in the past might not work with the Guard. This was all but mind-boggling to him. Even more disconcerting was the added challenge a compressed training schedule would create. There were but thirty days total from the date when the three battalions of the Virginia National Guard closed on Fort Benning to the projected date of deployment. Within that time the units had to undergo a variety of individual and unit training while completing all of the administrative processing known as preparation for overseas movement, or POM, that they had not finished at their home station. At best Nathan figured that they would be able to achieve a degree of proficiency at squad and perhaps platoon level but nothing more. The idea that he and his compatriots selected to assist in this feat would somehow have to learn a new way of doing things in the process seemed nothing less than ludicrous.

Nathan was still engaged in his own personal search for understanding when he felt a hand on his shoulder. "Hey, amigo. Wake up. Class is over. Day is done, gone the sun, etc., etc., etc."

Glancing about Nathan noted that he was the only one still in his seat. Terrance Putnam, another captain who had been yanked from the advance course and tagged for duty with the National Guard, was standing over him, smiling. "If you're going to drift off to Lala land during these briefings," he stated, "at least try to pretend that you're still paying attention."

"I suppose that you know all about that sort of thing," Nathan responded as he belatedly began to gather up his classroom handouts and unused notebook.

"Hell yes," Putnam enjoined as he turned away and began to make his way to the door. "They train us well at West Point."

Trudging along behind his cheery friend, Nathan grunted. "I see. Our tax dollars at work."

When they hit the corridor, the two infantry captains fell in side by side and in step.

Tall and lanky, Terrance Putnam dominated Nathan by a full half a head. While both men wore their hair short, Putnam's light blond mane gave the impression that he was almost bald. This made the Army issue black plastic framed glasses he wore while on duty, known as NFGs among the more irreverent, stand out even more than normal. In contrast to the starkness of his eyewear were a pair of china-blue eyes that lit up whenever he smiled, which was quite often. It was his lively, easygoing manner that drew Nathan to the West Pointer during their first days in the advanced course.

They were much alike in many ways. Proven in battle and self-assured, the two came across as that rarest of breeds, natural-born leaders who could inspire others with nothing more than a single glance and a few well-chosen words. They were also competitive to the point of near self-destruction. On the physical fitness test both redoubled their efforts after reaching the maximum number of repetitions that the standards of the test required. Neither man allowed any of their superlative performance in class or during tactical exercises to go to their heads. Nor had either of them found the need to take on airs. On the contrary, each possessed healthy doses of humility and a whimsical sense of humor that belied the cold, hard charging professionalism that drove them to excel where so many others failed.

If there was a downside to this duo it was their inability to take the infantry officer's advance course seriously. Like many of their compatriots they found much of what they were being taught out of synch with the reality of how things were actually done in the field. When they had taken as much of the school solution as they could and sensed that they could get away with it, Nathan and Terrance Putnam employed their quick wit and dry humor to make this point. Working in tandem the two had the ability to disrupt a class and fluster even the most determined instructor. It did not take long for them to gain a degree of notoriety, earning them the nickname "The Terrible Two" among the faculty. The only thing that saved them from being plowed under for their impolitic behavior in class was their academic standing in the course. Despite their irreverence, the two were in contention for top graduate honors of their advance course.

As with Nathan, notification that he was being reassigned to a National Guard unit didn't shock Putnam. The only difference was the easygoing West Pointer blamed the cause of his selection on their conduct during the course. As they made their way through Building 4, better known as infantry hall, Putnam revisited that issue. "I hope you realize that it was the solution we came up with in the period of instruction on airborne operations that got us thrown out of the course and into this. I warned you that major teaching that class had no sense of humor."

Nathan still became agitated when recalling the solution to the problem presented to his class by the instructor in question. "He not only lacked a sense of humor," Nathan growled, "he was also bereft of anything resembling common sense. People have been shot for being that dumb."

"Well," Putnam said, chuckling, "not everyone can be blessed with the same overabundance of wit, charm, intelligence, and tactical savvy cleverly disguised by those devastating good looks that you have been endowed with."

Glancing over at Putnam, Nathan gave his partner in

crime a dirty look. "If I were you I'd complain to your chapter of the West Point Benevolent Protective Society. It seems that oversized ring they issued you upon graduation from the Academy isn't functioning properly."

"That's the trouble with all you heathens and Canaanites. You really do think we have a direct line to the Department of the Army."

"Please," Nathan protested. "I know better. I'm willing to bet the only problem you ran into when you called officers assignments branch was that an Aggie picked up the phone."

"Don't think so. I could understand the guy I spoke to."

"I wouldn't be fooled by that," Nathan countered. "I hear tell that they offer courses in English at Texas A & M. I've even seen copies of the 'Texan–English, English–Texan' dictionary they use."

"Be that as it may, I hope we won't need to take a crash course in Southern drawl in order to understand the people we'll be working with in the not-too-distant future."

Nathan glanced over at Putnam. "I was about to say that if I were you I'd start working on the way I pronounced the letter A. That New England accent of yours is going to go over like a lead balloon. You'll be screwed for sure the first time you announce to your first sergeant that you need to pack ya ca in the packing lot."

"I'm afraid it's not the accent that's going to amuse them. You heard what that one Guard officer said this morning when he was on the subject of the Guard and their politics. What do you think all those good ole boys are going to say when they find out that their new comrade in arms is the son of a liberal lawyer who is a card-carrying member of the ACLU as well as a key member of the Massachusetts Democratic Party?"

Nathan smiled as they reached the entrance to the building. "For one thing," he advised before opening the door and stepping out into the hot Georgia sun, "I'd be very careful about how I used the word 'comrade.' I don't think it has the same meaning in Virginia that it does in the Bay State."

Once outside the pair stopped. After whipping out a pair of prescription aviator sunglasses and replacing his regulation NFGs, Putnam looked at his watch. "It's a little past two and way too early to head home. Annie still complains that I get home way too early. Seems she got used to not having me underfoot. Care to try to even the score at the racquetball court?"

"Putt," Nathan countered without bothering to consider his friend's offer, "what do you do when you report to a new post?"

"Scope the place out. You know, drive around, get a feel for the lay of the land, find out where the headquarters I'm expected to report to is located and figure out how long it will take me to drive there so I arrive on time. After all, like those cav pukes told us in class, time spent in reconnaissance is time well spent."

"Exactly," Nathan snapped without explaining.

After pausing to salute a lieutenant colonel who passed them on his way into the building, Putnam stepped around and confronted Nathan. "Okay, G.I. What's going on in that square cage you call a brain?"

"Let's say we put off the daily thrashing you seem to enjoy inflicting upon me at the gym for an hour or so and instead make a quick recon of the area where the 3rd of the 176th is slated to be billeted. I have it from a reliable source that their advanced party arrived last night."

Putnam smirked. "And you have the nerve to mock me about having a direct line to the top. It would appear that having a father who's the ultimate insider trumps my class ring."

"An insider, yes, but not my dad. It just so happens that one of my brother rats is on the staff of the 176th Infantry Brigade. When he saw my name on the list of newly assigned officers he called the alumni association at the Institute, pried my home phone number from them, and called last night. He gave me a pretty good rundown on the unit, where it's going to be here at Benning, and all sorts of other good poop."

"Such as?"

Instead of answering, Nathan smiled as he slowly put on his sunglasses. "Ah, knowledge is power. To enlighten you by sharing it would be most unwise, little grasshopper."

"I see. You've already gone over to the dark side, conspiring with the enemy and turning your back on your fellow officer."

"What enemy?" Nathan asked jokingly. "Haven't you been listening? We're all one Army, one big happy team, yada, yada, yada." Then, becoming serious again, he returned to his original point. "How about we go take ten minutes, go over there and poke around a bit? Who knows, we might actually learn something."

"For someone who opted to be institutionalized for four years instead of pursuing a college education, you sometimes make sense. Okay, lead on. But if we get in trouble, you're doing all the talking."

Nathan smiled. "Since I'm the only one who can speak proper English, I'd say that's a good idea."

With a shake of his head, Putnam pointed toward the parking lot. "Just go. Go before I have a serious attack of sanity and change my mind."

CHAPTER 6

Fort Benning, Georgia

The "T" before the number of each of the buildings stood for temporary. But there was nothing temporary about them. Built as part of the massive prewar mobilization of 1940 and 1941, the two-story barracks, split-level headquarters buildings, and sprawling mess halls Nathan drove by had housed generations of American soldiers as they prepared to wage war in Europe and the Pacific, Korea, Vietnam, the Persian Gulf, and Afghanistan. Now they were being made ready once more to receive American fighting men as they prepared to sally forth to keep the populace of the Holy Lands from slaughtering each other.

During those years the Army had changed, and so too had its demand for larger, more modern, and more sophisticated barracks, administrative buildings, and "dining" facilities. Yet somehow the need for the old wooden buildings thrown together in great haste never went away. Some were torn down. Some burned down. Others were simply deserted and allowed to literally rot in place. Only those deemed essential to the needs of the Army were preserved through modernization, refurbishment, and layer upon layer of paint. Despite this transformation the faithful old buildings retained their proud and unique character as they waited in silence to take in a new generation of soldiers charged with upholding the traditions of those who had gone on before them.

After slowly cruising through the battalion area that was at the moment all but deserted, Nathan and Terrance Putnam parked their cars in the vacant lot of a small PX annex that was being prepared by employees of the Armed Forces Exchange for reopening. Emerging from their respective vehicles, each man paused as they stood next to their autos and took a moment to look back wondering what, if anything, to do next. "Why is it," Putnam finally asked, breaking the silence, "that just when you started to think you're about to master the game the Army feels the need to throw you a curve ball?"

"To keep us on our toes, I guess," Nathan answered glumly. "They don't want us to get too cocky."

"Is it me, Nate, or do you feel like a second lieutenant reporting to his first unit all over again?"

Stepping aside before slamming the door of his car, Nathan chuckled as he gave his fellow captain a wary glance. "Oh, I dare say this is worse, much worse. Back then no one expected us to know beans. Things are different now. We're the professionals, the pros from Dover."

Putnam continued to gaze off in the direction of the buildings destined to be occupied by the 3rd of the 176th, pondering their next move. "Somehow I expect," he finally stated dryly, "those folks are just as thrilled about our arrival as we are."

"Well, let's not disappoint our newest fans. In the words of Iron Mike, follow me."

"Not so fast there, *Captain* Dixon. You're forgetting yourself again. If memory serves me right I have date of rank. *You* follow me."

As the pair fell in side by side and began to make their way on foot back in the direction from which they had just driven, Nathan muttered as he shook his head, "Fucking West Pointers," loud enough for his companion and partner in crime to hear.

Putnam grinned. "Fuckin' A. And don't you forget that."

* * *

Just exactly what the two expected to see or accomplish by strolling through the battalion's area was as much a mystery to Nathan as it was to Terrance Putnam. The buildings were no different than any of the thousands of similar structures scattered across the United States on hundreds of Army, Army Reserve, and National Guard installations, all constructed using the exact same plans and set out using the same street layout. Nor was there anything to be learned by observing the comings and goings of the handful of Guardsmen who could be seen scurrying about between those buildings, preparing them for the impending arrival of the battalion's main body. With more important tasks awaiting their attention and little time with which to accomplish them, the Virginians belonging to the advanced party ignored the two captains whose close-cropped hair, crisply pressed uniforms, and purposeful stride marked them as being regular Army types.

For their part Nathan and Terrance were quite satisfied to continue their casual stroll unheralded and unmolested. Only when they reached the battalion headquarters building did they halt to inspect an oversized sign bearing the unit's crest and motto that someone had found time to set up. "Victory or Death," Nathan mused as he read the motto written upon a scroll below the red crest emblazoned with blue over white diagonal bars. "Catchy phrase, wouldn't you say?"

"I'll take victory if you don't mind," Putnam quipped. Then looking up at the crest, he shook his head. "I dare say my dear old bleedin' heart New England liberal dad is going to be somewhat less than thrilled when he sees a set of those adorning my uniform."

Studying the unit symbol that bore a striking resemblance to a Confederate battle flag sans the stars, Nathan agreed. "It kind of puts things in perspective, doesn't it? Something tells me that if you don't already know the words to 'Dixie,' you'd better start learning them."

Absorbed by their inspection of the battalion's crest neither captain noticed the Guardsman who approached them from behind until he spoke. "We weren't expecting you gentleman until later this week."

Caught off guard, both Nathan and Putnam all but jumped. Spinning about the first thing the pair took note of was the stranger's rank. Instinctively and in unison they snapped to attention and saluted.

In response to their smartly delivered military greeting mandated by regulations, Lieutenant Colonel Charles Lanston rendered a salute that was as casual and nonchalant as his gait. "I was hoping to get a chance to speak with you before the battalion arrived."

Unsure of how to proceed, Nathan and Putnam dropped their salutes and assumed a rigid position of parade rest, exchanging glances out of the corners of their eyes as they did so. Taking the initiative Putnam cleared his throat and spit out the first thing that came to his mind. "Ah, well, we were finished with our afternoon classes and decided to come down here for a look around, sir."

A smile lit up the face of the middle-aged Guardsman before them. "Good. Very good. I'm glad you did. Your showing up like this saves me the bother of hunting you two down." Then, with a measured ease he stepped forward and offered up his right hand to Putnam. "Charles Lanston. When I'm not running the Bedlow school district or tending to all the 'honey do' projects my wife never seem to tire of finding about the house I command the 3rd Battalion, 176th Infantry, of the Virginia National Guard."

Still a bit unsettled by this unanticipated confrontation and unable to cast aside the military bearing that was second nature to him, Putnam offered his own hand as if delivering a karate chop. "Captain Terrance Putnam, sir." In the midst of a handshake that was firmer than he had been prepared for, Putnam motioned toward Nathan with his free hand. "And this is Captain Nathan Dixon."

Without releasing his grip on Putnam's hand, Lanston

glanced over at Nathan. "Captain Dixon. Your reputation precedes you."

In life these four words can be welcomed, for it informs the recipient that his past exertions and achievements have already spoken for themselves, thus alleviating the need for him to waste time trumpeting them himself. Or they can be harbingers of ill tidings, akin to having an oh and two count assessed against you before stepping up to the plate. At the moment Nathan found that he was unable to discern which it was as he reached over to accept his new battalion commander's hand. So he maintained the deadpan expression that he had managed to affect after recovering from Lanston's surprise appearance. "I am sure I speak for Captain Putnam that we are looking forward to this," Nathan stated calmly as he slowly tightened his grip to counter his new commanding officer's powerful grasp.

Ignoring this bold-faced lie and satisfied that his little impromptu test of strength of wills had been met in an appropriate manner, Lanston released Nathan's hand. "If you gentlemen don't mind, I'd appreciate it if I could have a moment of your time. Let's walk and talk."

Though the words were casually delivered as if they were nothing more than a friendly suggestion, both young captains understood an order when they heard it. Instinctively the two captains attempted to form up in accordance with proper military decorum. As the senior ranking officer the post of honor on the far right was immediately surrendered to Lanston. Putnam, whose West Point commission gave him date of rank over Nathan even though Nathan was actually commissioned nearly a month before his fellow captain, made his way over to Lanston's immediate left. As the junior officer Nathan took up his post on the extreme left. Lanston, however, had different ideas. After watching Nathan and Putnam scramble to their respective posts, the National Guard officer took one step back before inserting himself between the two. This maneuver caused as much embarrassment as confusion for the young captains who realized that they were receiving their first lesson in National Guard protocol à la 3rd of the 176th. Once everyone had settled into their new slots the trio began to make their way down the center of the deserted road at what could best be called a saunter, ignoring the comings and goings of the Virginians belonging to the advanced party except when one of them took the time to slow down and salute their commanding officer.

Lanston returned these hasty greetings without skipping a beat as he spoke to the two officers accompanying him. The discussion was rather one-sided, more of a soliloquy than a speech. The care with which the Guard officer selected his words and the tone of their delivery did not escape the attention of either Nathan or Terrance Putnam. "I will be quite honest with you, and I do hope that you will both be so kind as to return the favor," Lanston stated as he began. "There are many within this battalion who are somewhat less than thrilled about your assignments and the manner in which they were handled."

The temptation to say something to the effect that neither of them were particularly enthralled over the prospect of serving in a National Guard battalion proved to be all but overwhelming for Nathan and Putnam. Fortunately iron discipline and just plain old common sense allowed both officers to restrain themselves as they contented themselves to listening to Lanston's measured oration.

"The two captains whom you are replacing are good men. They're well liked by those who served with them as well as being accomplished members of our little community back in Virginia. Within the framework of a peacetime Guard their performance was acceptable. But . . ."

Lanston's deliberate pause, ostensibly to return the salute of a sergeant who wandered across their path, was telling. It was clear to Nathan that his new commanding officer was uncomfortable with the idea of speaking out against men who were more than former subordinates. If there was a true Achilles' heel to the Guard system, Nathan suspected that it was the sense of personal loyalty and dedication an officer like Lanston felt toward subordinates who were also fellow citizens, neighbors, and even close friends. The active Army is not immune to this phenomenon. They just are a bit more sanguine when it comes to disposing of officers who do not measure up.

This point was driven home on several occasions during the orientation Nathan and Putnam were undergoing. The National Guard, they were told, cannot be as cavalier in rooting out those who fall short of the mark. As a community-based and -oriented organization local politics and personal friendships play an important role in determining an officer's assignment. Such sentiments can blind a superior to shortcomings and deficiencies that professional officers who are worth a damn quickly learn to guard against. In the past, during the few encounters that Nathan had with Guardsmen he had listened patiently as they tried to explain how this loyalty was a virtue while denigrating the impersonal and uncompromising manner that the regular Army tended to rely on when dealing with its personnel. Trained to be part of that system, Nathan was as committed to its philosophies and practices as the Guardsmen were to theirs. Now, as the three officers meandered their way through the battalion area, Nathan realized he was witnessing what happens when those two very different views and the cultures that foster them collided.

"If this deployment was nothing more than part of a homeland security operation I would have done everything within my power to keep those two," Lanston explained. "Captain Tripplett, the battalion S-4 whom you will be replacing, Captain Putnam, was able to rely upon his NCOs and the routine nature of our exercises to overcome his lack of organizational skills. Our deployment to the Middle East, however, and the requirement to operate within the Army's logistical system in an active theater of operations are beyond his abilities. He knew that without having to be told."

Lanston's comment about the former S-4's competence when it came to logistical matters caused Nathan to wonder why Tripplett had been placed in a position that required those very skills in the first place. Was he a relative of a state official who was simply too powerful to piss off? Or was it simply his turn to serve on the battalion staff and when the time came there were no other slots open? It was a riddle that Nathan filed away in a corner of his brain housing a group for future study.

"Ben is not a stupid man," Lanston stated with a sadness he made no effort to disguise. "Given time I have no doubt that he would be able to master the routine and learn to muddle through in the same inimitable manner that he always did. Unfortunately, he didn't feel he was up to the challenge of handling the multitude of tasks and duties required of an S-4 in the sort of environment we're being thrown into." Lanston paused and exchanged glances with Putnam as they continued to walk. "You are fortunate, young man. In his heart Ben knew this. That is why he asked to be replaced, a fact that *should* make it a bit easier for you."

If Terrance Putnam felt any sort of joy or relief over this revelation, he kept it to himself. The most he was able to muster in response to the pregnant pause he felt obliged to fill was a simple, "I understand."

Bowing slightly at the waist as he continued to walk, Lanston turned away from Putnam and over at Nathan. "I wish I could say that the circumstances surrounding your assignment were as simple as Captain Putnam's."

Nathan swallowed hard as he returned Lanston's stare. "Would you care to elaborate upon that, sir?"

Straightening up, the Guard officer glanced up at the sky as he spoke. "Jim Preston is well liked. Hell, it's damned near impossible not to like him. He's intelligent, articulate, easygoing, and has the ability to charm the pants off you. Those very special skills are the bread and butter of his profession. They've allowed him to sway many a judge and jury he was pleading a case before. They have also allowed him to maintain the highest retention rate for a company-sized unit within the Commonwealth of Virginia."

A knowing smile came to Lanston's lips as he glanced back and forth between Nathan and Putnam. "In case neither one of you gentlemen have had the opportunity to spend a great deal of time with the Guard until now, retention of unit personnel is an important measurement of a company commander's effectiveness. It's more critical to us than reenlistment is to you folks in the regular Army. You see, our pool of available, qualified, and willing manpower is quite limited. Units can only draw from a definitive geographical area. To fill his ranks and keep them there a commanding officer must foster an environment within his command that is positive and enjoyable. He's got to make them want to be there despite the fact that by doing so they have to sacrifice time that would otherwise be spent with their families as well as expose themselves to sudden and unexpected disruptions to their personal and family lives. It's a popularity contest that not everyone understands or appreciates, especially professional soldiers such as yourself."

Unsure of how to respond without sounding critical of a philosophy that he found to be alien and professionally distasteful, Nathan merely nodded.

"Unfortunately," Lanston explained as the trio continued to meander along the near deserted streets of the battalion area, "Jim's efforts have resulted in an organization that has become more a social club than an infantry company. The men of Alpha Company are good people and they're a happy lot. But when it comes to patrolling, executing a movement to contact, or preparing a defensive position, they're all but clueless. During their last trip to Camp Pickett last year for annual training the company came in dead-ass last in damned near every area evaluated."

Finally unable to restrain himself, Nathan asked the obvious. "If that is the case, then how is it that he's still in command."

Stopping short, Lanston looked at Nathan as he arrested his own forward momentum, turned to stare at the regular Army officer. He was tempted to ask him if he had been paying attention to what he had been telling them, but instead shook his head and gave Nathan a weary smile. "There is much you have to learn about us, Captain Dixon. Much."

The urge to respond with a snappy reply was stymied by an overpowering sense of foreboding that twisted Nathan's stomach into a knot tighter than the colonel's joyless expression. Still, it was not in him to leave things as they were. Taking great care to modulate his voice, he nodded. "I imagine we all do, sir. That's what we're here for." •

Understanding the captain's comment, Lanston collected himself into what he considered a proper position of attention and once more offered his hand to the two young officers. "I am glad we understand each other and have had this opportunity to meet. I look forward to working with you. Good day, gentlemen."

With that he pivoted about and made his way back toward his battalion's headquarters building. After watching Lanston disappear inside, Putnam turned to Nathan. "Well, amigo, now we know the score."

Nathan grunted. "Yeah. Home team one, visitors nil." Then, regaining his balance, he looked over at his friend. "Do ya think there's still a chance we can get our hands on a couple of tickets for the *Titanic* and make good our escape?"

"Escape? You've got to be kidding, Nate? Where's you spirit of adventure? Your desire to take on a challenge? What we have here is another wonderful opportunity to excel."

"If memory serves me right," Nathan stated glumly, "those were the very words Custer cried out to Reno and Benteen as he rode off."

"There ya go, buddy," Putnam exclaimed with exaggerated joy. "You've got the idea. Now, let's get down to the gym before all the racquetball courts are scarfed up by those slackers from the advanced course. I feel like serving up a can of whoop ass on ya."

Needing to do something physical in order get his mind off the dark thoughts their brief chat with Lanston had engendered, Nathan readily agreed. "Okay, you win. Lay on, Macduff, and damned be him that first cries hold, enough."

Nathan was glad to find his wife at home after being soundly trounced by Terrance Putnam at racquetball. Normally as big a workaholic as himself, Chris had been doing her best to slip out of the office early each day with an eye toward spending as much time with Nathan before he had to pack up and move in with the other officers of the 3rd of the 176th. Both of them knew that this sort of thing was bound to happen. Of all the obstacles that a dual military career couple faces, sudden deployments and assignments that did not match were the most daunting. And while Chris understood the needs of the service far better than most wives and had intellectually accepted the idea there would come a time when their respective assignments would keep them apart, Nathan's pending departure was no less cruel.

Upon entering their apartment Nathan was struck by a cacophony of sweet aromas. Dropping his gym bag in the small entryway, he slowly made his way toward the kitchen where he spotted Chris standing at the small counter carefully icing a cake. For a moment he quietly stood in the doorway and studied his wife. Anxious to have everything ready before his appearance, she was obviously scrambling back and forth between the kitchen, where she was preparing dinner, and the bedroom, where she had been in the process of changing. At the moment she was in an OD T-shirt, BDU trousers, and barefoot. "Hey, congrats," he called out, startling her, "I see this one didn't flop over and die a premature death."

Pretending to be angry that he took every opportunity to kid her about her first aborted effort to bake a cake for him, Chris crinkled her nose and made a face. "It must have been a good cake, seeing how you all but inhaled it in a single day."

"I had no choice, dear girl. As I recall, other than the cake there wasn't a blessed thing to eat in the entire apartment."

"Was too. Since we've been married I've always made it a point to maintain ample supplies of peanut butter and fresh bread on hand."

Closing the distance between them Nathan put his arms around his wife's waist and drew her to him as she spun about to face him. In a playful mood, Chris waited until he had closed his eyes and leaned toward her before lifting the spoon containing a healthy gob of chocolate she was holding to Nathan's puckered lips.

Caught off guard his eyes popped open as he jerked his head back before the taste of frosting registered. Regaining his balance he opened his mouth and accepted Chris's sweet surprise. As his tongue licked the spoon, he made a great show of moaning with delight. "Oh, baby. You're so good to me. Do that again."

Now that she was in his arms Chris caught a whiff of him. Pulling away, she withdrew the spoon and held it back. "You've been playing racquetball with Terry and you didn't take a shower when you were finished, did you?"

Feigning a hurt expression, Nathan lifted his arm and sniffed at the wet spot that had formed at the pit of the sleeve. "I don't smell anything."

"Well I do not concur, Captain Dixon. And until you shower and change they'll be no more icing for you."

Flashing that smile that she had found so irresistible, Nathan nodded. "Roger wilco, over and out."

"Roger" was military shorthand for I understood the last radio transmission a station received. "Wilco" meant will comply. "Over" was added to the end of a portion of a transmission to notify other listeners on a radio net that you were pausing to allow them to respond while "over and out" announced that the conversation was finished. The only time anyone with even a modicum of military training used all four together was in jest or when they were trying to get someone's goat. Being a professional soldier herself Chris made a face. "God! What is the Guard teaching you? How to sound like Gomer Pyle?"

Rather than answering, Nathan changed the subject. "I met my new battalion commander today."

"I hope you did that before you played racquetball."

Ignoring her retort he explained how he and Terry Putnam had gone down to the battalion area to scope the place out and how Colonel Lanston had stumbled upon them. "He's about what you'd expect a National Guard battalion commander to be, Southern accent and all."

Having come across Guard officers in the classes she taught Chris didn't need any further explanation. Nathan's dry comment conjured up a standard, preconceived image of her husband's new commanding officer. "Well?"

"Well what?"

"Are you going to be able to get along with him?"

Nathan shrugged his shoulders as he reached around Chris, took the open can of frosting off the counter, and dipped his finger into it. "Do I have much of a choice? I mean, he's the boss."

"That's not what I mean. And don't eat all of that. I still have half a cake to finish."

Nathan considered Chris's comment as he licked the icing off his finger. "It's not going to be easy," he stated glumly. "He took great pains to point out to Terry and me that *The Guard is different.*"

Chris laughed at the exaggerated manner in which he made his point.

If Nathan took note that she was amused by this he didn't show it. He was too caught up in going over in his mind what had transpired between himself and Lanston. "He all but told me that I'm not going to be able to treat the people in his battalion in the same manner as I think he believes we do with our people in the active component." Pausing, he turned away from Chris as he placed the can of icing down. "I'm not sure how I'm going to skin this cat. From everything we're being told during the intel briefings the situation in the West Bank is quite volatile. Everyone that I have talked to seems to think it's going to get worse when we arrive. No one expects that the battalion is going to have an opportunity to finish training in country like the Guard was led to believe." Facing Chris once more, Nathan's expression betrayed his concern. "We're going to have to hit the street locked, cocked, and ready to roll. Given the time that I'll have before we're wheels up and on the way, I don't think that's going to be possible."

Sensing her husband's growing apprehensions about his new assignment and determined to make his last few days with her as enjoyable as possible, Chris wrapped her arms around Nathan and gave him a gentle squeeze before looking up into his troubled face. "I'm sure you'll find a way. You've always managed to do so before."

Unable to muster up a brave expression or find a word of hope, he simply looked down into his wife's brown eyes. Her expression, the subtle scent of vanilla that permeated the kitchen, and the warmth of her gentle touch banished all thoughts and concerns from Nathan's troubled mind.

Realizing that she had managed to capture his complete and undivided attention, Chris raised herself onto her toes as she reached up to kiss him, pausing only long enough to lick several stray clumps of frosting that remained upon his lips.

CHAPTER 7

Fort Benning, Georgia

The thirty-nine-year-old truck driver turned platoon sergeant was already awake and beginning to stir long before the automatic coffeemaker clicked on, heating the water he had carefully poured into its hopper the night before. From his bunk he listened to the sound of liquid as it boiled, bubbled, and slowly spilled over into the waiting grounds, generating a brisk aroma that cut through the dry stale air of his tiny room. The common kitchen appliance he had brought with him was a small thing, but an important one to him. These precious seconds alone he was enjoying would be the last quiet moments he would have total control over. There, in the darkness of his room, he could close his eyes, inhale the smell of his favorite blend, and pretend, if only for a minute, that he was still back home.

The sudden blare of his radio alarm brought this illusion to an abrupt end. Still struggling to wake himself, Sergeant First Class Matt Garver tumbled out of bed, poured himself a cup of coffee, and set out to rouse his platoon. Clad in nothing but his Skivvies and flip-flops, he shuffled out into the foyer at the front end of the two-story barracks lit only by faint red light cast off by the emergency exit sign above the stairs. Still a bit disoriented by his surroundings Garver stopped where the foyer opened into the platoon bay. With his free hand he reached up and began groping about along the wall searching for the light switch while sipping coffee. When the tips of his fingers brushed against an exposed length of conduit, he allowed them to follow it down until they came upon a metal junction box jutting out from the wall. Like a blind man reading Braille, his fingers explored the face of the box searching for the light switches. Recalling there were three switches for the overhead lights scattered throughout the bay where his platoon was still enjoying their first fitful night of rest at Fort Benning, he waited until he had his palm firmly planted beneath them all before quickly sweeping his hand up.

In an instant the full length of the bay was awash in the harsh glow of naked fluorescent lights. Garver stood there for several seconds listening to the sounds the men in his platoon made as they were unceremoniously catapulted into the conscious world. Here and there groggy voices rose above the dissonant chorus of throats being cleared and piteous moans. Above them all one lament gave words to the obvious. "Oh, for Christ's sake. It's still dark out!"

"No shit, Sherlock," another responded from a different corner of the bay. "It's five fucking o'clock in the morning."

Stunned by the glare of the light that hung just above his upper bunk, Specialist Four Jerry Slatery rolled over and pulled the blanket over his head. "Someone do me a favor and wake me *after* the sun comes up."

From his post at the head of the platoon bay, Garver bellowed out the same greeting that he always used during weekend drills and annual training at Pickett. "Rise and shine, boys. Rise and shine. Grab your jock and pull up your socks, Second Platoon. It's time to earn your pay." After taking another sip of coffee, he stepped off and slowly began to make his way between the rows of bunks. "First formation in thirty minutes. Uniform is PT."

Sitting on the edge of his upper bunk with his legs dangling over the side, PFC Paul Sucher called out to Garver as he went by. "Run before breakfast? On our first day? Whose brilliant idea was that?"

Glancing up without pausing, Garver smiled and lifted his coffee cup in a mock toast. "You have the colonel to thank for that, dear boy."

After rubbing his eyes, Sucher looked around the room

to see if anyone was putting on their sweats. "What's the weather like out there?"

From somewhere across the bay, a sarcastic voice sneered. "It's dark."

Sucher was less than amused. "Cute. Is it cold or what?"

Already on his feet and making his way to the latrine, PFC Tim Ratliff swerved to his right and made for a window. Throwing the towel he was carrying over his shoulder, he tried to open the window but was defeated in this effort by a fresh coat of paint that had been liberally applied while the window had been down. Rather than bothering to move on to another, Ratliff pressed his face against the cold windowpane and peered out into the early morning gloom in an effort to see if anyone was out there and what they were wearing. "Damn! B Company is already forming up."

Sean Zukanovic was unimpressed by this revelation. "Good for them. No doubt the colonel will give them all a gold star for effort. Now, is it cold?"

"Everyone I see is wearing sweats."

"Then the answer is yes," Zukanovic muttered. "It's cold."

This exchange cued Garver that he needed to amend his initial announcement. "Uniform is sweatpants and sweatshirt. You now have twenty-eight minutes." He had almost reached the far end of the bay when he took note that PFC Daniel Travers wasn't making any effort to stir. Walking over, he lifted the corner of the Army blanket Travers had pulled over his head. In as low and sweet a voice as he could manage Garver began to sing. "Oh, Danny boy, the pipes, the pipes are calling. From glen to glade, across the meadow calls . . ."

From beneath the blanket, a hand emerged and snatched the blanket out of Garver's hand. "Piss off and leave me alone."

Stepping back the senior NCO looked down at Specialist Four Samuel Rainey, the man who occupied the bunk below Travers, and smiled. "What do you say, Sam. Think you could help me roust your bunkmate?"

Rainey grinned. "Wilco." With that he lay flat on his back as he brought his knees up to his chest. When he was set, he firmly planted the soles of his feet on the underside of Travers's mattress. After softly counting to three, Rainey thrust his legs up, sending his reluctant bunkmate into the air and over onto the floor. Everyone who happened to be passing the bunk at the moment and witnessed this unorthodox technique let out a lusty cheer or shouted, "Airborne!" or "Look, Wendy, I can fly. I can fly."

After landing with a thump Travers collected himself. From the floor he glared up at Garver who was standing over him, casually sipping his coffee. "That's not fuckin' funny. I could have gotten hurt or broken something important. I'll bet you wouldn't be grinning if they shipped me off to the hospital for weeks."

The smile Garver wore broadened. "I'm not that lucky. Now, get off your arse and get dressed. First formation is in twenty-six minutes."

In ones and twos the men of second platoon made their way down the stairs in silence and out the doors of their ancient barracks building. The brisk chilly air of the early fall morning hit Daniel Travers like a slap in the face. Recoiling, he stopped and folded his arms tightly against his chest. "Damn it's cold. I thought Georgia was supposed to be hot!"

Hearing the electronics salesman's lament as he went past, Gene Klauss chuckled. "Wait till noon. By then you'll have all the warm Georgia sun beating down on that skinny little ass of yours you can handle."

Stomping his feet as he looked around, Travers continued to complain. "I've been here less than twenty-four hours and I've had all of Georgia I care for."

Coming up behind him Oliver Rendell, one of the second platoon's squad leaders and a deputy sheriff back in Bedlow, gave Travers a shove and called out as if he were directing traffic at an accident, "Move along. Nothing to see here, folks. Move along."

Stepping down onto the creaky wooden steps, Travers followed his companions and made for the milling mass of soldiers gathering on the gravel road that ran alongside the row of buildings belonging to A Company. Under the glow of streetlights and the bare bulbs illuminating barracks doorways the members of that unit slowly began to sort themselves out and form up into some semblance of squads and platoons.

From his post at the front and center of this company-sized scrum Alex Faucher watched and waited for platoon sergeants to finish rousting out the last of their stragglers from the barracks and into ranks. Like sheepdogs rounding up their charges, the four senior NCOs pleaded, prodded, and barked at their people. With nothing better to do until a reasonable state of order was achieved Faucher mentally noted the most egregious uniform violations. Few within the company were wearing the complete physical training uniform prescribed by regulation. Most of those who did show up attired in the issued light gray sweats with black block letters spelling out Army across the chest were the younger members of the units, men who had finished their basic or advanced individual training within the last few years. Most set aside those items of clothing for the unit's annual training, using them year in and year out until too many washings, fair wear and tear, or expanding waistlines dictated that replacement garments be procured. Since A Company seldom conducted physical training as a unit little effort or emphasis was made to secure proper replacements. This resulted in a motley assortment of shirts and sweatpants of various colors sporting a variety of logos and school names when the unit did form up to run or exercise en masse. Every now and then someone at state, brigade, or battalion would generate a memo instructing subordinate unit commanders to correct this practice. But like so many other memos considered to be trivial or Mickey Mouse put out by people serving only thirty-nine days a year in headquarters that were hundreds of miles away, independent-minded and easygoing subordinate unit commanders like Jim Preston elected to ignore it.

Being a person who enjoyed order and neatness in all things, the odd assortment of riotous colors and logos that had nothing to do with the Army worn by the milling mass bothered Alex Faucher. The meaningless cacophony was anything but military in appearance. Even when everyone finally settled down and was in his proper place, the company before him would look more like a high school gym class rather than an infantry company. He had once tried to enforce the edicts from above regarding the physical training or PT uniform but was dissuaded from doing so. His commanding officer felt that the money spent by the soldiers under his command out of their annual clothing allowance on new Army-issued PT uniforms would be better allocated in replacing worn or ill-fitting BDU items. Of course both Faucher and Preston knew that few in their company actually used their clothing allowance for its intended purpose and instead simply counted it as part of their take-home pay. Since he was but the first sergeant and the PT uniform was seldom used, Faucher did not feel that the issue was important enough to pursue. So he followed his company commander's lead and selectively ignored the issue.

From the front rank of the second platoon Jerry Slatery called out to Faucher as he was still mulling over this recurring irritant. "Hey, Top! Is the XO going to grace us this morning with his presence and lead us on this run?"

Before Faucher could respond Slatery's squad leader, Oliver Rendell, stepped out from his place at the head of the squad and glared down the ranks at Slatery. "Don't you worry about what Lieutenant Grello does or does not do. You just concentrate on keeping up with me."

Lifting his hands up with palm out, he glanced at Faucher while bending at the waist and turning to face his squad leader at the far end of the rank. "Okay, Ollie! Don't shoot. I'm just a simple soldier asking a simple question."

"Simple is right," Rendell snapped.

After waiting until Slatery had straightened up and pulled back into line, both Faucher and Rendell exchanged a long, wary stare. It had become something of a routine during Jim Preston's tenure as commanding officer for the officers of the company to either run on their own or as a group but separate from the rest of the company. While it made little difference to most of them, some enlisted men took exception to this. All sorts of speculation as to the reason behind this practice was tossed about by those who kept track of such things. Most agreed that some of the officers, to include the captain himself, didn't want to embarrass themselves by falling out of ranks before the run was over. While it was a sad fact of life that a fair number of the part-time soldiers always fell out, especially at the beginning of their two-week annual training period, even in the Guard it was something of note when an officer did so.

Like the PT uniforms, this was just one more unique feature of A Company that made Faucher uncomfortable, especially since nine times out of ten the enlisted men came to him to complain about what their officers were or were not doing. As the first sergeant he felt obliged to defend his commanding officer. In his book this was part of the job, just as it was his duty to shield the enlisted men in the company from that officer's more outrageous policies or off-the-wall ideas. "A first sergeant is like a shock absorber," he was told by his battalion sergeant major just after assuming his current post. "A good top sergeant smooths out the bumps from below while helping to keep the driver from veering off the road when he hits a pothole." As impeccable as this logic was, it did little to reduce the wear and tear Faucher endured while playing buffer.

Matt Garver was in the process of making one last check in an effort to ensure that all his charges were present and accounted for when he noticed a lone individual stretching and loosening up in the lee of a streetlight not far from where the company was forming. After watching the lean gray-clad figure with close-chopped hair for several seconds he called over to Faucher. "Hey, Alex. We have company."

Looking over in the direction that Garver was staring, the company first sergeant studied the lone figure for a moment. Everything Faucher saw pointed to the fact that the person in question wasn't part of the brigade. Yet there was no doubt that the individual was definitely taking an interest in what A Company was doing. Turning away and looking back to where Garver stood front and center of his platoon Faucher thought for a moment, then looked up at Garver. "Well, one thing is for sure. He's not one of ours. Odds are," he added after peeking over his shoulder once more, "he's regular Army."

"Think he's the new CO?"

Faucher considered this as he resisted a near overpowering desire to turn around and take a long hard look at the man. "Don't know. I've yet to meet the guy who's slatted to replace old Jimmy boy."

"There's one way to find out," Garver offered. "Let's see if he follows."

"Good idea. It's about time to get started anyway." With that, Faucher drew in a deep breath and bellowed in his best first sergeant voice, "A Company . . . *fall in.*"

The crisp order barked out by the man who was clearly in charge of the cluster of oddly uniformed men did not elicit the response Nathan Dixon had been conditioned to expect. There was no muted reverberation as the heels of a hundred pairs of sneakers came together and the hands of the men wearing them slapped their thighs as they assumed the position of attention. Instead the milling about slowly, very slowly ebbed while the muttering in the ranks diminished but did not totally disappear.

Much to his disappointment his preconceived notions of what a Guard unit looked and acted like were holding true to form, a sad fact he didn't much care for. He would have been content to be proven wrong. The hope of that being the case, however, faded as the man in charge of the company he would soon command prepared his charges for their first day of training. The response to each new command was sloppy and disjointed. It wasn't a total disaster. The company did face in the correct direction when instructed to do so. And they more or less stepped off together when the order "Forward . . . *march*" was given leaving no doubt in Nathan's mind that these men understood the basics. Unfortunately those simple maneuvers were just not being carried out with the same precision that he was used to seeing. As he watched them shuffle off the problem of just how much he would have to adjust his own standards to accommodate his new command and how hard he would be allowed to push in an effort to bring the company up to the level of performance to which he was used to once more came to the fore. Both issues were inexorably intertwined, different sides of the same coin.

With a sigh the troubled young officer set out to follow A Company. In the process of doing so he noticed that the leader of this brightly colored collection of Guardsmen kept glancing over his shoulder at him. Nathan had considered being a bit more circumspect while conducting his predawn reconnaissance. In the end he had decided to hell with that. He figured that while it might be true that the Guardsmen were less than stellar when it came to military matters, they were not dumb. His unexpected brush with Lieutenant Colonel Lanston two days prior had clearly demonstrated that. So Nathan opted to chuck stealth and instead maintain a safe and respectful distance.

* * *

Making no effort to hide what he was doing Matt Garver twisted his head about until he caught sight of the lone figure that had been standing under the streetlight. "Yep! He's following us."

Unable to acquire a good look at the figure trailing them, Alex Faucher abandoned his efforts to be circumspect and instead pivoted about in place and began to march backward, pretending to check that portion of the formation behind him. After watching the unknown interloper for several seconds, Faucher once more faced about and slowly picked up his pace until he was even with Garver. "That's a general's son if ever I saw one."

"Think we should stop and ask him to join us?"

Faucher shock his head. "If he wanted to join us he'd have done so already. He's just out here looking to get a sneak preview of us."

After the company turned onto the main street, Garver took another long look back at Nathan. "If he's trying to be sneaky, he's failing miserably."

"Well, be that as it may we have better things to do at the moment than play peekaboo with our captain-in-waiting." Easing back into his position, Faucher called out to the company, "Okay, A Company. It's our first day out so we're going to take it nice and easy today. Stay together and stay in step. At the double . . . *march!*"

The pace was neither grueling nor the route demanding. Like much of Benning the road the company took was flat and for the most part straight. Yet within minutes the Guard unit began to shed individuals who either could not or would not keep up. One by one these wayward souls made their way out of formation, disrupting it as men gave way or jockeyed around to fill the gaps left behind. Most of these castaways made a show of struggling on for a bit in the unit's wake before settling down to a leisurely walk as their comrades pressed on and disappeared in the distance. Whenever Nathan pulled even with these men few bothered to do more than give him a quick once-over. Nathan didn't return any of their stares. Instead he kept his eyes fixed on the man leading the formation. If he did notice that his command was diminishing in size he did nothing about it. Nor did any of the men leading the platoons or squads. What this said of them as leaders was hard for Nathan to gauge.

By the time the company passed what Nathan judged was the one-mile mark of their run he figured that he had gleaned all the useful information that he was going to from this early morning sortie. When they reached an intersection Nathan cut to the left and away from A Company. Since Chris preferred running in the afternoon and lingered in bed until she absolutely had to get up, Nathan broke out into a dead run. With luck he'd catch her just as she was stepping into the shower. The image of her standing before him as he scrubbed her back during a communal shower was more than enough to push aside any concerns he had over his future command's pitiful attempt at conducting an organized run.

"He's . . . gone," Garver managed to utter between gasping for breath. "Think . . . he's had . . . enough?"

Keeping his eyes glued to the roadway before him, Faucher made no effort to confirm Garver's observation. "Not likely. The only thing . . . I'm sure he's had enough of . . . is watching our pitiful performance."

"Hey! What . . . does . . . he . . . expect. It's our . . . first . . . day."

Looking up and down the contracted column at his much diminished company, Faucher grunted. "That won't make . . . any difference. He's a regular. His view of the world . . . is colored by his . . . indoctrination and . . . training."

Garver thought about this for a moment as he plodded along doing his best to keep up with the platoon in front of him. "It's going to be fun . . . to see . . . .who breaks first . . . him . . . or us."

After taking another hard look at the company Faucher smiled to himself. "I hope it doesn't . . . come . . . to that."

Unable to carry on this exchange Garver let his head droop as he concentrated on sucking in all the air he could manage. This left Faucher free to think about the coming ordeal that he would soon be confronted with. Like this morning's run he knew that the adjustment the company was going to have to endure as it prepared for its deployment to the Middle East was going to be both painful and grueling yet necessary. Very necessary, he repeated to himself as he watched two more of his charges drop out before facing back to the front and peering off into the dark in an effort to see the road ahead. These men, he reminded himself, were no longer simply his friends and neighbors. Their safety and welfare were his responsibility, his and the man who would soon be their commanding officer.

CHAPTER 8

West Bank

Finding it necessary to rest a bit before going on, Syed Amama slowed his pace and swerved to his right toward a weathered telephone pole. Before leaning against the pole, he instinctively cast a wary and circumspect gaze to see if anyone on the crowded street seemed to be taking an unnatural interest in him. Only when he was sure that none of the other pedestrians jamming the town's marketplace were following him did Syed relax. After planting his shoulder firmly against the pole, he shifted his weight onto his good leg before cocking the knee of the other one until its foot was barely touching the ground. With little more than a grimace he shook off a spasm of pain radiating from a wound that was still not completely healed even after three months of convalescing. Slowly, ever so slowly, the sharp burning sensation in his leg faded but did not completely disappear. Only the paranoia that stalked him like a second shadow created greater concern. Like the Israeli security forces that sallied forth into the Palestinian controlled areas of the West Bank, Syed feared that the wound he had suffered during his attack on the checkpoint would never leave. Like the Jews who occupied his homeland he had come to the sad conclusion that the best he would be able to do was to learn to cope with it, to find some way of dealing with it no matter how intolerable it was, just as his people had come to live with the fear of Israeli military reprisals.

Of course, unlike the Israeli occupation there were solutions to his problem, solutions that Syed chose to ignore. For him the danger of taking the addictive drugs his doctor offered was a risk he was unwilling to take. The young Palestinian feared that if he dulled his senses with opiates, he would lose his edge, his ability to maintain his vigilance. A man being sought by the Israeli Mossad needed to remain alert and ever watchful, lest he suddenly disappear like so many other patriots before him had. So he sought solace and escape from his pain and suffering by indulging in daydreams. Even here, amid the hustle that characterized the busiest part of this small market town Syed was able to close his eyes and conjure up a moment of tranquility, one free of the throbbing pain and nagging personal concerns that were now his constant companions.

This effort to withdraw from the torments of the world around him did not last long. The young Palestinian had just managed to settle into what passed for a comfortable place, physically and mentally, when he felt the pole supporting him begin to quiver. Within moments even the very ground beneath his foot began to quake. Opening his eyes he once more glanced about, searching for a danger that was close but as yet unseen.

Above the buzz of people swirling about him the deep-throated rumble of a tank's diesel engine betrayed the source of this new and most unwelcomed threat. Within seconds Syed caught sight of a slow-moving caravan of Israeli military vehicles trundling toward him down the center of the narrow street. As was their habit a Merkava tank led the solemn procession of sand-colored vehicles. This steel beast, mounting a 120mm gun and bristling with machine guns manned and held at the ready by the tank commander and loader, ignored all before it. Civilian traffic that had the misfortune of being in its path had no choice but to scurry off to one side or the other lest they be crushed by the advancing behemoth. The fact that the Israelis were in the throes of leaving the town did little to temper the stream of oaths and obscene gestures hurled their way by drivers forced to pull up over the curbs and onto the sidewalks. The shoppers on foot, in turn, found they had no choice but to scatter in order to avoid this unexpected invasion of their space. Angered by this disquieting disruption in their routine they too added their voices to the chorus of jeering directed at the Jewish soldiers, causing it to grow louder and more vicious as the Israelis continued to plow their way forward. Though he felt the urge to join his countrymen in giving the Israelis a final and fitting farewell, Syed kept his anger in check for he was under orders to maintain a low profile. Besides, the news that these troops would soon be replaced by a permanent American presence did much to mollify any elation he felt at seeing the Israelis depart.

Like so many of his companions who were eager to rid their land of the Jews, Syed wasn't sure if the change was a good thing or not. For years everyone had thought that the Israelis were invincible and immune to the feeble direct military pressure that lightly armed Palestinians such as he could apply. Yet this was turning out to be little more than a myth, a legend based on the recollections of past wars perpetuated by feeble old men. The sons and grandsons of Israel's founding fathers did not seem to have the heart or the stomach for waging the sort of perpetual war that the Palestinians and their Arab backers favored. The IDF was now little more than a shadow of an army that had once shocked the world with their courage, skill, and determination. Like many of their American backers, the Israeli soldiers sent to the West Bank did not possess the collective moral and political will to hold to a course of action no matter how necessary or righteous the cause. To the surprise of those who had taken up the standards of the outlawed PLA, it had taken little more than a nudge and the letting of a bit of Israeli blood and American pressure to send the Jews scurrying back across an imaginary line on the ground that had been drawn by diplomats eager to end a blood feud that they did not understand.

From top to bottom the unexpected announcement that the Israeli government had asked for the introduction of American peacekeepers had stunned the PLA, leaving the upper echelons of Syed's chain of command perplexed as how best to respond. It presented them with an entirely new set of problems and issues they were not prepared to deal with. While it was true that the flight of the Israelis partially fulfilled a stated goal of the PLA, it came at a time when they did not have the wherewithal to take advantage of it. The militant Palestinians had expected they would need to wage a protracted military campaign to rid the entire West Bank of the Jews before turning on and displacing the Palestinian Authority. To this end all their efforts had been focused on recruiting and training their fighters for it and not life after the establishment of an independent state under their control. Now, when they needed bureaucrats and moderates skilled in the art of diplomacy who had not been contaminated by their association with the PLO, Hamas, or Hezbollah all they had were dedicated young soldiers like Syed willing to lay down their lives. Without an organized governmental infrastructure of its own, the PLA's leadership was in no position to replace the Palestinian Authority, an organization that they considered to be little more than a collection of corrupt old men forced upon them by the U.N. and the United States. Since the military the PLA had created was tailored for a guerrilla war, it stood little or no chance of preventing another foreign force from replacing the Israelis or displacing the already established but weakened Palestinian Authority.

Thus the stunning success that Syed and others like him had achieved would, for the moment, be for naught. Americans were coming to take up the task of propping up and protecting the shaky and ineffectual Palestinian Authority as well as shielding the Jewish state. Both these results were an affront to the men who now rallied behind the banners of the new PLA. Establishment of a truly independent Palestinian state on the West Bank followed by the cleansing of their ancestral foe was viewed as being little more than phases of the same war other groups such as al Qaeda were waging against the enemies of Islam. Yet direct and decisive action against the Jews would have to wait until they were free of the sort of foreign interference that enfeebled the Palestinian Authority. As Syed's platoon commander was fond of saying, "Always tend to business first, then pleasure."

This thought was coursing its way through Syed's mind during his casual inspection of the Israeli convoy when he caught sight of a Jewish soldier perched high in the machine-gun ring mount of a heavy tactical cargo trunk. As if drawn to him by some unknown force the blond-haired, blue-eyed Israeli private gazed down upon the Palestinian leaning against a telephone pole. Like Syed, the Israeli's face betrayed no emotion or feeling as they regarded each other with care. Both men would have been surprised if they knew they shared a common sentiment. One was as glad to see the other go as that man was happy to oblige him by doing so. The only real difference lay in the fact that with the Israeli, his concerns and worries would soon be over. For Syed, the Israeli's departure changed little. If anything it complicated life for the PLA, presenting them with the same problem but an entirely new set of variables.

Having no firsthand experience with Americans themselves the young fighters of Syed's section found themselves having to rely upon information provided to them by their network of backers, fragmented snippets of data gleaned from the media and America's aggressive and all-pervasive culture mirrored by the Israelis. No one source could be considered to be wholly reliable since all were based upon stereotypes, misleading preconceptions, and half-truths. Even the information passed on from those members of the PLA that had once lived in the United States was of little use. The most sanguine members of the PLA saw the Americans as unpredictable and dangerous cowboys who just might prove to be as intolerant of the PLA's antics and were as quick to respond as the Israelis had been.

One of these doomsayers was Syed's own section leader. Upon hearing that the Americans were coming he called his tiny command together to discuss how they might deal with them. In the course of this gathering he cautioned them not to let their guard down when the Americans finally did arrive. "Because they are an impatient people the Americans will bring with them an aggressive approach to peacekeeping. They will not be content to stand on the sidelines and simply count the number of dead Jews as we purge them from our lands or turn a blind eye as we stockpile weapons and explosives," he pointed out. "The American soldiers will employ a lethal arsenal of advanced weapons directed by a highly sophisticated intelligence and targeting network. Their crack special operations forces who do most of their hunting and killing have honed their skills in countless encounters in Afghanistan and Yemen. To justify their presence here and whip up their hatred of us the American people are being told that our struggle is part of the great worldwide war on terrorism. This gives their President the freedom to take whatever steps he deems necessary to wipe us out. The fact that ours is a righteous war being waged to take back land taken from us by the Jews doesn't matter to them. They see our guerrilla tactics and techniques as being no different than the terror tactics employed by al Qaeda to strike at America itself. Our endeavors," he concluded with a chilly warning, "are just beginning."

As he went on the section leader spoke to his men in hushed tones as if they were gathered about a campfire and he were spinning a ghost story. "The American way of war relies upon directing massive amounts of firepower against decisive points. Yet they do not seem to fear face-to-face combat. Not only are their foot soldiers trained to be ready and willing to close with and crush anyone foolish enough to stand up to them, their culture teaches them that one can derive pleasure while doing so." Most of Syed's friends scoffed at this last point. Syed, however, was unable to casually brush aside his squad leader's words, for the young Palestinian had learned the hard way that the Americans did not hold a monopoly when it came to enjoying something that so many others saw as unpleasant and evil.

The last of the Israeli convoy was long gone before Syed was able to push aside the troubling thoughts his squad leader's warnings had engendered. Shaking his head as if waking from a deep sleep, he looked about once more to see if anyone was watching him. Gathering himself up he gingerly put weight back onto his injured leg as he prepared to make his way along the crowded street. As he limped along oblivious to the bustling crowd, he tried to cast aside the melancholy that followed him ceaselessly like a homeless dog. Doing so was not easy. In addition to the apprehension that the pending arrival of the Americans was creating throughout the PLA, Syed's return to active status with his squad had been short-lived. Within a week of reporting that he was ready for a new mission, he was told that he was being reassigned to other duties. It did not matter that he had no idea as yet what these duties would be, the young Palestinian managed to convince himself that they would not be to his liking. Having miraculously survived an attack that all had assumed to be suicidal, Syed felt a burning need to rejoin his squad, to be with his friends and comrades when the time came to face the new crisis that the coming of the Americans would surely create. He needed to demonstrate to anyone and everyone who might think otherwise that his brush with death had not affected him or diminished his dedication to their cause. A hardened veteran had once told Syed that any fool who has not been in battle before can be convinced to go forward. It takes something else, he warned Syed, something more than courage to keep doing so over and over again, especially after one had tasted the sting of enemy fire.

Syed had imagined that the cynical veteran had been speaking of personal courage and dedication to one's cause. Only now did he realize that other forces were able to compel a man to place himself in harm's way. Some of these compulsions were far different from the high-minded ideals poets and propagandists were so fond of. As much as he would have liked things to have been otherwise, his role in the massacre of the Israelis at the bridge had a profound impact upon his psyche. His actions on that day stirred emotions and awoke passions within him, some of which he did not fully approve of.

With the specter of death and threat of capture behind him, Syed was free to reflect upon what he had done as he convalesced from his wound. During his critical self-examination, he came to appreciate that he harbored no sense of remorse or guilt for having taken the lives of others. On the contrary, he took pride in having done so with such ease. There had been no hesitation on his part. If anything, in retrospect it had all been incredibly simple. At first Syed assumed that this was due to his training and his dedication to the cause. Only later, when it came time to decide whether he would remain with the PLA did it become clear to him that his rationale for doing so had nothing to do with nationalism or religious fervor. As much as he wanted his motivation for taking his place within the ranks of the PLA once more to be founded in an unflinching dedication to the PLA's stated agenda, Syed came to the conclusion that some of the things his squad leader had said about the Americans applied to him. Killing, it turned out, could be a pleasurable experience.

Like so many of his friends, Syed had been drawn to the juvenile desire to take chances that others saw as foolish or risk his life. As a young man, he had found it convenient to hide his pursuit of these deadly pleasures behind his nationalistic bombastic slogans of freedom and dedication to Islam he freely bantered about. Of course he spoke to no one about feelings. And since none of his companions admitted that they harbored them, Syed didn't either. Only now, when he found he needed to confront these truths did he dare give his sentiments a fair airing.

As he did so, he wondered if he was evil and twisted since his true reasons for taking up arms appeared to be visceral and base, almost animalistic in nature. He knew they were real, for whenever he left his mind free to revisit the images and sensations he had experienced during the attack, the ones that proved to be most dominant centered on the feeling of rapture he experienced during his brief and furious brush with death. He found himself savoring those memories. In the quiet of his room, he was able to close his eyes and once more see, hear, and smell all that he had experienced while charging the Israeli checkpoint. Everything about that moment remained as sharp and clear to him as they had been while they had been unfolding. Not even the prospect of losing his leg to infection in the aftermath of the attack diminished the incredible intoxication he felt every time he recalled the attack. What had been a mystery before that day was now clearly defined, with images and sensations that his mind could build upon and nurture, which was something it often did as he wiled away the hours during his painful recovery.

All of this created for Syed something of a moral dilemma. Before he could go back to the PLA, he would have to come to terms with this unspeakable desire to once more taste the exquisite joy that comes from flirting with and metering out death. Throughout this search for a more suitable rationale, what little shame he did suffer came from his total dearth of remorse and was trumped by the analytical approach he relied upon to justify his return to duty. Such explanations, of course, were for the consumption of others, for he slowly embraced the fact that he could not deny that his strange and unsettling joy in killing was at the heart of the matter. Efforts to convince himself that it was wrong to entertain such notions failed. No voice of moral indignation intervened to warn him that his soul would be corrupted or that his yearnings to kill for pleasure would lead him away from the teachings of the Prophet. Even when he allowed himself to listen to such rhetoric, it found no traction. Instead of rallying his conscience, he found it easy to dismiss all such reasoning as effeminate, brought on by a momentary weakness caused by pain and his long recovery. When his physical strength finally did begin to return, Syed not only accepted his feelings as sincere and acceptable, but had even managed to justify them as being correct and proper. A true warrior, he told himself, had to feel this way. Such men had to embrace such sentiments if they were to face battle again and again without fear, without hesitation. It was, after all, the will of Allah.

Thus reconciled to his destiny, his mind was free to dream of how he would once more throw himself into the midst of his enemies with total abandon. He would rise up off of his sickbed and go forth as a battle-hardened holy warrior. His purpose in life was clear. He was meant to strike terror in all before him, leaving them shocked and stunned by the violence being unleashed upon them. The allure that he felt drawing him to long to do so was proof that he was a true warrior of God. Once he was able to brush aside any lingering doubts and the doctor tending him pronounced that he was on the mend, Syed's urge to once more go into battle could not be checked.

At that moment destiny was leading Syed to a meeting with a complete stranger. Like the other fighters in his squad, Syed had never met an officer of the Palestinian Liberation Army. The fighting squads or sections that made up the PLA were recruited and trained by a local section leader. In carrying out these chores that individual exercised a great deal of independence and discretion. Only he

knew the identity of his superior and met with him to receive orders and guidance only when necessary. That officer in turn dealt only with the man who served as his
company commander. Just how far up this sort of structure
prevailed in the PLA was a mystery to all front-line fighters like Syed. That did not keep him and his comrades
from speculating on the matter. Some theorized that security was such a concern to the leadership of the PLA that
no one, save the members of the supreme command itself,
knew with any degree of certainty just how many units
made up the PLA and where all of them were. Having
learned the hard way through past mistakes made by
Hamas, al Qaeda, and Hesbollah, the current incantation of
the PLA remained in the shadows. With the exception of a
handful of spokesmen who gave voice to their struggle in
public forums in venues far removed from their homeland
and others who solicited support from sympathetic nations
and organizations, the leadership of the PLA concealed
their identity from friend and foe alike. It was even rumored that the Supreme Council wasn't even in the West
Bank, though Syed found this story a bit too extreme. What
no one questioned was the need for these precautions. Syed
certainly didn't find anything unusual about it. As a Palestinian who had grown up in the West Bank controlled by
the Israelis, he knew what it meant to be surrounded by enemies and informers, going through life having to cast one
eye over his shoulder. Trust for the people of that belea-
guered part of the world was more precious than gold itself
and far harder to earn.

The meeting Syed was headed for was a case in point.
He had no idea who his contact was or what he looked like
let alone what was going to be discussed. All he had been
told was where he was to go, when he was to be there, and
what he was to do when he got there. Along with these details, Syed was warned that any deviation would be a signal
to his contact that something was wrong. Not only would
the meeting be aborted, but Syed's future with the PLA

would be compromised. Whatever credibility he had managed to garner through his heroic efforts against the Israelis would be wiped away even if he was not to blame. He was, after all, a soldier and in war all soldiers were expendable.

Before reaching the corner where the small café he was headed for was located, Syed glanced at his watch. He was early, five minutes early. Not wanting to linger in front of the café itself and risk drawing undue attention, he chose instead to pause in front of a used bookstore he was passing. While absentmindedly glancing at the offerings the store's proprietor had selected to place in his window in an effort to entice customers, Syed noticed a number of books in English. One was an Arabic–English dictionary. That book he decided without having to think about it would be useful in the months ahead no matter what the leadership of the PLA had in store for him. Realizing that he did not have the time to rush in, buy the book, and still make it to his meeting he decided to wait until he had finished with his meeting at the café before returning to buy the book.

Upon entering that establishment he looked about, doing his best not to be too obvious while doing so. The place was quite deserted at the moment. His fellow countrymen were still outside, scurrying from one stall or store to another comparing goods, haggling over prices, and going about their business. Only when they had gathered up all they needed, and a little of what they didn't, would they flock to this café and others like it to enjoy a cup of coffee, chat with fellow shoppers, and pretend for a few precious moments that the world they lived in was safe, sane, and secure.

Taking his time, the young Palestinian made his way to a table that sat squarely before the front window. The small round table covered with a dingy tablecloth had but two chairs. It was the sort of place Syed imagined a young man and woman might choose to occupy while sipping coffee and enjoying each other's company. Even as he was taking his seat, he wondered why this particular spot was picked given that it was the most exposed spot in the entire café. Then, as he rested his elbows on the table and folded his hands before him while waiting to be served he looked out the window and understood. His contact was out there, lost in the milling crowd, watching him.

This thought triggered an all but irresistible urge to look about in search of the watchful eyes Syed knew to be on him, creating a stress that pitted his natural curiosity against the sort of discipline required of a foot soldier in the PLA if he was to survive the vicious wars being waged against the Israeli occupiers. This internal struggle left Syed weighing each movement and gesture he made, making his every action halting, hesitant, and painfully deliberate. Even his effort to find the right tone of voice when ordering coffee left him wondering if his attempts to act normal were having the opposite effect.

The young Palestinian was in the midst of his endeavors to strike a happy compromise between his nervousness, his curiosity, and his need for vigilance when a stranger walked into the café and without the slightest hesitation or pause made his way to where Syed was seated. With all the casualness and poise that he lacked, the stranger slumped down sideways onto the chair so that his back was to the window. After placing one arm on the table while draping the other across the chair back, he looked at Syed and smiled as he spoke without any sort of introduction or preamble as if they were old friends who were picking up a conversation that had begun sometime in the past. "I see your limp is still bothering you. That is unfortunate."

Alarmed by what the stranger's statement seemed to imply, Syed straightened up and leaned forward. "It is a small thing, really," he whispered. "In another month or so I am sure it will be gone. Even now I feel as strong as ever."

The stranger made no effort to suppress the amusement he seemed to derive from the discomfort his comment generated. For his part the young Palestinian was at a loss as how best to respond, if at all. Before he could muster up the courage to say something, a waiter shuffled up to the table with two cups of coffee and set them down before each man. It had not escaped Syed's notice that as best he could tell the stranger had not ordered the coffee by either word or gesture, leaving him to conclude that the man was either a regular customer at this particular café or that the waiter was also connected to the PLA. For all Syed knew as he surreptitiously glanced about, everyone in the place was PLA.

In the awkward silence that the pair lapsed into while the waiter was present and both men took a moment to taste their coffee, Syed's thoughts turned to more practical matters. Chief among them was the question of what exactly did this quiet stranger across from him want? There was no doubt in the young Palestinian's mind that the man was sizing him up. He could tell by the stranger's manner that he was measuring his every response, gesture, and word. This caused Syed to redouble his guard, something that was complicated by his desire to present the impression that he was calm and unfazed by this intense scrutiny.

For several long and nerve-racking minutes the two men eyed each other like boxers in a ring as they sipped coffee and waited for the other to say something. During this interlude Syed found himself wondering where exactly this person across from him fit into the PLA. The stranger looked to Syed to be in his mid-thirties, maybe younger. If this was true it would seem to indicate that he was a mid-level officer of the PLA, perhaps a company commander or some sort of staff officer. Never having met a PLA officer Syed had no way of knowing for sure. He could never have guessed the truth.

At age thirty-six Hammed Kamel occupied a unique place within the loose network of anti-Israeli organizations operating in the West Bank. He was a political neutral, officially unaligned with the numerous organizations that shared no common agenda save one, their uncompromising hatred for the descendants of Abraham's favored son.

Were it not for the fact that he needed them to provide him with manpower, money, and protection he would have had nothing to do with the PLO, Hesbollah, Hamas, and splinter groups such as the PLA.

Kamel's disdain for those organizations and his desire to remain aloof from the petty infighting that hobbled them did not derive from the sort of sense of superiority or self-righteousness that caused so much of the endless bickering and endemic distrust between them. He had no time for such childishness. Whenever asked why he refused to cast his lot with this group or that, his response was always the same. "In the end will it be of any consequence to our people who gets the credit for purging our lands of this ancient scourge? No. That is no more important than the means which will ultimately be used in achieving this end. After all, what is written by the hand of man will not be insignificant when it comes time for each of us to be judged by Him. We are but His humble instruments, and as such we must remain dedicated and focused on achieving our goal."

The manner by which the Palestinians would accomplish the goal Kamel and so many like him longed for was as much a cause for the division within the Palestinian community as was who would lead it. Even within the halls of the prestigious British university where Kamel studied, this topic created heated discussions and endless debates among his fellow Muslim students. Though all agreed that the mere existence of the Jews was an abomination to their God, like their leaders back in the West Bank and in capitals scattered across Southwest Asia, none of them could agree to a single coherent course of action. Frustrated by this prevailing lack of direction, Kamel came to the conclusion that he would have to find his own solution, one rooted in his studies of microbiology.

Placing his cup down on the table, Kamel turned away and looked off into the distance before speaking. "It is a rare thing for a suicide bomber to succeed in accomplishing his mission and live to tell of it."

His words, spoken with an air of nonchalance, stunned Syed. What, he asked himself as his mind raced to assess the situation, was this man eluding to? That he was a coward? That by living he had somehow failed? Even more disconcerting was the next series of questions that raced through his mind like a herd of panicked goats. Was this really an interview for a new position? Or was he being judged for violating an unwritten rule that he was unaware of? Unsure of what to say, Syed opted to hold back and say as little as possible until the purpose of the stranger's comments became clearer. With a casualness that belied the fear that he could feel welling within, Syed leaned back into his seat and looked out the window. "It was the will of Allah that I survived." Then looking back at the stranger, his eyes narrowed in a show of determination that he truly did not feel. "I can only guess that my work here on this earth is not yet finished, that like you, He has other things in mind for me." With that, Syed took another sip of his coffee, eyeing the stranger as he did so.

After weighing his young companion's retort for a moment to think, Kamel glanced back and studied the expression on Syed's face. Despite the alarm that he knew his statement had to have generated in the young man, Kamel was pleased to see that he had not been rattled. If anything, the sangfroid pose that Syed was endeavoring to strike was exactly the sort of response Kamel had been hoping for. "Do you have any idea why you have been asked here?"

With the same sort of steely determination that he had needed to steady his nerve on the day he had attacked the Israeli checkpoint, Syed answered, "I am here to receive my new orders."

Without any preamble or effort, Kamel switched to English. "Are you prepared to carry out those orders, no matter what they are?"

Sensing that this was some sort of test, Syed followed suit, doing his best to translate his Arabic thoughts into English words. "I am prepared to die if necessary."

"Yes, I know that all so well," Kamel sneered as he turned away and stared out the window. With a vague wave of his hand, he motioned at the teeming masses of people crowding the busy marketplace outside. "If all I wanted was someone to die for our cause, I could find half a dozen willing candidates out there in thirty minutes, maybe less." Turning his attention back to Syed, he continued. "What I need is not martyrs. Though that path has enjoyed some success, it cannot achieve the final solution we are all striving to attain. I do not need wide-eyed youths who can do little more than strap explosives about them and throw themselves into a crowd of unsuspecting Jews. What I need is a corps of disciplined soldiers, warriors who have the courage, the determination, and the skills necessary to carry out their orders again and again in the face of impossible odds."

Slumping back into his seat, Kamel again looked away as he gazed over the other patrons of the café and took a sip of coffee before going on. "A suicide bomber is like a bullet fired from a gun. Once fired, it is gone, beyond the control of the shooter. It cannot come back and say to its master, 'You should have aimed a little more to the left.' Only a living, thinking soldier can do that."

The words that fell upon Syed's ears were like a seductree's song. They enflamed his passions, passions that had already been brought to the fore by his own critical self-examination. "I understand," he stated crisply as his efforts to be guarded were now turned to restraining his enthusiasm.

"Good!" Kamel replied, making no effort to hide a smile that was not reflected in his eyes. "Now, when you leave here you will return to your home and stay there. You will receive a package tomorrow by courier that will contain instructions and money. You will follow those orders to the letter or," Kamel concluded, without making any effort to change his expression, "you will find the consequences of your failure to do so to be swift and terrible."

Without blinking, Syed nodded. "I understand."

"Now go."

Standing up, Syed prepared to leave when he suddenly paused. Taken aback by this last-minute display of hesitation, Kamel looked up. Like a child addressing a parent concerning an embarrassing matter, Syed's words were mumbled. "On my way here I passed a bookstore. There is a book, an English dictionary there that I would like to purchase. I was wondering . . ."

Relieved by the nature of this unexpected request, Kamel's smile returned. "Yes, of course. By all means do so. I think that would be an excellent idea."

Still feeling a bit foolish, Syed whispered a quick "Thank you" in Arabic before pivoting about and making for the door. When he was gone, the waiter who had served the pair returned to the table where Kamel remained, sipping his coffee as he stared vacantly out the window. "Well?" the waiter asked without preamble.

"He will do," Kamel responded.

"As what? A package or an operative?"

Kamel placed his cup down on the saucer and stared at it for a moment. "He thinks. I could see that in his eyes. And he has nerve. Otherwise he would have trooped out of here without hesitation. He is too smart to be a package. I think he will serve us better as an operative." Then, reminded of where Syed was going before heading home, Kamel looked up at the waiter. "When you deliver the material tomorrow I want you to look around. See how he lives. Talk to him about America and its culture. Find out how extensive his knowledge of their language and way of life really is. If he's good, we may even be able to find a more suitable use for him."

The waiter nodded. "As you command." With that he withdrew, leaving Kamel alone to enjoy his coffee as he watched his fellow Palestinians go about their daily chores, unaware of the price they would have to pay if Kamel's final solution succeeded.

CHAPTER 9

Fort Benning, Georgia

Scott Dixon's habit of peppering his father-son lectures with quotes uttered by famous generals and other warriors of note was one of those little idiosyncrasies that Nathan did not fully appreciate until well after he was commissioned. Only when he found himself facing challenges in the field that the Army's manuals and classroom instruction had not prepared him for did he come to regard those quotes as something more than colorful expressions randomly tossed about in an effort to dress up an otherwise dull discussion. They were shards of wisdom, pithy insights uttered by men who had themselves confronted the same sort of situations that Nathan faced day in and day out as he matured into an effective combat leader. In time he found himself turning more and more to those who had gone before him for guidance, drawing upon their insights and observations to illuminate his way along a path that was often shrouded in the dark mists of an uncertain and trackless future.

On the eve of his assumption of command he found himself reflecting upon a number of maxims that pretty much summed up how he felt about his immediate future and how best to deal with it. The one that came closest to the mark had been penned by Ralph Waldo Emerson concerning the relationship between men. "Trust men, and they will be true to you." This simple statement struck at the heart of the problem that Nathan expected he would soon find himself facing, providing him with a focus that would govern his conduct over the next few days.

By the time their five-day orientation wrapped up, Nathan, Terrance Putnam, and the other active Army officers assigned to the 176th Infantry Brigade had all come to the conclusion that no one within that organization would question the legitimacy of their orders. Despite the collective view they held concerning the Guard on certain issues, every one of them bought into the premise that the majority of the men they would soon be working with were mature enough to understand why the changes in personnel had been made. The brief conversation Nathan and Terrance had stumbled into with their future battalion commander was ample proof of that. What was not as clear was just how much resentment and resistance they, the professional soldiers, would encounter as they went about trying to prepare their counterparts and subordinates within the 176th for what promised to be a demanding and potentially hazardous tour of duty. Most feigned that they didn't much care what the Guardsmen felt or said. Even Nathan, who knew full well that he was replacing someone who had been popular, asserted that he hardly gave the matter a second thought. "We've got more important things to worry about," he remarked whenever the subject was broached. "If it was charm they were looking for they damned well wouldn't have picked us." Not wanting to be seen as breaking ranks with the only men they would be able to depend upon and commiserate with once they had joined the 176th Brigade, no one challenged Nathan's assertion.

Only when he was alone with Christina in the privacy of his own apartment did he manage to find the courage to openly discuss the nagging concerns regarding his ability to win over the hearts and minds of the men he would soon command. "It's more than simply finding a way of overcoming whatever residual resentment some of those men still harbor over the loss of their old CO," he lamented to his wife. "I've got to do so within the context of an institutional culture which I don't understand. Those people come from a common background and enjoy a shared heritage that has no equal in the active component. Talk about being the ultimate outsider!"

Christina did what she could to calm his fears by taking up her role as Nathan's Cassandra. "Your acceptance by them cannot be rushed without compromising your effectiveness as their commanding officer and principal trainer. Your strong suits are your technical and tactical expertise. Use that edge. Remember, you're their commanding officer, not their new best buddy. If you hold true to your core principles as a professional soldier and do what is right they will come around, eventually."

"Ah," Nathan responded glumly. "Eventually. But until they do, if they ever do, I'm going to be about as popular as a priest in the parlor of a Texas whorehouse."

In the days before his assumption of command, whenever she sensed that his mood was becoming far too dark, Christina would do her best to lighten the mood. On this night she did so by snuggling up next to her husband and planting a light kiss on his troubled brow. "Well, dear, one thing you don't dare do is go in there with that Attila the Hun, take no prisoners approach to leadership you inherited from your dad."

Glad to be offered an opportunity to change the subject, Nathan set aside his concerns and instead turned his full and undivided attention on his wife. Seizing her wrists, he spun Christina about and pinned her against the cushions of the sofa they were sharing. "If that be the case," he growled in a playful tone, "perhaps it would be best if you purged those barbaric traits from my system right here and now."

With a gleam in her eyes and a hint of a smile, Christina took up the invitation to a frolicking fun night by easing herself into a more comfortable position. "Well," she murmured, "anything for the greater glory of Rome."

For the moment whatever concerns or apprehensions Nathan felt about the challenge he would soon be facing was forgotten as the young couple eased into a night of mutually enjoyed passion.

The first hurdle to be overcome by each of the newly assigned officers from the active component was the manner in which they would report into the 176th Brigade. To Nathan and his compatriots this seemingly simple and routine act was crucial. How they assumed their assigned duties would set whatever tone they wished to establish with the men who they would work with, lead, and if things did not go well, risk their lives with. Those appointed to staff positions would have it relatively easy. Terrance Putnam halfheartedly joked that all he needed to do was find out where his office was. Everyone understood this sentiment. Once there he would have the luxury of slowly easing into his new duties by allowing the small staff assigned to his section to carry on the routine they were familiar with, leaving Putnam to choose how and when he would sally out from behind his desk and exercise his authority.

It was different for those who had been tagged to take over line units. Unlike Captain Queeg of the USS *Caine,* a rifle company commander cannot run his command perched upon a seat tucked away in the corner of an enclosed bridge. He is expected to place himself front and center of his unit whenever the opportunity to do so presented itself. This style of leadership begins on the very first day an officer takes command of a company in a ceremony that is centered on the symbolic passing of the unit guidon from the outgoing commanding officer to his successor. Since the circumstances leading up to his assumption of command were as contentious as they were unusual, both Nathan and Lieutenant Colonel Lanston agreed that it would be best if they skipped that ritual. Instead Lanston suggested a simple, to the point assembly in which he would introduce Nathan to Company A, say a few words in order to make it clear to the members of Company A that Nathan had his full support and confidence before having the battalion adjutant read the orders officially designating him as their commanding officer. What Nathan did after that was, as Lanston put it, "pretty much up to you." Discretion and unfamiliarity with his new superior kept Nathan from blurting out, "That's easy for you to say."

On the appointed day Nathan drove himself to the battalion area where he parked his car behind the battalion headquarters building. After shutting off the engine he took a moment to collect himself before climbing out and heading for the battalion commander's office. From there Lanston, Nathan, and the battalion adjutant trooped off in silence to a unit classroom where Company A had been assembled. The muttering of voices filling the hall came to an abrupt end when the unit first sergeant called the company to attention as Lanston strolled through the double doors at the rear of the room. Without pausing he trooped straight up the center isle to the raised platform at the front. Behind him came Nathan and the adjutant, a young Guard captain by the name of Les McDonnell who until recently had made his living managing a truck stop just off an exit of Interstate 81.

The footfalls of the three officers beat upon the tired old wooden floors in unison, resonating throughout the classroom like the beating of an anxious heart. Nathan didn't need to be clairvoyant to know what the men he would soon be commanding were doing. Few were making any effort to maintain the regulation eyes front mandated by the position of attention. While he marched by in the wake of Lieutenant Colonel Charles Lanston of Virginia row after row of citizen soldiers were turning their heads as much as they dared to catch a glimpse of him. They were watching his every move, his expression, the manner in which he carried himself in an effort to gauge just what sort of person was about to be anointed as their commanding officer. Painfully aware of this Nathan assumed the rigid and measured parade-ground stride that had become second nature to him at the Virginia Military Institute. Until he had a feel for the unit, he would have to keep on the straight and narrow. He would need to weigh every word, every expression, when dealing with the men who were about to be entrusted to him.

Without bothering to use the steps located on either side of the platform, Lanston bounded up onto the low stage and made for the lectern. While Nathan and McDonnell took their time to mount the stage properly and take up their respective posts behind him, Lanston looked out over the sea of attentive faces before him. When the pair of captains were set, he leaned over the lectern as if he were a country preacher about to deliver a sermon to his assembled flock. With the hint of a smile, he gave the command "take your seat" and pitched into his speech. "Since taking command of this battalion we've had some exciting times. I can recall one instance last summer as we were fighting the floods when I came to within a hairbreadth of ordering you people to stop filling sandbags and begin building an ark."

A ripple of muted laughter broke the tension that filled the room. Satisfied that his fellow Virginians were in a slightly more receptive frame of mind, Lanston wasted no time in getting to the heart of the matter. "In three weeks we will be leaving here. We'll be turning our backs on the serene pine forests of Georgia in order to go to a part of the world that has been racked by war and violence for decades, a place peopled by two hostile populations locked in a struggle that has defied every effort to resolve."

Taking a moment, Lanston studied the expressions of the men he would be leading to that place. He knew many of them by more than name. Without any effort he was able to conjure up images of many of them as members of the community he called home. Despite their current surroundings and attire, to him they were anything but soldiers. They were the men who built homes for Bedlow's growing population. They ran the businesses he and his own family frequented. They were the people he bumped into while walking down a street. He knew their wives. He ran the schools that their children attended. They were his friends. They were his neighbors.

For the briefest of moments Lanston was distracted. He found himself thinking that this was not where these men belonged. This was not where he belonged. None of them were ready for what they were being asked to do. Not now, not in three weeks. How could anyone, he found himself wondering, expect these men to bring peace to a place that had no concept of what peace was? These men, his men, were nothing more than hardworking Americans, doing their best to raise families in a quiet little part of the world few had ever heard of. Why they had been assigned to take on a mission he himself considered to be little more than a fool's errand made what he needed to say all the more difficult for Lanston to reconcile.

From his post just behind and to the right of his new battalion commander Nathan saw that Lanston had managed to secure their undivided attention. He missed the unintended hesitation caused by the battalion commander's sad reflections. Such subtleties could not penetrate the tension that gripped Nathan. All he could manage to perceive was that there had been a shift in attention of the men before him. He was no longer the center of attention, a fact that allowed him to relax and listen to what was being said.

With the shake of his head and a clearing of his throat, Lanston pushed aside his personal doubts as he struggled to pick up where he had left off. "We are not being sent there to sort this mess out. We are not being sent there to enforce a final solution."

Lanston's choice of words caused Nathan to wince, but he shoved that concern aside as his new battalion commander continued.

"Our task is simple. We're like the deputy sheriff called in to quell a domestic dispute." Pausing, Lanston looked straight at Staff Sergeant Oliver Rendell, whose duties with the county sheriff's department required that he periodically respond to such calls. "Ollie, I guess I have no need to tell you what *that's* like."

Blushing at being singled out like this, Rendell shook his head and smiled. "If that's the case, sir," he blurted out, "is it too late to transfer to the Air National Guard?"

Not the sort to refuse an opportunity to reinforce the unique rapport he had with the men in his battalion, Lanston grinned. "What? And miss all the fun?"

Again a ripple of subdued laughter rose up from the Guardsmen of Company A. When he felt it had gone on long enough, Lanston returned to the matter at hand.

"This call we've been invited to respond to isn't going to be as easy as one of Ollie's midnight spats. The people we will be separating over there are armed and dangerous. Not only do their armories sport weapons of every sort and description, they are driven by an age-old hatred that defies understanding. This hatred is all-consuming. It is an unimaginable and depraved hostility that compels the most radical element of one side to drape explosives around their children and hurl them at their foes like grenades, leaving the other no choice but to unleash its tanks and fighter bombers against towns and villages teeming with hapless civilians. While most of the Israelis and Palestinians want nothing more than the freedom to live out their lives in peace, it has become painfully clear that those who populate the fringes on both sides of the fence have a different agenda. For them there can be no compromise, no reconciliation. For them there is but one solution, one possible end state. For them victory can only be realized when every man, woman, and child of the other side is dead."

Pausing, Lanston allowed his Guardsmen a moment to absorb this brutal fact of life before pressing on. "We are not going to change anyone's mind over there. We're not even going to try. That sort of thing is the responsibility of our national leaders and the leaders of the two aggrieved parties. Our mission is simple. We've been charged with separating those two people and keeping them from killing each other, period. For six months we will stand watch over a troubled land. I am told that during that tour of duty the fanatics on both sides will do anything and everything within their power to draw us into this age-old blood feud or make our stay there so painful that we, the United States, will leave for good and allow them to get back to the serious business of slaughtering each other. From the day we get off the plane in Israel until the moment we're wheels up and headed home each and every one of us will be both a guardian of the peace and a potential target, a symbol of both hope and hatred."

Lanston paused yet again as he straightened up, glanced down at the lectern as if searching his notes before speaking again. This time his tone was decidedly softer, betraying a hint of concern. Whether this was real or simply an orator's device was hard for Nathan to discern. He didn't know the man well enough. "To see us safely through this ordeal we're going to have to embrace a level of discipline and vigilance that we Guardsmen are not used to. We're going to find ourselves in situations that call for quick, decisive actions. Chances are some of you will find yourself under fire from one or both parties that we are trying to separate. Though I pray that this does not happen, it would be foolish for us to go over there unprepared to deal with that sort of thing. To do so would be nothing less than criminal."

By now Nathan knew what was coming. In anticipation he braced himself. "To assist us in our endeavors both before we deploy and during our tour of duty the Department of the Army has assigned a number of highly qualified and experienced regular Army officers to this battalion."

Throughout the room Nathan could see a number of Guardsmen turn their gaze away from their colonel and toward him as Lanston continued to speak.

"I know that this move has not been popular with many of you. I understand the confusion and resentment some of you harbor at the manner in which this action was implemented. Be that as it may, let there be no doubt in any of your minds that I, personally, am thankful to have these regular Army officers as part of our battalion." The force of Lanston's words left no doubt that they were being spoken from the heart. "My goal for the next six months is to do everything within my power to keep each and every one of you men alive and see that you are returned home safe and sound to your families and our community. To achieve this goal I will be appealing to God, depending on the technical and tactical expertise of Captain Dixon, and relying upon your strength of character and good judgment. God willing, we will see this thing through."

Finished, Lanston stepped back from the lectern and between Nathan and the adjutant. As he assumed his official face, First Sergeant Faucher called the company to attention. When all in the room were on their feet and settled, Lanston turned to McDonnell. "Adjutant, post the orders."

On this cue, Alex Faucher jumped to his feet and shouted, "Company, a-ten-*shun!*"

Amid the chatter created as metal folding chairs were shoved about across the tired wooden floor, the soldiers of Company A, 3rd of the 176th Infantry, rose and assumed a near perfect position of attention. Only their eyes refused to conform to Faucher's exaggerated order. Without exception they were riveted on the man who was about to become their commanding officer as he stepped forward and faced Lanston.

With a well-measured and methodical precision that hid his nervousness, Les McDonnell read the orders in the deep, solemn monotone voice that many officers assume to be mandatory on such occasions. Nathan heard the laboriously articulated words but did not pay much attention to them. His mind was already speeding far ahead, fixing his mind not on what would happen in the next few minutes, but on the plan of action he would need to execute in order to translate the trite verbiage of the orders the battalion adjutant was reciting into reality. The fact that the battalion commander had chosen to drop the ceremonial passing of the guidon did not bother Nathan in the least. On the contrary, as far as Nathan was concerned, the quicker this onerous rite was over the better.

At the conclusion of McDonnell's reading of the orders, Lanston took a step forward and offered Nathan his hand. This threw Nathan. As a professional soldier, steeped in the exacting ritual of military protocol, he expected a salute rather than the causal demeanor that Lanston was resorting to in order to terminate this affair.

Lanston half expected this. Taking the lead, he forced his right hand into Nathan's even before the young captain managed to bring it up. Leaning forward, Lanston whispered into Nathan's ear. "We have much to learn from and about each other, and not much time. Good luck, Captain."

With that he straightened up, rendered the hand salute Nathan had been expecting. Upon receiving Nathan's response in kind, Lanston pivoted about and trooped off the stage with McDonnell following on his heels.

For a moment Nathan stood rooted to the spot he had taken up after mounting the stage as he watched Lanston make his way down the isle and out the door. Only when the battalion commander disappeared into the glow of the bright Georgia sunlight did Nathan step forward to the vacated podium and look down at his command. He knew better than to reach up and clutch the edge of the wooden stand before him. A podium, he had been told time and time again, was little more than a crutch, a prop used by a weak speaker to keep himself from falling flat on his face. At this moment Nathan didn't care much about such petty concerns. He was alone now before a company of soldiers who were, as best he could tell, less than thrilled with the circumstances that had brought them to this place. The way he figured it, no matter how trivial or artificial, he needed to use all the support he could get.

Mustering up his courage, Nathan issued his first order

in a voice that was as devoid of emotion as he could manage. "Be seated." The thought of adding the word "gentlemen" never entered the mind of an officer who had been raised in an Army where adherence to political correctness was viewed by some to be as important to an officer's career as tactical proficiency. Nathan had intended to use the time it took his company to settle down to frame his remarks. Like his father, he did not believe in preparing detailed notes or well-manicured speeches. He tended to shoot from the hip, on the platform and in the field.

The words with which he would launch his command did not come to mind. Instead of focusing on them, Nathan instead found himself scanning the faces before him. While there were some that could just as easily belong to any member of the Army's active component, most seemed to belong to men who were older than he was used to seeing. He had been forewarned by Guard officers during their orientation that members of the National Guard were, as they put it, "more mature." Those words did little, however, to prepare him for facing the reality. Equally stunning to Nathan was the unvarying sameness of those faces. To a man they were white, or more correctly Caucasian. This arresting revelation all but rendered him speechless as he tried to recall any previous occasion when he had been so acutely aware of the racial composition of an Army unit. This, Nathan suddenly found himself thinking as he nervously shifted his weight from one foot to the other before speaking, is going to be a challenge.

"Colonel Lanston's last words to me before departing," Nathan began, again doing his utmost to betray no emotion or nervousness, "was that we, he and I, had much to learn from and about each other. I dare say the same holds true when it comes to us, you and I. Before today all we had in common was this," Nathan stated as his pointed to the black embroidered "U.S. Army" sewn over his right breast pocket. "That all changed five minutes ago when Captain

McDonnell posted the orders assigning me as your commanding officer."

Nathan paused to collect his thoughts and measure the response from the crowd of men before him. Their expressions were as impassionate and uncommitting as was his tone. "From here on in, until this mission is over or I am replaced, our fates and our fortunes are one." Forcing himself to relax, Nathan let go of the podium and moved out from behind it. Not knowing what to do with his hands, he grasped them behind his back as if standing at parade rest. "We have much to do before we leave wild and wonderful Fort Benning and not much time, so I will not waste it here in a lame effort to introduce myself. I dare say you already know a great deal about my background, some of which I imagine is true."

For the first time a handful of Guardsmen in the audience broke the silence as they chuckled or let out an involuntary guffaw in response to a comment that Nathan had not meant to be funny. These offenders quickly realized what they had done and, blushing in embarrassment, stifled themselves as the room once more lapsed into silence.

Sensing that he had managed to achieve something of a minor chink in the stone wall that the members of his new company were presenting to him, Nathan decided to cut his losses and bring this affair to a quick and merciful end. "The training schedule for today has you listed for small-arms training, something that I am sure will be far more enjoyable and worthwhile than sitting around listening to me trying to impress you."

Pausing, Nathan looked down at the toes of his boots, suddenly at a loss as to how best to put a period on this session. Glancing up, his eyes met those of Alex Faucher who returned his stare. In an instant, he managed to regain his balance and knew what to do. "First Sergeant, when we leave here I would appreciate it if you would make sure the arms room is open. XO," he stated briskly, turning to Gordon Grello, "make sure the transportation to the ranges is laid on and waiting. Once the issuance of weapons has begun I want to see all officers and the first sergeant in my office."

Responding to the sudden spate of orders, both Grello and Faucher jumped to their feet and blurted out a crisp "Yes, sir" in unison. This response had been automatic and, given the circumstances, far more enthusiastic than either man would have liked. But while it was true that they were not regular Army, they were Army nonetheless. It was this fact that Nathan and the other active Army officers condemned to doing time with the 176th Infantry Brigade were counting on.

The meeting in Nathan's office was as mercifully short as it was stilted. Obsessively Nathan stated that its purpose was to review the training schedule for the balance of the week and ensure that all necessary coordination had been made and support for that training was on track. In truth all he wanted to do was to avail himself of this opportunity to meet his officers so that he could begin the process of matching names that he had only seen so far on old officers' evaluation reports with the faces of the men who those reports described. It was the first of the undeclared jousting matches that he would engage in as he, a new commanding officer, struggled to wrap his arms around a company of strangers who were in the throes of an intensive training program that even the most optimistic professional soldier knew was insufficient to prepare them for the mission they had been assigned.

The meeting came to an end when the company clerk rapped on the door of Nathan's small office, opened the door, and stuck his head in. Out of habit, he looked over to where Faucher was sitting. "Top, all the weapons have been issued and the platoons are forming up."

Realizing that his clerk had committed a major faux pas by addressing him and not their new company commander, Faucher looked over to Nathan. "Excuse me, sir, but . . ."

Nathan saw the pained expression on Faucher's face. "Yes, by all means. Like I said in the classroom, time is not on our side." Standing up, he looked at each of his officers. "Gentlemen, carry on."

After rendering salutes that were anything but crisp, the XO and platoon leaders began to file out of the room, when Faucher was about to reach the door, Nathan called out, "First Sergeant, could I have a word with you?"

Closing the door and taking his seat when he saw Nathan do likewise, Faucher realized what was coming. He had expected it and, in truth, was looking forward to this opportunity to speak with the man who would lead his company for the next six months. That Faucher considered this his company and not yet Nathan's was only natural. Though it was true that Nathan was now wearing the patch of the 176th Infantry Brigade and the unit guidon draped at a jaunty angle behind his seat was his, like the rest of the men in Company A Faucher still saw Nathan as an outsider, something of an unwelcomed intruder in their tightly knit world. Just how long it would take him to accept this regular Army officer was not the question. The real question weighing heavily on Faucher's mind at the moment was if he would ever be able to do so.

Before leaning back in his seat, Nathan reached down and pulled a bottom drawer out several inches. Relaxing, he propped his feet up on the open drawer, reclined in his seat, and brought his hands to rest on his stomach, fingers interlaced. "Well, here we are."

Caught off guard, Faucher's expression betrayed his puzzlement. The best the bewildered NCO could manage was a muffled "Yes, sir."

"I've been told you're a good man, First Sergeant, a top-rate NCO." Nathan's tone was casual, friendly.

Having recovered his balance somewhat and appreciating that they were now engaged in a far more candid exchange than he had anticipated, Faucher dropped all pretenses and responded as he would to one of his fellow firefighters back in Bedlow. "The same source that has probably been feeding you information about this unit tells me you're a first-rate line officer, a man who knows his stuff cold and is able to get the job done, come what may."

A hint of a smile lit across Nathan's face. "I see. Well, I sort of suspected Tim Mifflin was playing a double agent."

"He might have been your classmate and brother rat way back when, sir," Faucher smirked, "but he's a Guard officer now."

"And I'm not."

The statement hit Faucher like a spray of cold water. He studied his new company commander's face for a moment, searching for a clue as to how best to reply. For his part Nathan did nothing but return the stare, maintaining the same deadpan expression he had worn throughout the abbreviated change of command ceremony. Realizing that it was probably too late to backpedal, the Guardsman decided that this was as good a time as ever to see just how far he could go with a man whom he would be working with day in and day out for the next six months.

"No sir, you're not. While it may be true that you went to school in Virginia and we all took the same oath to defend and uphold the same Constitution, there is a cultural gulf that I don't know how we're going to bridge."

Nathan took his time responding, carefully choosing his words and delivering them in as calm and as even a tone as he could manage given the tension that permeated the room. "We start, First Sergeant, by doing our duty and keeping our focus on the mission. Whatever animosities or concerns the men of this company may harbor because I am a regular Army officer who has replaced one of their own is going to have to be set aside. We—you, me, and the company as a whole—are going to have to find a way to get the job done despite our diverse backgrounds and institutional prejudices. The lives of the men entrusted to our care and the success of this mission depends upon this."

Pausing, Nathan made no move as he held his unblinking gaze fixed on Faucher, waiting for him to respond.

"That, sir, is a tall order. I'll be the first to admit that those of us who call Bedlow our home tend to take our time warming up to strangers. There are people living in the county for fifteen years who are still referred to as the new folks at the end of the road. This isn't like a company in your Army where soldiers come and soldiers go like passengers on a New York subway. Before a new man is allowed to join Company A he has to have someone who is already a member of the unit and whom we trust recommend him. And even then it's not a sure thing."

"So I've heard."

"It's no reflection on you personally, sir. I have no doubt that you're a crackerjack officer when it comes to tactics and such."

"But . . ." Nathan intoned without finishing his sentence.

Finding that he was far too committed to his line of attack, Faucher pressed on. Straightening up in his seat as if bracing himself, he looked Nathan square in the eyes. "If what Captain Mifflin says is true, in time the majority of the company will come around and warm up to you. They'll come to see your assumption of command as the best thing that could have happened to this company. They will come to understand that there are times when friendship and our laid-back approach to our military duties has to give way to hard-knuckled reality. Unfortunately, there are some men who will never accept you as their commanding officer. They will always see you as an interloper, a man who was foisted upon them against their will. Oh, they'll salute you and do what you say, but they will never be able to overcome the fact that you're sitting there, in a seat that to them belongs to one of their own."

There was a moment of silence as Nathan considered

this, then leaning forward a bit, he half smiled. "And what camp do you belong to, First Sergeant?"

Without a wit of hesitation, Faucher gave Nathan a friendly sort of smile that one would expect to see from a friend you accidentally bumped into on the street. "I'm with the colonel. As far as I'm concerned your assignment to this company is the best thing that could have happened to A Company."

Having expected a more guarded response, Faucher's enthusiastic endorsement left Nathan at a loss. Sensing this, the company first sergeant stood up. "Well, now that we have *that* out of the way, sir, I fear that we have to get down to some really serious business."

"And that would be?"

"There's a pile of paperwork that Lieutenant Grello, the company XO, thought would best be handled by you."

Nathan's immediate response was to suspect his new number two's reason for leaving such mundane work for him. Bury the old man in paperwork and keep him out of our hair, he thought as he sat up. A good tactic, worthy, he half chuckled, of myself.

Confused by his commanding officer's reaction, Faucher gave Nathan a funny look. "Sir?"

Brushing aside his uncharitable thoughts, Nathan smiled. "Oh, nothing. It just seems that perhaps the cultural gulf between your Army and mine may not be as great as you think. It seems we both run on the same fuel, paper."

Laughing, Faucher turned to open the door. "Well, sir. It's our only defense against the battalion staff. If we don't keep them busy by barraging them with reams of paperwork, they'll have nothing better to do than come down and conduct training inspections and the like."

"Well, we can't have that, now can we, First Sergeant. Bring it on and I'll do my part to keep those folks away."

Just as he was about to leave the room, Faucher stopped and turned. "Sir, in about an hour I'll be running chow out to the ranges where most of our people are. Would you care to join me?"

For the first time Nathan let his guard down. Though it had been little more than an innocent remark, Faucher's use of the word "our" rang out in Nathan's ears. With a nod, he accepted the invitation. "I'd like that, First Sergeant."

CHAPTER 10

Fort Benning, Georgia

During the ride out to the stationary combat rifle range where the bulk of Company A was training Nathan prepared himself for his first real dealings with the men he now commanded. In his mind that morning's change of command ceremony didn't count. At the range he would have no script to follow. He would not have his battalion commander beside him, drawing much of the attention away from him. There would be no barriers keeping the soldiers he now commanded at bay. In place of the rigid formality that had kept him isolated and apart from his new command that morning, the range would present him with an unruly, free-flowing situation in which individual soldiers would have their first opportunity to get up close and personal with the new "Old Man." Surrounded by them as they ate their meals or waited for their turn in the firing order, Nathan would have to deal with whatever came his way. In many ways he saw himself as being no different from the pop-up targets scattered about downrange, exposed to anyone who had a mind to draw a bead on him and take potshots.

This sort of apprehension bordering on dread was nothing new or unique. Every officer who ever served experiences it to some degree or another every time he steps before his new unit. From the moment an officer first reports for duty he finds himself engaged in a sparring match with his subordinates. The natural curiosity that every member of the unit entertains concerning their new leader propels them to engage in all sorts of interesting and unique ways to assess his skills, knowledge, and personality. Sharpening this quest for knowledge is the certainty that things will change. No one has any idea what those changes will be or how they will manifest themselves, giving rise to the favorite pastime of soldiers the world over: speculation. Will the new man be tougher when it comes to discipline? Is he the sort of person one can freely talk to and perhaps even kid around with? What sort of standards does he intend to impose? Is he a spit-and-polish martinet or a muddy-boots type? A thousand such questions compel many to seize every opportunity afforded them to probe, prod, and test their new superior. For them it is important to figure out which habits they had slipped into under the previous regime needed to be altered or abandoned before the honeymoon period with the new man is over and he gets serious about commanding.

The task of feeling out all newly assigned officers is usually taken on by the more aggressive of the junior enlisted soldiers, men who seldom hold rank but have managed to assume a position of leadership among their peers that is as real as those who wear stripes. Every unit has them, its ration of cocky, outspoken soldiers who believe the only way to measure a new officer is to push all his buttons to see just how much freedom they will be able to enjoy in an authoritarian organization created to defend that principle, not practice it. From here on in Nathan knew he would have to be on his toes, listening closely to every word, every request, every comment, that was directed at him. He would have to quickly determine what the speaker's intent was, whether the man before him was engaged in an innocent exchange or was nothing more than a little prick determined to goad him into overreacting. As with everything else during these first few days, Nathan would need to take the time to frame a suitable response appropriate for both the situation and the person he was speaking with.

Unlike so many of his own peers, Nathan had entered

active duty prepared for just this sort of thing. It wasn't until after he had reported into his first unit that Nathan had come to appreciate just how much of an advantage he had over other officers who had not been Army brats when dealing with their subordinates. As a child he didn't fully understand his stepmother's assertion that his father treated his family as if they were soldiers and his soldiers as if they were his family. He had always assumed that she was accusing him of being unable to separate his professional life from his home life. Only later did it dawn upon Nathan that his father's behavior had been intentional, that he had been preparing his sons for life in the real world the only way he knew how. It took Nathan even longer to appreciate just how valuable all the little lessons his father had imparted to him along the way from childhood to professional soldier could be.

One of the more valuable lessons Nathan took away from his father was that not every challenge to authority needed to be answered. Like all young men teetering on the edge of adulthood, Nathan occasionally felt the need to push the envelope and see just what he could get away with. When the struggle was purely verbal and Nathan was fast approaching a line Scott did not want his son to cross, he would make a face and cock his head slightly to the right. The official explanation Scott gave for this particular habit was that his hearing in his right ear was shot. Even in the midst of some of the most heated discussions with his son he'd stop after doing so and jokingly state that as a young officer he had fired the old .45 far too many times without proper protection. "My hearing in that ear isn't what it used to be," he'd claim in a calm, nonchalant manner. Then, as his face lost all expression he would peer into his son's eyes with a cold, steady gaze as he stated in a cool, deep voice, "You were saying?" It wasn't until he was a cadet at VMI seriously studying leadership for the first time that Nathan came to understand that in all likelihood his father had heard him perfectly well the first time.

Rather than allowing a situation to deteriorate, Scott used a physical handicap, one that wasn't too severe as best anyone could tell, as a means of providing his son an opportunity to reconsider his words and conduct.

Though too young to use that sort of ploy, Nathan understood the principle and the need to develop his own unique ways of handling uncomfortable situations. As the Hummer hauling him, his first sergeant, and driver pulled off the main road and onto the range, Nathan wondered how many tricks from his personal leadership playbook he'd need to employ in the course of the next hour. As if to confirm this, after the driver had brought the Hummer to a complete stop, dismounted, and headed to the rear of the vehicle to drop the Hummer's tailgate to fetch the unit's noon meal, Faucher leaned forward, placed his hand on Nathan's shoulder, and whispered in his ear, "Remember, sir. These are Guardsmen. Some of them tend to be a bit more direct than the soldiers you may be used to dealing with."

Nathan nodded. "I understand. Now," he stated, forcing a smile, "as they say on Broadway, it's showtime."

The appearance of the first sergeant's Hummer did not bring an end to training. There was no mad rush to form a chow line, no call for an immediate cease-fire. Though the troops belonged to Nathan and Faucher, on this range the NCOs of the Infantry School's training command were in charge. No one did anything or went anywhere on their range unless they ordered it. Even when the post commander heralded by his twin stars swooped down upon the range in the course of a training inspection, the handpicked cadre didn't break their stride or alter their conduct one wit. For them this was more than a simple mark of professionalism and acknowledgment of their authority. It was a necessity. Their mandate to prepare young soldiers to close with and destroy their enemy did not allow them the luxury of excess time. They had the task of passing on to their trainees skills that so many of their fellow countrymen saw as a barbaric anachronism that had no place in "their" society. Soldiers who had been conditioned to believe that guns were evil had to leave this range confident in their ability to harness their rifle's potential and direct its lethality effectively each and every time their duty required it. Given little time to accomplish this feat, the range NCOs used every minute allocated to them, rain or shine, night and day. For this reason the appearance of a captain sporting a National Guard patch on his left sleeve was shrugged off by those running the range.

The same was not true for the soldiers of Company A. Like all soldiers through the ages, meals were a highlight of their day. The arrival of the first sergeant with chow broke the grim, grinding routine that dominated a training exercise of this nature. Not even the sight of their new commanding officer could stifle the enthusiasm most of the men felt now that the prospect of a break and food was at hand.

Nathan, of course, did not share this enthusiasm. For him, it was the beginning of an ordeal, one that started with the problem of how best to appear that he was doing something important when in fact he had nothing to do. At the moment everyone on the range had something to do. The first sergeant's driver was busy setting up the chow line in a covered area set aside for mess and breaks while Faucher walked over to the tower to let the NCO in charge of the range know he was there and would soon be ready to start serving chow. The soldiers of Company A were scattered about the range in groups. Some were sprawled on the ground behind small piles of sandbags that delineated the firing line, engaging the computer-driven and -scored targets as they appeared in their respective firing lanes. Others who were waiting to be cycled through the training lounged in the bleachers just behind the firing line, quietly watching the performance of their friends or chatting among themselves in hushed tones. Those who had finished and had no need to repeat the exercise due to a poor showing were farther back in an open-air shelter filled with large benches made of thick planks upon which they cleaned their weapons. Their conversation here was a bit more lively and sprinkled with touches of humor as each man's performance on the firing line was praised or derided by his peers.

Sprinkled about in these various groups were members of the cadre. The senior NCO and an assistant running the exercise manned a small state-of-the-art control tower. They were focused on ensuring that the computer program was functioning properly and that all training was being conducted in accordance with the established lesson plan. Out on the firing line a bevy of assistant instructors knelt or stood behind each firing pit, watching and critiquing their assigned shooter as he engaged the targets in his lane. Immediately to their rear, at the base of the tower, was the secondmost member of the cadre, charged with overseeing the safety of the range. It was his duty to watch that everyone on his range, regardless of rank, was adhering to the stringent safety protocols that this sort of training demanded. When a violation occurred he had both the unquestioned authority and responsibility to correct it, even if it meant bringing the entire operation to a standstill until it was safe to continue training.

For one awkward moment, Nathan stood beside the first sergeant's Hummer, looking this way and that as he took in the situation before him and tried to decide what to do next. It didn't take him but a minute to determine that of the three groups of his men present on the range, the ones who would be least distracted by his presence would be those who had already fired. Screwing up his courage, he took a deep breath before stepping off for the open-air shelter.

Looking up from the parts of his weapon neatly lined up before him, Jerry Slatery caught sight of his new commanding officer as he approached. Grinning, he began to make a squawking noise like a Hollywood starship going into battle. "Errp, errp, errp. Intruder alert, intruder alert. Errp, errp, errp."

Turning away from their own labors, the other members of second platoon glanced out from under the shelter to see what Slatery was blabbering about. When he caught sight of Nathan, Paul Sucher grunted. "Oh, great! It's Captain Courageous."

Travers watched Nathan for a moment before rendering his opinion. "More like Captain Walketh Erectus."

Knowing who they were talking about without the need to look up, Sergeant Gene Klauss went on with reassembling his weapon as he spoke. "He's VMI. They all walk like that."

Ronald Weir shook his head as he glanced between the officer and Klauss. "I beg to differ with you, my dear sergeant. Captain Mifflin at brigade doesn't go walkin' around like that."

Slowly Sucher drew the cleaning rod from the barrel of his rifle as he continued eyeing Nathan. "That's 'cause he's a Guard officer. He's been domesticated."

Slatery was in the process of commenting on this when Matt Garver set aside his rifle, wiped his hands on a rag he'd been using, and began to make his way toward Nathan. "Okay, people," he stated flatly as he made his way between the benches, bobbing and weaving as he went so as not to bump into the men standing around them, "can the sarcasm and look sharp."

Not one to miss a chance to throw out a crack, Jerry Slatery threw out his hands, flashed a smile, and in a mocking French accent announced, "But how can we do that, *mon ami*? After all, we are the Guard."

Unable to hold back, the men around Slatery broke out in a chorus of laughter, causing Garver's face to redden with barely concealed anger as he reached the edge of the shelter and prepared to greet his new commanding officer for the first time.

* * *

Nathan was well aware that the ripple of laughter was in response to some sort of comment one of the men made about him. He had watched as all their faces, one by one, turned and stared at him as he grew closer to the shelter. Having studied leadership at VMI and in the Army he understood the dynamics of group identity and psychology that were at work here. Having undergone the ordeal of being in a unit when a new commanding officer came on board he had a fairly good idea what the Guardsmen who were staring at him were saying. None of this, of course, made what he was doing any easier. The only difference between this occasion and the first time he walked into a unit was that he had no illusions this time, no false hope that he would be showered with instant respect or acceptance simply because a one-page set of orders stated that he was now their superior. He'd have to do what every officer has to do every time he meets his new command for the first time. He'd have to prove himself and earn their respect, bit by bloody bit.

When Nathan was but a few paces away, Garver drew himself up into a position of attention before rendering a hand salute. "Sergeant Garver, platoon sergeant, second platoon."

While it was not the sharpest salute or the crispest report he'd ever received from an NCO, Nathan was somewhat relieved. He had half expected the silent treatment, or worse. While raising his own hand to return Garver's salute, a cynical little voice in the back of his mind mockingly whispered, "Well, at least someone in this unit has a working knowledge of military courtesy. Maybe this won't be as hard as you've thought."

With the formal greetings concluded, Nathan dropped his right hand to his side, then quickly swung it behind his back where he clasped it with his left hand. He had considered offering it to the sergeant first class standing before him but decided not to at the last minute. Something told him that this was neither the time nor place for such a casual display of familiarity. Instead, he took a moment to look around at the men who were doing their best to appear busy while watching his every move. "I take it your men have all completed the exercise and qualified?" he stated in an effort to fill the awkward silence that had descended upon the shelter.

For his part Garver was just as anxious to say something lest he be left standing there looking like a dumbstruck bumpkin. "We're Virginians, sir. Most of my boys learned to shoot before they learned to read."

From behind him Slatery's cheery voice sang out with an unsolicited and most unwelcomed crack. "That's true accept for Travers over here. He hasn't learned to do either yet."

The storm of laughter unleased by Slatery's remark smacked Garver in the back of his head like a two by four, causing him to wince. Stuck between his new commander and an unruly platoon, he wasn't sure whether it was better to ignore the comment, which in reality no one could, or turn on the man known throughout the battalion as "The Mouth" and rip him a new one right then and there. Only when he opened his eyes and saw Nathan having trouble suppressing a grin did the irate platoon sergeant decide to wait until he was alone with The Mouth before opening up a fresh can of whoop ass on him.

Taking advantage of the unexpected but welcomed break in the tension, Nathan made his way into the shelter. Still holding his hands behind his back, he slowly walked among Garver's platoon, glancing to the left and right as he conducted a quick, cursory inspection of the disassembled rifles. With Garver in tow, the soldiers of second platoon once more lapsed into an uneasy silence as every man strained to hear who said what next.

When he had managed to set aside the anger that Slatery's comment had engendered within him, Garver broke the silence. "We're luckier than most units. The boys enjoy shooting, something that our location in the Valley allows us to do whenever we're in the mood. When we can't scrounge additional small-arms ammo from the Guard Bureau or other units that weren't able to use up their annual allocation, we buy our own."

Stopping, Nathan looked down at a scorecard left lying faceup on one of the benches. Reaching past the man to whom he belonged, Nathan picked it up and studied it for a moment. "Then I would imagine everyone here can shoot this well."

Not sure if this was a question or a challenge of some sort, Garver nodded even though Nathan wasn't looking his way. "They do well enough, sir."

Returning the scorecard to its original resting place, Nathan glanced over at its owner, who had been watching his every move with growing apprehension before moving on. "In my short time in the Army," Nathan remarked loud enough for most of Garver's platoon to hear, "I've discovered it's easy to get soldiers to do the fun things. It's their willingness to do everything well that is the true mark of a good soldier."

Not sure how to respond without offending his superior, Garver sought refuge in a bland and often used reply, "Yes sir. I suppose that's true."

When he came up to the bench where Paul Sucher was putting the finishing touches on his rifle, Nathan stopped and looked at the Guardsman. Without hesitation he took his hands from behind his back and began to reach for the rifle. "May I?"

Sucher first looked at Nathan, then over his shoulder at Garver as if asking him if it was okay to hand his weapon over to the new officer. Only when Garver gave Sucher a quick nod did Sucher relinquish his rifle. "Sure, go ahead . . . sir."

His delivery of the word "sir" had been late, coming almost as an afterthought. It wasn't meant to be an intentional sign of disrespect. Unlike the training NCOs who were running the range, this sort of formality was not second nature to Company A. Like so many other things, they wondered as they watched Nathan go through the steps of inspecting Sucher's weapon if this would have to change.

When he was finished examining the weapon, he offered it back to Sucher. "It's a little worn, but well maintained."

From behind Nathan, Garver saw the twinkle in Sucher's eye. Though he suspected he knew what was coming, the NCO couldn't find the words before Sucher began speaking. "It's a damned fine piece, sir. Care to try her out?"

Maintaining his composure as best he could, Nathan drew the rifle back and stared down at it once more as his mind quickly weighed the pros and cons of accepting Sucher's offer. Under ordinary circumstances, a soldier wouldn't dare challenge his superior like that. These, however, Nathan told himself, were not ordinary circumstances. And these men, he reminded himself as he glanced around at the faces that were watching his every move, were not ordinary soldiers. "Sure. It'll be fun."

The appearance of their new commanding officer at the base of the tower just behind the firing line created a ripple of excitement throughout Company A. Even before they knew for sure what was going on, men who had cued up for chow abandoned their place in line and made for the bleachers. Blissfully unaware of this the cadre NCO in charge of the range was in the process of leaving the tower when he suddenly found himself confronted by Nathan.

"Excuse me, Sergeant. I know you're looking forward to a break, but I was wondering if it would be possible to run me through the exercise before everyone stops for chow?"

Arresting his descent down the steps, the senior NCO took a moment to assess the situation. He would have been well within his rights to deny this request. Nathan knew this. He also knew that a request from a captain was understood by most professional soldiers to be something more than a request. But this was not always so, especially when the NCO in question was not in the chain of command of the officer.

Now that he had managed to muster up the courage to accept his first real challenge, Nathan was in no mood to delay it. Guessing that the NCO before him was in the process of weighing the consequences of denying his request, Nathan saw that he would need to press the matter, being tactful, yet determined. "Of course I'd understand," he added in a tone of voice that did not match the sentiment he expressed out loud, "if you didn't, Sergeant."

Taking care to keep the weapon's muzzle pointed downrange lest the NCO use this common safety violation against him to gain the psychological edge in the little drama being played out, Nathan stood his ground at the base of the stairs, blocking the tower's only exit. This unyielding stance, coupled with his expression and body language, convinced the NCO that the path of least resistance would be to honor the unusual request. Retreating back into the tower, he tore the hat from his head and threw it down on the table next to the target control panel. "Goddamn Guard officer wants to show off." After rattling off a quick string of colorful old Army sayings under his breath, he looked over to where his assistant was patiently waiting for calm to prevail and an order. Jabbing his finger toward the monitor like a light saber, the senior NCO barked, "He wants to play? Okay, fine! Let's play too. Give 'em the *special* program."

The assistant grinned as he punched in the necessary commands. "One enemy horde coming up."

When he had settled into a good firing position, Nathan glanced over his shoulder at the lane grader crouched behind his firing point and gave the man a thumbs-up. "Anytime you're ready, Sergeant."

The junior cadre NCO, in turn, gave the NCO in charge the high sign.

Even before the first target appeared Nathan decided to aim low. Not having personally zeroed the rifle he was using, he needed to determine what sort of sight picture he'd need to take up in order to hit with any degree of consistency. By aiming low, if he did miss the round would strike the ground in front of the target, kicking up a bit of dust or dirt as it did so and thus marking its precise point of impact. By recalling the sight picture he had taken prior to squeezing the trigger and mentally noting where the round actually struck, Nathan would then be able to calculate a proper "aim off" that he could apply when sighting on the rest of the targets.

The rest of the drill he'd need to use was rather standard and familiar to anyone who had ever spent time on a small-arms range. As he waited he mentally ran through the list of pointers that had been drilled into him by the NCOs who had trained him to shoot. Don't tense up while waiting for the targets to appear, lest the strain of doing so prematurely exhaust you and lead to wobbly arms and a drop-off in accuracy. Keep both eyes open and scan the entire depth and width of the firing lane for targets. Do not become fixated on a single point downrange lest you miss catching sight of a target that suddenly appears outside of your narrow field of vision. When a target does appear smoothly bring your weapon to bear, take up a good sight picture, watch your breathing, and remember to hold a bit of breath in your lungs before you begin to squeeze the trigger. Every small-arms instructor, including his own father, seemed to have their own personal opinion on which of these tips was *the* key to accuracy. Nathan guessed that they were all crucial, that none could be ignored if a soldier hoped to consistently put steel on target. He therefore did his best to apply each and every one as time and the circumstances permitted.

In the twinkling of an eye these disjointed thoughts evaporated as the first target sprang up from behind its well-concealed berm. It was a close one, a real give me situated somewhere around one hundred meters or so from the firing line. An easy mark, Nathan thought as he aimed and fired. Even so, his first shot struck just in front of the target. But the Fates were with him. While it was impossible to tell if the round had somehow managed to skip up and through the target or its sensors mistook the shower of debris thrown up by the near miss as the impact of an actual round, the computer program read the result as a solid hit and ordered the target down, recording its total lapsed time of exposure.

In the bleachers a flurry of hushed comments and remarks were exchanged. "Now that's what you call a lucky shot. One more millimeter, a fraction of an inch, and it would have buried itself in the dirt for sure," Sucher snorted.

"Lucky or not," Samuel Rainey replied crisply, "if that was a martyr in waiting, he'd be on his way to meet Allah minus the family jewels."

The snickering Rainey's remark generated was cut short when the next series of targets sprang up.

This time it was a pair, another close one and a second in the distance at a range of three-hundred meters plus. This awkward spread served notice that the picnic was over.

Confident that he now had a fair idea of the amount of aim-off he'd need to apply when sighting, Nathan engaged the close-in target without having to give much thought to what he was doing. His second shot rang out, ripping through the olive-drab silhouette target that vaguely resembled a man's upper torso and head.

In the bleachers, those with keen eyesight let out a murmur of approval when they saw the close-in target quiver.

"He's got the first one," someone muttered as all eyes turned to the three-hundred-meter target.

Even before the near target began to drop Nathan brought the muzzle of his weapon to bear upon the far target. This one would demand his full attention, his strict adherence to each and every steady hold principle he'd ever learned. This shot would be a much better test of his skills, guesswork, and luck. When all was set, when the rifle was firmly planted in his shoulder with his cheek resting on the weapon's cool plastic stock, Nathan stopped exhaling before all the air in his lungs was gone. Ready, he squeezed the trigger for a third time.

In the tower just behind the firing line, the assistant training NCO ignored everything but the computer monitor before him. When the "Hit" indicator lit up, he cried out with an enthusiasm that irked the senior NCO. "He's got it! This boy is hot."

Unimpressed, the senior NCO looked down at Nathan, then out over the downrange area. "Okay, Captain Hotshot," he growled, knowing full well what was coming next, "let's see you beat this."

"This" was a program that ran a sequence of targets that rapidly popped up all over the range in a staggered manner. From here on in there would be no distinct break between engagements. Obstinately it was designed to portray a mass attack. In reality it was used by the training cadre to test their own skills when conducting instructor training as well as cutting cocky trainees down to size. Unfortunately for the senior NCO, sometimes the special program failed to achieve its second less than laudable goal.

On the firing line Nathan quickly realized what was afoot. He also began to have second thoughts about the wisdom of accepting a challenge that a wiser man would have ignored. Of course that option was no longer available to him. He was in a meat grinder with no hope of avoiding the spinning blades that he was fast approaching.

He had willingly placed himself in a position that could fatally weaken his moral authority if he did not do well. Even as he began to take on the targets as quickly as he could, a voice in the back of his head told him he would have to do more than simply knock down as many targets as his ammo and time permitted. He'd need to look good while doing so. When all was said and done, he'd need to be able to stand up, face his men who were watching his every move, and with a straight face turn to the lane grader behind him and state in a calm and convincing voice, "It was a piece of cake."

Quickly the targets came on, close, far, and midrange. There were no more singles, no easy groupings. Their location on the range was scattered and the timing of their appearance was totally random. Realizing that he would never be able to take them all on, Nathan opted to go for those that were closer. This gave him the ability to engage them quicker without having to take the time to take up a perfect sight picture as he would have needed to if he had opted for the seemingly smaller, long-range target. Now all he concerned himself with was pointing at the center of mass of each target he elected to engage, dropping his aim point down a bit and to the left to compensate for the corrected sight picture, and fire. He didn't bother to count the number he had knocked down. He didn't waste any time wondering when there would be a break. He correctly guessed that there would be no pause until he ran out of ammo or the NCO running the range had decided he had extracted whatever revenge he felt he was justified in culling.

The cycle that Nathan now found himself caught in was a classic OODA Loop, pronounced by the Air Force fighter pilots who coined the phrase "Ooo Da." It stood for observe—orient—decide—act. In Nathan's case this translated to observing a target to be engaged, orienting his weapon onto that target, deciding when he had a good sight picture, and acting by shooting at it. There was no escaping the OODA Loop, not as long as there were targets. This endless cycle continued unabated as he observed the effect of his last round, thus starting the process all over again by reengaging when he missed or moving onto a fresh target. The only interruption came when he squeezed the trigger and in place of the distinct "pop" M-16s are noted for and the slight nudge against his cheek and shoulder, he heard a sharp "click" as the hammer leaped forward, hit the firing pin, and sent it thrusting forward into an empty chamber. When that happened, he'd withdraw his trigger finger from the trigger housing, reach forward with it to the magazine release while fishing for a fresh magazine with his left hand.

All of this was executed with far more grace and ease than Nathan's harried mind could have imagined at that moment. In fact, those who had not been in the shelter when Sucher had made the challenge began to suspect that something dubious was afoot. "It's a setup," a Guardsman from the first platoon suddenly announced to no one in particular. "The Old Man is in cahoots with the guys running the exercise."

"If it's a setup," his squad leader countered, "it's the captain who's being set up."

"Bull," intoned a third. "Those regular Army types stick together. They're commanding the targets down whether he's hit them or not."

From behind him another man added his unsolicited thoughts. "Even if that's the case look at him go. He's cooler than a January day. I'd like to see you crank out hits like he is."

This muted debate ragged on until the firing suddenly ceased for good. Though there were still targets showing and more popping up every second, Nathan backed away from the pile of sandbags he was nestled behind, rolled over to one side, and shouted out, "AMMO!"

In the tower the assistant instinctively hit the pause button on the keyboard, freezing the exercise and all results. The programmers who had designed the range computer's software, having taken into account human factors, had built in a delay that lopped off the last couple of seconds, thus giving the shooter a more accurate readout of his performance.

After getting the high sign from the assistant instructor who had been overwatching Nathan that he was, in fact, out of ammunition and his weapon was clear, the senior NCO glanced over at the monitor's screen and studied the results of the exercise. Realizing that he had been bested, he gave a grudging acknowledgment of Nathan's achievement. "I stand correct. The man can shoot."

Being a professional, the senior NCO took up the printout as soon as the computer spit it out and made for the firing line where the safety NCO was checking Nathan's weapon before allowing him to leave the firing line. After saluting he offered him the scorecard. "It goes without saying, sir, you qualified."

Casting his eyes over his shoulder, Nathan noted that there were still a few targets that had not yet been commanded down. With a straight face, he looked back at the range NCO. "Some of 'em got away."

For the first time, the range NCO smiled. "Oh, I wouldn't worry about them, Captain. I think they're running home to warn their buddies to stay away from your company."

The words "your company" had a ring that Nathan liked. Looking over at the bleachers, he wondered how long it would be before it really was his.

CHAPTER **11**

The West Bank, Israel

From where he sat huddled in the corner of the armored personnel carrier Avner Navon couldn't see a damned thing save the listless forms of the other men in his squad. Like him they were hopelessly wedged in between the jumble of assorted gear that cluttered every nook and cranny of the vehicle. The expressions they wore mirrored the same weary melancholy Avner felt whenever they were dispatched into a Palestinian controlled area. None of them looked forward to the next few hours. None held any illusions that what they were about to do would make any difference. They saw themselves as nothing more than bit players who were part of a sad little drama that their squad leader once described as something more akin to self-flagellation rather than a military operation.

In the parlance of the day they were "going over the wall," or passing through the barrier that separated Israeli territory from Palestinian communities. Their mission was punitive, a raid whose soul purpose was to mete out punishment upon a refugee camp from which the latest batch of human bombers had come, making it no different from a dozen other such forays Avner had participated in over the last few months. Neither he nor any of his fellow reservists had any illusions that what they were about to do would have a meaningful impact on the blood feud that was being waged between their fellow countrymen and the Palestinians. At best it might delay the next wave by disrupting the terrorists' planning cycle. At worse their actions would drive a new crop of desperate refugees into the waiting arms of groups such as Hamas and Islamic Jihad. Some of the men in Avner's platoon had even begun referring to these forays as Hamas recruiting drives.

To have done nothing, however, was not much of an alternative. Being shy and somewhat less vocal than his friends, Avner was unable to discuss his true feelings about this and other such matters with anyone other than the girl he hoped to make his bride. "It is a terrible thing to be faced with no good alternatives," he once told her when the subject of retaliation came up. "To sit quietly in our little corner of the world and do nothing while our enemies plot our extermination is insane. The Arabs would see it as a sign of weakness. Inaction would only encourage them to press their war against us with even greater vigor. Yet," he sighed as he turned to counter his own conclusion, "we can't continue stumbling along as we have been forever, trading an eye for an eye. We can't!"

The young woman Avner turned to in an effort to assuage his anguished soul was named Gilah, which meant "joy" in Hebrew. Like so many of her fellow countrymen she understood Avner's torment, for she had been taught well that the term "God's chosen people" was in reality a cruel epitaph scrawled on the tombstones of her ancestors. She learned this from the grandmother she was named for, a woman who bore tattooed numbers the Germans had given her when she was Gilah's age. "Those numbers mean we must never forget," Grandmother Gilah stated quietly the day her namesake asked what they meant. "They are there to remind us of the day my father allowed himself to be led away by his executioners. They serve to keep the memory fresh of the day when my mother struggled to hush my baby brother by telling him over and over that everything would be all right as we stood in line waiting for the Selection. They tell us that we must never forget that the greatest mistake a person can make is to close one's eyes to the evil of this world." Whenever Avner sought solace from Gilah, her grandmother's cold, sinister words would creep through her mind like an apparition from a grave, compelling her to clutch Avner closer and whisper sweetly in his ear, "Hush, my love, hush. Everything will be all right."

Memories of those tender moments did little to ease the dread that grew as every turn of the armored personnel carrier's drive sprocket carried Avner farther and farther into hostile territory. In his mind he could picture the scene that would be played out when they arrived at the refugee camp. He could almost taste the fear that gripped him every time the ramp of the personnel carrier dropped and his squad leader ordered them out. The only thing he could not imagine was not obeying that order. As repugnant as their assigned duties were, the idea of sitting idly behind the wall and doing nothing as wave after wave of fanatical young Palestinians blew themselves and Avner's fellow countrymen to pieces was inconceivable.

Lost in his own troubled thoughts, it took Avner a moment to realize that they were slowing down and stopping. Throughout the crowded crew compartment his squad mates exchanged nervous glances. "We haven't been on the road long enough," someone stated nervously. "Perhaps it's a roadblock, or . . ." He didn't need to finish his thought. Without having to be told everyone reached for their weapons, bringing them about as they prepared to dash out the rear of the APC and take on whatever unseen threat was waiting for them out there.

This sudden flurry of activity was brought to an abrupt halt by a sudden rapping on the rear door of the carrier, causing everyone to jump. "Jacob, open up. It's me, David."

Upon hearing the voice of their platoon leader everyone breathed a sigh of relief as the man closest to the door located in the rear ramp undid the combat lock and cranked the heavy steel handle until the weight of the door caused it to swing out. Even in the blinding light that flooded the crew compartment Avner recognized their lieutenant, an electrical engineer for a major telecommunications company when he was not wearing the uniform of the IDF. Peering into the crowded APC, the young officer looked about until he saw Avner. "Avner, they want you back at brigade headquarters."

Conditioned by years of random violence, the young Israeli's mind instinctively jumped to conclusions. "Is it my family? Is it Gilah?"

His lieutenant shrugged. "Don't know. They just sent a jeep after us with orders to pick you up and haul your skinny little ass back."

Wasting no time, Avner gathered up his personal equipment and made his way toward the open door, taking care as he went in an effort to keep from stepping on the other men crammed into the crew compartment. None of them spoke as he pushed past them. Only a few managed to muster up the courage to look him in the eyes for they did not know if they should envy him for being pulled out of the field like this or feel sorry for a fellow soldier who was about to come face-to-face with an unnamed personal tragedy.

Avner arrived at brigade just as the unit he had been pulled from began to sweep into the targeted refugee camp. The flurry of activity out there demanded the complete attention of the staff crowding the busy operations center, leaving Avner wandering about for several minutes searching for someone to report to. Eventually he stumbled upon a sergeant assigned to the adjutant's office who directed him to the brigade's intelligence section. There a female clerk escorted him to a small room. "Wait here," she stated briskly before closing the door.

Unsure of what was going on, Avner walked over to the small table in the center of the room and threw his rifle down on it. Left with nothing better to do, he looked about the room searching for a clue of some sort that would help him figure out what was going on. With the exception of the table and a straight-backed wooden chair the window-less room was bare. Only slowly, after he spied a number of irregular dark stains splattered about on the floor all around the chair, did it dawn upon him that this was an interrogation room.

He was in the process of bending over to see if those stains were really what he thought they were when the door opened. Straightening up, Avner watched as an older man with graying hair strolled into the room. Ignoring Avner, the man closed the door before making his way to the table. He wore a faded olive-drab IDF uniform with no name tapes over the breast pockets or insignia betraying his rank, unit, or branch of service. Having no idea of who he was Avner said nothing as he watched the man slide the rifle Avner had left on the table off to one side before slapping a folder he was carrying down next to it. Turning about, he boosted himself up onto the table. Only when he was comfortably seated with his legs dangling down and his hands grasping the edge of the table did he look up at Avner. With a humorless smile he gestured at the chair. "Sit."

Without taking his eyes off the man, Avner slowly eased himself onto the chair. Unsure of why he was here or what was going on, the young reservist said nothing. Just how long the pair sat there staring at each other in total silence was hard to gauge, for time has a habit of slowing to a crawl at moments like this. Eventually the older man picked up the file, opened it, and began leafing through its contents, pausing every so often to study a page more closely even though Avner suspected that the man was already familiar with its contents.

"Tell me why you left the yeshiva."

The suddenness with which the man blurted out this command startled Avner almost as much as the question itself. What, he wondered, did that have to do with the Army?

Even before he was able to frame a suitable response,

the stranger continued. "You were doing well. All of your teachers were impressed with your dedication and your understanding of the Torah. So why did you abandon your dream of becoming a rabbi?"

Rattled by the stranger's manner and questions, Avner blurted out the first answer that came to his mind, lest he be assaulted with another question. "They had no answers."

"They? Your instructor? Or the Bible?"

"Both I guess."

"Just what sort of answers did you expect to spring forth from the pages of our sacred scripts? The mysteries of the cosmos? The key to world peace? A workable settlement to our problems with the Arabs?"

Chafing under this mocking, Avner's bewilderment quickly turned to anger that he made no effort to check. "One can only hear the tired old phrase 'it is God's will' so many times before you begin to wonder just what sort of God it is we are praying to."

"So you turned your back on our faith and sought the answers to life driving a bus? Or perhaps you hope to discover the riddles of the universe in the arms of that lovely young girl you plan to marry?"

The mention of Gilah inflamed Avner's anger into a full-blown rage. Jumping to his feet he lashed out at the stranger. "What I do when I am not in uniform is my business and no one else's. And just who the hell are you?"

Unfazed by this outburst, the stranger replied in the same calm voice he had been using up to this point. "You are an Israeli soldier, in uniform or not. So long as Israel is surrounded by enemies determined to destroy us we all are. Furthermore you are a Jew, living in a Jewish state that is under siege by people hell-bent on finishing what the Nazis started. That makes everything you do my concern and the concern of your fellow countrymen."

The man's unflappable demeanor in the face of his outburst and not the strength of his argument caused Avner to back off. Though he made no effort to identify himself, it was now clear that he was not directly connected with the Army, leading Avner to suspect that the man was with one of Israel's intelligence agencies, perhaps even the Mossad. Settling back in the chair, Avner folded his arms across his chest. "What is it you want of me?"

Sensing that the young reservist was ready to listen the stranger lay the folder down on the table. When he spoke again he did so in flawless English. "In less than two weeks the Americans will be arriving. When they do they will be hiring locals as translators, one Israeli and one Palestinian per rifle company. You have been selected to be one of them."

Taking his cue, Avner replied in English. "Which one am I suppose to be, the Israeli or the Palestinian?"

Letting Avner's snide comment pass without comment, the stranger continued. "The résumé that was presented to the Americans with your application for that position emphasizes the fact that you were born in the United States. It also shows that you are still studying at the yeshiva. Any record of your activities since your departure from the yeshiva, to include your service with the IDF, has been expunged."

"What if they reject my application for the position you want me to fill?"

"Oh, it's already been accepted." Reaching into the folder, the stranger fished out a sheet of paper and handed it to Avner. "Here is a copy of the letter their embassy sent to you at your new address."

Taking the sheet of paper, Avner glanced at the address that the letter had been sent to before reading the body of the letter. When he was finished, he handed the letter back. "And if I don't go along with this little game of yours?"

For the first time since he had begun talking, the stranger's voice took on a sinister tone. "That is not an option."

Expecting more, Avner quietly stared at the stranger. When he made no effort to expand upon his curt reply, but instead returned his stare with a cold, unblinking gaze the young reservist shivered. Any doubt that the man before him was Mossad disappeared together with all thought of further resistance. "So," Avner finally stated glumly. "What is it you want of me?"

Dropping down onto the floor, the stranger collected up his folder and headed for the door. After taking the doorknob in hand, he looked back at Avner. "As we speak your things, or at least those that a rabbi in waiting would have, are being delivered to your new address. A driver will take you there."

"And what do I tell Gilah? How do I explain this to her?"

For the first time the smile that lit the stranger's face was sincere. "Leave that to us. We have ways of making people understand such things. And Avner," he added before turning to leave, "remember that you're a rabbinical student again. Start living like it."

"I suppose you'll be watching to make sure I do."

The smile disappeared. In its place was a dispassionate stare that was as cold and unfeeling as that of a shark. "I'll be in touch. Till then, talk to no one about this. Not even Gilah." Pausing, he thought about what he had just said, then added, "Especially Gilah." With that the stranger left the room.

Less then twenty kilometers from the small room where Avner's life was being turned inside out, Syed Amama's was unfolding in ways that were equally surprising and just as unsettling. Determined to pick up his struggle against the Jews right where he had left off, Syed was puzzled and quite disappointed when his first assignment with the most notorious Palestinian separatist group placed him in a job as a day laborer on the Israeli side of the wall. Exactly how building homes for newly arrived Jewish settlers would further the Palestinian cause was never explained to him. It was a mystery the young man was determined to solve.

He started by eliminating the obvious. His need to use English when talking to the Jew who owned the construction company was quickly dismissed as the reason he had been directed to that specific job. There were, he figured, far better jobs that would have placed greater demands upon his growing English vocabulary. Just as quickly tossed aside was the nature of his work. Since any fool could carry bricks and mix mortar as well as he could, Syed was at a complete loss to justify his current plight. The location of the new settlement he was helping to construct didn't seem to hold any significance either. There was nothing at the location or anywhere near it that could be exploited as far as he could tell. Were it not for his dedication to the cause he had already come close to sacrificing his life for, he would have walked away from Hammed Kamel.

In the course of carrying out this unusual assignment, Syed was saddled with another equally unexpected and unusual chore. As with his primary assignment it was passed onto him by the waiter who had served him the day he had met Kamel. The waiter did not bother to explain to Syed why it was important that he accompany the comely young woman through the Israeli checkpoint each day and make sure they sat in the rear of the bus during part of his commute to work. He was simply told to do so.

The first thought that came to mind was that she was someone's daughter, someone with important connections. It was not unusual for important men who tended to have many enemies to have trusted agents watch their families. The need to have a loyal man keep an eye on this particular young woman was obvious from the moment Syed met her. Though she wore the traditional head scarf and long robe while on the Palestinian side of the wall, as soon as she had been cleared by the Israeli security personnel the girl shed every stitch of clothing she could manage, revealing the western attire she seemed to prefer. Dressed in this manner she easily passed as a dark-skinned Israeli, a fact that she seemed to enjoy as she shamelessly flirted with men who gave her a second look. Only Syed's presence for part of their daily journey kept the young Jewish males who shared the bus with them at bay. What happened after he got off and who watched her during the day while he was hauling bricks was not his concern. All that mattered to him was that he did exactly what he was told and nothing happened to her while she was in his care.

This did not mean that his natural curiosity was not roused in regards to this as well as where she went and who she really was. Though wisdom dictated otherwise, Syed found that he was unable to keep himself from pursuing answers to the question that such secrecy tends to engender. Sadly, she always managed to find a way of frustrating his efforts to fill in the blanks. When he spoke with her often during their daily trek their conversations never moved beyond small talk, idle chitchat that was always friendly and enjoyable but not very informative. Attempts using more circumspect means to ferret out the information such as making innocent inquiries about her family or what she enjoyed during her free time also failed to yield any tangible results or information of value since her answers tended to be brief, almost curt. Already accustomed by his association with people who needed to maintain a high level of personal secrecy, he assumed her crisp but nebulous responses were designed to protect her secrecy and not meant to be rude. So Syed continued to probe and prod, taking care to do so in a manner that was both discreet and seemingly innocent.

Since she always carried books in the canvas bag she stuffed her traditional garb into every chance she could and the bus they rode continued on toward the American University after his stop, Syed naturally assumed she was a student there. Up to now he had hesitated to ask her about the books. To have done so was tantamount to asking her to betray what her role was within the organization, something no one dare do. He was confident that if he needed to know that, someone would tell him. But Syed could not deny his own curiosity. Eventually it eroded his better judgment until he found he could no longer resist asking her about the books and what she did while he was hauling bricks and mortar.

Thus on this day Syed managed to muster the courage to test the validity of his theory about the books and her being a student. Waiting until his stop was coming up, Syed turned to the girl and asked her about the books. With a smile and in a manner that reminded Syed of how a mother went about explaining something to a small child, she replied that they were on microbiology. "You know, germs. Tiny microorganisms and the such. They are nasty little animals that cause all sorts of infections and diseases."

Whether it was the unflattering directness with which she addressed him or the condescending tone of her voice, Syed felt a sudden and unexpected surge of anger, the sort that had until that moment been reserved for Jews. It took every ounce of self-restraint that he possessed to keep from lashing out at her, reminding her that he was not an illiterate peasant or a child, but an adult male and senior to her. He wanted to remind her that she owed him both the deference and respect proper Palestinian women owe their male chaperones and what happened to women who conducted themselves in a manner that was in violation of both their faith and social norms. He even considered slapping her.

Wisdom, however, prevailed. Not knowing who she really was or what part she was playing stayed Syed's hand and kept his rage in check. The idea that she was being sent along to keep an eye on him instead of the other way around could not be entirely discounted. The success that the Israeli Mossad and General Security Services continued to enjoy in infiltrating Palestinian organizations made those who belonged to them paranoid and distrustful. Of course the chances that she was an Israeli agent were, in his assessment, slim. In all likelihood she was little more than someone who was romantically connected with an important man in the organization or one of their relatives. Such men, he suspected, were not the sort of people who were interested in hearing despairing comments or unfavorable stories about their women. Whoever she was, Syed came to the conclusion that his best course of action was not to say anything about her behavior or reprimand her in any way himself. Instead, all he could safely do at the moment was to turn away and vent his fury by glaring at every male on the bus who dared to stare at his companion.

For their part his fellow commuters, used to seeing the pair on this particular bus day in and day out, seemed to recognize that something was amiss between the two Palestinians they assumed were a couple. Most of the male passengers who had taken note of the flare-up shook their heads or grinned knowingly before turning back to their newspapers and books. Only one man, someone whom Syed had never seen before, continued to glance back over his shoulder to where Syed and the girl sat.

Seated near one of the exits, this new face appeared to be a young foreigner, someone not much older than Syed or the girl he was assigned to accompany. His blond hair and piercing blue eyes stood out in the crowd, as did the expensive coat he wore over his sweater. Syed had learned a long time ago not to wear bulky garments like that even when the weather dictated otherwise. Such attire on a Palestinian, male or female, was an open invitation to every Israeli policeman and soldier to aggressively single them out and search the wearer for the homemade bomb belts members of Islamic Jihad and Hamas were so fond of.

This observation caused Syed to turn once more toward his charge. Blinded by the traditional values that formed the pillars upon which so much of his life revolved, it had never occurred to him that the girl next to him had no choice but to sacrifice her personal virtue by dressing as she did if she was to be left free to carry out whatever duties she had been assigned. Stunned by this sudden rationalization of her behavior, one that should have been obvious from the start, Syed gazed at the girl next to him with a newfound regard.

Sensing that her travel companion was paying attention to her once more, the girl slyly glanced over at Syed while giving him a sweet, almost mischievous smile. Embarrassed by her expression, Syed blushed. Finding the sort of satisfaction that only a woman can experience when making a man uncomfortable, she reached over and gave Syed's knee a squeeze. Shocked by this unexpected and inappropriate gesture, the young Palestinian panicked. Brushing her hand away as if it were an ugly insect that had suddenly lit upon him, Syed pulled away from her. Jumping to his feet, he grasped the hand strap overhead and stepped into the aisle next to his now vacated seat.

Both this response and a burst of laughter from his companion drew the full attention of every passenger on the bus, everyone except the blond-haired male near the exit. Turning this way and that as he returned the bemused stares of his fellow passengers with an angry glare, Syed failed to notice that the blond-haired foreigner was hunched over with his head between his shoulders as if trying to do everything in his power to keep from looking.

At that moment, as he stood there in the aisle of the bus with everyone staring at him, Syed could not imagine a worse possible situation. Though no one had told him that he needed to maintain a low profile while on the Israeli side of the wall, such orders were unnecessary to anyone associated with an anti-Israeli organization. To have done so would have been akin to someone telling the bus driver each and every day not to run over the pedestrians he came across. As it turned out, it was the bus driver who saved Syed from having to remain in the aisle for very long, languishing in the misery his companion and all the unexpected attention had brought down upon him. Bringing his

bus to a stop, the driver yelled back at Syed above the muffled laughter and chatter that now permeated the bus at
Syed's expense. "Hey, lover boy. I think this is your stop."

In a flash, Syed dashed for the open doors of the bus, ignoring his fellow passengers as he rushed by. He didn't
look back at the girl. Nor did he bother to glance up at the
blond-haired foreigner as he scampered down the steps of
the bus onto the curb.

The blond-haired foreign boy, however, was watching
Syed's every move as he fled. He kept an eye on the harried
Palestinian until the bus pulled away and he was sure that it
was safe to make his move. Only then did he stand up, face
about, and search the passengers at the rear of the bus until
he spotted the girl who had so unnerved Syed. She was still
laughing to herself over what she had done to her escort
and took no notice of the blond. Only the woman who had
been seated next to him bothered to look up at the blond as
he stood in the aisle. When she saw that he was intently
eyeing the comely young girl dressed in the bright yellow
blouse, the woman assumed that the fair-haired foreign boy
was going to go back and try his luck with the girl.

Luck, however, was to play no part in what he was about
to do. Everything leading up to this moment had been
planned. All possible contingencies had been considered
and addressed. Nothing, the blond-haired foreigner told
himself as he reached under his sweater with his free hand,
save Allah himself would be able to stop him now.

It took the roar of the explosion to shake Syed from the de-
spondency he had slipped into as he recalled the manner
with which the girl he was responsible for had treated him
in public. Stopping short, he turned and looked up, over
the heads of his fellow pedestrians who were scattering for
cover. Already Syed could see a plume of black smoke
laced with the last dying flickers of flame mushrooming
into the sky and filling the narrow canyonlike street. For a

moment Syed wondered if the bus he had just gotten off was in danger. Then, from out of the grim black cloud that was spreading fast like a death shroud, a bus door came tumbling down. In an instant the young Palestinian knew what had happened. He didn't bother to take the time to worry about the girl whose cruel laughter was still ringing in his ears. Nor did he even bother to raise his eyes up toward the heavens to praise his God for sparing him. As a Palestinian this was the last place on earth he wanted to be. Without giving the matter a second thought, Syed turned his back on the growing chorus of screams and cries for help and continued on his way as quickly as he dared.

Flanked by members of his trauma team, Dr. Joseph Meir impatiently waited just outside the entrance of the emergency room for the first of the casualties to arrive. He did not know the particulars of the incident. He didn't need to. An announcement that a bus had been bombed and wounded were inbound was all that was necessary to activate an all-too-familiar drill. In fact, it was too familiar. Long before the first victim arrived, Dr. Meir already knew how the next few hours would play out.

The first to arrive would be people with minor wounds, those who had been on the periphery of the incident. Their injuries were generally shallow cuts, bruises, and abrasions—bloody but nonfatal wounds caused by shattered windows, flying debris, or people thrown to the ground by the force of the blast or in an effort to seek cover. These hapless vitims tended to be snatched up by concerned citizens and driven straight to the hospital. Some even managed to drive themselves there in search of medical attention. While all wounds required attention, Meir's team would pass these along to a troop of paramedics and trained assistants who would clean and bandage these relatively minor wounds.

Slowly the flow of casualties lucky enough to escape

with minor cuts would give way to those with more serious injuries, bystanders who had the great misfortune to be in the immediate vicinity of the target. Their wounds would be far more severe, ranging from traumatic amputations and crushed skulls to abdominal wounds that lay bare internal organs that harried EMTs on the scene could only scoop up and pile back into the wound as best they could. It would be up to Dr. Meir to sort this grizzly parade of torn and bloody bodies into one of three categories. This process is known as triage, which is the evaluation and classification of casualties for the purpose of prioritizing treatment. Victims with minor, nonlife-threatening injuries would be sent onto a holding area manned by paramedics, a handful of nurses, and a doctor if one could be spared. This small medical team would do what they could for the lightly wounded as time permitted. Incoming patients whose life or limb hung in the balance, who would most likely die if they did not receive immediate medical attention, were seized by members of Meir's team and whisked away to treatment rooms where other highly trained physicians and their assistants stood ready to do all they could to tip the scales in favor of life. Finally there were those who were beyond help, mangled bodies that left Meir wondering how they had managed to survive the trip to the hospital. As much as Meir and all who worked for him wished otherwise, they knew they could not save everyone, that decisions would have to be made in the coming hours if their limited resources and personnel were to be effectively employed. Victims who had but moments to live were taken to a section of the hospital known as Area B, where they were sedated and left to the care of a rabbi and a nurse.

The need to make those decisions was at the heart of Meir's hatred for the bastards who planned and executed these attacks. Their actions, their misguided beliefs, and their hatred of his fellow Jews forced him to stand there like Solomon on judgment day. Forced to watch as a steady flow of mangled bodies were brought to him to be evaluated and classified. His decision would mean life or death for people he had never laid eyes on before, forced to finish what the terrorists started. That he was so good at making these calls and took pride in this grizzly skill bothered Meir. The thought that he was becoming inured to such horrors and was no longer able to see the victims who passed before his eyes as people but merely collections of wounds that needed attention haunted the trauma surgeon. The hope that this would all stop once the Americans arrived was a dream, one that few people in the besieged land bought into.

The arrival of the first ambulance refocused Meir back to the problem at hand. Assuming his best poker face, he began the grim task of sorting the victims brought before him and issuing orders to the appropriate members of his staff. "A light wound. Direct him to the clearing station. Zev, this one has multiple wounds and possible fractures. Take her to X-ray and clean her up as best you can while you're waiting for the results. Nurse, take this boy to Area B." As quickly as one gurney was wheeled away, another appeared. "Golda, take this girl to Dr. Roffman." Again and again, Meir leaned over the patient, carefully pulled away the field dressing when he could, and assessed the wounds as quickly and thoroughly as circumstances permitted.

On occasion, Meir would find himself unable to simply make a snap judgment before passing a particular victim on. Sometimes something caught his attention, something totally unrelated to his gruesome duties. The girl in the shredded yellow blouse was a case in point. "The police on the scene say the bomber stood right in front of her," the EMT exclaimed, "and looked at her as if he knew her. They want you to do everything you can to keep her alive long enough for questioning."

One look at the young woman told Meir that this would be a challenge. Her face was all but gone, its skin shredded and peeled back exposing the underlying muscle and bone.

Her upper torso was little more than a collection of open wounds, some minor, some great ugly gouges. And everywhere the girl oozed blood, blood that poured from her wounds and onto the gurney, creating pools of dark red fluids that spilled over onto the ground every time she was moved. Stepping forward, Meir carefully lifted several of the dressings, ignoring the puddle of blood he was standing in and the stream of contaminated fluids running off the gurney and onto his trouser leg.

When he was finished he stepped back unconsciously wiping his hands on his scrubs. "I don't see how I can save this girl, but I will try. Anything to catch the shits who did this." Turning to a nurse he directed her to take the girl to a team that was waiting to receive the worst of the worse. "Tell Abe to do everything that he can and that I will be along to lend a hand as soon as I am done here." Without waiting for the nurse to acknowledge his orders, he moved aside as the gurney was whisked away to make room for the next. He wasn't concerned about the thin rivulets of blood that trailed the gurney as it was rushed into the heart of the emergency room. Nor did the group of emergency specialists waiting to receive her have any idea that they were exposing themselves to a danger greater than any bomb Hamas or its sister organizations could ever produce. Such concerns were the furthest thing from their minds as they cut away the remains of her clothing and began to work on the girl Syed had thought he had been protecting. In the process of attempting to save her, the highly trained emergency-room doctors were hastening the spread of millions of microscopic organisms that permeated the blood and that clung to everything it touched.

The mindless task of hauling brick and mortar to the bricklayers left Syed ample opportunity to dwell upon the fate that awaited him when the workday was over. He had no illusions about what would happen to him after he had passed through the Wall and back into the Palestinian area. Once there he would be at the mercy of a system that held no respect for any laws other than what was recorded in the Koran by the Prophet Himself or those dictated by men carrying Kalashnikovs.

The price a member of the PLA paid for failing to carry out his assigned tasks was well known throughout the shadowy world of the Palestinian movement. There would be no inquiry or hearing at which he would be allowed to state his case or present matters in mitigation. Once it had been confirmed that the girl had been injured in the bombing, and Syed had no doubt that she had been, he would be called forth to atone for his negligence.

As grim as his prospects were, Syed had no real alternatives but to go back and accept his fate. The PLA's quaint policy of punishing one or more members of a traitor's family if the guilty party opted to flee or hide from their justice insured that most who fell short of the mark returned to meet their end like men. Since Syed had no idea who the girl he had been escorting really was or her relative value to the PLA, it was impossible for him to gauge how much of his own kin's blood would need to be spilled to assuage his blunder. Not that this mattered. Even the death of one family member would be too heavy a burden for him to bear. By late afternoon, while his fellow laborers had little more on their minds than what their wives would be serving them for dinner, Syed was preparing himself to meet his executioners. In the end, his decision to do so had not been hard to reach. Having already committed himself to die for the Palestinian cause, Syed saw that there was not much difference between doing so for an abstract idea he believed in or a family he loved.

Still, the trepidation that gripped Syed as he approached the Israeli checkpoint at the wall caused him to waver in his resolve. It would be so easy, he found himself thinking, to go up to one of the soldiers standing watch and surrender to them. After all, he had information that they wanted, information they would want to protect. Fortunately for the young Palestinian, the actions of the very Israelis he would have to place his full trust in provided him the excuse he needed to keep from giving in to this fit of weakness. Angered by the events of that morning and eager to extract vengeance from the people who hid the terrorists from them, the Jewish soldiers and policemen heaped on as much abuse and physical harassment as circumstances permitted. Everyone trying to make their way past them were showered with insults and taunts as they were pushed and shoved from one soldier to another. It was as if the Israelis equated being Palestinian with being guilty and personally responsible for the attack on the bus. By the time it was his turn to negotiate the gauntlet where he was jostled from one soldier to another who freely used their rifle butts and riot batons, Syed's determination to do the right thing had reasserted itself. Better, he thought during the course of this humiliating ordeal, to die one quick death at the hands of my own people than suffer a million tiny ones every day while cowering behind the protection of these Jews.

The man who greeted Syed once he had cleared the wall was none other than the waiter. He was wearing a smile that reminded the young man of a predatory cat who had just sighted its pray. Without ceremony, the waiter stepped up to Syed once he was sure the soldiers at the checkpoint could no longer see them. "I have been sent to fetch you."

A halfhearted effort by Syed to say something noble or profound in way of a response was cut short when the waiter turned away and began walking. Left with little choice, Syed followed. On the outskirts of the small village near the wall the pair met a third man standing next to a late-model car parked on the side of the road. When the stranger saw Syed and the waiter approach, he climbed into the driver's seat and started the car. As soon as both men were in he began to drive. No one spoke as the vehicle carried the three along the narrow, poorly maintained roads that characterized the Palestinian zone. Each kept to himself, concealing whatever thoughts or feelings he might have been harboring. Eventually the driver turned off the main road and began to ascend a steep hill topped by the ruins of an old castle, the sort that Christian Crusaders had built during their brief tenure in a place some called the Holy Lands. After grinding its way up along the badly rutted road through well cared for orchards the car rolled through the open gates of a sprawling compound that sat in the shadow of the castle.

The young Palestinian hesitated for a moment, taking his time to look about and study the compound. It was a working farm, but unlike any he had seen. Nestled between crude buildings that looked as if they dated back to ancient times were freshly whitewashed modern structures. On one side of this strange collection of buildings was the massive outer wall of the castle. Most of the buildings, both old and new, butted up against it. The rest of the complex emanating from this main cluster consisted of a collection of outer buildings that looked to be support facilities such as sheds and storage areas. The whole collection of structures was surrounded on three sides by a stone wall, one that was two to two and a half meters high. On the other side of that wall lay the crazy quilt pattern of orange and olive groves that were separated from each other by ancient waist-high stone walls through which the car carrying Syed and his silent companions had passed.

Despite his current situation, Syed could not but keep from thinking that under different circumstances this would have been a wonderful place to explore. It created the appearance of a modern facility that seemed to have everything a farmer could want. But this was not another time, the young Palestinian reminded himself as the waiter and the driver opened their doors and began to climb out. Their sudden moves reminded Syed that he lived in an age dominated by a reign of terror and bloodshed. That his blood would soon stain this serene pastoral setting bothered him but it did not reduce him to tears or panic. He had chosen to align himself with those who were responsible for those changes and in doing so he understood that he had accepted that the price for doing so was death. Perhaps, he found himself musing as he prepared to step out of the car and meet his fate, the person assigned to kill him would feel the same exhilarating rush he had experienced when he himself had wielded the awful power of life and death.

Slowly, cautiously, Syed opened his door and began to step out, looking to his left and right as if searching the faces of those scattered about the compound who had stopped what they were doing to look his way. While most were dressed as he imagined farmers should be, here and there he spotted men wearing white lab coats leaning in doorways as they enjoyed a cigarette or going from one building to the next. Having resigned himself to his fate the only things he now concerned himself with were the technical aspects of the deed and what his executioner would look like. He wondered if the two men who had brought him here would turn out to be his executioners or someone else, perhaps one of the bystanders in a white coat. Would they kill him here, out here in the middle of the compound? Or would they take him out there, into one of the many orchards where a shallow grave already awaited him?

Circling about behind the car the waiter took Syed by the arm. "This way. He is waiting."

The waiter's grip was light, meant to guide him along, not restrain. Without the slightest hesitation Syed allowed himself to be shepherded toward one of the modern buildings. "Here," the waiter stated as he pointed toward a door. "In here." So, Syed thought, this is it. Gathering himself up as he went, the young Palestinian passed from the bright sunlit courtyard and into the dark room beyond the heavy steel door that someone inside had opened.

Before his eyes could make the adjustment, Syed felt the waiter's hand fall away, a pair of hands reach across the threshold, grasp his right hand, and begin to shake it. "I am so glad to see that all went well and you managed to find your way back to us."

Stunned, Syed refused to believe he was hearing the familiar voice. Not until his eyes adapted and allowed him to confirm that the man greeting him with a broad smile was in fact Kamel. Only then did he allow himself to relax, but only a little.

"When you did not return this morning after the bombing we thought that you had been caught up by the Israeli security sweep or worse."

Still unsure of where his superior was going with this and wondering if the "worse" meant death or going over to the Jews, Syed said nothing as Kamel released his hand and motioned him into the building and toward a seat in an air-conditioned room that reminded him of a well-appointed waiting room belonging to a wealthy doctor.

"I would like to be the first to congratulate you on the success of your task," Kamel continued as he made his way across the tile floor over to another chair. "I can appreciate how difficult it must have been for you to carry out your orders not knowing why you had been given this task."

For the first time Syed saw an opportunity to speak. "But the girl! She had to be injured, or even killed. I don't see how she could have escaped unscathed."

Smiling, Kamel leaned back in his chair. "Oh, she is very dead. We have managed to confirm that."

"She was the bomber? But how? Where did she hide the bomb? Certainly not under those skimpy cloths she was wearing."

Shaking his head, Kamel chuckled. "No, she did not carry the device that blew up the bus. That was done by one of our foreign volunteers."

Suddenly the image of the blond-haired boy on the bus who had been behaving strangely came to mind. Unable to restrain himself, Syed blurted out, "It was him!"

Now Kamel laughed. "Ah! So you did see our latest martyr."

"I did. But," Syed asked in an effort to clarify his confusion, "what about the girl? If you knew that the bus was going to be attacked, why didn't you warn me. I could have saved her!"

Suddenly Kamel's expression changed. In an instant, his smile disappeared. "Your task was to make sure that the girl was on that bus where the American boy could find her."

Rather than answering his question Kamel's answer only added to Syed's confusion. "I do not understand."

Maintaining his impassive expression, Kamel motioned to another man who had been standing in the corner. "It's not important for you to understand. All that is important is that you do as you're told."

Suddenly a stranger who had been standing quietly in a corner behind Syed where he could not be seen stepped forward and handed Syed an oversized envelope as Kamel continued to speak. "Your new task involves working for the Americans as a translator. Everything you need to know of this assignment is in here."

Recovering from the momentary spate of panic that had seized him when the stranger had sprung out of nowhere, Syed cleared his throat. "How do I go about securing this position?"

"All those details have been taken care of already. You have already been accepted by the Americans and will be notified by them at your new apartment within the next week. The address and a key to it are in the envelope. Until then you are free to take a break from your labors and enjoy yourself. You have earned it."

Fingering the envelope that he held, Syed looked into Kamel's eyes and wondered if it would be wise to ask more about this new mission. The stern, uncompromising gaze reflected by Kamel's eyes served to warn the young Palestinian not to do so. Having survived his attack against the Israeli checkpoint and this morning's bus bombing, Syed figured that it would be unwise to press his luck. As he saw it, he guessed that he would need whatever luck he had left to see him through the coming weeks. "It is a privilege to accept this new challenge on behalf of our people," Syed finally managed to say.

Kamel smiled and nodded as he stood up. "Good, good." Then without another word he withdrew through a door leading to another room in the building with the stranger who had handed Syed the envelope. Once they were both in the next room and the door was closed the stranger took a pistol that he had been concealing in the small of his back, reengaged the safety, and slid it into his holster. There would be no need for him to use it, at least not today.

Escorted to the front gate of the compound by the waiter, Syed was told that there was a bus stop along the main road not far from where they had turned off it to ascend the hill. Slowly making his way down the rock-strewn road, Syed finally had an opportunity to collect his thoughts. That he was being kept ignorant of his real purpose was obvious. Such precautions were necessary given the aggressive manner with which the Israelis managed to infiltrate Palestinian organizations and break captured fighters during interrogation. Perhaps, he told himself, it is best this way.

Still, Syed was a young man with a fertile imagination. No longer preoccupied by the ominous thoughts that had consumed him on the way up the hill, he was now free to take a moment on his way down to look back at the farm compound and castle. When he reached the bus stop along the north-south road that ran along the base of the hill he found an old man sitting on a weathered bench waiting for the bus. After taking a seat next to him, Syed turned to the old man. "Tell me, uncle, are you from around here?"

Unlike the people in the city where he lived and had been associating with as of late, the old man smiled as he spoke to Syed. "Yes, yes. I have lived here my entire life, just beyond the castle on the other side of the hill."

Glancing back up at the hill he had just descended, Syed

nodded. "That is a far more impressive sight from here than on top of the hill."

"Oh," the old man exclaimed. "You've been up there? Do you work for the people who run the experimental farm there? I have been told it is a wonderful place to visit."

"No, I do not work there. I am a laborer."

"You should go back to the farm," the old man enjoined, "and seek a job from them. It seems they are always in need of all sorts of help. Every day they have to bring people in from all over to help with their work and care for the orchards."

"Yes," Syed responded, anxious to find out all he could about the unusual complex without seeming to pry. After all, he had no way of knowing if this old man had been planted here by Kamel in an effort to see if he would speak to someone he did not know about what had just transpired or make inquires about the farm compound.

"Some foreigners from Europe bought that farm years ago," the old man explained without any prodding by Syed. "Germans I believe. It was a gift to our people, an effort by the Europeans to modernize the way the farmers around here plant and care for their crops. They told us they wanted to see us catch up and surpass the Israelis in every way. They said all we needed was a start, that our orchards and farms could be as fertile as theirs. For years they have worked side by side with our people at a time when no one else paid us any attention."

"And has it worked?" Syed asked, emboldened by the forthright manner with which the old man was volunteering information.

"You have eyes. Look at those orchards," the old man bragged as he waved his hands at the hillside covered with tightly packed orchards. "Have you ever seen the likes of our fruit trees anywhere else on the West Bank?"

"No, I have not. They do look impressive."

"It's the work the Germans have done in that compound that makes the difference. They have created special chemicals just for our soil and climate," the old man stated with pride. "They are teaching our young men how to make those chemicals using all sorts of modern equipment they brought with them from Europe." Pausing, the old man took a moment to reflect upon the miracle he had been witness to. "I am told that there are still all sorts of wonderful secrets up there that we have yet to see. I pray that I live long enough to see some of them bear fruit."

Like a thunderclap Syed suddenly realized just what sort of secrets those walls concealed, secrets that the old man next to him could never have dreamed of, not even in his worst nightmare. For the first time since he had volunteered to join Kamel's secretive little band, Syed came to appreciate that the man he had pledged his loyalty to had something far greater in mind than merely blowing up buses and killing a handful of Jews.

With a grin that the old man misunderstood, Syed stared at the castle, muttering as he did so. "Yes, great things will come from there."

The old man nodded. "Yes, you can be sure of that."

CHAPTER 12

Arlington, Virginia

The colonel tagged by the G-2 to hand carry the report to Scott Dixon's office stood in the middle of the room watching him leaf through the pages as quickly as he could without missing any of the critical information it contained. Every now and then, after pausing to reread an important passage, Dixon would look up at the colonel. Sometimes he did so in order to ask him a question, even though he suspected the G-2 rep knew nothing more than what was already before him. Sometimes he used the opportunity to demonstrate his anger at being handed a document such as this so late in the game by throwing out a sharp rhetorical question or simply scowling.

"How long did the CIA sit on this?"

"They received it less than three hours ago. I was told that as soon as they saw what it was they dispatched a copy over to us. We've had it less than one. Which," the colonel hastened to add, "isn't half bad given some of their past performances."

Dixon was not amused. "Bully for them. Did they include any of their own analysis of this information or its reliability?"

"Nothing to speak of. It seems they've stopped doing a thorough analysis of certain military-related intelligence and have opted instead to pass the raw info straight onto us," the colonel ventured. "I guess if I had been burned as many times as they have been for sitting on information concerning an ongoing military operation I'd do the same."

"I see. It's the old 'it's not my job' routine," Dixon mumbled even as he was turning his full attention back to the final page of the report, the one that included the summary and conclusion. He took his time reading both of these passages, considering each point the Israeli analyst who drafted them made before moving on to the next. When he was finished, Dixon threw the report across his desk in disgust. "There's a reason the Mossad passed this onto us at this time. I have my suspicions, but I'd like to hear what Buck thinks."

The colonel took a deep breath as he prepared to reiterate the view held by Lieutenant General Edward "Buck" Quintela, the Army G-2. "While the Israeli intelligence services have been doing their best to make it seem as if they have been cooperating, General Quintela believes that they've been very selective about what they have passed on to us. He thinks they've deliberately held back information such as this until we were so committed, so locked in that it would be impossible for us to back out or delay the deployment of our troops."

The mention of the forthcoming deployment caused Dixon to look at his watch, then up at the bank of clocks on the wall. "The President is in Texas, the Sec Def's in China, and the Secretary of State is still in New York yacking it up with the usual suspects in the U.N."

"And," the colonel added, "it's Friday afternoon."

"Perfect, just perfect. Those bastards in Jerusalem are spot on. They knew just when to deliver this bomb."

The colonel waited until Dixon's anger subsided some before he continued on. "The main body of troops are not scheduled to be wheels up until oh six hundred Monday morning. General Quintela has already pulled together a crack team and assigned them the task of pulling together a briefing for both the National Security Council as well as one for the senior commanders of the peacekeeping force. The latter will be hand-delivered by selected members of

General Quintela's staff as complete a package to the division and each of the brigades involved in this operation within twenty-four hours."

Dixon thought about this for a moment. "Any idea who the senior officer going to Benning will be?"

Like everyone else on the Army staff, the colonel knew that Dixon's own son was involved. "Yes sir. That would be me."

When he spoke, Dixon's voice betrayed the trepidation he felt in doing what he was considering. "In that case, I would like to ask a personal favor from you."

"Of course, sir. Anything."

"Before you leave, drop by my office and see me."

Fort Benning, Georgia

With the final formation of the day over, Company A, 3rd of the 176th, broke apart like a shattering plate. Some of Nathan Dixon's Virginians made straight for the barracks where they looked forward to enjoying a long hot shower. Others headed off at the double quick to the main post exchange, anxious to beat the Friday evening rush and purchase those last-minute items they assumed they would need "over there." A number of men simply remained in place, clustering together to discuss half-made plans or see what their friends and neighbors were up to before committing themselves.

One of these clusters was centered on Paul Sucher. Like a quarterback in a huddle preparing to take the field, he looked at his fellow squad mates. "Well, it's now or never. We either leave in the next couple of hours or we drop the whole thing here and now."

Ronald Weir nervously looked at his fellow conspirators. "I don't know. I mean think of it. It's a ten-hour drive, which puts us in Bedlow at early Saturday morning. To make it back here in time for first call on Monday morning, we have to leave there by noon on Sunday. Which means we'll be on the road for twenty hours in order to spend maybe thirty hours with our families?"

"And what's the alternative?" Sucher countered. "Stay here, in wonderful Fort Benning, and enjoy an intimate weekend with a couple of thousand horny soldiers?"

There was a pause as Gene Klauss, Sam Rainey, and Jerry Slatery considered the opposing views thrown out by Weir and Sucher. Finally Rainey broke the silence. "Paul has a point. As much as I like you guys, given a choice I'd rather spend what free time we have left with Jenny instead of sitting around here contemplating my navel. The way I see it, we'll have plenty of time to do that over there."

First Klauss, then Slatery, nodded in agreement. "He has a point, you know."

Making no effort to hide his disgust, Weir threw his hands up. "Hey, if you guys are so hell-bent on doing this, be my guest. But count me out."

Angered that he had not prevailed, Sucher glared at Weir as he backed out of the circle. "Fine! Go ahead and stay. I'll give Pat a tickle and a peck for ya when I see her."

The mention of his wife's name enflamed Weir. "Fuck you, Sucher."

Having succeeded in getting Weir's goat, Sucher smiled. "That, dear sir, is exactly what I plan to do."

In silence the remaining conspirators waited until Weir had left their circle and was out of earshot before they continued to lay their plans. Finally, Sucher turned to Klauss. "Is Jack still in?"

The assistant squad leader shook his head. "There's a briefing for all officers tomorrow morning, after which the captain has scheduled a last-minute sand table exercise with all the platoon leaders and platoon sergeants. So unless we're willing to wait till both of those are over, Jack is a no go."

As had become his habit, Sucher mumbled a collection of well-chosen oaths every time someone mentioned

Nathan's name or something he had said or done. "You'd think by now it would have dawned upon that asshole that we're not regular Army types getting ready to storm the beaches of Normandy."

To everyone's surprise, Jerry Slatery came to Nathan's defense. "He's doing what he thinks is right. And to tell you the truth, he's managed to cram more worthwhile training into these last two weeks than the rest of the battalion combined."

"And to what end?" Sucher shot back. "To impress the colonel?"

"To get us ready for whatever we might run into over there," Klauss snapped.

Sensing that he was on the losing end of this oft-debated topic, Sucher backed off. "Look, we don't have time to discuss this here if we're going to make it to Bedlow by dawn tomorrow. So get changed, gather up your dirty laundry, and meet me behind the barracks in an hour if you're going."

Without another word, the small knot of conspirators dispersed and trooped off to join their fellow Guardsmen in the barracks.

The sand table located in the brigade classroom was a detailed three-dimensional representation of the West Bank area the 176th Brigade would soon be responsible for. Every detail imaginable had been replicated on it, from the checkpoints that were to have been the focus of the brigade's attention to the spiderlike network of unpaved farm roads and goat trails that had suddenly taken on a new significance. With other company commanders anxiously waiting to use the mock-up, Nathan Dixon, his executive officer, platoon leaders, and platoon sergeants didn't have any time to waste going over trivial or nonrelated issues. Still, before launching into his spiel Nathan took a few precious seconds to survey his grim-faced officers and NCOs.

For the first time since he had assumed command of Company A he felt that he had their full and undivided attention. He didn't mind that it had taken a briefing such as the one they had heard that morning to achieve this. All that mattered was that his Virginians had finally managed to shift their thoughts and concerns to where it should have been all along; the tactical situation they would be facing in less than two days and not his military pedigree.

After giving them a moment to orient themselves on the table Nathan began. "I'm sure you've all heard the term 'mission creep,' a phrase that became popular during our intervention in Somalia in the early nineties. Basically it's the process by which the nature of a unit's mission changes after they have been deployed. In Somalia a force that had been dispatched to guard and oversee the distribution of food went from being strictly defensive in nature to an offensive operation charged with seeking out and attacking tribal leaders who were considered to be a threat to the peace and stability of the region. Based on what we were told during this morning, the only difference between us and those poor bastards is that instead of suffering a gradual mission creep, we're experiencing mission leap."

Nathan's comment was not meant to be witty or funny. The same Israeli intelligence summary that had angered his father had changed, in the twinkling of an eye, the manner in which his son's company would carry out their assigned duties. From the very beginning it had been understood that American troops deployed to the West Bank would be at risk. Now, if the new information contained in the briefing they had just received was true, that risk had become a near certainty. Being practical men, no one assigned to the 176th Brigade, active component or Guard, now had any doubt that they were about to become the primary target for every Palestinian terrorist who could tote a bomb or fire a rifle. So while the members of the National Security Council back in the nation's capital sat around a long table, hotly debating whether or not this new reality compromised the political and military practicality of the peacekeeping mission, a handful of the people who would have to carry out those duties stood about a sand table trying to sort out how they would go about executing that very mission while minimizing the risks doing so entailed.

Much of the original plan stood unchanged. Since neither the Israelis nor the Palestinians wanted to have American forces in their respective areas for political reasons, all American base camps and units assigned to the peacekeeping mission were located within the three-kilometer security zone that had been established by the international accord that set this entire expedition in motion. Everything the 176th Brigade did during its tour of duty would revolve around its three battalion-sized base camps dubbed Camp Washington, Camp Lee, and Camp Jackson. Originally viewed as little more than well-guarded administrative and bivouac sites from which detachments would depart on a daily basis to carry out their assigned peacekeeping tasks, these camps would now have to be transformed into self-contained strongpoints. The security zone itself was defined by the Israeli-built wall in the west and in the east by a pair of heavily reinforced chain-link fences topped with razor wire separated by an antivehicle ditch running between them. Until that morning the primary mission of the American troops centered on manning the checkpoints along both the wall and the fence within their respective battalion sectors. Unfortunately, the criteria planners had used to locate the base camps the 176th Brigade would be operating from had been predicated upon the needs of that mission and not a concerted threat directed against the Virginians or their base camps.

Complicating their efforts to deal with the new threat members of the 176th Brigade would soon be facing was the failure to clear the security zone of all indigenous population. When the United States initially took on the obligation to separate the warring factions on the West Bank, American military planners had assumed that the security zone would be depopulated as the Israeli government had advised. Unfortunately, members of the U.N. Security Council who were decidedly pro-Palestinian and international human rights groups scuttled this effort, pointing out that to do so would unduly punish the Palestinians and create a new generation of refugees. While this altruistic arrangement satisfied politicians and the liberal glitterati, it magnified the security concerns of operational planners ten times over. Repeated efforts by Scott Dixon and others at the Department of the Army to point out that the farms owned and operated by Palestinians scattered throughout the security zone had the potential of becoming base camps for anti-American terrorists were ignored. Their pleas to dissuade their own government from buying into this bit of insanity were ignored by Scott Dixon's counterparts at the State Department who argued that to do so would disenfranchise the rightful owners of the land and create tensions between the American troops and the Palestinians that could lead to violence. That there were senior people in the government who actually believed that the radical elements among the Palestinians might hold back from attacking the American troops once they were on the ground was appalling to Dixon. "After listening to those people," he once remarked after a meeting with representatives from the State Department, "I understand why our government adopted the motto 'In God We Trust,' 'cause we sure as hell can't trust the people who run it."

The politics and machinations at his father's level meant little to Nathan and even less to his assembled platoon leaders and platoon sergeants. The reason why things were being done really didn't matter to them. What did concern them was how they were going to deal with the realities that they would soon be facing. "We've gone from being little more than gate guards," Nathan stated blandly as he continued his briefing, "to having to conduct full-scale active military operations aimed at ensuring our own security."

Sensing that his fellow Virginians were at a loss as to

how to respond, Alex Faucher took the lead. "Question, sir. Given what we've just been told, what takes priority? Manning the checkpoints or protecting the force?"

Nathan shook his head. "Good question, one for which I have no definitive answer. I don't think anyone has quite sorted that out yet. My guess is that they, the folks at brigade and higher, are still wrestling with it." Pausing, Nathan looked around the table at the faces of his senior leaders. "Of course, even if that's true it doesn't do any of us any good. We can't waffle. We have to give our people something firm to hang their hats on, something that provides them with clear, concise orders and positive measures that suit the situation that they will be facing. So here's how we're going to play the hand we've been dealt.

"At this time," Nathan explained, "the concept of operations remains basically the same with very few modifications. The battalion will still continue to rotate the line companies through what has been dubbed the red, amber, green cycle. As before the red company is responsible for the four checkpoints in our battalion area. No change there. The major change is how the amber company operates. Previously they were little more than an alert force, patrolling the wall and fence in the evening before sunset and again at dawn, looking for signs of infiltration while maintaining a platoon-sized ready response force prepared to reinforce the red company or deal with problems they cannot handle."

"And now?" Gordon Grello, the company XO, asked hesitantly.

"In addition to patrolling the wall and fence and the ready response force, the amber will conduct aggressive patrols throughout the battalion area."

Matt Garver studied the many roads that crisscrossed the area connecting the myriad of farms that surrounded Camp Lee. "Could you define aggressive, sir?"

Nathan chuckled. "Unfortunately, no. Like so many

things, Sergeant Garver, that is a question for which I have no answer."

"Mines and ambushes," Faucher stated to no one in particular. "Like Iraq, I imagine that the greatest danger those patrols will face will be from land mines and small ambushes by indigenous personnel."

"You mean Palestinian terrorists," Keith Stone, the platoon leader for first platoon, stated sharply.

"Not necessarily," Allen Teeple, his counterpart from the third platoon, replied as he looked up at Stone. "It would be wrong to discount the possibility of the Israelis dispatching a provocateur into the security zone for the express purpose of staging an attack and then blaming it on the Palestinians."

Both Faucher and Grello gave Teeple a long, disbelieving stare as Garver shook his head and responded. "It would seem that Al's still suffering from an overload of liberal dogma that the University of Virginia has become so famous for, not to mention a touch of conspiracy paranoia."

The post-grad student glared at the older platoon sergeant but was unable to reply with a suitable retort. Though he was somewhat taken aback by the remarks Garver had made to an officer, Nathan sought to bring this discussion to a quick close. "Mines and ambushes," he stated sharply, "*will* be a major concern regardless of who is responsible for them. It is a concern we'll be discussing in a bit." When he was sure that his tone and expression had defused the unexpected flare-up, Nathan continued. "The green company has also taken on greater responsibilities. Previously all it was supposed to do was handle all the admin chores within the camp that support units weren't dealing with using some of its personnel while continuing to conduct small unit and individual training with the balance. Now, however, that company will have to take on as its primary responsibility security of the base camp itself. This will include maintaining one additional platoon on one-hour standby ready to back up either the red or amber company should they find themselves in need of additional forces or if the battalion is suddenly ordered to conduct a preemptive strike against a pending threat."

Faucher shook his head. "So what you're saying, sir, is that we're not going to have much of an opportunity to finish up the training we didn't get to here."

"Not quite," Nathan countered. "Though the time we thought we would have for training has all but disappeared, this company's need for it has not. What this does mean is that you, the platoon leaders and platoon sergeants, will have to be creative and aggressive in the training of your people. You'll need to make the most of each and every opportunity as they occur to hone those skills that your soldiers are deficient in. Being on standby as a ready reaction force does not mean sitting around in your Hummers twiddling your thumbs. You can run a reaction to ambush drill without having to move those Hummers, or conduct first aid or weapons training right there next to your vehicles. There's any number of things you can do. As I said, you simply have got to be aggressive about seeking out and using every opportunity that comes your way."

Teeple was tempted to remark on Nathan's overuse of the word "aggressive" but decided that this wasn't a good time to be cute.

When no one made any effort to respond or comment, Nathan pressed on with his discussion of the threat they faced as he saw it. With the pointer he touched the various items throughout the 2nd Battalion's sector as he mentioned them. "A direct assault against Camp Lee by anyone other than by a lone bomber is almost nonexistent. If it came, such an attack would be quick, isolated, and over before any force, other than those at the point of attack, could be mustered against it. Vigilance is the only solution here. The same holds true at the checkpoints, especially those where vehicles will be passing. An unflinching vigilance and strict adherence to all protocols and procedures will reduce the likelihood of an attack, but can never totally eliminate the possibility. There's little we can do beforehand to stop a person who is hell-bent on dying for his God. In my humble opinion it is not a question of 'if.' Rather it is simply one of when." As he made this statement Nathan glanced up at each of his platoon leaders. "A platoon within our brigade *will* face that attack. When it comes, and if it turns out that one of our platoons is on the receiving end the best we can hope for is that our people will be ready and able to stop it before the martyrs-in-waiting manage to worm their way into a position where they can maximize havoc and carnage."

Nathan allowed his platoon leaders to reflect upon his comments before going on. For their part the three platoon leaders were silent as they reflected upon what their commander was saying. "In an effort to keep them at arm's length," Nathan continued, "I have recommended to the battalion commander that we establish a two-man roving checkpoint fifty to one hundred feet away from each of the permanent checkpoints we will be manning. These roving checkpoints, located in a slightly different spot each day along the road leading to the main checkpoint, will conduct a prescreening that all pedestrians and vehicles must pass through."

Jack Horne, platoon leader of the second platoon, cleared his throat in an effort to get Nathan's attention. "Begging your pardon, but it seems to me that doing that will only serve to unduly expose the men assigned this duty since I am assuming they will not have the benefit of sandbags or bunkers at the checkpoint to protect them if attacked."

Nathan nodded. "That is very true. I didn't say it was foolproof or without risk. They will in effect be something like a point element, a small detachment that may, I say again, may prematurely trip an attack before the terrorists manage to make it to where the bulk of our people and innocent civilians are."

"And how," Horne asked innocently, "do we determine who draws *that* duty?"

"You will, Lieutenant. You and your NCOs."

Nathan's reply stunned Horne. He didn't respond. Instead he cast a fugitive glance at Matt Garver, his platoon sergeant, before looking over at the other young platoon leaders. For their part they met his eyes with an expressionless, deadpan stare. It was during this exchange that it hit Nathan just how unprepared these men were to make the sort of life and death decisions that this mission would sooner or later require of them. What he could do to prepare them to meet that challenge would be his greatest challenge.

Throughout this entire exchange only Alex Faucher was able to step back and appreciate just how far apart their new commanding officer and his platoon leaders were. As hard as he had been trying, Faucher could tell that Nathan was still unable to view this mission as little more than another assignment, a task that had to be executed in the most efficient and effective manner possible. For their part the expressions on the platoon leaders' faces betrayed the trepidation they felt, an apprehension that any man would harbor when suddenly confronted by a set of circumstances that forced him to make decisions that would place men who were his friends and neighbors in harm's way. Just how this divergence of attitudes and perspective would play out and affect the company was hard to foresee.

"Okay," Nathan stated briskly in an effort to regain the full attention of his officers and NCOs. "We have a lot more to cover and less than an hour to cover all I need to before the next company takes over here at the sand table. So let's press on. Now, the first sergeant brought up the subject of land mines and ambushes. Yes, they will be a problem, a big problem. Here's what we are going to do about them."

* * *

Pausing, Christina Dixon studied her handiwork in the bathroom mirror for a moment before carrying on. It had been a long time since she had taken this much time putting on makeup. Like most couples the grind of life together after marriage had forced each of them to change. After all, courting is high stress, a demanding ritual that cannot be maintained indefinitely. Once all the thank you notes have been written and mailed and all the photos are safely tucked away in the album both husband and wife are free to refocus their attention to more practical matters. One by one those little things that people do to please their perspective mates during the courtship slipped away unnoticed, until the new couple settles down into a routine that is both comfortable and practical. This did not mean that the love each felt for the other diminished. It simply transformed itself into something more meaningful, something that could be sustained.

Laying aside the eyeliner, Chris rested her elbows on the cool white countertop adjoining the sink. With her chin cradled in the palms of her hands she stared into the reflection of her own eyes. It was as if she were trying to see what was really going on behind them. She found herself admitting that her efforts to make these last few days together special were nothing more than a defensive ploy, an effort on her part to avoid the harsh reality that these would be the last days they would have together for a long, long time. Perhaps they would be the last days they would . . .

With a start she stood upright, grasping the edge of the sink's countertop with her hands while maintaining eye-to-eye contact with herself in the mirror. "No!" she shouted as her cheeks glowed red with anger. "You promised you wouldn't go there. You promised you weren't going to do this to yourself."

But promises are easier to make than keep. Often they blissfully ignore reality, a reality that Christina Dixon was finally having to deal with. For despite her chosen profession, despite her determination that she would keep things in perspective, Chris was coming to realize that she was first and foremost a woman, a woman in love with a man who would soon be taken away from her by a calling that trumped all, even life itself.

Releasing the countertop, Chris threw back her head, stifled a sniffle, and carefully dabbed the corner of her eye with a Q-Tip lest the tear welling up in it undue her handiwork. "You're all right," she chanted. "You're all right and everything is under control." With that, she continued her prep.

Long before he saw her Nathan knew that Chris was up to something. Like a cat he entered their apartment and crept forward. Those lights that were on drew him into their small living room where he discovered the love of his life stretched out on the sofa. With her auburn hair artfully tussled and framing her face, Chris stared at Nathan as he came around the corner. Wearing nothing more than a short lacy black silk robe that didn't quite cover everything, she greeted him with a sensual smile. "I've fixed you all your favorite things."

Her expression, the breathless, sexy tone of her voice, and the undeniable come-hither look in her eyes solicited an immediate and uncontrollable response that Nathan could not have concealed if he wanted to. "So I see."

Lifting a long-stemmed red rose she was holding, Chris waved it at the dining-room table set for two. "Not me, silly," she stated playfully. "I was talking about dinner."

"Pardon my French," Nathan stated as he approached her, "but screw dinner."

"Nathan, Nathan, Nathan. Must I explain everything to you? You eat dinner first, then we, well . . ."

He was about to lean over to kiss her when she brought her hand up and stopped him short. "No treats for you, my dear sir, until you've showered, shaved, and changed."

Pouting like a boy being reprimanded, Nathan pulled

back. "Okay, okay." With that, he disappeared into the bedroom, leaving Chris free to rise up and finish setting out dinner.

Unable to match his wife's sexually charged attire, Nathan opted to counter with something unexpected. Digging through his dresser drawer he pulled out an old red, white, and yellow VMI rugby shirt and a pair of well worn and very short shorts. With an enthusiasm that rivaled that of a kid anxious to get at his gifts on Christmas morning, he threw himself into preparing for a night of intimacy that promised to erase all thought of his pending departure. Forgotten for the moment was the note his father had sent him via the G-2 briefing officer. There would be time to ponder the meaning of those hastily scribbled words. For as surely as the coming of the morning sun, his company would begin a journey that promised to be both challenging and hazardous.

But that was tomorrow. Until then Nathan was hell-bent on enjoying a night of unrestrained passion and romance that his wife had so carefully laid out for him. After all, he snickered as he jumped into the shower, it was his duty as a husband to go along with Chris's little game. "Ah duty," he mused as he soaped himself up in the shower. "Will I ever escape the burdens of my duty to God, country, and the girl next door."

Bedlow, Virginia

In the stillness of their small bedroom, Brian McIntire reached out and laid his hand on his wife's distended belly. He held it there until he felt a sudden jab. With glee, he followed the movements of his unborn child as it shifted and turned as if trying to escape from the hand it could not yet see or touch directly. Had his wife not begun to stir and threaten to awaken, McIntire would have followed each and every wild and spasmodic gyration that brought him joy.

Though he pulled his hand away, he continued to watch as one side of his wife's stomach seemed to deflate before his eyes. "You're a squirmy little thing," he whispered as if the child could hear him. "Just like your old man."

Stirred by the sound of his voice, McIntire's wife reached out and touched him. "Is everything all right?"

Rising up on his elbow, the National Guardsman leaned over and gently kissed his wife's cheek. "Everything is fine, hon. Go back to sleep."

For the moment, everything was fine. Any doubt or concerns he had about joining in on Paul Sucher's harebrained idea of going back to Virginia for the day were wiped away by the sheer joy of the moment. Taking care to avoid disturbing the baby, McIntire draped his arm about his sleeping wife, closed his eyes, and drifted off to sleep.

CHAPTER 13

Israel

In silence the Israeli Army colonel who was called Matt by a handful of friends stood before twin panes of thick glass. He watched intently as medical technicians encased in biohazard suits carefully slid the lifeless body of Dr. Joseph Meir from his bed, across sheets of plastic, and into an open body bag draped over a waiting gurney. Once they had all of Meir's limbs tucked securely in the heavy rubber bag, the medical techs carefully folded everything the doctor's body had come in contact with and stuffed them into the bag as well. Sheets, pillow, bedcover, plastic sheets, everything went.

Raising an eyebrow, the colonel turned to the solemn-faced physician next to him. "Isn't that being a bit sloppy?"

The physician's response betrayed the pain he felt over what they were being forced to do. "I regret what we are doing, but we are being quite practical. By doing things this way we reduce the amount of contaminated material we have to handle and dispose of."

"I don't see how when someone is going to have to open the body bag, pull all that other material out, and repackage it in another container."

Surprised, the wizened old doctor stared up into the face of the Army colonel. This, he thought, was a strange twist in roles. "Usually it is the doctor who is supposed to be empathic and sensitive to the needs of the patient," he stated cynically, "not the professional soldier."

The colonel looked away from the grim scene on the other side of the glass and looked down at the doctor. "I do not understand."

"He," the doctor stated, indicating Meir's corpse with little more than a nod of his head, "will be taken straight to the disposal site. The body bag with the good doctor and everything he came into contact with while he was in our care will go straight into the incinerator. Even the pad on the gurney and the biohazard suits the med techs are wearing will go with him." Looking back into the isolation ward crowded with dying patients, the doctor sighed. "If I could, I'd tear down every wall and pull up the very floor of this room and send them into the flames along with my unfortunate colleague."

"You will not perform an autopsy?"

Stunned by this line of questioning and shaken by his inability to do anything to help the people on the other side of the double-paned window, the old doctor came close to losing his temper. "That would be pointless and cruel. I do not have to slit that poor soul open from groin to neck to know that his lungs, his stomach, and damned near every inch of his intestines have been reduced to little more than a bloody pulp. If anything," the old doctor continued as his anger grew by the second, "I'm tempted to peer inside those who haven't died yet in order to find out why they haven't!"

Finally appreciating just how stupid and naive his questions had been, the colonel looked down at the floor. "My apologies, Doctor. I just wasn't prepared for . . ."

Still worked up, the doctor cut the colonel's apology short. "None of us were. Oh, we thought we were. We thought we had done everything to prepare ourselves for this day. All the protocols were neatly laid out and understood by all. My people trained again and again for this sort of thing. Procedures for handling the victims and protecting ourselves were codified, published, and distributed. It was all there. Everything. Everything was ready, everything but the shock of having to face a day such as this. When this," he stated as he waved his right hand in a vague gesture at the patients and med techs on the other side of the window, "when it finally does hit. Nothing, nothing, can prepare us for this, this . . ." He didn't finish his thought as the odd pair lapsed back into silence.

Sensing that there was nothing more to be gained from standing there, the colonel looked at his watch. "I need to be getting back to the Ministry of Defense. The Chiefs of Staff are awaiting my report. But before I go, I must remind you again that it is critical that you and all your personnel are under orders by the government to maintain absolute secrecy. No one, not even members of your own families, is to know what really happened to these people. If word got out about this at this time, who knows what would happen."

The doctor looked up into the colonel's eyes. For a moment he was tempted to make a snide comment about the political necessity someone in the government thought trumped practical reality. But he didn't. He kept his tongue in check and let the colonel walk away.

When the Army colonel had disappeared behind the double doors at the end of the corridor, the doctor's young protégée came up next to him. "Well, what's the verdict?"

Turning to the young woman who would one day take his place as the nation's leading expert on viral infections, the doctor smiled. "It seems that those who are far wiser than we have decided that this outbreak is little more than an isolated incident that does not warrant a nationwide alert. We are to continue to care for our patients as best as possible, dispose of the remains in accordance with established protocols, and then forget that this ever happened."

Shocked, his young assistant stared at him with her mouth agape. It took several efforts before she could manage to put together a coherent statement. "That's insane! It's criminal"

"It's politics, my dear. If word of this leaked out, do you

think the Americans would still come? No. Our government is committed to drawing our longtime benefactors into our war against the Palestinians. They want the Americans to taste the sting of mindless Arab terrorism. And nothing, nothing short of a biblical disaster will keep them from their task."

"And this," the young doctor cried out as she pointed at the dying patients on the other side of the windows, "this is not a disaster?"

The old doctor shook his head. "This," he stated with a straight face, "never happened." With that, he turned and walked away.

Fort Benning, Georgia

The early morning hour and his determination to make his last night with Christina a memorable one conspired to dull Nathan's senses. Throughout Company A's first formation, the issuance of weapons from the unit arms room and their movement to the airfield he failed to notice the look of concern both his first sergeant and executive officer sported. Having already become used to the clumsy gyrations they and the other officers and NCOs in the company would go to in an effort to avoid him, Nathan suspected nothing until the aircraft commander, a major on the brigade staff, began to call off the names from his master list and assign each man a manifest number. Even then, it took far too long before the young company commander came to the realization that something was amiss.

In the process of shouting out the names of the four hundred plus members of the 176th Brigade who were slated for this particular charter aircraft, the aircraft commander paused only when he did not hear an immediate response from the man being called. This reply usually came in the form of a crisp military "yo" or a sullen, reluctant "here" depending on the amount of enthusiasm the individual was able to muster. The first time someone failed to reply, Nathan thought nothing of it.

To insure that everyone heard him, the aircraft commander repeated the name when no one responded. "Klauss, Gene William. Klauss, Gene William."

A murmur ran throughout the ranks and files of soldiers burdened with weapons and personal gear standing in a single great mass waiting patiently in the early morning darkness to embark on the Boeing 747. From where he stood, the aircraft commander yelled out. "Okay, people, settle down. We don't have all day," as he prepared to continue to march down the long list of names before him.

From somewhere in the great mass, a cheerful wag countered. "The hell you say. The sun isn't even up yet."

Amid the chuckles another Virginian added his own comment. "Take your time, Major. We have six months."

Unable to keep a straight face himself, the major let the men he would be responsible for during the ten-hour flight to Israel enjoy this bit of comic relief for several minutes before making an effort to regain control. "Okay, people, at ease. Let's hold it down. I still have a lot of names to go through here and I for one have no intention of spending any more time in the great state of Georgia than I have to."

After a final ripple of laughter he picked up calling off the names where he had left off. This continued along without incident until he came to Brian McIntire's name. "McIntire, Brian. McIntire, Brian. Sound off."

This time there was a pronounced silence as those who were familiar with the names of the two people who seemed to be missing realized that they not only belonged to the same company, but were in fact assigned to the same squad. Unfortunately for Nathan, he was still too new to the unit to make this connection. It wasn't until Faucher came up behind him, tapped him on the shoulder, and whispered in his ear, "Sir, we need to talk," that he began to suspect something was not quite right. Stepping out of the line where the officers and senior NCOs stood, Nathan followed his first sergeant off to one side where Gordon Grello, his XO, and Jack Horne, the platoon leader of the second platoon, stood. Judging by their expressions, Nathan knew before anyone said a word that whatever it was they were about to spring on him, it wasn't going to be good.

Taking the lead, as was his habit at times like this, Faucher just blurted out the whole story as quickly and concisely as he could. "Some of the boys took off Friday afternoon at the completion of our last formation and headed back to Bedlow."

Behind them, Nathan could hear the aircraft commander drone on as he called off more names, stopping when he didn't hear an immediate response. "Rainey, Samuel K. Rainey, Samuel K."

Holding his anger in check, Nathan folded his arms across his chest. "Let me guess. They're not back yet."

"Sir, the car they rented broke down last night just south of Knoxville, Tennessee, in the middle of nowhere. Paul, I mean PFC Sucher, called and said that it was almost two hours before anyone bothered to stop and give them a hand."

Nathan all but bit his tongue in an effort to keep from swearing. "When did they call?"

"Just before midnight."

Making a great show of looking at his watch, Nathan checked the time, then looked into the eyes of each of the Virginians before him as he spoke. "And you're just getting around to telling me this now?"

When Faucher said nothing, Grello stepped up. "We thought they'd make it. Last time they called on Gene's cell phone, they were midway between Chattanooga and Atlanta."

"But they didn't make it, did they, Lieutenant?"

Grello was about to say something, but didn't.

"Do any of you know what the penalty for missing a movement is?"

The three Virginians didn't answer as they looked down at the ground, shuffled their feet, and glanced at each other.

"Well," Nathan continued, making no effort to curb his rancor. "I don't know what the UCMJ calls for either. But I will tell you that it's not going to be half as painful to them as this blatant betrayal of your trust in me has already been."

"Sir, it's not that we don't trust you," Faucher tried to explain, "it's just that . . ."

"I see," Nathan hissed. "You thought you could get away with it! The three of you, you and whoever else is involved thought you could slip one by the old man. Didn't you?"

When no one answered, Nathan balled his hands into fists and planted them on his hips. "Well, people, if this is the way you want to play the game, fine. I can play too. Just be sure you remind the good citizens of Bedlow who belong to this company every time they come to you bitching and moaning because the captain is on the warpath as to the reason why."

Faucher knew better than to try, but Grello felt the need to say something. His efforts to do so, however, were cut short by Nathan's curt order. "Rejoin the company." With that, the young company commander pivoted about on his heels and stormed off.

It took Nathan a good two hours after they had finished boarding and taken off before he finally managed to settle down. In this effort he was aided by rereading the note his father had sent him via the colonel who had delivered the latest in-country intelligence briefing to the 176th Brigade. Fishing the note from his pocket, he studied the hastily scribbled words of advice written below the three-star symbol belonging to the Army's Deputy Chief of Staff for Operations. *"I cannot tell you how best to meet the challenges that you will find yourself facing in the days and weeks ahead. Though there is much I'd like to say, precious little would be of value. About all I can think of that will be of use is to do what you know is right and not what is expedient or easy. That, son, is why you get paid the big bucks. You are a commander. So command. Not everything you do will be right. Not every decision will be the wisest or the best. Those are the only things you can be sure of. But if you hold true to those principles that your mother and I, the Virginia Military Institute, and the United States Army have tried to instill in you, you will prevail."*

Leaning back in his seat, Nathan let his hand holding the note come to rest on his lap as he closed his eyes. He knew his father was right. He also knew that in the scheme of things the incident involving the five who had missed their flight was trivial. What was not so easy to ignore was the manner in which his officers and NCOs had chosen to handle the affair. He knew that the new commanding officer had to go through a mating ritual of sorts in which he and his subordinates felt each other out as they established ground rules, a dialogue, and a foundation upon which an effective working relationship could be built. As a platoon leader and a company executive officer, he had gone through that very process from the other side. Unfortunately he expected that those past experiences could not be relied upon as guides. The common ground that served to expedite the transition all new commanding officers go through was missing here. None of his people were professional soldiers. Their view of the world was still driven by a common civilian-oriented background that Nathan did not share. Because of this he suspected that many of the leadership techniques that he had honed during his tenure as a lieutenant would not work. Just how he would go about figuring out which did and which did not while executing a mission that would have been a tough one for a fully trained line unit was but one challenge that Nathan would have to deal with each and every day for the next few weeks.

Lost in his thoughts, Nathan didn't notice that Colonel Lanston had made his way back to where he was sitting until his battalion commander spoke. "A note from your dad with a few last-minute words of advice?"

Caught off guard, Nathan's eyes flew open as he hurriedly stuffed the note back into his breast pocket. "Yes sir. Something like that."

Lanston gave his newest company commander a moment to collect himself before he got down to business. "Could I have a word with you in private, Captain?"

While framed as a question, the colonel's words were an order. "Yes sir. Of course."

The two men made their way through the crowded cabin until they reached one of the banks of bathrooms that divided the cavernous 747 into sections. After waiting for a startled soldier who popped out of one of the bathrooms to beat a hasty retreat, Lanston got right to the point. "I have been advised of the problem concerning Sergeant Klauss and his band of wandering souls."

His colonel's effort to make light of the incident failed to amuse Nathan. With a straight face, the young officer listened in silence as Lanston spoke. "I have decided to handle this matter myself and have instructed the battalion adjutant to personally handle the investigation. No doubt you will have more than enough to do once we're on the ground."

When Nathan made no effort to respond, Lanston continued. "Those five men made a mistake, a serious mistake. They will be punished. On that, you can be sure. Chances are you will not agree with my decision, but I can live with that. What I cannot live with, Captain, is having one of my companies torn apart over such a trivial affair."

Unable to let that comment pass, Nathan spoke. "Sir, with all due respect, I do not consider missing a major troop movement a minor affair."

Having spent his entire military career in the National Guard, Lanston was not at all put off by a direct challenge that would have earned Nathan a swift and stinging rebuke had that young officer tried it with a career Army officer. That Nathan was challenging him was clear. It was, however, a confrontation that Lanston refused to engage in. Instead of verbally ripping his subordinate's head off, Lanston flashed a sympathetic, fatherly sort of smile. "Well, I suppose you're right, Captain Dixon. And I suppose I'm overstepping my bounds by reaching down into your company and snatching this out of your hands. But I'm afraid you're going to have to trust me when I tell you that it's best for everyone involved, especially for you, if you let me do things my way."

"And the next time someone screws up, sir? Are you going to let my people skip over the chain of command and come running to you hoping to get a better deal?"

Ignoring Nathan's effort to provoke him, Lanston's smile grew. "Oh, those lads aren't going to be getting away with a darn thing. You forget, Captain, when all of this is over they have to go home with me. Even when I'm no longer the battalion commander, the memory of what they did this morning will live on. For as long as they remain in the Guard, every time one of them comes up for a promotion, every time one of them is under consideration for an advanced military school, every time one of them asks to be excused from some particular nasty duty someone is going to rub their chin and ask, 'Wasn't he one of those fellows who missed the plane to Israel?' That, my young friend, will hurt them more than anything you or the Uniformed Code of Military Justice could ever do to them."

Though far from mollified, Nathan realized that Lanston had a point, one which he would never have stumbled upon on his own. Unable to think of an appropriate retort, and just as unwilling at the moment to concede that the colonel was right, Nathan drew himself up into a position of attention. "Is that all you have for me, sir?"

"Yes, Captain, that's all. For now."

* * *

Like a scene reminiscent of their days in high school, Paul Sucher and his four companions who were already being referred to as "the Bedlow Five" sat in a row of chairs just outside the office of the assistant adjutant for the 176th Brigade. Each man knew that he was in serious trouble without having to be told. It was merely a question of how much trouble, a question that no one assigned to the brigade's rear detachment could answer. With their company's barracks already cleared and locked up, the five had nothing to do and nowhere to go. Even if they did, none of them were willing to venture any farther than the latrine at the end of the hall. Like errant children who had been threatened with the loss of their Christmas if they made one more misstep, Gene Klauss, Brian McIntire, Sam Rainey, Jerry Slatery, and Paul Sucher sat with their heads bowed and shoulders hunched, resigned to their fate and unusually quiet.

Still, though they were momentarily humbled, they were not completely dead. Glancing to his left and right at his co-conspirators, Sam Rainey snickered. "We'll leave at noon," he stated mockingly. "We'll be back in plenty of time. I'll bet no one even notices we're gone."

Angered at having his very words thrown back at him, Paul Sucher gave Rainey a dirty look. "Fuck you and the horse you rode in on."

From across the hall, Gene Klauss laughed. "We probably would have done a whole lot better if we had used horses. You know, there's a good reason the car rental company we used is named Cheap Heaps."

With a quick snap of his head, Sucher turned his glare on Rainey. "Fuck you too."

"What's the matter," Slatery smirked. "Didn't get enough when you were home?"

Sensing that his manner of responding up to now was

doing him little good, Sucher opted instead to sit upright, fold his arms across his chest, and glare at each of his tormentors.

This standoff lasted until the brigade's assistant stepped out of his office and into the hall. "Well," he stated in a cheery voice meant to goad the A Company strays, "you seem to be in luck. The C-17 leaving this afternoon with the last of the brigade's heavy equipment does have five vacant slots." Then, slipping back into a more official tone, he issued his orders. "You have two hours to gather up your personal gear that's being held at the brigade's S-4 shop, get something to eat at the mess hall, and be back here."

As the only NCO and senior member of the Bedlow Five, Klauss asked about their weapons. "Where are they being kept, sir?"

The brigade assistant adjutant shrugged. "I don't know anything about that."

"Who does know?"

The assistant adjutant gave Klauss an uncompromising stare. "I have negative knowledge concerning your weapons, Sergeant. I doubt if anyone here knows anything about that. My responsibility begins and ends with getting your skinny little butts on that plane. Other than that, I really don't give a damn." With that, he walked back into his office.

Sensing an opportunity to get a few of his own swipes in, Sucher chuckled. "Nice going, Sergeant Klauss."

Now it was Klauss's turn to show his anger. "Fuck you."

Wanting to keep out of the heated exchange that threatened to spin out of control, Brian McIntire stood up. "I don't know about you guys, but I'm hungry. Anyone care to join me and head over to the mess hall before going to pick up our gear?"

Seizing the chance to bring an end to the acrimony that was bubbling up, Sam Rainey jumped to his feet, grabbed McIntire by the arm, and began to head for the door at the end of the corridor. "Now there's a plan I can live with. Anyone else want to join us?"

One by one, the others rose up off their chairs and followed suit, leaving Paul Sucher alone until he finally came to the realization that sitting around sulking was pointless and not a little childish. Slowly, he pulled himself together, sucked down his pride, and did his best to catch up with his friends.

CHAPTER 14

Israel

Arrival in Israel left Nathan no time to dwell on the manner the entire battalion's chain of command had chosen to deal with the five soldiers who had missed the flight. By the time the charter flight carrying the main body of the 3rd Battalion, 176th Infantry Brigade, touched down at the Israeli military airfield, Nathan Dixon had to dedicate his full attention to the myriad of problems his company would face during their first forty-eight hours in country. Even the deep resentment and sense of betrayal he now felt toward his officers and senior NCOs could not be allowed to cloud his judgment or divert his attention away from the tasks at hand.

As a light infantry unit, the 3rd of the 176th lacked the necessary organic or assigned transportation needed to pick up and move all its personnel and equipment at once, movement to Camp Lee inside what was being called the West Bank Security Zone was accomplished by bus companies the U.S. government had contracted for from local companies. Most were tour buses that were designed to haul visitors from one biblical site to another. After being crammed into a charter version of the 747 that many of the members of the 176th equated to an airborne cattle car, the air-conditioned buses with plush seats and huge tinted windows were a treat. Like kids on a class trip they vied for seats next to the windows. Most had never been outside of the United States. For some, other than the brigade's four-week stint at Fort Benning and their basic training, this was their first time outside the state of Virginia.

In their excitement, few of the men belonging to

Nathan's company appreciated the danger they were in. The presence of Israeli armored vehicles and armed personnel was ignored as the Virginians took in the strange and exotic landscape around them. Nathan and other senior officers could not afford to allow themselves to be distracted. While their men stowed their gear in the cargo bays of the buses and scrambled onto them, Nathan gathered up his officers and NCOs. "Okay, listen up, people," he called out in an effort to be heard over the hoots and jabbering going on all about them. "Until we reach Camp Lee we're under the protection of the Israeli Army. To the best of my knowledge, there isn't a live round of ammunition among us." Nathan, of course, was lying. As was his habit he had two fifteen-round magazines of 9mm ball ammunition tucked away in a pocket of his BDUs. Unbeknownst to him, his first sergeant likewise had ammo already loaded into magazines for his pistol as well as four full thirty-round M-16 magazines tucked away in the small canvas tote bag he kept with him at all times. Like Nathan, Faucher had no intention of walking into the shadow of the valley of death without the ability to defend himself or his charges.

"Should something happen while we are en route to Camp Lee," he continued, "and the convoy is brought to a dead stop, get your people off the buses and under cover. I don't want any heroics. Until we're in sector and draw our own combat load of ammunition, we're going to have to rely upon the IDF to do our fighting."

Not everyone was thrilled with this state of affairs. One of them was Keith Stone of the first platoon. "And what happens if some of those rag heads manage to spill into the ditches where we're cowering?"

Reaching out, Nathan grabbed Stone's web belt with one hand and the hilt of his bayonet with the other. With a quick jerk, he unsheathed the bayonet and thrust it point first into the air. "In that case, the order of the day will be fix bayonets. Any questions?"

For the infantry this order has always been the precursor of the most desperate sort of fighting that a soldier can engage in, hand-to-hand combat. It requires that the combatants be close enough to peer into his opponent's eyes, to be able to feel his breath on your face, hear his every grunt, and feel every twitch he makes as he grapples with you in a struggle from which only one of the two combatants will escape with his life. In an age of precision munitions launched from multimillion-dollar aircraft and guided to their targets with the aid of satellites, the idea of infantrymen resorting to this sort of combat was viewed as little more than a quaint anachronism, a Hollywood image that had no place on the modern battlefield. But even among twenty-first-century warriors, the term "fix bayonets" was enough to send a chill through their soul and highlight just how desperate their situation was.

Satisfied that he had made his point, Nathan flipped the bayonet in the air, grasped it by the blade, and offered it handle first to Stone. He did not intend for this bit of showmanship to be impressive. As a professional soldier who was used to hanging out with men who gave the term "hard-core" its meaning, it was simply the way he did things. His Guardsmen however were wowed by this little flamboyant display of military swagger and the cool casualness with which Nathan delivered such an intense and somber message. For them the holiday lark was over. While their men watched strange and wonderful new countryside glide past their windows, the officers and NCOs of Company A found themselves eyeing every sharp bend in the road or commanding hilltop along the way as a potential ambush site. In this way, Nathan managed to achieve his first objective of the day; he was getting his subordinate leaders to think like soldiers.

In concept, design, and appearance, Camp Lee was a throwback to the Vietnam-era base camp. It had been laid out and constructed under the supervision of U.S. Army engineers using a mix of American and Israeli Army engineers augmented by Israeli civilians. In reality Camp Lee was less a camp in the modern military sense and more of a fort, not at all unlike the sort of fort American colonists built to protect themselves from the indigenous population they were displacing or even those thrown up by Roman legions as they went about conquering the ancestors of the same people the 176th Brigade had been dispatched to bring peace to.

Squatting low atop a sprawling hill, Camp Lee was like all newly thrown together military installations, its dominant feature was dirt that tended to turn into seas of mud at the slightest hint of rain. The outer perimeter was a thick dirt berm encased in sandbags front, back, and top. At each corner and on either side of both the front and rear gates were massive circular sandbag bunkers that jutted out like the keeps of a medieval castle.

Within these outer defenses were four company-sized camps, each set back from and parallel to one of the main walls. At each end of the blocks set aside for the companies were motor pools that separated the companies much the same way that the corner bunkers on the outer walls did. Within the hollow square formed by the company areas and motor pools were the battalion command post, mess hall, communications center, and a dispensary. Mixed in among these battalion-level support facilities were an assortment of recreational facilities that included a pair of basketball courts and two clubs, one for officers and NCOs and one for enlisted men.

In a military compound such as this, one is able to gauge the relative value of a structure at a glance. Facilities such as the battalion headquarters and comms center are almost always entirely enclosed in sandbags and fenced off by razor wire. Others, like the pair of clubs located at opposite ends of the inner square, had neither. Within the separate company areas only the bare wooden platforms upon which the venerable GP large tents would be erected were ready. Thus, like the U.S. Army of old that was sent out to patrol the vast barren expanses of a new nation, the first chore the soldiers of the 3rd Battalion, 176th Infantry Brigade, would have to perform would be to erect shelter for themselves.

This realization as well as the dismal appearance of the place that would be their home for the next few months effectively put an end to the holidaylike atmosphere that had dominated the trip to Camp Lee from the airfield. Exhaustion bred by their early morning mustering, a long flight, and being catapulted across several time zones all but zapped whatever energy remained within Nathan's company. Like a herd of disgruntled teenagers being shepherded off to their first day of school after a long summer's break, the soldiers of Company A dragged their duffel bags through the dirt as their NCOs led them down their assigned company street. One by one each squad and section peeled off as they came across the hand-scrawled sign bearing their squad's number tacked to a vacant platform. With all the enthusiasm of men erecting their own gallows, Nathan's Virginians piled their duffel bags and gear off to one side and set about stretching out and erecting the heavy canvas tent they found sitting in the center of each platform. This task was made all the more difficult for the members of Staff Sergeant Oliver Rendell's squad since five of their numbers were still sitting at an airfield in Georgia waiting for the last of the brigade's vehicles to be loaded up. Accompanied by the usual assortment of oaths that still permeated the modern politically correct Army, Rendell and his remaining men struggled with the tent, vowing to each other that the Bedlow Five would pay dearly for missing what Don Olkowski sarcastically dubbed as a wonderful team building opportunity. Daniel Travers, a man with a genetic abhorrence to physical labor, glumly agreed wholeheartedly. "Oh, yeah," he repeated again and again between strategically timed grunts. "Those boys are gonna pay, big time."

At Fort Benning the soldiers of the 176th Brigade had been at home. Though their stay there had been longer and the training more intense than what they were accustomed to, nothing they did at Benning was any different from the battalion's two weeks of annual training. Even the World War II era barracks they occupied each year at Fort Pickett, Virginia, were pretty much the same as the ones they found at Benning. This, and the schedule mandated by the Infantry School and Department of the Army, allowed the leadership of Company A to carry on with little need for guidance or input from their new commanding officer. For the most part he was just another officer along for the ride.

All that changed the moment they stepped foot on Israeli soil. The exotic nature of the land, so different from the lush green Shenandoah Valley, and the somber utilitarian appearance of Camp Lee itself served to remind the Virginians that they were quite literally out of their element. Here, in an active theater of operations, the roles quickly reversed. It was Nathan who now felt at home and the platoon leaders and platoon sergeants who were at a loss as to how best to proceed. Nathan understood this and they knew it. While no one was prepared to admit it yet, there wasn't an NCO or officer in Company A who suddenly did not find it reassuring to have a professional as their commanding officer, a soldier who had earned the right to wear a patch on his right sleeve and a combat infantryman's badge over his left breast pocket. In the twinkling of an eye, what he said and did became the focal point of the entire company.

Nathan wasted no time in exploiting this advantage. Once he saw that his first sergeant and platoon sergeants had the company well in hand and the erection of the tents was pretty much completed, he gathered up his officers and began to make his rounds. His first stop was battalion headquarters where he found Colonel Lanston and his staff in the throes of setting up shop. Walking up to his commanding officer, Nathan saluted Lanston and rendered a quick update on his unit's progress. "Everything appears to be well in hand. All personnel, with a few exceptions and their personal gear, are accounted for. By tonight we'll be settled in."

He was still in the process of highlighting some of his concerns when Captain Russell Hough, the battalion's operations officer, entered the small room that Lanston would have to share with his adjutant. Stepping aside to make room for Hough, Nathan greeted the Virginia State Police sergeant turned staff officer. "Just the man I was looking for. Before walking the perimeter with my platoon leaders I wanted to check in with you to make sure that my company's area of responsibility hasn't changed."

Anxious to escape the chaos created by his own NCOs as they went about getting his ops section up and running, Hough raised his finger as if motioning to Nathan to hold his thought. "If you give me a minute to dash over to my office and grab my helmet, I'll join you." Then, as an afterthought, he glanced over at Lanston. "That is if you don't need me at the moment."

Looking about at his bare office, the superintendent for schools turned battalion commander shrugged. "The thing I need the most is a chair, something I suspect you can't help me with."

"That sounds like an S-4 problem to me, Colonel. Remember, I don't do logistics."

Lanston sighed. "Go on, enjoy yourself. But if either of you happen to stumble upon the S-4 during your little walk about, be so kind as to send him this way. I would like to have a word with him about his priorities."

Nathan and Hough exchanged glances, smirked, and

made for the door as quickly as possible before Lanston changed his mind.

Once they were outside, the two captains with Nathan's platoon leaders in tow headed straight for the compound's eastern wall. "Your area of responsibility hasn't changed from what I told you back at Benning," Hough explained as they marched side by side. "Your company is responsible for securing the entire eastern wall to include both Strongpoint Alpha, the northeastern bunker, and Strongpoint Bravo anchoring the southeastern portion of the wall. Headquarters Company has responsibility for the entire northern wall and Bravo Company has the southern wall as well as the camp's main gate."

From behind them, Jack Horne of second platoon snickered. "Lucky them."

Keith Stone agreed. "That's fine by me. I'll gladly take two bunkers over playing gate guard for six months."

Hough looked over his shoulder at Nathan's platoon leaders. "Don't be too quick to count your blessings. Remember, your people are going to be standing watch on the wall facing the Palestinian zone."

"And in case you don't understand what that means," Nathan added as he paused before climbing up onto the wall itself, "just bear in mind that the number of incidents involving Palestinian snipers, bombers, and mortar attacks outnumber those initiated by members of the Jewish population by about a zillion to none."

As before, Nathan's unexpected dose of harsh reality served to remind the young Guard officers that they were playing for real here. Like out-of-town tourists emerging from a New York subway for the first time, each of the platoon leaders was on his guard, alert to everything going on around them as they cautiously followed their commanding officer and Russell Hough up onto the wall.

The base of the outer perimeter wall was little more than a dirt berm constructed by dumping spoil scrapped away during the leveling of the interior portion of Camp Lee. This dirt was dumped into a wide crib. On the outward face of this berm or parapet sandbags were stacked up until they reached a height equal to an average man's chest. In order to be fully protected by those sandbags one had to duck, which is what the young officers behind Nathan and Russ Hough instinctively did. Only when he stopped after making his way to the midway point of the wall and turned to study the ground off to the east did Nathan take note of the posture his executive officer and platoon leaders had assumed. After staring at them for a moment he made a face, glanced about as if checking to see if he had somehow missed something, then looked over at Hough. Like Nathan, the Virginia State Police sergeant turned ops officer had been standing upright as he surveyed the open ground before them. With a wink and a grin Hough leaned back and looked past Nathan at the crouching Virginians. "I imagine you gentlemen would get a much better view of the world if you stood up and took a peek over the parapet." Sheepishly the gaggle of lieutenants looked at each other and then, one by one, stood up and joined the pair of captains.

The narrowness of the security zone and the width of Camp Lee meant that the fence marking the border of the Palestinian state was clearly visible from the wall with the naked eye. The gleam of the bright sun on the razor wire shone like a bright metallic ribbon stretching as far as the eye could see from the northern horizon to the southern horizon. On either side of it the land was mostly barren with only a smattering of dwarf trees and scrubs clustered about here and there to break up the monotony of a parched, rocky land dissected by meandering dry gullies. The only feature of any note that was visible from the eastern wall of Camp Lee was a conical hill just beyond the fence. Its steep slopes were covered with orchards. Precariously perched atop this hill were the ruins of a Crusader castle and a more modern walled compound that appeared to jut out from the castle's southern wall. At the base of the hill ran the north-south road that paralleled the eastern boundary fence.

For a moment everyone's gaze fell upon the massive stone edifice that had silently stood watch over this land for centuries. With a tone that betrayed his awed reverence, Jack Horne broke the silence. "To flush out my schedule one semester and take care of one of my electives I took a course in medieval architecture. The professor was a character, a real Indiana Jones sort. He had done his doctorial thesis on Crusader castles in the Middle East. He even went on several digs here before things got really stupid. I wonder if this was one of the places he visited?"

The setting sun, now low in the western horizon, bathed the imposing stone bastions and keeps of the castle in a yellowish red hue. Mesmerized by this spectacle, it took a real effort on the part of Russell Hough to set aside his enjoyment of the moment and get back to the business at hand. "Infiltration is going to be our major concern," he stated dryly as he continued to peer off in the east. "The orchards over there and the gullies and dry streambeds that run down from the high ground they're on will provide more than enough cover and concealment right up to the wire to anyone interested in bypassing the checkpoint. And the castle, well, even though it's five klicks from here it's close enough to be of concern to us."

"In other words, gentlemen," Nathan added, "anyone who has a mind to won't have any problems finding some really great spots to snipe at us from."

"To say the least," Hough added. "Which is why it's going to be SOP that anyone assigned to pull duty up here will be required to wear their helmet and flak vest, day and night, twenty-four/seven."

Allen Teeple, the company's junior officer and third platoon leader, looked around, taking note that none of their party had any. "Begging you pardon, sir, but doesn't that put us in violation of that policy?"

Hough rolled his eyes and gave Nathan a quick shrug. "Thank you for pointing that out to us, Mr. Teeple."

Turning his back to the eastern horizon Nathan faced his platoon leaders and XO. "For now I am assigning primary responsibility for manning Strongpoint Alpha, to my right, your left, to first platoon. The wall between the strongpoints belongs to second platoon. Mr. Teeple, your third platoon gets Strongpoint Bravo. These will be your alert positions, the place where your people will deploy ready to fight in the unlikely event that we're attacked. Of course, since our mission will require us to man checkpoints and conduct patrols throughout the security zone some or all of your platoon may not be here, which means that whichever platoon is here will need to be able to extend itself in order to cover some or all of the company's sector."

"One platoon covering all of this? That's a tall order," Jack Horne stated blandly.

"It's more than an order," Nathan shot back. "It's a necessity if it turns out that the Israelis are right about the Palestinians."

"And what does our CIA say?" Horne asked.

Hough chuckled. "That Oswald was a lone gunman."

Everyone but Horne broke out laughing. "I'm serious."

"So are they," Hough quipped with a wink and a smile.

"Okay, okay," Horne relented when he saw he wasn't going to get a straight answer. "What about ammo? When will that be issued?"

Nathan looked over at Grello. "Well, XO? Have you been able to find out when and where we're going to be able to draw our basic load?"

Like a deer in the headlights, Gordon Grello stared back. "Sir?"

"I say again, have you been able to find out when and where we're going to be able to draw our basic load?"

Having relied on the unit's full-time training NCO to handle such matters during Company A's weekend and annual training events back in Virginia, Gordon Grello was not used to dealing with duties that are routine to a regular Army executive officer. At a loss, he blurted out the first thing that came to his mind. "Ah, no sir, I have not. I was hoping you knew."

Understanding what was afoot, Nathan decided to use this opportunity as an objective lesson. "Gentlemen, we're not in Kansas, or more correctly Virginia, anymore." While keeping his eyes on them, Nathan pointed out at the razor-wire fence and the open land beyond. "We're a line unit assigned to stand watch in a potentially hostile environment. Practices and procedures that got you by back home won't hack it here. While I do appreciate the fact that it will take some time and not a little bit of effort on your part, you're all going to have to overcome some of your old habits and start getting used to doing things in a manner prescribed by Army tactical and administrative doctrine. The sooner you and your people get used to doing so, the easier it will be for all of us. Is that clear?"

To a man Nathan's lieutenants understood what their commanding officer was trying to say. Each knew he was right. But none of them appreciated the manner in which he was pointing out these hard truths. Gordon Grello took Nathan's comments as nothing less than a rebuke, one which he saw as undeserved.

Sensing that his fellow Guardsmen were smarting under Nathan's impromptu lecture, Russ Hough made a show of checking his watch. "Nathan, I'm supposed to meet the local nationals that'll be serving as translators for us at battalion in about ten minutes. Since some of them will be working directly for you it might be a good idea if you come along and meet them. Who knows, maybe the old man will let you take the pick of the litter."

Sensing that he had perhaps gone a bit too far and that Hough was throwing him a lifeline, Nathan went along with the suggestion. "Sure, why not." But before leaving, he turned to his officers once more. "While I'm gone and the XO is checking on the status of our ammo, I want you platoon leaders to scout out your primary area of responsibility here on the wall. When you're ready, bring your NCOs up here and make sure they know how to get to their positions just in case. If time permits, I'll go over them with you later. If not, we'll hit it first thing in the morning. Any questions?"

Anxious to be rid of the commanding officer, if only for a short while, no one said a word. "Okay then, carry on."

Of all the strange and unexpected twists and turns that his life had taken since he had dedicated his life to the Palestinian cause, Syed Amama knew that his current situation had to be the most bizarre. Surviving a suicide attack and coming back for more was one thing. Willingly walking into an American military installation, unarmed and in the company of a Jew who just had to be connected to the Mossad or General Security Forces, was something beyond the pale.

The only thing that kept Syed from spinning about on his heels and fleeing for his life was the sight of armed American soldiers scurrying about as they rushed to put the finishing touches on a base they had built on Palestinian land. The claim that these troops were here to protect his people, trumpeted by the American government in the world press, rang hollow in Syed's ears. The extension of the security zone at the expense of the Palestinian state, the erection of a new and even more sinister barrier along its western limit, and the wholehearted adoption of Israeli techniques and methods for controlling the movement of Palestinians across the security zone were all the evidence Syed and his companions needed to convince them that the Americans had no intention of doing anything to help their fledgling state. It was an article of faith that American politicians were little more than puppets to the Jewish state. Now it seemed that their soldiers were being hired out as mercenaries, sent to take the IDF's place and finish the job of isolating them from the rest of the world in order to starve them economically and politically into submission. Only this realization coupled with the knowledge that he was part of some grand scheme whose aim was to rain down the most hideous punishment that man could imagine upon the Americans kept Syed from giving in under the strain that his current predicament created.

His Israeli counterpart suffered none of the trepidations or stresses that Syed labored under. On the contrary, Avner Navon had managed to effect a complete about-face in regards to his selection for this unusual duty. His anger at the manner in which his life had suddenly and unexpectedly been disrupted didn't last long as it soon dawned upon him what the successful completion of his assignment here would mean to his future. His close association with Americans would open any number of opportunities to him. It didn't take much of a stretch to see that carefully cultivated contacts with the Americans he was working with could lead to the chance to study or work in that country. At the least, if he opted to stay in Israel he suspected that his collaboration with the Mossad on this matter would lead to a change in his current Army reserve affiliation from the infantry to something more suitable and far less hazardous.

As different as their views concerning their assignments were, both Avner and Syed did share some common ground, though neither man knew this. Each man suspected that the other was working for someone else, that the impeccable credentials they carried were as false as the beguiling smiles and feigned friendliness each of them put forth whenever dealing with Americans. After all, they both reasoned that if their superiors could doctor their own records and manage to hide their past as well as they had, there was absolutely no reason to believe that the other side had not done the same. Of course neither Syed nor Avner made any mention of this to the Americans. They didn't even speak to each other when they were picked up by the American military representative and driven to the camp located in the middle of the security zone. Throughout that journey Avner sat on his side of the vehicle, doing his best to pretend that Syed did not exist, and Syed did the same.

The other thing that the Israeli and the Palestinian would have agreed on had they bothered to compare their observations was the friendliness that every American soldier they came across showed to them. Having lived in a land where there was no such thing as a safe haven and death threatened every man, woman, and child around the clock, the openness of the Americans was stunning. To Avner it seemed that each and every American he came into contact with felt an obligation to tell him his entire life story in as brief a period as possible. Even Syed's hand was grabbed and vigorously pumped by every American that he met as if he were a long-lost relative who had finally come home. It was difficult for the two jaded agents to be sure if these Americans were simply naïve or whether they were, as some of their own countrymen contended, the world's greatest fools. That they were here, in this part of the world in the belief that they could somehow bring peace to it, tended to support the latter view.

Their arrival at Camp Lee began as all encounters did when meeting a fresh batch of Americans, hardy handshakes all around accompanied by the rattling off of names that were as foreign to Syed and Avner as their own names must have seemed to the Virginians. It was during this latest round of introductions that Avner began to suspect that some of the things his Mossad handlers had briefed him on concerning the Americans might not be true. They had told him that the people he would be working with were National Guardsmen, a class of reservists that his superiors equated to as something akin to the small militias each Israeli settlement was forced to form in order to survive, a community-based military organization. The appearance and manners of the man who introduced himself as the operations officer for the battalion Avner would be working with and the company commander he was assigned to support belied this notion. Both were lean and well-built men whose manners and appearance were unmistakably military. The one who introduced himself as Nathan Dixon in particular struck Avner as anything but a part-time soldier. A paratrooper? Perhaps. Maybe even a commando. But a reservist? Never. At least not like any reservist Avner had ever come across.

After sharing a bit of chitchat and forced pleasantries, Russ Hough had one of his NCOs escort both Avner and Syed to the adjutant's office so they could complete some paperwork. After the pair of translators disappeared inside the headquarters bunker building, Hough turned to Nathan. "I dare say if I pulled either one of those characters over during a routine traffic check, you can bet I'd run a check on any wants or warrants on them before letting them go."

Nathan smiled as he looked back at the doorway the two had disappeared into. "What's the matter, Officer Krupke? Don't you trust the clean bill of health our boys at the CIA and State Department gave them?"

Hough grunted in disgust. "The only reason I'm holding on to the background checks they gave us on those two is in case we experience an unexpected shortage of toilet paper."

"Ouch! I heard you Virginians were tough. But paper?"

Hough made a show of looking about as if searching for something. "Captain Dixon, do you see any trees or leaves lying around waiting to be used in an emergency?"

Nathan chuckled. "You do have a point. And with that, my good friend, I am afraid I have to bid you adieu for now. I've left my lads alone long enough. Time to see what sort of mischief they've managed to get themselves into."

"Crack that whip, Nathan. No slack."

Wandering away, Nathan waved his right hand above his head. "Yeah, something like that."

CHAPTER **15**

Palestinian West Bank

Off to the west the last light of day was fading. From where he stood safely tucked away among the fruit trees, Hammed could see the outline of the American camp as it slowly began to merge with the shadows of the shallow valley below. In the gathering darkness its modern construction became obscured. Had he not seen it in the bright glare of the sun's light, Hammed could easily have mistaken it for a scaled-down version of the Crusader castle that sat atop the hill behind him. Like the Christians who had erected that castle in an effort to hold on to a land that was not theirs, Hammed saw the Americans who occupied the dirt fort to the west as little more than the latest in a long line of invaders who had come here to die. If he had his way and his latest efforts bore fruit, Hammed mused as he took a long drag on his cigarette, they would not have long to wait for that blessed event.

The sound of hurried feet approaching from behind brought an end to his all-too-brief solitude. "Hammed, you must come quickly."

After one final puff, he flicked his cigarette away, turned toward the excited lab technician who stopped as soon as he was sure he had been heard, and glowered. "Are you sure this time?" Hammed asked incredulously.

Sheepishly the technician bowed his head. "Yes, we are sure. Two other goats are beginning to show evidence that they are infected. Already one of them is having difficulty standing. It tried to but collapsed again and again."

"Good! Perhaps we finally have it right." With that the

viral biologist headed back to the agricultural compound built in the shadow of the castle that dominated the hilltop. All thoughts of the current wave of Christian invaders occupying the sandbag fort were for the moment forgotten as he entered the compound and his mind returned to the technical aspects of his labors. The collection of modern whitewashed one-story buildings mixed in with some of the original structures that had been built centuries ago after the Crusaders had been vanquished and the orchards gracing the hill once more reverted to their rightful owners. Even those that had once been little more than hovels had been gutted and refurbished in an effort to maximize the limited space available within the confines of a wall that had been built using stones scavenged from the castle.

Though it was called a farm by the consortium that had financed its construction and all who worked there, it was a far cry from any of the other Palestinian owned and operated farms in the area. It had been built some ten years prior with funds donated by the development agency of the European Union to serve as both a model farm and a research facility dedicated to improving agricultural productivity of the region. As a result, in addition to the usual sort of people you would expect to see on a farm were white-coated lab technicians and researchers. These were highly educated specialists drawn from a number of disciplines who spent their days developing variations of nutrients, fertilizers, and pesticides that were tested in the surrounding orchards in an effort to uncover a blend of chemical and organic compounds that would optimize crop yields. Unlike the workers who spent their days tending those orchards, the lab techs and specialists were mostly foreigners who spent their days laboring indoors, hidden away in high-tech labs equipped with everything they needed to conduct their research, from high capacity fermenters to clean rooms where they could safely study samples under tightly controlled conditions and without the fear of outside contamination.

Both the people of the region and the Palestinian Authority were proud of this experimental farm. A week didn't go by without seeing visitors trekking up the steep hill to inspect it and the work that was being conducted there. Even Israeli scientists had been given the grand tour of the research labs and support facilities. All who did so were duly impressed with what they saw. All appreciated the value of this sort of project to the future of the Palestinian state. Yet despite the openness with which outsiders were treated during these tours, none were allowed to learn the true nature of the work that was now being done in the shadow of the Crusader castle under the guiding hand of Hammed Kamel. Not even the vaunted Israeli Mossad who suspected everything that the Palestinians did was able to discern the true mission of the experimental farm. This wasn't through a lack of effort. Even before the last coat of whitewash had been applied to the refurbished farm Israeli agents had covertly combed every millimeter of the place. Every package and parcel that went up the hill and came down from the farm was inspected, openly when passing through the State of Israel and surreptitiously if brought in through Jordan. When the Palestinian state was formed and the last of the Israeli troops departed, their intelligence services made arrangements to keep tabs on the place and the people who frequented it.

Hammed knew of their efforts, as did every Palestinian who worked there. He even encouraged some of the farm workers to become friendly with those Israeli agents that were known to them. Every effort was made to keep up the air of normalcy that Hammed had labored so hard to create after he had returned to Palestine to assume overall management of this facility when his position at the University of Baghdad had been terminated.

This task was relatively easy, all things considered, since so many of the labs were small and highly compartmentalized. They had to be, lest someone accidentally compromise hundreds of delicate experiments that were being conducted in each of them or cross-contaminate samples. Every time Hammed or anyone else for that matter made his way through the facility, he had to adhere to the same biohazard procedures the lab techs and researchers adhered to as they went about their work. It was only after he had passed through one of the small level-two biohazard labs and into a room adjoining it where thousands of samples were kept in oversized refrigerators that Hammed departed from the research facility that everyone knew about and into another that was very different. This second, most secretive lab was one that Hammed himself had built modeled after the lab he had run in Iraq. It was one that had nothing to do with weaning fresh life out of the soil that scores of conquerors had trampled underfoot since before recorded time.

Entrance to this second, covert facility was gained through one of the half-dozen walk-in refrigerators that lined the northern wall of the storage room. Like those to its left and right it was fully functional, filled with hundreds of real samples that were no different from any of the others being used in the experiments carried out in the orchards and farm fields that surrounded the compound. Unlike the others, its rear wall was not a wall at all but a door, one that had no handles or locks on the side that was part of the refrigerator. Opening it required Hammed to pull out and leave open several of the drawers containing samples in a set sequence, something a well-disciplined lab tech would never do. If done properly and within a set time, the latch keeping the rear of the walk-in refrigerator closed released, allowing someone who knew about the door to push and swing it open.

Hammed passed through this door and across the threshold with the technician who had brought him the news concerning the goats in tow. The world they entered was a very different one, a dark, dank subterranean universe all its own that bore little resemblance to the gleaming white labs that lay behind them. The narrow corridor they moved along was lined with rough-hewn stones, stones that had been cut by hand hundreds of years ago. Its barrel ceiling was so low that Hammed had to stoop over lest he hit his head. This was the castle's sally port, a small concealed exit built as part of the castle's southern wall, which was used by the Crusaders to launch sporadic raids upon the Muslim warriors who besieged them. Later, after the last of the Christian defenders had been put to the sword and peace had once more come to this troubled region, the locals who built the original farm compound used the sally port as a means of gaining access to the castle to scavenge the very stones used to build the wall surrounding their new farm. When they were finished, they used the last of the stones they had recovered from within to block off the entrance itself and promptly forgot about it.

Hurrying through this dimly lit passage, Hammed came to a sharp right turn, purposely designed to slow down any intruder who might wish to gain access to the castle through this passage. Upon making that turn the German-educated microbiologist came face-to-face with a trio of armed guards wearing camouflaged uniforms. When they saw their superior appear, all three assumed a stance that was about as close to a position of attention as anyone belonging to the PLA could manage. For his part Hammed took no note of them as he pushed by and passed through a door they had been guarding.

The next room Hammed came to contained a set of narrow stairs cut into the very rock upon which the castle was built. They led almost straight down into another ill-lit, rough-hewn passage that had also been painstakingly excavated. This second corridor was a bit wider, but not much. Only the amount of light available changed. Down here the light fixtures were quite modern, connected to each other in series by a heavy-duty conduit that ran down the middle of the low ceiling. Hunched over, Hammed made his way down this narrow corridor until he came to another sharp turn, this one leading off to the left. Only after he had

rounded the corner did the crudeness of the construction
cease.

In the space of a few meters he came across something
more akin to a well-built, carefully crafted stone chamber
with a smooth if well-worn stone floor. This aberration
would have been comforting to anyone who had made it
this far if it weren't the presence of a machine gun manned
by another pair of PLA soldiers. Their gun, propped upon
a waist-high pile of sandbags, was trained on the narrow
corridor Hammed had just emerged from. Anyone trying to
reach the labs that lay beyond the thick steel door behind
the machine gun had to get by that weapon and its vigilant
crew first. Unlike their three companions in the anteroom,
the pair protecting this subterranean room made no effort
to acknowledge Hammed. Even when they were sure it was
Hammed and not an unwelcomed intruder, they continued
to crouch behind their weapon, aiming it on the opening
that was less than four meters from its muzzle.

Once past this weapon, Hammed came to a stop before a
steel-plated door that had no doorknob or handle of any
sort. With the palm of his hand he slapped the door three
times. "Open up, quickly."

From the other side a weak voice could be heard. "The
password, please."

Anxious to gain entry, Hammed lost his temper. "Open
the door, you fool, now."

Realizing he had angered his chief, the lab tech on the
other side of the door cranked open the handle on his side
and swung the door open. "Excuse me, I . . ."

Hammed was not interested in the man's excuses. Pushing by he began to rattle off a series of quick questions as
he stormed forward through a second door and into yet another corridor. These subterranean chambers and the castle
above had been constructed centuries before under the
guidance of European engineers who had built both to defend a land their masters had won by the might of their
arms. With little effort it had been converted by Hammed

to fill a new and far different role. Unlike any of the passages leading to it before, this corridor was quite large. The Crusaders had taken their time building it, using smooth, carefully finished stone blocks to finish it. Along the sides of the main corridor at regular intervals were numerous small barrel-vaulted chambers. They too had been built with the care using the same well-manicured material. Most of these smaller chambers were crowded with an assortment of lab equipment, computer terminals, refrigerators, and desks heaped with reference material of every kind. It was in these cramped chambers where most of the detailed research work Hammed had come here to carry on was performed by a small army of technicians and biologists who were no different than their counterparts who labored away at the other labs aboveground.

Unlike those labs, the ones set up throughout this subterranean complex were totally undetectable by remote air- and space-based platforms. It also had one more advantage, one that had drawn Hammed to this place. Except for a handful of people, the sally port and the chambers he was passing through had been totally forgotten. Like so much of the region's history many of the details concerning the Crusader castle had died with those who had built it. Even the farmers who rummaged about in its ruins after the victorious attackers had moved on to other conquests soon lost all conscious memory of the finer points concerning the looming edifice in whose shadow they labored in an effort to eek a living out of a harsh and unforgiving land. Generation after generation of illiterate peasants toiled and died without ever knowing that these long-forgotten chambers lay beneath their fields.

Besides providing the castle's original inhabitants with ample space for storage, this massive underground complex was meant to allow them a means of escaping through the sally port, the same one Hammed had used in order to gain access. Like the sally port itself, few of the Crusaders who defended the castle were allowed to know about the massive chambers under it. Were it not for a fortuitous discovery on Hammed's part while studying in Germany, he would have never known about them either. Knowledge of this place came to his attention when he had been struggling to pay for his education. For a nominal fee, Hammed was asked to translate rare manuscripts dating back to the Crusades for a friend of one of his professors. One particular obscure work brought back to Germany by an officer who had served as an advisor to the Ottoman Army in World War I had fascinated Hammed. Written by the Muslim general who had taken and sacked the place, it described the siege of this very castle. It also was the only known document in existence that gave a detailed description of the place. Hammed in the midst of its translation stumbled across mention of the underground chambers, a point that the professor he was working for was unaware of. He thought that the sally port and its associated passages leading into the castle courtyard were buried under the northern wall, part of which had collapsed. And he was totally ignorant of the subterranean chambers. For some reason Hammed chose not to translate this part of the text, keeping its secret to himself. Back then he didn't know why he had done so. Perhaps it was a bit of chauvinistic arrogance on his part, a desire to keep foreigners from knowing too much about his people and their past. Only later did he attribute this decision to being nothing less than the will of Allah, divine intervention that would eventually provide him with a place where he would be free to continue his work.

The need to do so came about when Baghdad fell to the Americans in the spring of 2003 and he was forced to flee that city in haste. It was during this flight that he remembered what he had done when he had been a young student. Though he couldn't recall many of the details concerning the castle, he did manage to remember enough to locate it. At first he was discouraged when he discovered that Europeans had established the experimental lab right where he had hoped to set up his new facility. Only after he realized that they, like the old German professor, had no idea what lay beneath the little utopia they had tried to create did Hammed come to appreciate that Allah was truly guiding him.

Though it took time as well as copious amounts of money provided by those who shared Hammed's vision of a final solution to replace the original management of the experimental farm, Hammed succeeded. After a decent interval, when he thought it was safe to do so, he set about updating and expanding the facility. Besides bringing in truckloads of new and more sophisticated equipment, some of which was actually used for the purposes that he made public, Hammed hired new researchers and technicians, all of whom were trusted associates he had worked with before.

These new people were key to the research now being done beneath the Crusader castle. As he was with his research, he was ruthlessly thorough when dealing with matters concerning security. The moment anyone's loyalty in his tight-knit working group became suspect, he disappeared. On occasion this resulted in mistakes being made. But to men who spent most of their adult lives working to achieve the unthinkable, a few lives lost here and there on the road to Armageddon was nothing more than the cost of doing business.

When they saw him coming the researchers Hammed had so carefully chosen ceased their excited babble and turned to watch their superior approach the massive work area they were all gathered in. The last room at the very end of the corridor was a large chamber with a high ceiling, now converted into an oversized lab where full-scale experiments on animals were carried out. Because of the nature of the work performed in there it was known as the Ark due to all the animals they needed brought in. To ensure the rest of the work areas weren't compromised if an experiment went terribly wrong, the Ark was sealed off from the rest of the facility by airtight glass doors guarded by a pair of armed men. Unknown to the highly educated lab techs and assistants who passed these sentinels day in and day out, the guards were not there to keep people out of the Ark but should the biohazard alarm sound, they were under orders to make sure no one left it.

On this evening the Ark was crowded with every technician and assistant who could manage to break away from their own work stations to view the effects of Hammed's latest full-scale experiment. Stepping aside when he entered the Ark, they made room for Hammed at the plate-glass window that separated the specimen pen from the rest of the room. On the other side of the glass was a small herd of eight goats. One of them was alone in the corner, lying on its side. Were it not for an occasional twitch or sudden spasm it would have been hard to tell if it was alive. Sensing its distress, the others had pressed themselves against the opposite wall of their enclosure. They had no way of knowing that this precaution would do nothing to save them. Even from a distance Hammed could see that three of them were bleeding at the mouth and rectum. One was on its front knees, struggling to stand up but failing in this effort. Another simply stood on four wobbly legs, swaying this way and that like a drunk that was on the verge of toppling over. Unable to escape the one in the corner and sensing that these two had to be avoided as well, the remaining five scurried this way and that in a futile effort to escape a doom that was already preordained.

Pleased with what he was seeing, Hammed nevertheless managed to contain his excitement. "How long has it been since case zero was infected and put in with the others?"

Though he already knew the answer, the viral biologist known as the Russian in charge of this phase of the experiment read the chronology of the experiment from a clipboard he always carried with him. "We fed case zero the contaminated orange skins two days ago in the morning. The disease began to manifest itself this morning. The first animal in the control group began to show some indications of infirmity shortly after you left."

"And all the bleeding from the others? That occurred at the same time?"

Another tech who was a veterinarian stepped forward. "As you can see, the animals are quite agitated. They sense that there is danger, but are unable to flee. The resulting panic has caused their heart rates and respiration to increase. If the cause of the danger is not removed or they cannot escape from it, their panic will give way to an uncontrollable frenzy during which their bodily functions become uncontrolled and random, hence the defecation and urination. In this they do not differ from humans who are suddenly overcome by hysteria."

"Except," Hammed stated as he allowed a hint of a smile as he glanced over at the veterinarian, "humans are not so easily detained. With their cars and airplanes they have the ability to cover much ground before they succumb."

Only one man in the room made any effort to curb the growing enthusiasm. From the rear of the pack watching the bewildered creature a lone voice with an unmistakable German accent called out a warning. "Unfortunately we cannot predict just how far our little friend will spread before it is contained. It would have been far better had we been allowed to use primates. Their physiology and social patterns are far closer to humans than these creatures."

"These animals are indigenous and plentiful," Hammed countered without taking his eyes off of the struggling goats. "It would have been impossible to import the number of monkeys we needed without rousing the suspicions of Israeli intelligence."

The German would not be mollified. "Well, even so all of our efforts may be for naught if the Americans are able to control the event with the same efficiency with which the Israelis seem to have managed to contain our latest field test."

Hammed had considered this possibility when he had

been preparing for the little outside experiment he had run in conjunction with the bombing of an Israeli bus. "Though they are no different from the Jews in so many ways, the Americans are a very undisciplined people. As with any action such as this, the number of people actually affected does not matter. It is the perception of danger and the fear that perception engenders that creates terror. If two men with one rifle can paralyze five million people and the entire region surrounding their national capital for months, think of what our little friend will do once the American media discovers it. Even in a day when there was no mass transit or round-the-clock coast-to-coast news programs, the influenza epidemic of 1918 all but brought America to its knees."

Though he remained unconvinced that their efforts would slay the millions that Hammed sometimes claimed it would, the lone cynic kept his counsel. He was, he reasoned, little more than a physician dealing with only a very small part of a very large and complex operation, an operation he was more than happy to leave to Hammed and others like him to handle. So long as he was allowed to carry on his research on the physiological effects of Hammed's "little friend," he would be content.

With a clap of his hands, Hammed turned to face his assembled team. "We must make sure all data is collected, checked, and double-checked. Then we must run the entire experiment again. We must demonstrate that this event was not a fluke. In the meantime," he added, "have a second videotape of this made. Our backers in Riyadh will want to see what the petrodollars the Americans sent them has bought them."

Camp Lee

When people have really screwed up and know it there are any number of ways they can respond. Embarrassment over a failure can humble a person, leaving them humiliated, ashamed, and quick to apologize to those whom they had failed. Others do everything within their power to hide their misconduct by doing everything within their power to go about their business as if nothing had happened. Then there are those who are like Paul Sucher, a brash individual who didn't know the meaning of the word "humble."

Arriving at Camp Lee well after midnight local time, the Bedlow Five were dropped off in front of the tent where the other members of their squad were doing their best to repay their sleep debt. As the senior ranking enlisted, Gene Klauss dropped his bags and gear next to the entrance of the tent and took off at once to find First Sergeant Faucher in order to report in. Left on their own, the other four began to file into the tent with Sucher in the lead.

Unsure of where anything was, the tactless construction worker stopped just inside the dark tent and shouted out, "Hey! Where's the light switch?"

Stirred from a deep and much needed sleep, Daniel Travers groaned as he realized where he was and what time it was. "Who in the hell wants to know?"

"I want to know. Now where are the frikin' lights?"

Up and down the row of cots that lined either side of the tent those who had not been awoken by Sucher's first blast were rudely shaken from their slumbers by this quick exchange. A medley of moans and oaths filled the tent from men roused in the middle of the night. From somewhere down the line a brave soul groped about in the dark and unfamiliar surroundings until he found the chain to the overhead light that dangled from the horizontal brace that ran down the center of the tent. The sudden glare of the naked lightbulb brought a renewed surge of profanity and complaints.

With his way now lit, Sucher began to move down the row of cots filled with restless figures writhing about in an effort to shield their eyes. Amused, Sucher chuckled. "Oh, quit your whining. As soon as we find our cots, I'll turn the damned light off."

Angered by being shaken from a much needed sleep by a man whose absence had caused him so much grief, Oliver Rendell all but leaped onto the bare wooden floor. In three quick bounds he managed to cover the distance between his cot and the spot where Sucher was. Stopping just short of the latecomer, Rendell thrust his face forward to within inches of Sucher's while jabbing his right index finger into that man's chest. Surprised by his squad leader's unexpected aggressiveness, Sucher recoiled, bumping into Jerry Slatery who had been trailing him. Caught off guard, Sucher dropped his duffel bags and threw his hands up. "Whoa, Ollie. Let's not get excited here. I'm only trying to find a place to lay my head. We've had a rough day."

"A rough day?" Rendell roared. "You sorry sack of shit. You and your little friends don't know what rough is. By the time I get done with you you'll wish you never heard of the National Guard or me."

From behind Sucher another, more menacing voice kept Sucher from responding. "Sergeant Rendell. You're going to have to wait until I'm finished with him."

To a man all eyes turned to the entrance where Alex Faucher, wearing nothing but his boots, BDU pants, and field jacket, stood. For the first time a look of concern crossed Sucher's face. The other recently arrived members of Rendell's squad who had been standing behind Sucher quickly stepped aside as if trying to get out of the line of fire. With a quick flick of his hand Faucher pointed at Sucher, then stuck his thumb over his shoulder back toward the entrance. "Outside, mister."

Doing his best to hide his concern, Sucher scared up a hint of a smile and made his way out into the company street. No one said a word, no one moved as the two men left. Once they were alone in the middle of the street Sucher turned to face Faucher. He was about to say something when Faucher reached out with both hands, grabbed Sucher by the collar, and jerked the wayward Guardsman up unto his toes. In a low, menacing voice that no one in the company had ever heard before Faucher laid into the stunned man. "Now you listen to me and you listen good, mister. I'm tired of your cocky attitude and your smart mouth. Me and every man in this company is tired of putting up with your shit. You and your little buds in there have screwed the pouch big time. You've managed to piss off everyone up and down the chain of command, from the battalion commander to me. And while the battalion commander has managed to save your sorry little ass from the just punishment that you so richly deserve, there isn't a power in heaven or on earth that can protect you from the mountain of shit I'm going to bring down upon you every day we're here."

With a shove, Faucher released his grip on Sucher and stepped back. Unable to maintain his balance, Sucher toppled over onto the ground. Stunned by Faucher's rage he looked up at the dark, menacing shadow hovering over him. "Get out of my sight." Scrambling to his feet, Sucher found himself so shaken by Faucher's uncharacteristic rage that he all but fled back to his tent, leaving his first sergeant alone in the street to recover his composure.

With his biological clock shot to hell as a result of jet lag, Nathan was up well before anyone else in his company was stirring. When he was shaved, dressed, and ready to take on the world he made for the mess tent in search of a cup of coffee and a fresh bun that the unit's baker had spent the night preparing. Inside the warm mess tent the smell of freshly brewed coffee and hot breakfast pastries cleared away the last of the cobwebs that a fitful night's sleep had left.

From the rear of the tent Terrance Putnam stepped out from behind the serving line and made for the first table.

With a cup of coffee in one hand and a muffin in the other, Putnam motioned Nathan over. "We're not ready to serve yet, but feel free to grab something to tie you over till they are."

Happy to comply, Nathan helped himself to a hefty cinnamon bun that would put any found in a gourmet bakery to shame. When he joined Putnam, he lifted the bun. "Where did you manage to find these puppies?"

Terrance smiled as he gnawed on his. "This, my friend, is only the beginning. Wait till you see what we have laid on for tonight."

Ignoring table manners, Nathan spoke as he chewed. "If this is any indication of what your folks can do, I'm going to have to write to my dad and see if there is any way he can activate your cooks and assign them to my next unit."

"This is nothing, amigo. You'd be surprised at what these people can do. Thanks to one of my spec four clerks who installs TV dishes when he's not doing time in the Guard, I've got your basic satellite with every premium channel you can imagine."

Nathan paused just as he was about to take another bite. "You're kidding."

"Well, it's not all as great as you might think. The satellites serving this part of the world don't carry all the neat stuff ours do. On the other hand, we do get Al Jazeera live as well as the Saudi version of MTV."

"I'll bet that's a scream."

Putnam made a face. "Only if you're into belly dancers and songs that are indistinguishable from a Muslim cleric's call to prayer."

"Well, I'm sure it beats the hell out of what passes for entertainment in my neck of the woods. I haven't heard that much country and western music since my dad was stationed at Fort Hood."

"Not to mention," Putnam added, "your company's very own version of professional wrestling."

Stunned, Nathan looked at Putnam. "You've already

heard about my first sergeant's impromptu counseling session with the ringleader of the Bedlow Five?"

"Heard about it? No. I heard it. In fact, I think the entire camp heard it."

Concerned, Nathan sheepishly glanced about. "Damn! I was hoping no one noticed."

"Let's be a little realistic, my dear boy. The walls of these tents don't do much to muffle the noise of the outside world."

"I'm afraid First Sergeant Faucher got a bit carried away."

"If your first sergeant hadn't done what he had, I suspect the sergeant major would have been out there last night looking to extract his authorized pound of flesh from the Bedlow Five. Those characters of yours made the whole battalion look bad, something that these folks take very personally."

Nathan thought about that as he sipped his coffee, recalling what his battalion commander had told him on the plane. Though it was a bit belated, Nathan finally began to understand what Lanston had been trying to explain. "Putt, we're dealing with a different breed of cat here."

Lifting his half-eaten cinnamon roll, Nathan's companion grinned. *"Vive la différence."*

CHAPTER 16

Camp Lee

Having arrived after midnight and finding no one had done anything for them, once the first sergeant had finished chewing them out Gene Klauss, Brian McIntire, Sam Rainey, Jerry Slatery, and Paul Sucher had little choice but to wander about the unfamiliar base camp in search of the battalion's S-4 shop where someone had told them their duffel bags had been secured. The only man they found there was a specialist-four supply clerk who was anything but pleased to be rousted out of his sleeping bag in the middle of the night. Bleery-eyed and not quite awake, he stumbled about like a drunken sailor who was lost. It was several minutes before his head cleared and he remembered where the unclaimed duffel bags had been stacked. Leading the Bedlow Five through piles of material and supplies that had yet to be properly sorted, he motioned in the direction of a corner with a lackadaisical wave of his hand. "They're over there somewhere," he announced glumly as he scratched his belly before turning to walk away.

Klauss, the senior ranking man, looked about the disheveled storeroom a moment before calling back to the clerk who was already crawling back into a sleeping bag that he had thrown over a pile of camouflage nets stacked behind the counter at the front of the battalion's supply room. "What about cots?"

The supply clerk yawned as he pulled the zipper of his sleeping bag up. "Come back in the morning and I'll issue you some."

Ever the smart ass, Paul Sucher grumbled. "Hey, it's already morning. We've had a long day. It would be nice to have a cot."

The supply clerk was unmoved by Sucher's appeal. Rolling over onto his side with his back to the five, he reached up and flipped off the battery-operated lantern that had been illuminating the storeroom. Like a recorded message on an answering machine running at half speed, the supply clerk rattled off procedures established by Terrance Putnam, the battalion S-4. "Hours for issuing or exchanging equipment are between ten hundred and fifteen hundred hours. Special arrangements for drawing or exchanging equipment during hours other than those posted must be requested through the S-4 one day in advance and approved by the battalion XO. Good night."

Left standing in the dark room, the five co-conspirators had little choice but to rummage around as they tried to find their own duffel bags. Sucher's suggestion that they roll the lazy supply clerk out of his bunk and force him to leave the light on as well as issue them cots was quickly vetoed by the other four. "Are you nuts? Aren't we in enough trouble already?" Klauss hissed. "The last thing we need to do is piss all over the S-4's boots. Don't forget, he's an even bigger regular Army jerk than our own CO. Now shut your trap and grab your duffel bag."

Ordinarily Sucher would have stood his ground, arguing his point more out of habit than principle. But in this case he knew Klauss had a point. The battalion S-4 controlled many of the nonmission essential goodies that soldiers in the field rely on. And the battalion's supply sergeant, a regular good ole boy who had a long memory, also had a knack for procuring things that were not listed in any Department of the Army catalogue or table of organization. To get on his bad side by picking on his supply clerk would have been the height of folly. So Sucher checked his tongue as he joined his squad mates groping about in the dark.

One by one they secured their duffel bags and dragged them out of the storeroom past the supply clerk who was already sound asleep, through the quiet company streets, and back to the tent where the rest of the squad was down for the count and oblivious to their blundering about in search of someplace to settle down. By the time the last of them had managed to dig his sleeping bag out and unroll it onto the bare wooden floor, it was well past oh two hundred. The bare lightbulb that dangled from the center ridgepole of the tent lit up at precisely oh three thirty as Sergeant First Class Garver strolled through the tent yelling, "Rise and shine, boys. Duty calls."

Checkpoint Alpha on the Western Boundary of the Security Zone

Dawn found the third squad of second platoon mounted up and trundling out the front gate of Camp Lee headed for what was being called the Israeli checkpoint. To a man they believed they had been selected to pull the battalion's first tour of duty at the checkpoint because of the Bedlow Five. Even had they been handed a copy of the battalion's OPLAN drafted back in Georgia assigning Company A as the first unit to assume the red cycle, everyone would have still found a way to blame Sucher and his co-conspirators.

Being the sort of unit that the 3rd of the 176th was, there was some truth to this. The philosophy of swift justice and retribution pervaded the battalion, from its commanding officer on down the line to their platoon leader, Jack Horne. He took special glee in arranging the duty roster so that his third squad drew the first tour of duty. For them this meant reveille at oh four hundred hours with their first formation an hour later. Departure, sans a hot breakfast, followed immediately after that. "Until the mess hall gets its act together," Matt Garver announced as he handed an MRE to each member of the third squad as they prepared to climb onto the truck, "you're going to have to make due with the Army's idea of fast food." Too tired to groan or complain, the disgruntled Guardsmen took whatever they were handed and settled down on the bench seats of the open cargo truck. Without any fanfare or ceremony, the truck, escorted by an armored Humvee, cranked up and headed out.

They were already well on their way when Sam Rainey turned to his squad leader. "Hey, Ollie, when are they going to issue us some ammo?"

This inquiry peeked everyone's interest. To a man the members of third squad turned to their squad leader, Oliver Rendell. Before responding, he glanced over at Matt Garver and winked. Garver had lost the coin toss with his platoon leader the night before, earning him the right to go along with Rendell's squad to see what all was involved with duty at the Israeli checkpoint. Straight-faced, the deputy sheriff turned platoon sergeant looked over at Rainey. "What do you need ammo for? I'm told the Israelis are friendly."

"What about the Palestinians?"

"What about them?"

"What happens if one of them decides it's time to see Allah?"

Without changing his expression, Garver shrugged. "Well then, I guess we'll all get a chance to find out if all that hype about the twenty-seven virgins is true."

With the exception of Rainey and his recently arrived companions, everyone broke out laughing. "I'm serious! We're supposed to have ammo, right?"

Sensing that Rainey was becoming a bit too agitated, Rendell decided they had had enough fun at his expense. Still, he couldn't resist adding a jab of his own. "If you had been here last night when the rest of the company was being briefed you'd know that all we're supposed to do for the first two days is observe how the Israelis run the checkpoint. Today we watch as they handle the checkpoint. Tomorrow we will handle the checkpoint as they watch. If all goes well, we're on our own starting on day three. If something goes down during those first two days, they'll handle it."

Still smarting from all the abuse that had been heaped upon him since his arrival, Paul Sucher pitched in. "And what are we supposed to do if all hell breaks loose?"

For the first time Garver smiled. "I suggest that you start praying. But take care that you mention Jehovah and Allah, just in case we're the ones who are out in left field."

This time even Rainey, Klauss, and Slatery joined in the laughter. "Hey, hey!" Slatery called out as he found himself caught up in the moment. "Wouldn't it be a bummer if instead of Saint Peter we found a cow guarding at the Pearly Gates?"

It took the better part of the morning for the nervous anticipation engendered by countless briefings delivered by solemn-faced officers at Fort Benning to give way to a serious case of boredom. The aloofness of the Israeli soldiers assigned to man the checkpoint that greeted Rendell's squad was forgotten as soon as the Israelis took up the chore of screening the throngs of Palestinians making their way to their jobs in Israel. Left to themselves, the Virginians settled down to learn the routine by observing the Israelis in action. It didn't take long to figure out that the routine was, well, routine. By late morning when their commanding officer and platoon leader arrived to see how things were going even Matt Garver found himself wondering why someone had felt the need for a two-day orientation. "There's really not much to this," he explained to Nathan and Horne as Faucher handed out boxed lunches to Rendell's people. "Anyone who's been through an airport security check already knows the drill." Raising his right hand with his fingers spread out, Garver pulled down a finger with his left hand each time he enumerated a step in the process used to move hundreds of Palestinians through the checkpoint. "A—check the ID card with the person before you. B—pass them through the metal detector one at a time. C—search anything they're carrying. D—shuffle anyone who doesn't measure up or sets off an alarm off to the side for special attention." Folding his arms across his chest, he paused as he looked around. "All in all, this will be a piece of cake."

Nathan said nothing for a moment as he watched an Israeli soldier riffle through the bag of a woman dressed in a black burka that covered everything but her eyes and the upper bridge of his nose. The woman stood motionless, lest any sudden or unsolicited move on her part alarm any of the heavily armed soldiers manning the checkpoint. The Israeli who was searching her worn canvas bag was taking his time, more in an effort to pace himself than out of a desire to be thorough. A few meters to his left another man was checking ID cards held up by passing Palestinians as they stepped through the metal detector that framed the gateway into Israel. Behind this pair who were doing the lion's share of the work was a third soldier cradling his rifle in his arms. Of the three he seemed to be the most attentive, observing all that was going on as if he were expecting something to happen at any moment. Above them, tucked away in a concrete watchtower that provided a clear 360-degree view of the entire area were three more soldiers. One of the trio was leaning out over the tower's parapet, resting his forearms on the layer of sandbags that rimmed the parapet. Though his posture was rather relaxed, he was attentively eyeing the line of Palestinians waiting to come through the gate. Behind him his partner stood ready at a machine gun trained on the narrow opening in the wall of masonry and wire that separated Israel from the security zone and the Palestinian area beyond. The third man in the tower hung back in the shadows. Like the soldier at its base and the pair in the tower with him, he was watching and waiting.

"Vigilance and attention to detail," Nathan finally stated flatly as he looked back at Horne and Garver. "Maintaining a high state of vigilance and ensuring that your people pay attention to detail will be the greatest challenge that you will face here. An attack will not come as a bolt out of the blue. Nine times out of ten a terrorist will betray himself by doing something out of the ordinary, something that is unexpected and out of the norm. A hesitant pedestrian, one that is unusually reluctant or shy may be a person passing through here for the first time or someone with something to hide. Perhaps the assailant will attempt to overcome his or her fears by acting overly bold, pressing forward as if in a hurry to meet Allah. They might give themselves away as they fidget with their weapon or try to cover the bomb strapped to their waist with a package clutched a bit too tightly. Those," Nathan stated pointedly, "are the sort of things that your people will need to be alert to every minute of every day that they are on duty here."

Having no idea how their company commander could be so sure of himself on this matter, Garver and Horne glanced at each other before Garver replied. "Having been here little more than four hours, I can state without fear of contradiction that maintaining a high degree of attention to detail will be easier said than done. Duty here will be about as exciting as checking groceries at the store."

"That is why there are so many backups," Nathan stated as he motioned toward the trio in the tower and the soldier cradling his rifle in his arms. "At any given time there are only two or three soldiers who are actually dealing with the Palestinians. Everyone else is watching. And in the tower, the squad leader is watching the watchers. No doubt," he pointed out, "you've seen that man up there jack up some of his people when they were getting a bit too lax."

As if on cue, the soldier who had been standing in the shadows behind the machine gunner stepped forward, leaned over the parapet, and yelled down at the man checking ID cards. His admonishments and the way with which they were delivered needed no translation. Without hesitation the Israeli checking ID cards signaled the line of

Palestinians waiting to come forward to back off and remain behind the call forward line painted on the ground as he halted the person before him in order to take a second look at the card the Palestinian had initially waved in front of his face without slowing down or stopping. Having made his point without needing to say anything more, Nathan suppressed an urge to gloat. Instead he kept a straight face as he folded his arms across his chest. "Gentlemen, I rest my case."

After watching their company commander's point driven home, both Horne and Garver saw little point in pursuing that issue. Instead, Horne turned to another subject that had been troubling him. "Language is going to be a problem. We're going to need more than the handful of Hebrew or Arabic words they tried to teach us."

Nathan nodded. "I know. Somehow I don't think 'Shalom you all' is kosher."

For the first time Garver smiled. "What? It works for me."

After rolling his eyes, Nathan turned back to watching the comings and goings of the Palestinians. "I still haven't figured out how we're going to get by with the pair of translators we've been assigned. They can't be everywhere we need them, and we're going to need them everywhere."

Having no suggestions of their own, both Horne and Garver fell silent as they continued to observe the activities at the checkpoint. They were still doing so when First Sergeant Faucher strolled up to them carrying three small white boxes. "I saved a lunch for each of you," he announced as he handed the boxes out. "Fried chicken, a biscuit, and a piece of fruit."

Garver crinkled his nose as he accepted the box. "MREs for breakfast and cold chicken for lunch. Um, boy, we're livin' high on the hog."

Having finished passing out the lunches, Faucher smiled as he poked Garver's gut. "It's my new weight loss program, designed to take off the pounds."

Slapping the first sergeant's hand away, Garver feigned

being offended. "I like my flap. Keeps me warm in the winter."

In the midst of picking through his lunch box, Nathan looked up at Faucher. "Do you guys always eat like this in the field?"

In all seriousness, Faucher shook his head. "I must apologize for this pitiful fare. The mess hall usually does better than this. I'm sure once they have their act together, things will improve."

"Improve? First Sergeant, if they do, I'm afraid I'm going to have swap my BDU pants with Sergeant Garver."

Looking at his commanding officer's svelte waistline, then at Garver's extended girth, Faucher laughed. "That'll be the day."

As the two officers and Garver settled into munching on their lunch, Faucher took the time to watch the Israelis. After a while, he began muttering more to himself than anyone in particular. "You know, it seems to me that this whole region would be a whole lot more peaceful if the Israelis just closed their borders."

Having discussed this numerous times before among themselves, but never in the presence of their new commanding officer, Horne and Garver stared at each other before Horne shrugged as he took on the task of responding. "Yes, it would make a whole lot more sense, from a security standpoint, if the Israelis did so."

Looking up from a half-eaten chicken breast, Nathan studied Horne for a moment. "You're right of course. From a security standpoint that would be the ideal solution to many of this region's problems. But economically, it would be a disaster." Pausing, he looked over at the people making their way through the checkpoint. "The Palestinians are no different than the Mexicans are to us back home. The new Palestinian state is overpopulated and economically underdeveloped, just like Mexico. There simply are not enough jobs over on the other side of the security zone. Over here the problem is just the opposite. Israel is the home to highly technical industries and international business concerns that demand workers who are highly skilled, well educated, and reliable. The entire educational system of this nation is geared to prepare the children of Israel to enter that workforce, just as ours is struggling to meet the demands of a technically advanced workplace."

Ever the teacher, Horne was becoming curious as to where Nathan was going with this. "So how do the Palestinians fit in?"

"Again, think of the Palestinians as you would Mexicans. Who's going to flip the kosher hamburgers and clean the toilets while all the good little Israeli boys and girls chase after college degrees and technical training?"

Horne looked at Nathan, then at the Palestinians waiting in line. Without exception they were dressed as one would expect a person to be who performs manual or menial labor to be dressed. Before biting into his biscuit, Horne nodded. "I see your point."

"What we have here, gentlemen, is a true symbiotic relationship. As much as they hate each other, neither the Jews nor the Palestinians can survive without the other. Of course neither will admit it. To do so would be to acknowledge a mutual dependency that their political rhetoric cannot accommodate."

"So what's the solution? I mean, how long can they continue to go around blowing each other up?"

Nathan shrugged. "I'm afraid the answer to that is for folks well above my pay grade. All I'm supposed to figure out is how best to keep them from blowing each other up during our tour of duty."

"That," Faucher intoned as he started to collect up the empty boxes, "I dare say is going to be enough of a challenge."

"Amen, Brother Faucher," Garver wailed using the exaggerated manner of a TV evangelist. "Amen."

As he finished licking his fingers, Nathan found he

couldn't help but laugh. Working with these Guardsmen was going to be a trip.

Camp Lee

Completion of a brutally uneventful tour of duty at the Israeli checkpoint did not signal the end of the day for the third squad. Before anyone did anything else save shedding their flak vests, load-bearing equipment, and helmets, all personnel and crew issued weapons had to clean them. Compliance with this policy, initiated at Fort Benning by Nathan Dixon soon after he had assumed command, was enforced by means of an inspection conducted by either a platoon leader or Nathan himself when his duties permitted. The standard, one that Ollie Rendell made clear he fully endorsed, was to have this completed within one hour of a unit's return to camp.

As one would expect this dictate was not enthusiastically embraced by everyone. This was especially true for the Bedford Five as they dragged their weary bodies from the dismount point back to their squad's tent. Since arriving in country, even the hardiest of them had been unable to log more than an hour's worth of sleep. Matt Garver made sure no one afforded them an opportunity to make up for lost sleep during the day. From the time they had been rousted off the floor and out of their sleeping bags, he was on their case. At the checkpoint any efforts on their part to sneak off and find a quiet place where they could catch up on some of their sleep was frustrated either by him or Ollie Rendell. Whenever one of those two NCOs caught a member of the Bedford Five drifting off, they would grab the man by his arm and send him to stand next to an Israeli soldier with orders to watch what he was doing. "Pay attention! Tomorrow you're going to have to be doing this," they would admonish the bedraggled Guardsman. Too exhausted to complain and doing all they could to keep from making things worse, the five co-conspirators dutifully obeyed, for the twin curses of jet lag and a near sleepless night following on the heels of their ill-fated marathon trip from Benning to Virginia and back had left them too tired to even whimper or whine.

This sullen acquiescence came to an abrupt end back at Camp Lee when Jack Horne sauntered on over to where the third squad was arranging themselves in line to have their weapons inspected. "Upon completion of the evening meal," he announced without preamble, "we will be forming up as a platoon and moving out to our alert positions on the camp's eastern wall. Upon completion of that we will move to the battalion's ammo point where we will be issued a basic load of ammo."

Unable to hold back, Sucher rolled his eyes. "Oh, for Christ's sake!" He made no effort to hide the disgust he felt as he spit out his words and made a show of turning away from Horne. "What the fuck is he trying to prove?" The word "he" when used alone like this had come to mean Nathan Dixon.

Had they been at Fort Pickett or on the drill floor of their armory back in Bedlow, Horne would have ignored Sucher's remark or simply passed it off with little more than a mild admonishment such as "calm down," or "at ease." But they weren't in Bedlow or Fort Pickett. A day spent going over the battalion S-2's latest threat assessment and conducting a mounted reconnaissance of the security zone with the bulk of the battalion's officers had driven home to Horne the point that many of his old leadership techniques would have to change. Watching the comings and goings of hundreds of people wandering back and forth between the Palestinian checkpoint and the Israeli checkpoint convinced Horne that their task wasn't going to be easy. "Any one of those people," Lieutenant Colonel Lanston had stated during their initial mounted recon of the area as he pointed at a cluster of day laborers making their way toward Israel, "could be a suicide bomber headed for a rendezvous with Allah. Whether he takes out a busload of Jewish children returning from school or one of your squads as they go about their duties doesn't make a wit of difference to them. As the S-2 is so fond of reminding us, you, me, and every swinging Richard in this battalion is a legitimate target. It makes no never mind to them who they kill. We're all the same to them."

That moment had given rise to a true epiphany, a sudden and striking moment of clarity unlike anything Jack Horne had ever experienced. The people moving back and forth before the assembled host of American officers were not images on a TV screen. They were real. And because they were real the threat they posed to him was equally real. Thus, as he headed over to where his third squad was waiting he did so with a renewed resolve, a commitment to do whatever it took to make sure that his men would be ready for whatever came their way. If this meant losing the friendship of men who were his neighbors or being accused of being the company commanding officer's toady, so be it.

So when Sucher launched into his all-too-familiar rant, Horne was ready. Without hesitation he marched up to the disgruntled Guardsman and lit into him in a manner that startled everyone who witnessed the confrontation. "You're supposed to be at a position of attention, Private."

Stunned by Horne's unexpected reaction to his tantrum, Sucher turned to face his platoon leader, cocking his head back as he stared at him. "What in the hell has gotten into you, Jack?"

Pushing his face forward until his nose was but an inch away from Sucher's, Horne lit into him in much the same way Faucher had done but a few scant hours before. "You listen to me and you listen good, asshole. I have no intention of putting up with your shit. We're not playing weekend warrior anymore, not over here. In case it hasn't penetrated that thick skull of yours, there are people on the other side of that sandbag wall who are itching to get at you and blow your miserable ass to kingdom come. Now if it was just you I might not mind so much. But unfortunately those jackasses are in the habit of taking lots of folks with them. That means that a failure on one man's part is paid for by his buddies."

"What makes you think I'm going to screw up?"

"Give me a break, Sucher. You're not happy unless you're making a fuss about something or going out of your way to be a royal pain in the ass. Back in Virginia we could afford putting up with your shit. Here, things are different, a whole lot different. And until you figure that out, I'm gonna ride you like a cheap whore."

At the end of the squad Ollie Rendell was tempted to intervene but didn't know quite how. This was a side of his platoon leader that he had never seen before, a far cry from the mild-mannered teacher who in better times taught math to his two oldest children. Not that he wasn't pleased over the change. Like Horne, Rendell had come to the same conclusion that Horne had while watching the comings and goings of the Palestinians during the day. They weren't playing a game here. The expressions on the faces of the day laborers passing through the checkpoint and the uncompromising dedication of the Israeli soldiers had finally convinced him that the threat their company commander and the S-2 had been talking about was real, very real and very deadly.

Clearing his throat, he managed to catch the attention of Horne. "Sir, if my squad is going to make it to chow before we go to our alert positions we need to get on with this weapons inspection."

Sensing that he was making more of a scene than he had intended, Horne backed away from Sucher. Still, he was determined to make his point. Looking to his left and right, paying particular attention to the Bedford Five, Horne continued to press the issue. "This isn't a weekend drill. We're not going home tomorrow night or next week or next month. We can't magic away the enemy like the controllers do during maneuvers. We're here, on the line, at the pointy end of the stick. The people out there aren't the OPFOR. They don't use blanks. They're playing for keeps. Now I don't know about you, but I have every intention of leaving this shit hole the same way I arrived; on my own two feet and in one piece. If that means living up to the sort of standards that we've gotten into the habit of scoffing at, so be it. I for one will do whatever it takes to make sure that we all make it through this. Even you, Sucher. Is that clear?"

Sensing their platoon leader's grim determination and finding no fault in what he was saying, to a man the third squad nodded. Here and there one or two added a muttered "Yes sir." Even Paul Sucher managed to overcome his anger and nod. Not that this much mattered. Jack Horne had not only seen the light and had been converted, he had become an apostle of the testament according to Nathan Dixon.

CHAPTER 17

Camp Lee

The wailing of a siren and the confused cries of men jolted from their slumbers were all part of a bad dream. It had to be. Lost in a deep sleep, Brian McIntire resisted the urge to open his eyes and look around in an effort to determine if the cacophony filling his head was real or merely a grotesque fantasy conjured up by a mind starved of sleep.

A sudden tug on the foot of his sleeping bag by an unseen hand put an end to this self-serving pretense. Suddenly the words "ALERT! ALERT!" penetrated the fog that had been clouding his exhausted brain. In an instant he was sitting upright, looking this way and that as he tried desperately to make out what was going on around him in the darkness of the third squad's tent. Off to his left he heard a voice cry out, "Someone turn on the friken light!" In response someone else shouted, "No! No lights. It's an alert. No lights." Above all the commotion, McIntire found the only voice he was able to make out was that of Ollie Rendell, whose tone struck him as surprisingly calm. "On your feet, Third Squad. Grab you gear, your weapon, and move out to your positions on the wall. Now!"

In his haste McIntire began to crawl out of his sleeping bag without bothering to unzip it first. Only after he had managed to get his head and right arm and shoulder free did he find that doing so was impossible. Stopping midstride he groped around with his right hand searching for the zipper. He was in the midst of this frantic effort when he sensed that there was someone at the foot of his cot.

Looking up he saw a black, faceless form hovering over him. "Get on your feet and get moving, *NOW!*"

Abandoning his failed efforts to find the zipper's tab, McIntire managed to bring both hands up to the small opening of the Army-issued mummy sleeping bag. With one mighty jerk he forced the opening apart, tearing the interlocking metal teeth apart. Now free from the sleeping bag he clambered to his feet, bent over, and began to feel about in the darkness with his hands in search of his pants, boots, and other essential pieces of clothing. Not having taken any particular care as to where he had tossed these items before turning in and unable to remember where anything was, he came upon each item in a rather random manor. First he found a boot. But this discovery would do him no good until he had his pants on. Then he found his shirt, but at the moment he was fixated on finding his pants first so that he could put on his boots. Chucking the shirt aside, McIntire dropped to his knees as he continued his increasingly panicked search, ignoring the harried cries of others all around him as they cast about conducting their own mad hunt for clothing, equipment, and weapons.

The next thing his hands lit upon was his helmet. Grasping it with both hands, he thought about putting it on. Wearing their helmets was something the training cadre at Fort Benning had been most insistent about. "Your brain bucket only works when it's on your head," one of the regular Army drill sergeants reminded them every time he caught a Guardsman who wasn't wearing his. But his helmet was the last thing McIntire thought he needed at the moment. Pants! That's what he needed.

It was at this moment when Matt Garver appeared out of nowhere. Grabbing a handful of McIntire's T-shirt, the former truck driver jerked the former mailman to his feet. "What the hell are you doing down there?" Garver bellowed. "Put that helmet on, grab your flak vest and weapon, and move."

Without a moment's hesitation McIntire plopped the helmet he was still holding on to his head, spun about, and grabbed his flak vest and rifle. Pushing his way past Garver he dashed barefooted toward the open tent exit and out into the company street.

Outside, at the head of the company street stood Nathan Dixon flanked by Alex Faucher and Gordon Grello. The three of them watched in mute silence as their company scurried and scattered about this way and that. Some were under the impression that they needed to form up into squads before moving to their alert positions on the eastern wall. Others simply took off helter-skelter in the direction that they thought was the right one. Most managed to guess that part of the drill right. Too many did not, creating a wild spectacle as soldiers ran this way and that, bumping into each other as the man they were following suddenly stopped in an effort to get his bearings or ask another who was headed in the opposite direction which way was the right way.

Folding his arms across his chest, Nathan found he was all but unable to keep from laughing. While watching the mad melee unfold before him, he sighed. "Have any of you two ever seen a Marx Brothers movie?"

Understanding the analogy and pained by what they were seeing, both Faucher and Grello winced. Grello spoke up first. "I guess we weren't as ready for this practice run as I thought we were."

Nathan glanced over at his executive officer. "I dare say I would have to concur with that, Gordo."

Unable to bear watching any longer, Faucher turned his back on the farce and drew himself up before his commanding officer. "Sir, in my opinion I think we should put an end to this abortion and start all over."

Without a moment's hesitation Nathan nodded. "I agree, First Sergeant. Fall the company in and get the men sorted out. When they're dressed and fully under arms, we'll move them over to our positions on the wall as a company.

Gordo, take charge while I go find the battalion commander and let him know what we're doing."

Feeling somewhat embarrassed by the pitiful performance of his fellow Guardsmen, Grello stepped in front of Nathan after Faucher left them, bellowing out to the scattered and confused Guardsmen to fall in by platoon. Hanging his head, Grello looked down at the ground as he spoke. "Sir, I don't know what to say."

Reaching out, Nathan placed his hand on his XO's shoulder. Giving it a friendly squeeze, he managed to smile when Grello looked up. "Hey, this was only a drill. No harm done. Now, go help the first sergeant get this mess sorted out and let's see what we can do to make sure that this doesn't happen again, okay?"

It didn't matter to the Virginian that his commanding officer was going out of his way to play down the magnitude of the fiasco unfolding all around them. Nathan had enough confidence in them now to appreciate that his key subordinates understood what had gone wrong. He had also learned from Lanston's handling of the Bedlow Five, trusting that the Guard had their own unique ways of dealing with their own. As he walked away from the confused gaggle of half-dressed men, Nathan was confident that Grello and Faucher would take whatever action was necessary to make sure that there was not a repeat performance of the morning's ill-fated drill. And if they didn't, if the company failed to measure up a second time to his standards, he always had the option of resorting to tried and true methods that were more drastic, familiar methods that he had absolutely no qualms about using as he struggled to bring his company up to full combat readiness.

At battalion headquarters Nathan Dixon had to wait in line in order to explain to his battalion commander why his company was unable to occupy their alert positions within the allocated time. Of all the units stationed at Camp Lee, only Company B managed to beat the clock. This would have earned Frank Collins, their commanding officer, an attaboy except that the entire company turned in completely dressed and fully decked out for battle. The glaring disparity between this stellar performance when compared to the chaos and pandemonium that reigned throughout the balance of the command left little doubt that Collins had violated his battalion commander's confidence and forewarned his subordinates that an unannounced alert was in the offing. The only comfort Nathan was able to garner from this bit of subterfuge was that Colonel Lanston spent more time admonishing Collins for betraying his trust than he did beating Nathan and the other commanders up over the pitifully poor performance of their companies.

· What Frank Collins did and did not do and how he chose to run Company B was of little concern to Nathan. While it was true that failure on the part of Company B could impact upon Company A, Nathan could do nothing to influence how that unit was run or carried out its assigned tasks. His responsibility and authority was limited to what his own command did or failed to do. And at the moment, that meant sorting out what had gone wrong and taking whatever steps proved necessary to make sure that they did not stage a repeat performance of that morning's farce.

After swinging through the company area to check on Grello and Faucher's progress and finding that they had already moved the unit to their assigned positions, Nathan headed to the eastern wall. Making his way along the rear of the line of positions manned by grim-faced Guardsmen, Nathan was more than satisfied by the turnaround his XO and first sergeant had managed to stage during the short time he had spent with the battalion commander. Yet when he came across them, he went out of his way to project an impression that he was restraining his anger.

Not that he was really angry. While he wasn't at all pleased by what he had witnessed at the start of the alert, Nathan had more or less expected something along the lines of what had transpired. But he felt he could not let his subordinates know this. To him a commanding officer occasionally had to inspire fear in the hearts of those he led. He had learned early on in his career that soldiers often carry out assigned duties for no other reason than to escape the ire of their officers in much the same way that children do things that they do not enjoy lest they incur the wrath of their parents. This did not mean that he looked down on the men he had led in the past as immature or childlike. On the contrary, it was his experience that when compared to their fellow countrymen, nine out of ten of the men and women he knew who wore the uniform displayed a degree of maturity and sound judgment that was heads and shoulders above their peers. This was especially true in regards to the National Guardmen he now commanded. To a man they had jobs, families, and responsibilities in what they sometimes referred to as "the real world." But soldiers and his Guardsmen were still people, human beings who were driven by the same instincts and responded to the world around them in much the same manner as anyone else.

Another key element that Nathan had come to appreciate thanks to studying the manner in which his father conducted himself both at home and during the rare opportunities he had seen him with troops was that a leader had to be a fair actor. Though one will never find any mention of this aspect of leadership in any of the Army's manuals on the subject, all great commanders understood this. From Alexander the Great through George S. Patton they appreciated the effect that a little theater had when it came to dealing with their subordinates. Feigned rage or exaggerated praise could motivate soldiers to achieve things that they themselves would never even dream of had they been left to their own devices. This theater is the reason behind much of the pomp and circumstance of the military and awards ceremonies as well as the vicious dressing down that errant soldiers are subjected to from time to time.

At the moment, Nathan felt it would serve his purposes

best if he affected the impression that he was struggling to contain his anger. Stopping as soon as he reached Grello and Faucher, Nathan assumed a position of parade rest with his feet shoulder-width apart and his hands clasped behind his back. Ignoring the pair before him at first, he looked to his left, then to his right as he spoke. "We need to be able to occupy these positions in less than ten minutes. Even at that, we might be too late. So," he continued as he turned to face Grello and Faucher, "another performance such as the one we just witnessed could prove to be disastrous."

Grello and Faucher exchanged nervous glances before Faucher took the lead this time. "This will not happen again, sir."

"Well," Nathan stated stiffly, "let's make sure that it doesn't." He went on, modulating his tone a bit. "Now, the good news is that the mess hall will be open to feed the people headed out to the checkpoints a hot meal before they have to move out. The bad news is that they have less than an hour to go chow down and be ready to roll out the front gate. First Sergeant, take charge of the company and stand the men down while I have a chat here with the XO and the platoon leaders."

Again Grello and Faucher looked at each other as Faucher tried to express his sympathy through his expression alone to a man who was about to be read the riot act.

The Israeli Checkpoint

The actual difficulties Avner Navon encountered as he took up his unwelcomed role as a translator for the American troops assigned to police the border between Israel and the newly created Palestinian state were not what he had imagined they would be. Most concerned the woman he expected to marry one day. Though he tried to adhere to his instructions, Avner found he was unable to keep the truth from the woman he loved. Within days he told her of his encounter with the Mossad agent. He had hoped that this would explain why he had suddenly up and quit his job and moved without bothering to consult her. He had hoped she would understand, that Gilah would become a source of solace during these troubling times. Quickly Avner discovered that he could not have been any more mistaken.

Rather than sympathy, a stunned Gilah recoiled at the idea that the man she thought she knew could be so cavalier about making such a decision without bothering to discuss the matter with her first. While he did his best to explain that there had been no time for such niceties, that the whole affair had been presented to him as an accomplished fact, Gilah would not listen. As he spoke she frustrated his every effort to reach out and take her in arms in an effort to calm her fears by stepping back every time he tried to close the distance. Avner repeatedly tried to explain that this was no big deal. "I'm going to be a translator, for heaven's sake. Not an assassin. The only dealings I'll have with the Mossad is when I submit a report from time to time on what the Americans are doing."

To a woman who craved security in a land where security was little more than a word, Avner's assent to cooperate with their nation's nefarious intelligence agency was tantamount to a slap in the face. "How could you do this to me? The Army, yes. I understand that. Everyone must serve. But the Mossad? Are you mad?"

No matter how hard he tried, no matter how fast he spoke, Avner could not find the right words needed to console her. In the end, she fled the apartment they had shared, leaving him in an emotional limbo that was compounded by the manner with which his fellow countrymen reacted to him when he began reporting to the American base camp in the security zone.

The suspicion he was greeted with the first time he passed through the checkpoint en route to the American base camp came as something of a shock to Avner. Almost without exception traffic through the checkpoint consisted of Palestinians who left their own zone each day and made for the Israeli state where they worked. Avner's attempt to go against the grain was met with confusion and disbelief. What should have been a simple matter of flashing his identification card, a cursory search turned into a major interrogation. "What business do you have over there?" the sergeant in charge of the detail at the checkpoint demanded. Every effort on his part to explain was cut short by another question. "Who authorized your employment with the Americans? Where is this documentation? Show me." It didn't matter that while Avner was being grilled in this manner three more Israeli-born citizens showed up at the checkpoint also seeking passage to Camp Lee. Each and every one of them was treated as if they were charter members of Hezbollah. Unable to explain that he had been recruited by the Mossad, Avner had little choice but to endure this humiliation in silence, much as he had done when Gilah had turned her back on him.

The routine changed little in subsequent days. If anything the disdain his fellow countrymen went out of their way to heap upon Avner redoubled when he arrived at the checkpoint along with Ollie Rendell's squad to commence their second day of duty there. A leper would have been more welcomed than Avner. Unable to find comfort in the arms of his lover and shunned by his fellow countrymen, his solace came in the friendly manner the American soldiers he had been dragooned into spying upon accepted him.

This association turned out to be educational, though at times it could be quite trying and not a little confusing. When he had been told that he was going to be working with American reservists, Avner naturally assumed that they would conduct themselves in the same very informal manner that Israeli reservists do. He was quite taken aback when he found that this was not the case at all. The adherence to what Avner saw as strict military etiquette such as the emphasis their officers and even some of their NCOs placed on appearance and the precision everyone demanded in carrying out even the most mundane duty amused Avner. If these were reservists, he thought to himself every time he saw something new, he wondered what their regular forces were like.

There was of course a great deal of informal and good-natured bantering between the soldiers when they were not directly involved with the task at hand. Avner found himself quickly drawn into these exchanges as the Americans, anxious to learn all they could about the people they had been sent to protect, directed scores of questions at him concerning everything about his people, his country, and the problem between Jews and Arabs. Since the Israeli officer responsible for the checkpoint refused to relinquish the watchtower until his men were completely withdrawn, the American Guardsmen who would have been manning the machine gun there had nothing better to do than stand around, watch their companions screen the Palestinians coming through, and chat with Avner.

"So let me get this straight," Jerry Slatery stated after listening to Avner summarize the history of the Zionest movement. "The Romans enslaved the population of Israel after they revolted in . . ."

"Sixty-seven A.D.," Avner replied. "That marked the beginning of the Diaspora."

"Right," Slatery continued. "And that's how the Jews spread to Europe."

"And Africa as well."

"Okay. I understand that. It's the middle part I have problems with. Not all the Jews were thrown out."

"That is correct, Jerry. Some managed to stay and remain faithful. But not many as the Christians and Muslims fought to control Jerusalem."

"The Crusades. Yeah, I know. But when they were over nothing much happened until some European Jews called

Zionists got together and decided it was time to reclaim Jerusalem even though it and the land around it belonged to someone else."

This was the part that tended to frustrate Avner, especially when trying to explain it to Americans who somehow always managed to conveniently forget that most of them were descendants of Europeans who crossed the Atlantic and seized land that did not belong to them either. "Israel is our hereditary homeland. This land is our land. We belong here."

"And where do the people who were living here when the Zionists came belong?"

Doing his best to maintain his calm, Avner explained again how the early settlers tried to find a way of living side by side with the Arab inhabitants. "The Zionists tried to legally purchase the land from the Arabs and Palestinians. But many who wanted to sell their land were prevented from doing so, first by the laws of the Ottoman government, then by the British government who took control of the region after the First World War, and finally by their fellow Arabs who didn't want to see the land they called Palestine overrun by my people."

"Makes sense to me," Daniel Travers enjoined. "We're having the same problem back home with illegals coming up from Mexico."

"Except that the land we were trying to buy back was ours to start with," Avner countered.

"That's what they keep saying about Texas. They want it back."

"And are you going to give it back to them?" Avner challenged.

Surprised by the question, Travers gave the Israeli translator a queer look. "Are you kidding? It's ours. I expect those down home good ole boys in Texas will do whatever it takes to keep it that way."

Avner smiled. "I rest my case."

Gene Klauss, who had remained silent as he listened to

the exchange up to this point, found he could no longer hold back. "Excuse me, Avner. But that's where you lose me. Are you saying that your people have the right to this land because they once lived here two thousand years ago? Or is it the Palestinians because they were the ones who were here when the Zionists came?"

Rolling his eyes, Avner regrouped as he tried to find a way to explain something that was so simple and so obvious.

Unable to hold back, Paul Sucher stood upright, stretched out his arms, and yawned. In doing so, he exposed himself above the pile of sandbags that the third squad had erected along the road leading to the Israeli checkpoint some thirty meters in front of it.

Half asleep himself, Sam Rainey was startled by Sucher's sudden and expected movement. Grasping his rifle, Rainey pushed himself away from the sandbags that he had been leaning against and peered down the road. "What is it?"

"What's what?"

Only when he looked back at his companion who was in the midst of stifling back another yawn did Rainey realize that they were not in any danger. "Jesus Christ, Paul. Don't do that. You scared the ever-loving shit out of me."

Sucher laughed. "Not to mention waking you up."

After giving in to the urge to yawn on his own, Rainey shook his head. "Man, I hope they don't think we can keep up this pace for six months."

"What? You mean standing out here watching Palestinians troop by is already wearing you out?"

"Don't be an ass," the former landscaper snapped. "I mean not getting any sleep. Do you realize that we have had a grand total of four hours of sleep since arriving in country? Four hours! Hell, back home I take longer naps in the afternoon during the winter when business is slow."

Placing his hands behind his head as he continued to

stretch, Sucher looked at the barrenness of the security zone and the Palestinian area beyond. "I don't think you'd have much of a chance to nap here. This whole place is crying out for scrubs and a bit of decorative terracing."

Rainey looked about as well. "It would be a waste of time. This isn't the Valley. There's not enough water in the battalion's whole sector to support a single lawn of any significance."

"Have you ever been to Phoenix?" Sucher countered. "The folks have taken a desert and made it as green as my backyard."

Rainey snickered. "I'm not impressed. I've seen your backyard."

"Up yours."

Ignoring Sucher's retort, Rainey continued to survey the land before him. "It took a lot of money and people who give a damn to do that to Phoenix. If the poor sods who have been passing through this way today are any indication of what the rest of their kind is like, hell will freeze over before anyone gets around to doing anything constructive with this land."

Settling back down into a comfortable position with his forearms resting on the top sandbags, Sucher shook his head. "The Jews tried to make something of this land and look where it got them."

"That's because not all the land they were trying to reclaim from the desert belonged to them."

Cocking his head, Sucher gave Rainey a funny look. "That doesn't make sense. How can the desert belong to anyone? It's like the ocean. How can it belong to anyone?"

"When it's all you've got, what choice do you have but to make the best of it?"

Seeing a group of Palestinians headed their way, Sucher pushed himself off of the sandbags he had been resting on. "Well, they could do like all the other Arabs in the world have done. They can go to New York City and drive a cab."

"Very funny. Why don't you go out there and ask them if

they think this land is worth fighting for while you check their IDs?"

Sucher looked at Rainey who had settled back into a comfortable position leaning against the sandbags. "I just might do that." Slinging his rifle over his right shoulder, Sucher stepped out from behind the hastily thrown-up position and onto the road. Raising his right hand, he signaled the group of Palestinians to stop as he set off toward them.

The appearance of an armed soldier emerging from a position that wasn't supposed to be there startled the group of Palestinians. Recoiling, they exchanged nervous glances as Sucher approached.

Back at the checkpoint, the Israeli soldier serving as a spotter in the tower watched the confrontation for a moment before turning to the machine gunner. Without hesitation the gunner brought his weapon to bear.

Sucher was unaware of this, just as he was oblivious to the circumspect manner with which the young Palestinians before him were behaving. Even as a young man who had been hanging back behind the others began to pull away from the group, Sucher's only response was to continue forward while calling out to them as he went. "Hey! ID cards. Show me your ID cards." When he saw that they were making no effort to comply, Sucher assumed they didn't understand what he was saying. In an effort to clarify his demand he stopped, reached over with his right hand to grasp the sling of his rifle hanging from his shoulder, and raised his left hand, forming his fingers as if he were holding a card. "ID card," he repeated louder. "Show me . . ."

Before he could finish the youth who had been backpedaling suddenly reversed himself, lunging forward, and took off toward Sucher at a dead run. Befuddled, the Guardsman didn't quite know what to do.

The Israeli behind the machine gun in the tower did. With the flick of his thumb he threw the safety off, leaned into his weapon, and cut loose.

The whole drama played out before Sucher only took five seconds, maybe less. But to him the scene unfolding before his startled eyes seemed to take forever. It was as if the world before him had slowed to half speed. He imagined he could see every bullet ripping through the torso of the Palestinian before him, every wrinkle and furrow that creased the youth's face as the shock of what was happening to him began to register. Standing in the middle of the road as frozen as time itself seemed to be, Sucher watched helplessly as the youth thrust his right hand under his jacket. Even the most minute detail was crystal clear, so well defined. Everything except the explosion. That, like the barren patch of ground the Hezbollah suicide bomber had been standing on, disappeared in a blinding flash.

CHAPTER 18

Palestinian West Bank

The urge to drop everything and head straight off for the compound where he suspected he would find Hammed was almost too powerful for Syed Amama to resist. But resist he did. He had no choice. To do anything but continue carrying out his assigned duties with the Americans at the Palestinian checkpoint along the eastern edge of the security zone would have further compromised his standing with them. The most he could do when word came across the tactical radio that the explosion they had all heard in the distance had in fact been a suicide attack was to briefly lift his eyes up to the sky and silently give praise to his God.

No one saw him do this, at least as far as he could tell. Each of the Americans manning the Palestinian checkpoint was too caught up by their own thoughts and concerns to pay attention to what he was doing. None of the Americans seemed to care what he did anyway except when they needed him to explain something to one of his fellow countrymen either passing through the checkpoint headed for Israel or to the small detachment of Palestinian police who shared the task of controlling access to Israel through the security zone. This suited Syed just fine. It allowed him to hang back and listen to the idle chat that the Americans exchanged and information that came blaring out of the speaker attached to their tactical radio. From these sources he was able to learn much about them. In their conversations they revealed just what sort of people they were, the types of jobs they had held before being mobilized, and, most important, how their military did things. This last item was a point of interest that Hammed had told him to pay particular attention to. "Nothing that they do is too trivial," he had been told. "The tiniest fault in a system can often be exploited to bring it all crashing down."

No one had taken the time to explain just what sort of flaw Hammed was looking for. Perhaps, Syed reasoned, that was because Hammed himself didn't know what it was he was looking for. A foe's weaknesses or vulnerability is seldom readily apparent. If it were the enemy would take steps to correct it. The Israelis did that all the time. That was why young Palestinian males were always the first to be searched or detained whenever something happened. No matter how minor the offense, they were gathered up and detained for questioning by the authorities on both sides of the security zone. And even when that did not occur, it had been Syed's experience that the Jews he worked for would draw away from him and his companions whenever they could. Like a gang of conspirators, they would gather together in little knots in order to talk about their Palestinian minions in hushed tones while casting a leery eye in their direction every so often, just as the Americans were doing now. No matter how often he saw it, no matter how justified the Jews and now the Americans might be in feeling uncomfortable about having Palestinians in their midst, Syed's response was always the same: indignation and a desire to strike back. The problem with this was that Syed had no means to do so effectively on his own. Only through working with men like Hammed was Syed afforded a means of doing so.

As he listened, the initial reports concerning the attack at the Israeli checkpoint were soon followed by an order to seal off the security zone by closing down all checkpoints. Quickly the American in charge of the squad manning the Palestinian checkpoint gathered in his men and issued them their new orders. "Well, now that the horse is gone, we've been instructed to close the barn door." No one found any humor in this caustic remark, one which Syed didn't quite follow. When he was done issuing instructions to his own people, the American in charge motioned to Syed. Obediently, the young Palestinian rose to his feet and approached. "We're shutting this operation down," he announced. "Since there'll be no one passing to the west for the rest of the day I see no need for you to remain here. Why don't you go home?"

The American's tone and expression made it clear to Syed that this was not a request but an order. Having little interest in remaining there among nervous American soldiers, Syed nodded. "Yes, I see." Gathering up the worn backpack he used to haul his lunch, a couple of books, and a liter bottle of water, Syed made his way through the gate back into the Palestinian zone. No one said good-bye, no one called out with a friendly "see you tomorrow," or anything of the sort. They just slammed the reinforced gate shut as soon as he was through it.

Slowly Syed made his way to the open-air bus stop that stood within sight of the checkpoint. Since this was only midafternoon it would be a while before the next bus came by. During his wait he glanced up at the hill covered with fruit orchards that rose up behind him. The compound where he had last spoken to Hammed was but a few hundred meters away, well within easy walking distance. It would be nothing for him to go there directly and personally report what he had seen and heard. Though he was anxious to do so, he knew it would have been foolish. Looking back at the checkpoint Syed watched the Americans take up positions behind their sandbag emplacements on the other side of the fence. Seeing this, and fearing the sort of retaliation that the Israelis had used in the past every time a suicide bomber had struck, the Palestinian security personnel the Americans were supposed to be cooperating with at this checkpoint were also withdrawing into their own bunkers. Like Syed, those guards trusted the Americans about as much as the Americans trusted them, which is to say not at all.

It was this inbred suspicion that convinced Syed it would be unwise to go directly to the compound. Instead, he would have to wait until the bus heading south, toward his home, trundled by. When it did, he would board it, just as any American who might be watching him expected him to. To have done otherwise would have only served to reinforce any misgivings they already had concerning his reliability. So rather than taking the direct route to the compound, Syed took the bus as he always did, taking care to watch each time he made a transfer to another one in an effort to see if anyone duplicated his intricate and roundabout path back almost to where he had started.

The announcement that Syed was at the front gate of the compound annoyed Hammed. He had gone out of his way to make sure the young man understood the correct procedures he was to use to pass on information. Of course, he appreciated that he was himself to blame for Syed's sudden and unwelcomed return to the hilltop compound. It had been a mistake to have the young Palestinian brought here in the wake of the attack on the bus he had participated in. Hammed's chief of security had told him as much at the time. But in the euphoria he experienced in the aftermath of that successful full-scale experiment, Hammed had ignored those warnings. Now he would have to pay the price for his stupidity, something a man like Hammed hated to admit.

In a fit he threw a clipboard he had been holding across the room where it barely missed a lab technician seated before a table crowded with beakers and vials. "Idiots! I am surrounded by idiots!" Not knowing which idiots Hammed was talking about, the lab techs who were not aware of the source of their master's anger scurried for cover as he stormed through the lab complex, ripping off his white lab coat and tossing it aside as he went. Were it not for the fact that he had no way of replacing Syed without delaying his project as well as incurring a great deal of trouble and expense, the Palestinian microbiologist would have simply ordered the head of his security detachment to make the young fool go away, permanently.

Hammed's navigation of the underground passages, up the rough-hewn stone stairs and through the building that concealed the entrance to his subterranean facilities, did little to lessen his anger. When he reached the gate where Syed was waiting he found he had to draw upon every ounce of his self-control to keep from reaching out and grabbing the young man by the scruff of his neck and lifting him off the ground. "Why have you come here?" Hammed spit out by way of a greeting.

Startled, Syed stepped back until he bumped into an armed guard who had been standing behind him. Trapped between his enraged superior and the armed security man, Syed stammered as he tried to explain. "I thought you'd like to know . . . I mean, I was only trying . . ."

"You fool," Hammed hissed as he pushed Syed out through the compound's open gate and into the open beyond as he looked to his left and right. "You didn't think, did you? If you had you never would have come here. Were you followed?"

"No, no. I was not followed. I swear. I made sure of that."

Still not satisfied, Hammed stood still for a moment as he continued to scan the familiar surroundings, searching for any sign that something was amiss. Only when he was sure that neither he nor his precious compound was in immediate danger did he motion for the guard who had followed him through the gate to return to his post before turning his full attention upon a very shaken Syed. "What is so important that you must place us in such danger. I hope it is not simply to tell me that Hamas felt compelled to launch an ill-advised attack on the Americans? I already know everything I need know about that."

"The incident was reported over their tactical radio net

almost as soon as it happened," Syed offered as he began to recite whatever thought concerning the incident came to his mind first. "It was as if they were expecting it."

"Well," Hammed huffed as he reached into his pocket and pulled out a pack of cigarettes. "They would have been fools if they hadn't."

"Their response," Syed continued, "was no different than the Israelis. All checkpoints were immediately shut down. I listened to their tactical radio net as a series of code words from their command post went out, ordering some units to assume a higher state of readiness and others to take up positions covering the east boundary fence."

"No units were dispatched to cover the wall along the western boundary?" Hammed asked as he lit his cigarette.

"No, none. I think the Israeli Army itself covers that."

Hammed blew a puff of smoke as he gazed across the valley at the American compound in the security zone. "Of course. They have coordinated their responses with those of the Jews."

"But not with our own people," Syed added. "After I left the security zone, the officer in charge of our checkpoint asked me what was going on. I told him all I could, which did not seem to please him. I do not think he knew what to do."

"No, few within our government know what to do."

"Not all of the Americans did either," Syed continued. "I do not think all of their units understand what all the code words meant. Whey they called back for clarification, their commander back at the base camp had no choice but to explain to them over the radio what they were to do."

"Confusion?"

Syed thought about this for a moment, then shook his head. "Some, far more than the Jews, but not much. While they are making many mistakes that an IDF unit would not make, their officers and sergeants are quick to correct them. And though the soldiers themselves do not seem to be keen on being here and often complain about everything, especially the food, they follow orders without question."

Walking away from Syed and out among the trees of the orchard, Hammed thought about this. He had hoped to capitalize upon the fact that the Americans who occupied the base camp just across the valley from where he stood were not regular Army. Many of the popular perceptions concerning the quality of the American reservists that he had been relying upon were proving to be wrong. "We will have to rethink some things," Hammed mused to himself as he wandered about between the fruit trees, thinking as he went.

Suddenly an idea began to take shape. Turning, he looked at Syed. "Are they friendly?"

Syed shrugged. "To each other, yes. And to the Israeli translators as well. But so far none have made much of an effort to talk to me even though I have tried to start conversations with them."

Reaching up, Hammed grabbed an orange hanging on a low branch and gave it a tug. When it snapped off the branch he tossed it to Syed, who bobbled the orange in his hands as he tried to catch the unexpected projectile. "Try harder," Hammed stated. "Come by here each morning before you go to the checkpoint. The guard at the gate of the compound will have a fresh sack of fruit that you are to give to them."

"How do I explain this generosity?"

"Tell them that some of the local workers who tend this orchard found out you work for them. Tell the Americans that they want to curry favor with them. Tell them they want to be good neighbors."

"And if they do not take the fruit?"

The angry expression that had momentarily left Hammed's face returned. "Do what you must to gain their trust. Do you understand?"

Sensing that he had already pushed his luck too far, Syed nodded. "Yes, yes, I will do as you say."

Stepping closer to the young Palestinian, Hammed did his best to tower over him even though they were almost of equal height. "Make sure you do."

Camp Lee

All eyes turned to Nathan Dixon as he pulled aside the tent flap and entered the company orderly room. They were all there, the company XO, the first sergeant, and all the platoon leaders together with their platoon sergeants. Their expressions and demeanor reminded him of a concerned family sitting around a hospital waiting room anxiously awaiting word about a loved one. Walking over to the first sergeant's desk, Nathan plopped down in a folding chair sitting next to it before taking off his helmet and setting it on the desk.

Looking up at Faucher, Nathan smiled. "That man must lead a charmed life." Throughout the room there was a collective and audible sigh of relief.

"Then he'll be all right," Faucher asked in an effort to confirm what he had just heard.

"Yes, he's fine. The doctors at the hospital he was evaced to just want to keep him overnight for observation. They felt they could do a better job of monitoring him there than back here and our battalion's physician assistant agreed."

Just to make sure that he wasn't jumping to conclusions, Jack Horne questioned Nathan more closely. "Then there were no injuries? Nothing broken?"

Nathan shook his head. "Oh, they're not sure if his hearing will ever be what it was, but other than that, he'll be his old self again in no time."

Sensing an opportunity to relieve some of the tension, Matt Garver grunted. "God, I hope not."

A few of the men gathered about in the room who were a bit slow on the pickup gave Sucher's platoon sergeant a funny look. Winking to Faucher, Garver explained. "I was hoping that blast knocked some sense in him."

Finally catching on, everyone joined in on a round of nervous laughter. Nathan let this go on for a few minutes before he sat up and cleared his throat. Taking the hint, a hush fell over the senior leadership of Company A. "I'll not bludgeon you or the rest of the company with the more obvious lessons we all need to carry away from this little episode."

Faucher nodded. "Sir, I dare say that one asshole did more to drive home the point you and everyone at Benning have been trying to make about the need for us to maintain our vigilance. On the one hand I'm sorry it took this sort of thing to drive that point home. But on the other, I thank God for giving us a wake-up call like this."

Around the room, several of the men nodded and muttered heartfelt "amens."

Leaning back in his seat, Nathan took a moment to think as he ran his hand through his close-cropped hair. "I'm sure you all believe in what you're saying. And I have no doubt that every man jack in this company is going to be on his toes come tomorrow. But it's not tomorrow I'm worried about." Pausing, he looked about the room at the faces that had resumed a more solemn expression. "The great challenge that each and every one of us will face in the weeks and months ahead is to make sure our people don't lose that edge, that they are just as keen about going out there and doing a good job three months from now as they will be when we hit the street tomorrow morning. I can't do this on my own." Pausing, he reached in the "In" box sitting on the first sergeant's desk and grabbed a handful of papers that were waiting to be sorted. "Far too much of my time and the first sergeant's time is going to be consumed fighting the paper dragon." Tossing the assorted pages down, he pointed at each of the platoon leaders and platoon sergeants in the room. "You are going to have to be the heavies. You are going to have to be out there each and every day, ready to put a boot up the ass of anyone who even looks like he's even thinking about slacking off. Lieutenant Stone, you're not a loan officer at the local bank anymore trying to scare up business. Jack Horne, this isn't a classroom exercise. And, Mr. Teeple, no one out there gives a damn about the law. Each of you is a platoon leader. How you do your job and what you need to keep your people pumped up and ready to kick ass and take names is not my concern. That you find a way to do so each and every day we're out on the line is. Am I making myself clear?"

Not having realized how strident his tone had become as he had been speaking, Nathan was taken aback somewhat when the three young officers responded with a crisp "Yes sir!" Sensing for the first time that he had finally managed to capture both their hearts and minds, Nathan continued. "The same holds doubly true for you platoon sergeants. The enlisted men in your platoons will take their cue from you. If they see you slacking off, they'll slack off. If they hear you bad-mouthing your platoon leader or bellyaching, they'll do the same. We can't afford a 'we versus them' mentality within this company and you can't allow that sort of thing to happen in your platoon. If anything, I'll hold you more responsible for any failure within your platoon because you guys are older than your lieutenants. Each and every one of you has more time in uniform than all three of them put together. They're still learning. You know better, or you should."

Unlike the officers, the three senior NCOs looked at each other, then Nathan, and nodded. Seizing the opportunity, Faucher added his own thoughts on the subject. Just as Nathan had done, he pointed his finger at each of the platoon sergeants. "When we're finished with this tour the captain here is going to go away. Odds are we'll never see him again. But I'm going back to Bedlow with you guys. Just make sure that when we get there, I have no reason to be ashamed over having known you."

Nathan hadn't asked Faucher to say this. He didn't need

to. The first sergeant was simply articulating an element that makes the National Guard such a potent force. Unlike units belonging to the active component, Guard units already come with an esprit and a connectivity that campaign ribbons hanging from a flag and unit history cannot match. A Guard unit, the people who belong and the community from which it comes, is tightly bound together, giving it a strength that, when tapped, is all but unbreakable.

Sensing that he had no need to expand upon what his first sergeant had said, Nathan stood up. "Now if you gentlemen would excuse me, I need to find the battalion commander and let him know I'm back. First Sergeant, if you would go over tomorrow's schedule with everyone before they scatter."

With that, he left the tent, allowing his senior leadership the freedom to go over among themselves the day's events and what had just been discussed in a manner to which they were more accustomed.

CHAPTER **19**

The Security Zone, 3rd Battalion of the 176th's Sector

The completion of their first full week at Camp Lee and change of duties from green to amber status was not as welcomed by some in Company A as Nathan Dixon had come to believe. He had thought that the suicide attack on the second day alone would be enough to turn even his most optimistic Guardsman off to the duties there. In some cases, he was correct. Manning the checkpoints had quickly settled into a routine that was a strange blend of tedious repetition that led to boredom coupled with the nagging fear that stalked the Guardsmen from the time they rolled out the gate of Camp Lee each morning until the moment they returned.

The unexpected factor that entered into the equation that Nathan had not factored in was the tedium that life at Camp Lee had so quickly settled into. As a company commander, having more to do than the hours of the day permitted, he missed seeing this. It wasn't until Alex Faucher pointed out that the men were already becoming restless that he took note of how fast the men of his command had overcome the cultural shock that their deployment to the Middle East had created. "While we're running around like a couple of headless chickens," Faucher remarked to Nathan, "the men are becoming restless. Instead of storming the beaches of Normandy, they're playing traffic cop for two groups of people whose hatred for each other is only slightly more obvious than their resentment of us. I'm more than a bit concerned that in time, we may find ourselves finding out if the old saying—idle hands do the devil's work—is true."

Alerted to this unanticipated crisis within his command, Nathan began to pay more attention to what his men were up to when they were on and off duty. It did not take long to see just how little their lives changed from day to day. Not the scenery, not their schedule, not even the faces of the people coming through the checkpoints they stood watch over.

To some degree the soldiers themselves took steps to mitigate the corrosive effects that tedious and repetitious duty tended to have on their morale. One age-old technique employed by the Guardsmen of third squad to break the monotony of their duty was to liven up their tour of duty and mask their nervousness through the use of uniquely American sense of humor. It started when those assigned the task of checking ID cards and rummaging through packages, parcels, and handbags found themselves beginning to recognize some of the Palestinians. Unable to read the Arabic or Hebrew used on ID cards, Jerry Slatery quickly took to assigning nicknames to some of the more notable regulars who passed through the checkpoint. These hapless workers forced by circumstances to commute back and forth across the security zone on a daily basis were soon labeled with monikers such as the Nose, Big Eyes, Bug Eyes, Shaky, Buckie, and so on. Within days, the soldiers were competing with each other in an effort to come up with witty names for those who had not yet been so blessed.

This was not all bad. By engaging in this contest, the wisdom of keeping the same personnel assigned to the specific duties as the Israelis had done whenever possible slowly started to become self-evident to anyone who bothered to analyze what was actually going on. The habits of the people passing their checkpoint, the ebb and flow of the traffic, and the typical response of people Ollie Rendell's men came to call "frequent fliers," not only kept his people interested in what they were doing, it also allowed them to zero in on those passing their way who were behaving in a suspicious or circumspect manner. Without having to be browbeaten or supervised every minute, they were becoming proficient in their jobs. This in turn slowly led to growing confidence that they could deal with another incident should anyone be foolish to try again.

Thus, when it came time to switch from red company to amber some in third squad greeted the change with a bit more trepidation than anyone would have imagined. For Matt Garver, still somewhat shaken by the suicide attack at the Israeli checkpoint, the change in duties was coming none too soon as far as he was concerned. He considered the pair of checkpoints along the western wall where the Palestinians mingled with his people and Israelis as being the most dangerous spot within the battalion's sector, a place where the question was when and not if something bad was going to go down.

While Ollie Rendell agreed, he had a different view when it came to the subject of rotating his squad's assigned duties. He surprised his platoon sergeant by requesting that the battalion consider leaving them at the checkpoint. Ever the deputy sheriff, Rendell made a convincing argument, pointing out that his people had the drill down cold. "We've finally gotten to the point where my people can sniff out those Palestinians who're acting quirky and give them the special attention they deserve. In two weeks when we pull red company again we'll have to start all over."

Garver had no sympathy for Rendell's argument. As a platoon sergeant he had more than Rendell's squad and the pedestrian checkpoint they manned to worry about. The second platoon also covered a second checkpoint farther north that handled vehicular traffic passing from east to west while holding a squad as a ready response squad who did nothing but sit around geared up and ready to roll to either checkpoint to assist either checkpoint in the event of another attack. As boring as the third squad's work at the Israeli checkpoint could be at times, it was nothing in comparison to the tedium the ready response squad had to deal with. Held back at Camp Lee, for them the only difference between duty hours to nonduty hours was that while on standby the soldiers of Jack Horne's second squad sat around decked out in their full panoply of weaponry and equipment. Were it not for the collection of dog-eared Tom Clancy, Stephen Coonts, and Clive Cussler novels that were passed from soldier to soldier, the members of second squad would probably have gone stark raving mad. The same was no different for the platoon Nathan was required to hold back at Camp Lee during red week as a response force. The only saving grace for them was that they at least had the ability to relax a bit more since their response time was fifteen minutes as opposed to the "Move now!" time crunch that Jack Horne's ready response squad was held to.

Another interesting twist to what Nathan and others had expected was the realization that the duty of manning the checkpoints within the 3rd Battalion's zone of operation placed a great deal of responsibility upon Company A's squad leaders. They were the only ones with rank who were there every minute of their squad's tour of duty. Their ability to keep their men motivated and on their toes made the difference between success and failure. In an emergency, it would be their initial decisions and response to it that would make all the difference between success and failure. Fortunately, the maturity of Nathan's squad leaders coupled with civilian professions that required them to do much the same back in Virginia paid off. This was particularly true in Ollie Rendell's case. When Nathan asked him about this during one of his frequent inspection tours, Rendell smiled. "Hell, sir. It's no different than running a sobriety checkpoint except that these people tend to be more coherent than most of the drunks I come across on New Year's Eve."

This all changed when Company A took over as the amber company. Now the platoon leaders would have to assume a more active role. Rather than flitting about from post to post checking on their scattered squads, they would be leading platoon-sized patrols that encompassed critical points throughout the battalion's area of responsibility. One involved patrolling the western wall, or the concrete and barbed wire barrier constructed by the Israelis before the Americans had arrived. A second platoon did the same along the twin fences marking the eastern or Palestinian boundary of the security zone. Both were inspected by a reinforced squad-sized element led by an officer four times daily. Two were routine, always performed shortly after dawn and just prior to nightfall. The other two patrols were not tied to a fixed schedule other than one went out sometime during the day and the second during the night. To allow their platoon leaders an opportunity to enjoy a longer period of sleep than would have been possible if they had to lead all four patrols as well as to break up the monotony of their own duties, Nathan and his XO took turns leading some of these patrols. The purpose of all of them was to make sure that no one, either terrorists or smugglers, was attempting to infiltrate through the barriers between the checkpoints. Backup for either of the platoons conducting the patrols was provided first by Nathan's third platoon, which was held back as a ready reaction force when it was not out conducting roving patrols throughout the security zone, or by an alert force drawn from the green company that was under the control of the battalion commander.

As before, Nathan Dixon opted not to rotate his platoons' assignment. His reasoning, reinforced by the company's experience at the checkpoints, was simply to maintain continuity and accumulate a degree of familiarity with their surroundings that could provide them with a critical edge in a crisis. To the delight of his men, Jack Horne's second platoon drew the roving assignment. Unlike the random manner with which Nathan had assigned the platoons to checkpoints during the previous week, his decision now was based upon his assessment of the platoon leaders he had to work with since he had seen little that distinguished the men in one platoon from those of another.

The officers were a different story. Keith Stone of the first platoon was a good man but a cautious one who was as meticulous in carrying out his duties as an infantry officer as he had been while working as a bank loan officer. His attention to detail, one that permeated his entire platoon, made the first platoon the ideal choice for the eastern fence, where Nathan and the entire battalion staff expected trouble. Allen Teeple leading the third platoon had the potential to be an outstanding officer, but in Nathan's opinion he simply did not have enough experience in handling men yet. This assessment was shared by both Gordon Grello and Alex Faucher. "He's not a weak sister," Faucher was quick to point out every time he found himself saying something that was even remotely negative. "He's just a wee bit wet behind the ears." This drove Nathan to give Teeple's platoon the task of patrolling the western wall, a well-constructed barrier built with an eye on resisting any effort to breach it, tunnel under it, or go over it. Of the three assignments the amber company covered, it was theoretically the easiest.

Of the three, Jack Horne seemed to be the most flexible and well rounded. As a high school teacher who was used to dealing with rowdy teenagers and classrooms that always seemed to be on the verge of exploding into chaos he had to be. In Nathan's view this experience gave him an edge over his peers when it came to dealing with fast-moving situations. While keeping a lid on a gaggle of precocious teenagers was a far cry from leading a combat patrol, Horne impressed Nathan as having the flexibility that Stone lacked and the maturity and judgment Teeple had yet to amass. Still, Nathan did have some reservations. "Though he's the best platoon leader I've got," Nathan confided to Terry Putnam in private, "I still have concerns."

As the battalion's S-4, Terry Putnam had little to do with the day-to-day operations of the battalion, allowing him to be a bit more cavalier when it came to such matters. "I've seen worse," he quibbled. "And I'm sure you have as well. Though I hate to admit it, I once had to deal with a brand-new second lieutenant straight out of West Point who couldn't find his way to the latrine with a map, detailed directions, and a GPS."

"If my biggest concern was whether or not they'd make it to the rest room before the floods came I wouldn't be worried," Nathan countered. "Unfortunately, the sort of accidents we're likely to run into are a bit more lethal. Ambushes, land mines, and car bombs tend to be rather unforgiving."

Sensing his concern and having no suitable response, Putnam simply nodded. "I can't argue that. Still, if I were you I wouldn't sell any of these people short. I'm beginning to think there's a lot more to these Guardsmen than meets the eye."

Nathan considered his companion's words for a moment. Perhaps he was being too critical of his own command, a common failing in commanding officers who had not been afforded the luxury of training and molding his own subordinates. That, coupled with his inbred skepticism concerning members of the National Guard and Army Reserve, left Nathan uneasy about the future. To him, his company was like an unbalanced sword, a weapon that could be as dangerous to the one who wielded it as it was to the foe. He would have to take great care if and when he came to use it in battle.

Residing side by side with Nathan's deep-rooted opinion on National Guard officers was his philosophy on command. A key principle that was part of that philosophy concerned the amount of latitude that he allowed subordinates in carrying out his orders. Like his father he did not believe it was necessary or even advisable to tell them how to do their jobs. As officers he expected them to be smart enough to figure that out. So other than assigning them their missions and establishing some very basic parameters, each of his platoon leaders was free to organize his platoon and run his patrols as he saw fit.

In many ways Jack Horne was very much like his company commander in that he was also a captive of his experiences and beliefs. This was especially true when it came to Horne's style of leadership. Like Nathan he did not feel he needed to tell his squad leaders how to do their jobs. This bit of wisdom was derived not from a military text but rather from dealing day in and day out with high school students who were ever eager to discover who they were and what they were capable of. He saw little need to alter the approach he used in the classroom when it came to the running of his platoon. In both he saw himself as more than simply a taskmaster, charged with the obligation of providing both his pupils and his Guardsmen with an opportunity to learn to think on their own and respond to any given situation as they saw fit provided that it achieved the goals he had established for them in a manner that was both effective and carried out within accepted standards of conduct. In the case of the Guard, this meant following established rules of engagement. To have done otherwise when doing his time with the Guard would have run the risk of alienating men like Ollie Rendell who were both older than Horne and had a great deal of practical experience when it came to dealing with people in and out of uniform.

Almost without exception the men in his platoon saw Horne's light touch as nothing more than the natural order of things, the way it should be in a Guard unit made up of men who were in their minds friends and neighbors first and soldiers second. Though some were not as mature as they themselves thought they were, all were rational human beings capable of taking care of themselves and getting the job done. Tim Ratliff certainly was. The school bus driver saw his selection to drive the lead Humvee whenever Jack Horne's third squad sallied out of Camp Lee as an opportunity to do the sort of thing he had always wanted to do. Seeing no need to ask Horne trivial questions like how fast he should drive, he rolled through the gates of Camp Lee for the afternoon patrol at speed. When he came up to the road junction, Ratliff did little more than glance to his left and right before cranking the wheel hard left without bothering to let up off the accelerator. Up top Ronald Weir hung on to the spade grips of the M-2 machine gun attached to the rooftop ring mount as the vehicle careened around the corner and onto the road headed east. Like a cowboy in a B western, Weir cut loose with a piercing "Yeeeee-haw" that was heard by the pair of Guardsmen who were left standing back at the camp gate in a cloud of dust thrown up by the four Humvees.

Inside, Jack Horne said nothing as he watched the barren landscape fly by. Only Syed Amama, crouching in the seat behind Ratliff, cringed. He had always thought that the popular image of Americans as cowboys was nothing more than a myth, an urban legend perpetuated by movies and America's legions of detractors. Antics such as those displayed by Ratliff and the other Americans he accompanied on these patrols proved him wrong. They made the Jewish drivers in Tel Aviv look absolutely timid.

Once the Humvee was settled back onto the main east-west road and after he had given Ratliff directions toward their first stop, Horne turned around in his seat and looked over at Syed. The smile he wore was an honest, friendly smile unlike the ones members of the battalion staff assumed whenever Syed dealt with them. "Hey, Sigh-ed. What did you bring with you today?"

Ignoring the manner in which the American officer butchered the pronunciation of his name, the young Palestinian returned Horne's smile as he reached down and retrieved a worn canvas sack that sat between his feet. "I regret that I have only oranges for you this day," he responded as he fished one out and offered it to Horne.

"No need to apologize, Sigh-ed. Oranges are just fine."

Even before Jack Horne was able to take the freshly picked fruit from the Palestinian, Ronald Weir thrust an open hand down in front of Syed's face. With a nod, Horne motioned to him to go ahead and give Weir the first orange. Bewildered by Horne's deferral to what he saw as a crass gesture by a subordinate, Syed paused.

"It's okay, Sigh-ed. Go ahead and give it to him. I have no problems with sloppy seconds."

Upon hearing this, Ratliff gave Horne a funny look. "I'm not sure I want to know how often that's a problem you need to deal with, Jack."

After taking an orange from Syed, but remaining twisted about sideways in his seat with his arm hanging over the backrest so that he could freely talk to both his driver and translator, Horne smiled as he began to pull the skin off the orange. "Hell, Tim, you know my wife. Don't let the fact that she teaches second-graders fool you. If she ever found out that I was messing around she'd pull a Lorraina Bobbit on me without giving it a second thought."

Feigning an expression of pain, Ratliff squeezed his knees together. "Damn, Jack! Don't go there."

Though he had no idea what they were talking about, Syed joined in the laughter. Hammed had been right. The simple gift he brought with him each day made all the difference in the way the Americans responded to him. Rather than being ignored as he had been by the first group of Americans he had been assigned to work with at the Palestinian checkpoint, this platoon seemed to be more amiable and accommodating.

Both Jack Horne and Ratliff were still enjoying their little joke when Horne lifted his right arm and pointed at something up ahead that Syed could not see. "Stop here and let's see what this guy is up to."

Knowing that he would be needed, Syed leaned over and peeked around Ratliff to see what the officer was referring to. Up ahead on the road, more than a hundred meters away and headed toward them, Syed caught sight of a herd of goats that spilled over onto either side of the roadway. It took him a moment before he was able to spot the lone herder. As they drew nearer, he could see that he was a stoop-shouldered elderly man being swept forward by the numerous animals he was caring for.

Up top Ronald Weir had also caught sight of the old man. Having taken to heart the lessons that had been driven home in the aftermath of the suicide bomber at the Israeli checkpoint, Weir's first response was to swing his machine gun about and train it on the goat herder. Without needing to be told he gave the charging handle a quick jerk back, cocking the weapon even as he glanced quickly to the left and the right in search of any indication that they might be rolling into an ambush.

Pulling up just short, the squeal of brakes and hail of stones thrown up by the Humvee's tires sent the lead goats scurrying off the road and into the barren fields beyond. Those animals that were in the middle of the herd and could hear but not see the Humvee began to bleat in fear as they pressed against each other in a vain effort to escape the unseen danger. Ignoring the Americans, the herder immediately began to dart about this way and that in a vain effort to keep his herd from scattering to the four winds. In this he failed, leaving him in no mood to answer any questions that Jack Horne began to fire at him as soon as he and Syed had dismounted and were near enough to do so.

"Ask him where he's from and where he is going," Horne ordered as he stopped at what he thought to be a safe distance from the milling mass of frantic goats.

More concerned over his charges, the old man made no effort to reply, causing Horne to glance over to Syed and repeat his demand in a more forceful manner. "Find out where he's from and where he is going."

Sensing the frustration of the American officer, Syed stepped closer as he tried to convey the urgency of his inquiry. "Hey, old man. These people do not mean to harm you. But you must tell us where you are from and where you are going."

For the first time the herder turned away from his vain attempt to gather in his flock. After looking up at the man behind the oversized machine gun, one no different than those carried on Israeli tanks he glared at Syed. Though no words passed between them, the younger Palestinian understood what the older man felt, for he had worn the same contemptuous scowl many times before when Israeli soldiers had levied similar questions upon him when he had been doing nothing more offensive than merely trying to survive in a land where survival was always in question.

Unsure of what was going on and growing a bit nervous, Horne laid his right hand upon the handle of his holstered pistol. "Syed, what's going on?"

Doing his best to swallow the anger he felt at being placed in such a difficult spot while in the service of men allied to his sworn enemies, Syed looked down at the road and shook his head. "He's nothing," he finally replied as he looked over at the American officer. "He is only a foolish old man tending his flock."

Not sure what to make of the situation, Horne glanced back and forth between Syed who had gone back to staring down at the ground before him and the herder who had turned his back on both of them as he returned to the daunting chore of rounding up goats that were now scattered all over the place. It was just beginning to become clear to him that the old man had no intention of cooperating with them when Weir called out from his perch. "Hey, L.T., you're wanted on the radio."

Relieved at being given an opportunity to back away from the awkward situation he unexpectedly had found himself in, Horne called out to Syed. "I guess we've caused the old sod enough trouble. Let's go."

Turning his back on both the herder and his translator, Horne headed back to the Humvee. Syed however remained behind for a moment, watching the old man as he scurried about in a valiant effort to collect his herd. He wished that there were some way he could convey to his fellow Palestinian that he was not a traitor, that he was in fact working to rid their people once and for all of those who conspired to deprive them of the land that was rightfully theirs. But he knew there was no way of doing so. Depressed by the plight in which he found himself, Syed also walked away from a man who knew no loyalty to anything or anyone other than the land that he was born to and the goats that provided him the means with which to live upon it.

When he reached the Humvee Horne had already taken the radio call and was headed down the small column of armed vehicles. Curious, the young Palestinian stopped next to the driver's door and asked Ratliff through the open window where Horne was going.

"That was battalion on the radio. Brian McIntire's wife, the one who's very pregnant, is in the hospital."

"She is having the baby?"

The American's hesitation and his expression told Syed that this had not been expected. "Don't know. My guess is that whatever the problem is, Brian will be headed home."

"For good?"

Ratliff shook his head. "Maybe yes, maybe no. The folks at battalion didn't know for sure. I imagine they'll give him emergency leave to start off with until things get sorted out back home."

This intrigued Syed. While it didn't seem to be all that important, Hammed had made it a point to impress upon him that he needed to learn all he could about the comings and goings of the unit's personnel. "What does that mean?"

Shrugging, Ratliff looked up at the sun as it hung low in the western horizon as he thought for a moment before answering. "Well, let me see. I don't imagine Brian'll be leaving until tomorrow morning. It'll take time to sort things out back at Camp Lee and cut orders for him. By then it'll be dark and the Israeli checkpoint will be closed down. If he does leave I expect he'll go back the same way we came. They'll truck him back to the Israeli military airfield we flew into where he'll catch a hop back to Ramstein airbase in Germany. There's a regularly scheduled Air Force transport that shuttles back and forth between the two on a daily basis bringing in visitors, VIPs coming over here on boondoggles to check us out, and whatever critical repair parts we need to keep these Humvees up and running. Unless it's really bad, I imagine Brian will have to cool his heels at the Israeli airbase awhile waiting for the scheduled flight to leave. In Ramstein it'll be the same. He'll have to cool his heels waiting for a spot on the first available flight back to the States that has room for him. Once he's in the States he'll be home free, able to catch any commercial flight that's headed back to ole Virginia and mama."

"This sounds like it will take a long time. There must be an easier way?"

Ratliff glanced up at Syed and snickered. "Son, there ain't no such word in the Army's vocabulary as easy. They have whole agencies tucked away in the Pentagon working around the clock searching for new ways to make life difficult for people like Brian."

Unable to comprehend the true meaning of Ratliff's cynical humor, Syed simply stared at the American. It really didn't matter why they did things the way they did, he told himself. All that was important was finding how they did them and pass everything he learned back to Hammed.

What he did with this knowledge was of little concern to him. In the end, he trusted that men like him would see that those who labored to keep his people under heel would be punished.

CHAPTER **20**

The Security Zone, 3rd Battalion of the 176th's Sector

The flurries of calls back to Bedlow and soothing reassurances from both family members over the phone and friends at Camp Lee did little to calm Brian McIntire. From the moment his platoon leader informed him that his bother-in-law had taken his wife to the hospital McIntire's mind was fixed on one thing and one thing only: getting home as soon as he could. Unfortunately, Tim Ratliff's prediction concerning the twisted and tortuous machinations that he would have to endure proved all too prophetic.

A call from home is not in of itself enough to initiate the process needed to place a soldier on emergency leave. It can alert him and his chain of command to the nature of the problem and allow administrative personnel to lay the groundwork necessary to send him packing, but the requirement that a serviceman be immediately relieved from his assigned duties and handed priority travel orders must be verified. This is usually accomplished through the American Red Cross. In the case of Brian McIntire's wife, this meant that a local Red Cross official in Virginia had to contact the primary physician tending to his wife and verify the nature of the emergency as well as the need for McIntire's immediate return. Once he or she was satisfied that the situation warranted action, the Red Cross official in Virginia passed his recommendation and supporting documentation along to a Red Cross liaison assigned to the Department of Defense who, in turn, relayed it to the Red Cross field rep handling all American military personnel in the Middle East. Only then could the adjutant of the 3rd of the 176th Infantry cut the necessary orders. As cruel and as heartless as this Byzantine process could be, it was necessary lest lonely wives and worried parents bombard the Army with a ceaseless barrage requesting that their sons be sent home immediately to tend to matters that were not true emergencies.

The speed with which Alex Faucher and the battalion adjutant moved to cut through the military red tape went a long way in getting McIntire out of Camp Lee and on his way. Yet confirming the need for emergency leave, cutting the necessary orders, and arranging for transportation from Camp Lee to the Israeli military airfield were only the beginning of McIntire's ordeal and by far the easy part. The trip to the airfield where the American Air Force detachment supporting U.S. forces assigned to the security zone alone took more than four hours. It wasn't the distance. From Mount Hermon in the north to the Gulf of Eilat in the south Israel measures only 250 miles, more or less the same distance that separates Washington, D.C., from New York City. It wasn't the distance that he needed to cover that prolonged the Guardsman's agony, it was the maddening wait at half a dozen checkpoints along the way as well as a route crowded with normal early-morning commuter traffic that choked roads connecting towns and villages mentioned in the Bible. And this was simply the beginning, a taste of what was to come once he was at the airfield where Brian McIntire would find himself at the mercy of the Air Force's Air Mobility Command.

The United States Air Force, like the Army and Navy, is divided into various component commands, each with a unique and vital role to play. The mission of the Air Mobility Command or AMC, headquartered at Scott Air Force Base in Illinois, is providing all branches of the armed forces of the United States with rapid, worldwide mobility and sustainment as well as providing humanitarian support at home and around the world when called upon. To accomplish this global task the AMC relies on over 142,000 active-duty and Air Reserve Component military and civilian personnel that includes approximately 52,000 active duty, 8,000 plus civilians, 44,000 Air Force Reserve, and 38,000 Air National Guard men and women operating a fleet of aircraft that includes giant C-5 Galaxys, C-17 Globemaster III and the C-141 Starlifter transports, C-9A Nightingale air ambulances, KC-10 Extender and KC-135 Stratotanker aerial refuelers as well as a diverse fleet of smaller tactical transport and support aircraft such as the tried and true C-130 Hercules, VC-9s, VC-25 (better known as Air Force One), C-20s, C-21s, C-22s, C-32s, C-37s, C-137s, EC-135s, and even a covey of humble UH-1 Hueys that had done yeoman's work during the American war in Vietnam.

It was into the maul of this massive beast that Tim Ratliff deposited Brian McIntire. The Air Force personnel manning the nondescript Quonset hut that served as both an operations center and reception station were helpful enough. They took McIntire's orders, listened to his story, and provided him with all the information concerning flights in and out. A female sergeant took great care in briefing him on the facilities that would be available to him while he waited for the next available flight out. But there was little she could do to speed him along his way. Like the other four Army personnel waiting in the tiny lounge set up at one end of the Quonset hut waiting to catch a hop back to the States, he was at the mercy of the tasking orders drafted at Scott Air Force Base that directed the massive fleet of aircraft hither and yon from continent to continent. Once issued only a general officer or an act of God, which some people tend to confuse as being one and the same, could change them. The female sergeant and the people who worked for her were little more than gatekeepers and support personnel, charged with servicing scheduled flights coming into and out of Israel as well as handling the flow of personnel and equipment they brought and carried away.

"We have two flights scheduled today," she explained to McIntire. "The first one has already departed Ramstein and is enroute now. It's slated to arrive sometime early this afternoon and leaves as soon as the ground crew is able to turn it around. The second doesn't arrive here till this evening but won't depart until tomorrow morning."

Not sure what this meant to him, McIntire stared at her for a moment. When he saw that she wasn't going to expand upon what she had told him, he asked, "So, what exactly does that mean? Do I leave today or not?"

Confused by his question, it took the Air Force sergeant a moment to realize that McIntire didn't seem to understand how the system worked. "Well, that's hard to say. Everything depends upon whether there are seats available for you on either of those flights. Later today a detachment of Marines who have been participating in an exercise at our embassy in Jerusalem will be arriving. Since they were part of a scheduled exercise, they are already on the manifest of the first flight, so it doesn't look good for you with that flight. If there are any open seats after the Marines have boarded people like you who are on standby will be added. If not, I'm afraid you'll just have to wait and see if there's an open slot for you on the next flight."

When he heard this, McIntire was unable to hide his disappointment. In an effort to cheer him up, the female sergeant smiled. "Of course there are always unscheduled flights coming in and out of here from Ramstein as well as other bases throughout Europe. Why just yesterday a senior officer from NATO headquarters came in for a quick one-day tour of inspection. When he left he took two soldiers on emergency leave who had been waiting here for a regular hop."

This bit of information did little to cheer the Guardsman up. Still troubled by the uncertainty of a system that seemed more like a crap shoot than a military operation, McIntire finished his in-processing with the Air Force personnel, took the manifest number they gave him, and joined four other soldiers on emergency leave who had arrived before him.

For the better part of an hour McIntire did nothing but sit in the corner of the Quonset hut that had been set aside as a waiting area mulling over his plight in silence. Being the sort of person he was, however, he was unable to dwell on his own problems for very long lest he slowly go mad. So he chose to pass his time in the manner he enjoyed best, which was by striking up a conversation with his fellow travelers. Each had a story that was no less compelling than his own. The oldest of them was a fourteen-year veteran of the regular Army, a sergeant first class by the name of Conners. He was the father of a teenage son who had been involved in an auto accident back at Fort Hood, Texas. Though his boy's condition was not life-threatening, Conners explained that his wife wasn't taking things well. "Even when he was a baby my wife depended upon the boy for stability when I was overseas," he explained. "As he got older, he more or less became the man of the house when I wasn't there."

As he made this statement, McIntire could tell by Conners's demeanor and his tone that there was more to this aspect of the story than the sergeant was letting on, a hint of melancholy that led him to believe that this confusion of family roles created problems between father and son. "Without him," Conners went on after a brief pause to refocus his thoughts, "my wife is a basket case." Then, looking up at his new set of companions he stared into each of their eyes as if trying to justify to them why he was there. "She's a good woman. She just isn't very strong when it comes to dealing with a family crisis like this on her own."

The senior ranking member of the group was a quartermaster captain en route to Florida for the funeral of his father. "I guess he knew we weren't going to see each other again when I visited him before coming over here," he confessed. "He put up a brave front, pretending that he'd be there when I came back. But he knew. I guess we both did." Rather than embarrass himself by breaking down in front of enlisted soldiers the captain stood up, excused himself, and made for the one stall latrine that served as both a men's and women's room. Not having experienced the loss of either of his own parents, McIntire found himself wondering how the captain knew that he was seeing his father for the last time. Was it a hunch? Or had he fallen prey to an active imagination that tends to conjure up all sorts of horrific and baseless premonitions that seemed to be so common among soldiers faced with service away from their home and families. Perhaps when the officer managed to regain his composure and settle down once more he'd be willing to share his experiences on this matter with him.

The only female and youngest of the group was a private first class who was a single mother of twins. Like McIntire she was a member of the Virginia National Guard who had been mobilized with her Richmond-based unit for this mission. "The girls are doin' just fine," she stated, making no effort to hide her relief over this aspect of her story. "Lordy, they are the fattest, happiest little babies I ever did see. It's my mama. She isn't as young as she used to be. I guess the girls were just too much for her. Drove her straight into the hospital with a nervous breakdown according to my sister." The young servicewoman's easygoing, almost cheerful manner belied the concern gnawing away at her as she sat unable to do anything to aid the people she loved. "My sister has three of her own to worry about and another on the way. She hasn't time to tend to my two. So I'm goin' home to take care of my little babies and Mama till she's well 'nuff to take over again."

The fourth serviceman waiting to continue on with his own sad trek home to tend to a family crisis was the quietest. In fact, the young E-5 infantry sergeant said nothing while his accidental companions shared their tales of woe and exchanged idle chitchat in an effort to wile away the time waiting to find out if they would make the next flight out. Every so often McIntire looked over at the forlorn man, wondering if he was the sort who was too proud to share his concerns lest his emotions get the better of him or if he was just unsociable. From what the Virginian could see, the young sergeant seemed like a nice guy, no different from any of them, just another poor soul stranded in a strange and alien land trying to do a difficult job that no one else was able or willing to do.

Noon came and went without any sign of the hoped-for un-scheduled flight. Only the arrival of the Marine detach-ment broke the monotony that had settled over the corner of the Quonset hut where McIntire and his companions waited. This flurry of activity did not last long. After taking one look around and spotting the gaggle of downcast sol-diers seated in the corner, the Marine officer in charge took his people outside. "If you don't mind," he informed the Air Force sergeant, "we'll wait outside."

When the last of the Marines had left, the staff sergeant from Fort Hood heaved a sigh of relief. "Thank God. This waiting is bad enough without having to put up with a gag-gle of jarheads."

Starved for some relief from the oppressive gloom that permeated their section of the Quonset hut, McIntire glanced at his fellow Guardsman who seemed to have been thinking the same thing. Still, neither commented on Con-ners's parochial attitude concerning the Marines as they re-turned to the stilted conversations they had been sharing with each other until the afternoon flight arrived.

With great expectation all five of the homeward-bound soldiers sat up and turned to watch the Air Force sergeant as she left the Quonset hut and head for operations. "Well, do you think we'll make it?" McIntire ventured in an effort to break the tension that held them in near breathless anticipation.

"God willing," the female private whispered, more by way of a prayer than in response to McIntire.

Neither God nor Air Mobility Command was with all of them that day. Within minutes the female sergeant returned with the bad news. "I am afraid there is only one open slot on this flight."

All eyes were fixed on the female sergeant. By now she was used to this sort of thing, having to go through the same drill on a daily basis. Without further ado she looked down at the clipboard she held at waist level before her and called out the name of the lucky individual who would leave on the next flight. "Sergeant E-5 Louis Pascucci. Gather up your things and follow me."

Without a word the quiet infantryman stood up, grabbed the small canvas bag that comprised the sum total of his baggage, and followed the Air Force sergeant to the counter at the far end of the room. In her wake the remaining four looked at each other before slumping down into their seats. Though no one said a word, McIntire had no doubt that each was thinking the same thing he was: "Why him? My crisis is just as important, my need to get home no less pressing. Why him?"

Unable to hide his disappointment, McIntire cast about in desperation for something to do, something to take his mind off the bitterness that he could feel building up inside. Frustrated, he reached down to his nonregulation gym bag, pulled back one of the side pocket zippers, and pulled an orange out. He had always been a stress eater, a person who sought escape through comfort food. Lacking a handy convenience store, McIntire seized whatever was at hand. Ripping into his orange, he dug his fingernails into the peel as he savagely tore away chucks bit by bit.

Seated across from him with his arms held tightly across his chest, the staff sergeant absentmindedly bit the back of his thumb as he too struggled with the disappointment he felt at not being selected. Only the scent of McIntire's orange stopped him from drawing blood. Ceasing his nervous gnawing, he tucked his right hand under his arm and looked over at the Guardsman. "You wouldn't happen to have another one of those, would you?"

McIntire was so consumed by his own dashed hopes that it took him a moment to realize that the staff sergeant was talking to him. Shaking his head as if casting off the anger that clouded his thoughts, he cleared his mind and looked over to his compatriot in misery. "Yeah, sure." Reaching down a second time he rummaged through the open compartment of his gym bag until his fingers touched upon the paper sack of oranges. After fishing one out, he tossed one across to the staff sergeant with an easy underhanded toss. "One of the locals working for our unit as a translator gave me a whole sack of these this morning before I left Camp Lee. He told me they would be good for my wife, something about how fresh fruit was the best thing a woman could do for her unborn baby."

The sergeant forced a smile as he began to peel away the skin. "I suppose he's got a point. Probably much better than some of the weird stuff my wife wolfed down when she was pregnant."

Upon hearing this, the female private from Richmond snapped out from her own gloomy reflections as she glanced over at McIntire and the sergeant first class. "Now what would you two know about what's good and what's *gooood?*"

For the first time all day McIntire found he was able to crack a smile. "Since this is my first, I'm afraid I'm going to have to plead ignorance on that issue." Then, catching sight of the way the female soldier was eyeing his orange, he reached back into his gym bag and retrieved another. "Here," he offered as he leaned over and handed it to her. "See if this passes muster."

From his seat the captain watched and listened as the enlisted personnel began to chatter as they ate their oranges. When no one bothered to offer him one, he cleared his throat while staring at McIntire with big, droopy eyes. "Ah, if you don't mind, could I have one too? I haven't had a bite to eat all day."

Without hesitation McIntire once more went searching through his gym bag for one of the oranges that Syed had offered him that morning. At the time he had thought nothing of the kind gesture. In fact, now that he thought about it McIntire found himself wondering if he had even bothered to thank the young Palestinian for them. Oh, well, he thought as he popped a wedge into his mouth and began to chew away, I'm sure he'll understand.

No one else responding to a frantic call from home and a request that they return ASAP joined the little covey of soldiers in the corner of the Air Force Quonset hut as they waited to catch a ride on the next hop. And no other aircraft came in until the regularly scheduled evening flight from Ramstein arrived. That left McIntire and his three remaining companions little choice but to cool their heels until morning when the C-17 Globemaster would make its return trip to Germany.

After spending an anxious night in a barracks room set aside for transients, Brian McIntire was awakened from his fitful sleep shortly after oh three hundred hours in the morning. Ignoring a dry raspy throat that began to plague him shortly after midnight, he leaped from the cot he had been provided and quickly dressed. Not trusting a system that defied his best efforts to understand, he was eager to get over to the Quonset hut as soon as possible lest some new and totally unexpected obstacle be thrown in the twisted and tortuous path he found himself traveling.

McIntire quickly found that he wasn't the only one who had opted to skip his normal morning routine in an effort to ensure his place in line. Upon arrival at the lounge where he had spent so much of the previous day he discovered that the others had the same idea. Only when they were sure that they were all signed up for the next flight and that the C-17 would depart on time did any of them pause long enough to assess his own sorry state. When the quartermaster captain became acutely aware of just how scruffy he was, he sheepishly looked around at each of his travel companions and explained that he, like them, wasn't going to risk missing this flight. "I figured that there would be plenty of time," he sheepishly admitted as he ran his hand across the stubble of his face, "to clean up, shave, and sort myself out before we ran into someone who gave a damn about what I look like." He added with a wink and a nod as he tried to ignite a spark of humor even under these most trying of circumstances, "Failing that, if anyone did give me static over my appearance, I figured all I needed to do was whip out my emergency leave orders and lay the best sob story on them I could."

Despite the early hour, an unsettled stomach, and his concern over his wife's condition, McIntire managed to chuckle. "Well, sir, if you ask me all we need to do is present them with a description of what the Air Force fed us last night and I'm sure we'll have no trouble winning the sympathy of even the most hard-core case waiting out there to give us grief."

Rubbing his own stomach, Conners looked at McIntire and made a face. "You too? And all these years I was under the impression that the Air Force was supposed to have the best mess facilities in the Armed Forces."

Unlike the previous day, the female private from Richmond made no effort to add her own comments as she shuffled over to one of the now familiar lounge seats. All she managed was a whispered, halfhearted request after she had settled herself in. "Would someone wake me when it's time to board?" Without waiting for an answer, she closed her eyes and dozed off. Taking their cue from her, McIntire and Conners also returned to the same places they had occupied the day before. Glancing about and seeing that nothing was going to happen for a while, the captain headed for the small latrine. "May as well use this chance to catch up on my personal hygiene."

Without a hint of enthusiasm, Conners nodded. "Go right ahead, sir. Be my guest."

For a while, everything seemed to go well for the four. The flight from Israel to Ramstein Air Base in Germany went without a hitch, taking close to six hours from takeoff to touchdown. During the entire flight none of them said much of anything. Besides suffering from the usual bouts of emotional ups and downs this sort of trip inflicted upon soldiers as they fought their way through the system in response to a family crisis thousands of miles away, all four were suffering from queasy stomachs and headaches. As he had earlier Brian McIntire pretty much passed these symptoms off as being little more than the by-product of nervous anticipation, strange food, and a severely disrupted personal routine. By the time he had deplaned in Ramstein, filed through customs, and endured the obligatory orientation all personnel returning from the Middle East were required to receive before continuing on with the next leg of his trip, McIntire was exhausted. When he ran into Conners in the latrine at Ramstein's passenger terminal he studied his traveling companion for a moment. "Christ, I hope you're feeling better than you look or I feel."

Standing before a sink, Conners tried to effect a smile but found he just didn't have it in him. Instead, he was seized by a sudden and uncontrollable spasm. Grasping the edge of the sink for all he was worth, he bowed his head and threw up.

Whether it was the sight of the bloody vomit that sprayed everything before the forlorn sergeant first class or the stench that filled the room, McIntire found himself unable to hold on to what little he had in his own stomach. Panicking, the former postal worker covered his mouth with his hand, turned toward the bank of commodes, and ran toward the nearest one that was open. He almost made it but not quite before he too began to retch. Unable to think straight any longer, McIntire fell to his knees before the toilet amid the sickening film of vomit he had sprayed over every inch of the stall's interior. Between heaves, he began to sob. "Oh, Jesus, make this stop. I've got to get home. Please make it stop."

But it did not stop.

CHAPTER **21**

The Security Zone, 3rd Battalion of the 176th's Sector

Rather than wandering around throughout the security zone all day, the amber company platoon charged with conducting mounted patrols had the option of stopping from time to time and establishing OPs or observation posts. To be effective these OPs needed to be located on a prominent terrain feature that offered the Guardsmen a clear view of large portions of their assigned patrol sector or selected critical points such as a road junction or a checkpoint. Officially they were designated roving OPs. Jack Horne's men came up with the brilliant idea of turning them into armed picnics.

The story behind this most unmilitary activity sprang from the liberties they were used to taking while performing their duty. Daniel Travers, a man noted throughout the battalion as being a connoisseur of fine wines, was given credit for the idea, though in typical fashion he did nothing to move it along once he had hatched the scheme.

It began on the day Brian McIntire was notified that his wife was in the hospital. After they had dropped him off at the front gate of Camp Lee, the men of third squad found they had little enthusiasm for carrying out that day's patrol. Upon completing a sweep of an area south of Camp Lee during which not a word was uttered in any of the four humvees, Horne ordered Ollie Rendell's squad to set up an OP on a small hill overlooking the Palestinian checkpoint. Once they had circled their Humvees and formed a loose laager with all vehicles facing outward so as to provide them with 360-degree security, the Guardsmen of third squad settled down to a noon meal of MREs. Squatting on the ground next to their vehicles, seated on their hoods, or perched behind the weapons attached to the rooftop ring mount everyone tore into the plastic pouches Alex Faucher had issued to each of them earlier that morning. Never having been a fan of the Army's idea of fast food, Travers found he wasn't able to take another bite. Disgusted, he flung the pouch containing the entrée he had been trying to eat as far as he could. "Damn! That stuff is nasty."

Used to Travers's ceaseless complaining, Ollie Rendell snickered. "Well, if that's the way you feel about the fine fare the first sergeant worked so hard to provide you with, there'll be no seconds for you."

Folding his arms across his chest in a manner more fitting a spoiled three-year-old boy than a twenty-one-year-old man, Travers fumed as some of his squad mates chuckled for the first time since McIntire had been dropped off. "That's okay by me. As far as I'm concerned you can stick your 'fine fair' pouch and all where the sun don't shine. I'll just start bringing my own lunch."

The others continued to munch on their meals, chuckling and trading comments on the subject for a couple of minutes until Ron Weir, who had been giving what Travers said some serious thought suddenly stopped eating, sat upright, and looked over at his squad leader. "You know, Ollie, Danny Boy over there may be on to something." Rising to his feet, Weir scanned the horizon for a few minutes before continuing. "As far as I can tell there isn't a soul that matters who can see what we're doing up when we're occupying these little hilltop OPs."

Sensing that Weir was trying to make a point, Rendell looked around as well before he shrugged. "Yeah, I guess so. So what?"

"So," Weir explained, "the next time we're sent out on

one of these little forays, instead of relying on MREs for lunch we bring our own food."

Catching on, Sam Rainey smiled. "Why not? It wouldn't be any different than what we used to do back home on drill weekends, would it? I mean, hell, even our old company commander used to carry a small grill in the back of his Humvee when we were at Pickett." With everyone shaking their heads in agreement, Weir continued to put forth his idea. "Instead of just sitting here like bumps on a log we can have our own little cookout, a picnic. I'm sure between us we can scrounge something from the cooks, just like we always have."

As the excitement over the idea began to grow others joined in with their own suggestions. "And what we can't weasel out of them," an excited Sean Zukanovic shouted out, "we can buy from the locals."

Turning to their Palestinian translator, Weir flashed a broad smile. "Hey, Syed. Instead of bringing us oranges every day, if we all chip in and made it worth your while do you think you could purchase whatever we need that we can't get from the mess hall?"

Unsettled by this unexpected discussion that he wasn't able to fully follow and his sudden involvement in it, Syed didn't know what else to do but agree. "Why yes, of course. I will do anything you ask. Anything."

Seeing no harm in this sort of thing, Ollie Rendell said nothing as the members of his squad quickly began to hammer out the details of their little scheme and organize themselves. Like others in the chain of command he was already beginning to look for things he could do to alleviate the boredom that would eventually impact on their morale and, in turn, the unit's performance. The sudden and troubling circumstances surrounding Brian McIntire's departure had served to highlight just how quickly morale could drop within his squad. A little thing like this, Rendell reasoned, could go a long way in keeping the men on their toes and spirits up. Without much need to prod Jack Horne, the proposal was unanimously embraced by the entire squad and discussion turned to how best to put this idea into action. By the time they had returned that night, everything, from the pooling of funds to purchasing incidentals, had been finalized.

Anxious to see if their little scheme would work, that night Rendell lobbied Horne for the honor of taking out the next day's midday patrol. Put on guard by the fact that someone was actually volunteering for something, Jack Horne prodded Ollie Rendell as to why he wanted to go back out on patrol. Knowing that his platoon leader would find out about their little scheme sooner or later, Rendell filled him in. Curious to see if Rendell's men could pull their little picnic off, Horne agreed under the stipulation that he go along. As soon as that was settled Horne went to Nathan to request that he lead the midday patrols. Though Nathan suspected that the reason Horne was eager to take out this particular patrol was to ensure that he didn't get stuck with the one his platoon ran between midnight and dawn, Nathan agreed. Having no idea that his people were up to something, Nathan's decision was based upon his own scheduling requirements. By taking out the night patrols, he could maintain his presence in the field while tending to the administrative details of the company during the day.

The presence of their platoon leader during their first armed picnic made no difference to the men of Ollie Rendell's squad since Horne tended to take shenanigans such as this in stride. Having been with the unit during the tenure of Jimmy Preston, its easygoing former commanding officer, Horne was used to this sort of thing. If anything, he found it amusing to watch as Gene Klauss, Don Olkowski, Sam Rainey, and Jerry Slatery went about digging out a little barbecue pit in the center of his platoon's laager while Paul Sucher and Ron Weir laid out the food they had managed to collect on the hood of one of the humvees. "You know, if I didn't know any better, I'd swear that the little stunt the Bedlow Five pulled and this were nothing more than a plot by you guys aimed at getting me in trouble with the old man."

Rendell took his platoon leader by the arm, spun him around, and led him out of the small circle of vehicles. "You know what they say, Jack, see no evil."

Smirking, Horne pretended to look about in every direction except behind him. "See what? I don't see anything!"

"I kinda thought you'd feel that way, sir. Now, how would you like your burger?"

"You know very well I like mine medium well. And tell Ron to take it easy with the ketchup. Not everyone enjoys watching their burger drown in the stuff."

They were in the midst of enjoying their second armed picnic when the call came in from the battalion operations officer for them to drop everything and immediately return to Camp Lee. Those who heard the order let out a collective groan that was quickly taken up by the rest of the squad as soon as word was passed around. Don Olkowski, who was tending the half-finished burgers and hot dogs, called out to Horne. "Hey, Jack, tell 'em we're tracking the head of Mamas or something."

With every pair of eyes on him, Horne figured the least he could do was try. Taking up the radio hand mike, he thought for a moment before responding. "Blue Five Alpha, this is Red Two Six. We are conducting a surveillance of a suspicious group of males one klick southeast of our position, over."

There was a moment of silence after Horne let go of the hand mike's push to talk button. When the radio did spring to life again with a response to his story, the voice that came out of the speakers belonged to that of Captain Hough, the battalion S-3 himself. "Red Two Six, this is Blue Five actual. You will drop whatever it is you're doing and get your butt back here in zero five, out."

It was not the fact that the battalion operations officer himself had responded to his request that concerned Horne. Nor was the fact that he had ended the conversation with an "out," which meant the conversation was over, period. As a sergeant in the Virginia State Police Russell Hough tended to be a bit more gruff than other Guard officers when issuing orders. Rather it was Hough's tone that convinced Horne that there was something amiss, something so serious that it demanded their immediate and unquestioning compliance. Chucking the hand mike onto the seat of the Humvee he turned to face the men of Rendell's squad. "Okay. You heard the man. All I want to see is assholes and elbows. Put out the fire, dump whatever food we can't salvage, and mount up. We're headed for the barn."

Without exception Rendell's men responded with a loud and heartfelt collective groan. The sole exception was Syed, a man who became quite nervous every time the Americans did something unexpected.

He knew there was no reason why he should be concerned about what was going on. None of the Americans showed even the slightest interest in him. As was their habit they were ignoring him. Yet, without even knowing the reason behind this sudden and precipitous return to base, Syed found himself wondering if he needed to worry. Left on his own while Rendell's men glumly went about extinguishing the small cooking fire and packing away the food that could be saved, the young Palestinian slowly made his way to the edge of the circle of vehicles. As the minutes ticked by and the unfounded fears that clouded his thinking began to manifest themselves into real demons he found himself looking about, seeking some sort of covered and concealed escape route. But there was none. As he had on previous days, Jack Horne had selected an elevated spot that provided his people with clear and unobstructed fields of observation and fire, one that also had the advantage of being a perfect defensive position without a gully or bush within a hundred yards of where Syed now stood.

He was still weighing what his chances would be if he found it necessary to flee when Jack Horne ordered Rendell's squad to mount up. Standing at the door of his own vehicle, the American officer caught sight of Syed who had managed to move well outside of the laager. "Hey, Sigh-ed. Let's go. Time's a-wasting. Let's go see what's so hellfire important." Seeing that he had no other option, Syed meekly climbed into the Humvee and began to mumble a prayer under his breath.

Of all the reasons behind the abrupt change in plans that ran through Jack Horne's fertile mind while they made their way back, of all the sort of receptions that he would have to face when they reached Camp Lee, nothing came close to the greeting that the mounted patrol actually met. Even before they made the turnoff the main east-west road onto the access road that led into Camp Lee, Horne saw that something quite out of the ordinary was going on.

Seeing the same thing, Tim Ratliff anticipated Horne's order and slowed the Humvee he was driving well before the sealed gates and fully manned walls. "Oh, shit! There's been another attack."

Horne leaned forward in his seat, shaking his head as he did so. "I don't think so. They would have given the code word for full alert if that had been the case."

"Then how do you explain the gag bags and full turnout, Jack. Everyone I see up there on the wall is decked out as if they were expecting World War Three."

The realization that the personnel at the gate and manning the southern wall of Camp Lee were wearing a full suit of chemical protective clothing as well as their protective masks stunned Horne. "Stop!"

Slamming on the brakes, Ratliff launched everyone forward. Up top Ron Weir, his mouth agape by the scene before him, almost lost his footing and fell. "What the fuck?"

Thinking it was because of the sudden stop, Ratliff looked up through the open hatch. "Sorry 'bout that."

"No," Weir protested. "Not the stop. That," he exclaimed, pointing to his fellow Virginians manning the gate. "What's going on?"

Equally perplexed, Horne sat for a minute thinking, torn between exiting the vehicle and making a call on the radio to the battalion ops center to request clarification of the situation. While he was pondering his best course of action, Ratliff turned toward his platoon leader. "Do you think we should put our masks on?"

Despite the growing concern that Ratliff made no effort to hide, Horne snapped. "How the hell should I know? I haven't a clue as to what's going on. For all I know this could be nothing more than another silly drill."

"Well maybe you should find out before . . ."

"Before what?" Having no idea what Ratliff was suggesting and not waiting to find out the hard way, Jack Horne's anger trumped logic. In a sudden burst of rage he threw open his door and climbed out. His boots had barely hit the ground when one of the guards manning the parapet over the gate called out. "Halt! Don't come any closer."

Astonished, unnerved, and not a little irritated by what was going on Horne stared at the masked Guardsmen for a moment, clutching his fists as he watched them slowly, almost reluctantly bring their weapons to bear on him. For the former schoolteacher this was the last straw. Without any regard for who was listening or the reasons behind this frightening turn of events he began to yell out as loud as he could at his fellow Virginians who seemed intent on keeping him at bay. "What the fuck is going on?"

"Orders, Lieutenant. We've been ordered to keep you and your men isolated." Though the response from the sentinel standing on the wall above the gate was somewhat muffled by the protective masks he wore, the tone of his voice and the message both his words and action conveyed were clear enough to dampen Horne's anger.

"Isolated? Why? What have we done? What's happened?"

Handicapped by all the protective clothing he wore, the soldier at the gate shook his head from side to side in an exaggerated manner. "Don't know. We just have our orders."

Sensing that he wasn't going to get anywhere with the pair of Guardsmen at the gate but not sure of what to do next, Horne turned and eyed the line of Humvees halted behind his. He could see the anxious stares of some of his men through the windshields and guess that they, like he, were having a hard time containing the apprehension that was growing by the second. Seated in the passenger seat of the next Humvee in line behind Horne's, Sergeant Gene Klauss in particular was leaning as far forward as he could, intently staring at his platoon leader with an expression that all but asked, "Well, what are you going to do?" Horne had little doubt that Klauss reflected the same concern shared by every man in the column. It also left little doubt that he expected Horne, the senior man present, to do something quickly.

Reaching through the open door of his Humvee, Horne was grabbing for the radio hand mike when the gate up ahead opened a crack. Through this crack two soldiers slipped out before the gate was slammed shut behind them. Attired in full chemical protective gear like the guards, the pair trudged down the access road to where Horne was standing. The rubber overshoes and the bulky chemical protective clothing coupled with the restricted field of vision the protective mask imposes when worn causes a soldier in full protective gear to walk in a most unnatural and exaggerated manner. Instead of presenting the image of agile combat infantrymen, the two looked and moved more like a cross between circus clowns and stunt doubles for the *Creature from the Black Lagoon.*

Only when they drew near and he could read their names handwritten on strips of tape hastily slapped onto their chemical suits could Horne tell that they were his company commander and first sergeant. Sensing the gravity of the situation, no one made any effort to pay homage to regulations and military courtesy by saluting. Jack Horne simply repeated his unanswered questions minus the expletive. "What is going on?"

Nathan stopped when he was at arm's length. Alex Faucher, who had been trailing his commanding officer off to his left, swung around and stood just back from Nathan's left shoulder and Horne's right. Both men stared intently into Horne's eyes before either spoke as if gathering up their nerve. Finally Nathan broke the oppressive silence. "We have been informed that Specialist Four McIntire has been hospitalized at Ramstein along with three other servicemen he had been traveling with. All four seem to have been stricken with symptoms described as suspicious."

Stunned and feeling more than a bit unnerved by this news Horne looked at Dixon for a moment, then at Faucher. Were it nothing more than food poisoning or the flu Horne knew that he and his third squad would not have been greeted in this manner. As was his habit, his imagination leaped to a worse-case scenario. Still, he wanted to hear his company commander tell him what the men with him and Brian McIntire were facing. "Suspicious symptoms? What sort of symptoms?"

Nathan and Alex Faucher exchanged glances before Nathan responded. When he spoke, his words were painfully deliberate. "We're not sure yet. The folks at Ramstein dealing with this problem were quite vague. But the orders concerning measures to be taken by the parent units of each of the affected service members were not. Nor were the symptoms unit medics are to look out for." At this point Nathan paused as if he needed a moment to muster up the necessary courage to proceed. When he did, he all but blurted out the rest of what he had begun to say. "The battalion's chemical warfare officer and battalion surgeon have come to the conclusion that McIntire has been exposed to some sort of biological agent, most probably hemorrhagic fever. If that's true and that contamination occurred before he left here, there's an outside chance that the rest of the men in his squad were exposed to it as well."

Faucher was quick to add a note of caution. "Jack, Doc says it will be some time before the folks at Ramstein know for sure what exactly it is that Brian is suffering from."

Still reeling from this blow, Horne looked away for a moment as if trying to absorb the impact of what he had just been told. With his head spinning like a punch-drunk fighter in the ring, he managed to steady himself and look back at Nathan. "Hemorrhagic fever? Like Ebola?"

Sensing that his subordinate was having difficulty coming to grips with what he was being told, Nathan reached out with his gloved right hand and took Horne by the arm. Shocked and dismayed by this action Alex Faucher looked at his commanding officer's hand, then at Nathan. The same orders that had put them on alert had specifically stated that no one was to make any physical contact with any personnel within the afflicted personnel's squad or detachment. Faucher understood why Nathan had done what he had. Given another moment or two he most likely would probably have done the same. Still, the fact that his captain had actually done so without knowing what the full consequences of his action meant left Faucher momentarily dumbstruck.

Doing his best to comfort his subordinate, Nathan tried to downplay the severity of a situation that he himself was troubled by. "No one knows anything for sure. I suspect, I hope, everyone is being overly cautious, taking extreme measures to make sure that whatever is going on doesn't get out of hand."

Slowly, Horne regained his senses and was able to focus on what Nathan was saying. "So, what does that mean for my people here?"

Releasing his grip, Nathan stepped back. "First, everyone who is in McIntire's squad as well as other personnel who may have had close and protracted contact with him are going to be decontaminated. Once that has been completed those personnel, mainly yourself and Sergeant Rendell's squad, will be placed in an isolated section of the camp."

"Where will that be?"

"Arrangements have been made to turn the southeastern bastion of the outer wall into a sort of isolation ward," Faucher explained. "Cots, fresh clothing, sleeping bags, and everything you need are being taken to the bunker under the bastion. Food, water, and whatever medicine you need will be brought to you."

Horne listened, then thought about this for a moment. "How long will we need to stay there?"

Again Nathan apprehensively exchanged glances with his first sergeant. "That depends on a lot of things," Nathan finally ventured.

"Such as?"

"Such as what happens to Specialist Four McIntire and the others at Ramstein and whether or not . . ."

Horne bowed his head and raised his hand signaling Nathan to stop. He knew what his commanding officer was about to say, but as if articulating the words would bring bad luck, he had no desire to hear them.

After another long silence Nathan cleared his throat. "If you would gather up your people, Lieutenant Horne, I'll fill them in on what's going on."

Jack Horne glanced over his shoulder at the convoy of Humvees, then back at Nathan. "If you don't mind, Captain, I think it would be better if I did that myself."

Relieved that he would not have to endure that ordeal, Nathan made no effort to argue. "Fine, fine. Once you're ready for decontamination give the battalions ops center a call via radio and we'll get started."

Horne simply shook his head as he turned away and

waved his arm over his head, signaling Ollie Rendell's men to dismount and form on him. Having accomplished what they had set out to do and with nothing more to do there, Nathan and Alex Faucher looked at each other before turning away and heading back toward the gate. Just before reaching it Nathan stopped at a spot already marked out by the battalion chemical warfare officer. Carefully he removed the glove from the hand he had touched Horne with and threw it into a barrel lined with three heavy-duty plastic bags. Within an hour that barrel would be filled with every item of clothing currently being worn by Jack Horne and the men who had been on patrol with him. Those cloths, along with numerous samples taken around Camp Lee, would be whisked away to an American naval support vessel in the Mediterranean Sea to be tested and analyzed. Until the results of those tests came back, all of Camp Lee would be locked down and quarantined from the outside world with third squad isolated and shunned by their own neighbors and friends as the meaning of bioterrorism finally left the realm of theory and added a new and ominous chapter to the battalion's unit history.

CHAPTER **22**

Ramstein Air Base, Germany

The periods of consciousness Brian McIntire was experiencing seemed to be getting shorter and shorter. Just as troubling to him was his inability to make sense of what was going on around him. Everything he saw and heard was strange and so unfamiliar. He had to focus, he told himself as he lay on his back staring up at the ceiling through the crinkled layer of a clear plastic tent that separated him from the world around him.

As he did, each time he came to and opened his eyes, a feat that was becoming harder and harder to perform as time went by, Brian McIntire took stock of himself. He began by sorting as best he could whatever physical sensations he could make out through the drug-induced haze he always seemed to find himself in during these brief lapses of consciousness. Without fail the cold was always the most pronounced sensation. Why he was so cold didn't make any sense to him since he was also sweating, or at least he thought he had been. He could tell he had been sweating because everything his skin touched was wet. It felt as if he were lying in a pool of his own sweat. As a native Virginian he was used to that sort of thing. Back home when the unit went to Pickett for annual training during the summer more often than not they drew barracks that lacked any form of air-conditioning. During their stays there Brian McIntire found that he was never able to escape the wet stickiness that drenched everything his skin touched. Still, the oppressive heat and humidity of a Virginia summer could not explain his current plight. It was cold here, cold and wet. You don't sweat when you're cold.

Then there was the pain and soreness. His chest, his stomach, his back, his throat, everything seemed to hurt. Sometimes the pain was sharp, acute razor-sharp jabs that took his labored breath away. Mostly though it was a dull throbbing collection of unending agony. McIntire attributed the latter to the same drugs that were robbing him of his mental faculties. Whether or not this was a blessing or a curse was difficult to tell since the pain never seemed to fade but his inability to think and reason clearly when he was conscious was keeping him from understanding what had happened to him.

No, McIntire told himself as he teetered on the verge of lapsing back into unconsciousness. It was his confused state of mind, that swilling jumbled collections of dislocated thoughts and sensations that were preventing him from cutting through the haze he found himself in, that was worse. Was he home? he wondered. Had he finally managed to fall asleep during his trying journey home to his wife? Or was this a dream? Had he become so exhausted by his tribulations and worries that he had fallen into the sort of deep, neverending sleep where the rational mind takes a holiday.

That had to be it, he finally concluded when nothing he saw through the clear plastic made sense. Even the pain he thought he was experiencing was unreal, as unreal as the strange images that were flashing before his eyes. They were all part of a really weird dream, a collection of phantoms that belonged to an imaginary world.

Suddenly, it didn't matter who the hooded people staring down at him were or why they were dressed as they were. Untroubled, McIntire closed his eyes once more and turned his fleeting thoughts back to his wife. It will be good to be home once more, he thought. He needed to be there with her, holding her hand and helping her as she embarked upon the greatest adventure of her life, her passage into motherhood. It'll be hard for her, he thought to himself. She is so young, so innocent in so many ways. It will be hard for both of them. It would be best, he finally concluded as he felt himself slipping back into the dark, bottomless abyss of sleep. He needed to rest while he could. There won't be much chance of doing that once the baby arrives. Everything will change. Nothing will ever be the same again.

As Brian McIntire's eyes fluttered shut, the Air Force doctor hovering above him glanced over at the monitor tracking McIntire's erratic vital signs. "He's still with us and as stable as we can keep him. But I'm afraid he's slipping back into unconsciousness."

Unable to contain his frustration, a military intelligence office standing on the other side of McIntire's bed slammed his fist against the steel bed rail he had been leaning over. "Damn it! Can't you keep him awake long enough so I can ask him a few simple questions?"

Already annoyed by the meddling of this officer and an unending stream of others like him, the doctor lashed out at the intelligence officer. "You keep smacking things like that and you'll compromise the seal of your suit."

Suddenly aware of what he had done, the MI officer quickly jerked his gloved hand up before his face to inspect it as well as the tape that sealed it to the Level-A protective suit that encased him. Unused to viewing the world through the lenses of the full facepiece of the self-contained breathing apparatus as well as the clear plastic hood of the suit, it took him a minute to confirm that all was in good order. When he was sure that he had not punctured or ripped anything, he glared at the Air Force physician standing on the other side of the bed. He felt like telling the man to fuck off, but knew that wouldn't do any of them any good. The doctor and his entire staff were just as frustrated by their inability to help the man before them as the intelligence officer was over being unable to ask him any questions.

Peering down at the naked body of Brian McIntire through all the layers of protection that separated the two men, the intelligence officer quickly concluded that in a few more hours none of them would be able to do their job. Not only was blood now flowing freely out of every orifice of McIntire's body, the rash that had been spreading across his chest and abdomen was now erupting into a sea of pustules that sprang up and spewed forth a bloody discharge like a tiny volcano. With his anger mollified by the sight of the poor wretch before him, the intelligence officer looked back over at the doctor. "How long before he goes under for good?"

The doctor didn't answer right away. Instead, he assessed the condition of his patient and considered everything he knew and suspected about the man's condition. Finally, he sighed. "Not long. Judging from the accelerated pace at which the virus seems to have incubated and manifested into a full-blown case, I would venture to say twelve hours, twenty-four at the most."

"That's not much time."

Glancing up at the intelligence officer, the Air Force doctor glared. "I dare say it will be long enough for this poor bastard to suffer a hell I can't even imagine."

Unable to reply, the intelligence officer turned away from Brian McIntire's bed and made his way toward the decon chamber. If he could not get the answers he needed from the dying man firsthand, perhaps the pathologists would provide him with the information he was desperately pursuing. Until then, he'd need to report this to his superiors so that they could take whatever actions they needed to in order to keep this from happening to anyone else, if that was still possible.

The Security Zone, 3rd Battalion of the 176th's Sector

No one was asleep in the crowded bunker of the southeastern bastion when the phone tucked under Jack Horne's cot rang. Reaching over the side of his cot, he felt around with his fingers until he found it. No one stirred, but all listened as Horne answered it. "Lieutenant Horne speaking." He listened for a moment, then slowly replaced the receiver on the cradle without saying another word. Instead, he slowly sat up and looked around before he swung his sock-clad feet onto the floor. Slowly he pulled on his pants and boots without lacing them. Then he just sat there on his cot for the longest time, staring vacantly off into the darkness as if wondering what to do next.

Sensing that something was wrong, Ollie Rendell propped himself up with his right hand and looked across the narrow space that separated his cot from his platoon leader's. Though he had his suspicions, he still needed to ask. "What was that about?"

Only when he was sure that he could speak without breaking down, Jack Horne answered in a hushed whisper. "Brian is dead."

Rendell did not ask how he had died or when. No doubt he would learn all those particulars soon enough. For the moment just knowing that one of their own, a man who was more than a squad mate and a neighbor, was gone was quite enough to absorb.

Unable to stand the oppressive atmosphere within the bunker, Jack Horne finally got to his feet and began to pick his way through the maze of tightly packed cots toward the ladder that led up to the fighting platform above. As he rose through the narrow opening the cool night air cut like a knife through the thin T-shirt he wore. Yet he hardly felt it. At that moment he didn't really feel anything other than an all-consuming heartfelt sorrow unlike any that he had ever experienced before in his life.

Making his way over to the eastern parapet Horne leaned against it, planting his forearms on the top layer of sandbags while clasping his two hands together. He gazed up at the moonlit night for a moment before bowing his head until his forehead came to rest upon his cupped hands. Without giving what he was doing any thought, he began to pray. He prayed for the soul of his departed friend and comrade. He prayed that the men gathered together below would make it through the night. He prayed that the Lord would watch over Brian's wife and find a way of seeing her through the twin ordeals she would now have to face alone. Mostly, he prayed that he would never again have to suffer the loss of another one of his men, not like this.

When he had finished and once more turned to face the clear night sky, he noticed that he wasn't alone. Standing next to him at the parapet was Ollie Rendell. He was gazing up at the stars as if lost in his own thoughts. Not wanting to speak, Jack Horne turned his eyes away, peering off into the distance at the hill where the Crusader castle sat silhouetted against the cold night sky. In the days since their arrival he had spent many an hour on the eastern wall studying that castle, doing his best to recall everything he had learned about medieval fortifications back in college. That ancient ruin proved to be a godsend to him, a means of escaping the cramped and harried confines of Camp Lee and giving his harried mind something to think about other than the daily grind that his new lifestyle entailed. Tonight, however, the sight of that forlorn structure could do nothing to assuage his anguish or provide him with an escape from his cares and troubles.

"Mind if I join you two?"

Lost in their own very private thoughts, Ron Weir's voice startled Jack Horne and Ollie Rendell. Both men turned toward the opening in the roof of the bunker. Sensing that he had screwed up, Weir paused a moment to apologize. "Sorry, I didn't mean . . ."

After collecting his wits, Jack Horne raised his hand.

"No need to. I don't think any of us will be getting much sleep tonight."

Joining the pair at the wall, Weir looked out at the barren landscape for several minutes before straightening up and turning around. After he was sure that they were the only three up there, he faced Horne. "Where's Syed?"

Rendell continued to study the stars as he replied, "Still in his cot I suppose."

"His cot's next to mine. He's not there."

"Then maybe he's in the corner of the bunker behind the curtain, taking a dump in that nifty little latrine they rigged for us."

With growing concern, Weir shook his head. "I took a leak there before I came up here. If he was up and around, we would have bumped into each other."

It took longer than it should have for him to absorb what Weir was saying. But when the import of his observations became clear to him, Jack Horne jumped upright and turned to Weir, then Rendell. "Dear God in heaven! The little shit's gone over the wall!" He shouted, as one the three Guardsmen broke from the wall and made for the ladder.

In the corner of the battalion's operations center Charles Lanston, Russ Hough, Terrance Putnam, and Nathan Dixon sat about on folding chairs in a tight little circle drinking coffee and speculating on how best to deal with the myriad of problems they would soon be facing. None of them paid any heed to the ringing of the phone across the room. The operations sergeant on duty was there to answer it. They simply continued to sip coffee and chat in low, hushed voices until the sergeant leaned back in his chair, placed his hand over the receiver, and called out to Hough. "Sir, it's Lieutenant Horne. He says that Palestinian translator that was with them isn't there anymore."

Stunned, the four officers looked at each other before Hough asked the obvious. "What?"

"I say again, Lieutenant Horne says that the Palestinian translator that was with them in isolation at the southeastern bastion is gone, vanished, disappeared. He doesn't know where he is."

Leaping to their feet, all four made a mad dash for the phone. Russ Hough got there first, snatching the proffered receiver out of his sergeant's hand. "Jack, are you sure?"

Even as his battalion operations officer was listening to Horne's response, Lanston began issuing orders to Nathan. "Have your ready reaction force mount up and stand by to move out."

Hough placed a finger in his left ear so he could hear Horne's response to the questions he continued to pepper the platoon leader with. "How long do you think he's been gone? When did you see him last? Did he say anything to anyone?"

Nathan listened as best he could to both Hough and Lanston while reaching for another phone to call down to his company. "I'll have another platoon roused in case we need it."

Feeling left out, Terrance Putnam took Lanston's arm. "What can I do, sir?"

"Call the headquarters company orderly room. Have them wake the entire operations staff as well as the scout platoon."

By this time Hough was finished with Horne. The other men in the ops center went silent as they turned to him to hear what he had to say. "Jack said that the Palestinian could not have been gone for more than a half hour."

Lanston glanced over at Nathan as he spoke to Hough. "Is he armed?"

Nathan answered without hesitation. "There were no weapons in the bunker. Everything Horne's people had with them was taken away during the decon."

Moving over to the oversized map posted on the wall of the ops center, Hough placed his finger where the southeastern bastion of Camp Lee stood. "No doubt he's headed east. The question is whether he's going to make for the Palestinian checkpoint or try to slip under the wire."

Nathan considered the problem for a moment. "We don't have much time. If Syed was hustling, he could be at the wire by now." Then, facing Lanston, he offered up his solution. "With your permission I'd like to have Terry here head out with one of the Humvees of the ready reaction force and make for the Palestinian checkpoint just in case Syed took off down the road and headed that way. I'll dispatch a second Humvee to the northeast till it hits the fence. From there it'll work its way south along the eastern boundary. The rest of the reaction force will move out with me. We'll fan out and slowly make our way crosscountry due east from the southeastern bastion till we hit the fence. If we haven't found the little shit by then I'll send one of my vehicles south toward Captain Putnam's position and one north until it runs into the northernmost detachment. If he's still missing and we haven't seen anything to indicate that he's managed to wiggle his way through the wire, I'll continue to patrol the fence with that platoon while the follow-on force crisscrosses the area between Camp Lee and the eastern boundary fence."

Hough nodded. "I'll take charge of that force."

Lanston was about to disagree, instinctively preferring to keep his operations officer at his side to run things from the ops center. Then he thought better. As a sergeant in the Virginia State Police Russ Hough was the best man for that particular job. "Okay. I'll run things from here. All units will operate on the battalion command net, secure mod. Now get moving while I let brigade know what's going on."

Then, as an afterthought the Guard battalion commander raised his hand to signal his subordinates to hold on a moment. "Gentlemen, I haven't a clue as to what this

man did or what he knows. He may not know a thing in regards to what happened to our man. He may be running for
no other reason than he's afraid that we're going to suspect
him simply because he's an Arab. Be that as it may, it's important that you bring him back alive. Is that clear?"

When no one else spoke, Nathan looked at Hough and
Putnam. "We move out from the front of my company orderly room in two minutes." With that, the three officers
broke from the small huddle and scrambled out of the operations center, leaving their battalion commander behind
to perform what had to have been the most difficult part of
their hastily conceived plan.

Even before he had managed to cover half the distance to
the eastern fence, Syed realized that he had made a terrible
mistake. He had done nothing wrong. Nor did he have anything to hide. During the decontamination he had suffered
through with the Americans he had been on patrol with no
one had treated him any differently. They suspected nothing, for he had given them no reason to suspect him. Only
after he had made good his escape had he come to see that
his decision to run had been both foolish and unwise in
every way he could imagine. Now the Americans would
have little choice but to conclude that he had done something wrong. Whatever trust he had managed to build with
them was gone, thrown away by him.

Yet as serious as any consequences he might have to pay
should the Americans manage to catch him, nothing they
could do would equal the wrath that would befall him and
his family if his PLA superiors found out he had left the
Americans without any justification. As he picked his way
across the rocky landscape toward the twin fences that he
would have to find a way through, Syed had no doubt what
would happen to him if anyone found out that he had fled
without cause. Any safety he did manage to find would be
short-lived and illusory. One simply didn't walk away from

the PLA. Die for it, yes. But desert its ranks? To do so was akin to suicide, death without honor or redemption. His only salvation would be to lie, to create some sort of story that would explain why he had no choice but to run when he did.

Syed was mentally piecing together a tale he could spin when he heard the sound of a Humvee behind him. Glancing over his shoulder he tried to determine where the noise was coming from. When he saw no headlights, he quickly came to the conclusion that the vehicle he was looking for couldn't be behind him at all. It had to be down on the road to his right. It was the night air. It was playing tricks on him. Reminding himself that he would need to pay more attention to what he was doing, Syed set aside the fable he needed to fabricate for Hammed's benefit and instead turned his full attention to making it to and through the eastern fence.

Perched on the front edge of the Humvee's passenger seat with a set of night-vision goggles pressed up against his face, Alex Faucher slowly scanned the landscape before him. When his commanding officer's Humvee appeared within his field of vision off to his right he knew he had completed a full circuit. Behind him Barry Lasner stood upright in the roof hatch doing the same. Suspecting that their quarry was somehow involved in what had happened to Brian McIntire, both men found themselves fighting the urge to push their driver to go faster. No doubt they would have done so long ago if Nathan Dixon had not stressed in his briefing to them the need to maintain a slow, steady pace while advancing toward the eastern fence. "By keeping our speed down we'll reduce our own noise signature as well as affording us all the opportunity to conduct a more thorough sweep of the area." The logic of his orders did little to allay the desire to press forward as quickly as they could.

Finishing a 180-degree sweep of the ground up ahead, Lasner called out to Faucher in a voice just loud enough to be heard over the Humvee's engine. "Not a sign of him, Alex. Nothing." Without pausing his own search Faucher acknowledged Lasner with little more than a crisp "Roger."

Nathan's Humvee was within a few hundred meters of the eastern fence when Staff Sergeant David Erickson, riding topside in his commanding officer's Humvee, tapped Nathan on the shoulder with his right boot. "Target ahead at ten o'clock."

Reaching over, Nathan lay his left hand on his driver's arm and told him to slow down even as he peered off in the direction Erickson had indicated. "I've got him. Driver, left just a hair." When the driver had finished bringing the vehicle about until the lone figure was dead ahead Nathan ordered his driver to hold that heading. Seizing the radio hand mike, he made a net call. "All stations this net. This is Alpha Six. I have the target in sight. Alpha Seven, he should be at your two o'clock."

Both Faucher and Lasner swung about to their right. When he saw the bright green image of a man walking east, Faucher reported his sighting. "Roger that Six. I see him."

From somewhere northeast of them Terrance Putnam called in. "This is Rebel Four. I can see Alpha Seven but I cannot see the mark, over."

Throwing aside proper radio-telephone procedures, Nathan began to orchestrate the convergence of the three humvees. "Terry, keep moving south along the fence. Be ready to cut the bastard off if he makes a run for it. Seven, stay behind and to the left of him as you close. I'll stay to the right. Don't give him any place to go. On my order, turn on your headlights."

Rather than growing fainter, the distinctive growl of a Humvee's engine seemed to be growing louder. Even more troubling to Syed was the fact that no matter which way he turned, the sound did not seem to diminish. It was as if he were surrounded by American vehicles. Sensing that something was very wrong and that his chances of escaping were fast slipping away, he decided to toss all caution aside and make a break for the fence. It wasn't far now. It couldn't be. A quick dash, he told himself, and he'd be there.

Unable to hold back his excitement, Nathan mashed the push to talk button on his radio. "He's spotted us. Hit your headlights now!"

In an instant the darkness of the security zone was pierced by the glare of headlights from two Humvees. Caught in their crossed beams Syed broke into a dead run. He hadn't gone more than a few meters, however, when another Humvee that had been creeping along the fence line swung about and flashed its headlights on him. Stunned by the unexpected appearance of the Americans and dazzled by the brightness of the high beams bathing him in a flood of light, Syed came to a dead stop as the trio of vehicles roared toward him, stopping only when they were inches from colliding into each other. Resigned to his fate, the young Palestinian dropped to his knees and buried his face in his hands.

Catching Syed proved to be easier than deciding what to do with him. Both Nathan and Faucher had dismounted and walked up to Syed with their weapons trained on him before they realized that neither of them had their protective masks on. When it dawned upon him what he was doing, Nathan stopped short and yelled over to Faucher. "Hold it, First Sergeant. He might be contagious."

Taking a quick step back, Faucher glanced over at his commanding officer. "If he is, how the hell do we get him back without putting ourselves in the hole?"

A bit slower than the others, Terrance Putnam heard Faucher's question as he climbed out of his Humvee. Remaining next to his vehicle, he thought for a moment. "Hey, Nate. Have the little shit sit on the hood of your Humvee. Your man up top on the cal .50 can cover him from behind. I'll lead off and have my machine gunner spin his weapon around and train it on him as well."

Nathan thought about this a moment before he agreed. "Putt, we're going to be really close. Even if your man manages to hit him dead on, his caliber .50 slug would sail on through Syed as well as my windshield. So make sure your gunner knows he isn't to fire unless Syed does manage to hop off my Humvee and make a run for it."

Despite the nature of the problems they had been forced to deal with all day, Faucher couldn't help but snicker as he listened to the two officers discuss what they would need to do in the event Syed ran again. "You hear that, boy? There's going to be a pair of M-2s trained on you the whole way back. I have no idea what you did or what you think you did. But to be honest, at this moment I really don't give a hoot one way or the other whether you live or die. So unless you're in a real hurry to be one with Allah, I'd advise you to sit tight and don't try anything, 'cause nobody here is going to give popping you a second thought."

Seeing no need to expand upon what Faucher had just told him, Nathan motioned to Syed to get on his feet and move to his Humvee. When everyone was mounted and Syed was on the hood of his vehicle, Nathan gave the order to move out toward the road where Russ Hough's Humvee would join them.

CHAPTER **23**

Camp Lee

When they reached Camp Lee Terrance Putnam's vehicle was directed toward the northeastern bastion. The covey of Humvees, with Syed seated atop the hood of Nathan's, followed. At the entrance to the bunker under the northeastern bastion they were met by Lanston, Jeff Reed, the battalion intelligence officer, and half a dozen armed guards. While the guards hustled Syed into the bunker, Lanston and Reed waited off to one side for Nathan, Hough, Putnam, and Faucher to dismount and join them before Lanston began to update them on what had transpired while they were out hunting the young Palestinian. "We've been bombarded with a slew of messages from the CDC in Atlanta and the Army Chemical Warfare people at Fort Dietrick in Maryland. Both seem to think that we're in the clear here."

As relieved as Alex Faucher was by this news, he kept his exuberance in check. "Does that include Ollie's people and Jack?"

Lanston nodded. "Everyone."

Nathan didn't allow his first sergeant much time to celebrate this minor triumph before asking the next logical question. "Do they know what killed McIntire?"

"While they cannot be one hundred percent sure until further tests are run they're of the opinion that it was a hemorrhagic fever." As he spoke, Nathan noted that Jeff Reed was being quite deliberate with his choice of words. "To be more specific, the folks at the CDC seem to think it's Marburg."

"They think?"

Reed looked at Nathan a moment, then he glanced about to make sure that no one outside their small circle could hear them. "Brian McIntire and the others with him had all the classic symptoms associated with Marburg. The only problem is the speed with which it took them. The normal incubation period for Marburg is five to ten days during which the symptoms manifest themselves. Once it has developed into a full-blown case the morbidity rate, even with immediate hospitalization, is twenty-five to thirty percent. But that didn't happen in any of the cases at Ramstein. From the first sign of trouble till Brian's death the whole process took two days. And of the three who were with him, none survived."

"Which means?"

Again Reed hesitated, looking over at Lanston as if he were seeking permission to speak. While he understood the need to maintain a tight lid on what they had been told, Lanston also appreciated the alarm not telling Nathan and Faucher would engender. "A follow-on message from Fort Dietrick indicates that McIntire was killed with a refined strain of the virus, one that had been weaponized."

Faucher was stunned. "A biological weapon? Brian was killed with a biological weapon? How?"

Lanston hesitated before answering, peering over his shoulder at the entrance of the northeastern bastion a moment before giving Reed a nod. Ever the diligent intelligence officer, Reed was far more familiar with what was going on thanks to some back-channel calls he had made to friends at the Guard Bureau in Washington, D.C. "Unlike Ebola, Marburg is more stable when stored and is less susceptible to environmental factors, making it ideal for weaponization. The former Soviet Union discovered this and conducted extensive experiments with Marburg at their biowarfare facility at Stepnogorsk in Kazakhstan. By 1990, they had succeeded in producing a virus that did not respond to any known treatment and was so potent that a single milliliter of the virus contained billions of contagious particles, each capable of infecting a full-grown man."

Alex Faucher stifled the urge to gasp. A billion doses of a germ that killed within days, without discrimination, without hesitation, a germ that Brian McIntire would have carried back to Bedlow, Virginia.

Nathan absorbed the news without flinching. "Is there a connection between the old Soviet biowarfare program and this case?"

Reed shook his head. "A straight line? No, probably not. But here is what we do know for sure. Beginning in 1981 the Soviet Union began to produce ICBM warheads filled with weapons-grade biological agents. They stored them at four locations, one of which was Stepnogorsk. They were still there when the USSR broke up and Kazakhstan became an independent nation, one with a predominantly Muslim population."

This was all Nathan, Putnam, and Alex Faucher had to hear. Reed nodded. "Yeah, you guessed it. Like so many other elements within the Red Army, security at its biowarfare facilities became something of a joke after the breakup. Unemployed scientists, lab techs, and security personnel were aggressively courted by some of the world's more nefarious characters, to include the mother of all assholes, Saddam Hussein, who did more than simply send checks to the families of suicide bombers."

There was a moment of silence as the four men who had gone out to capture Syed finished connecting the dots Jeff Reed had so carefully laid before them. Inevitably, all eyes turned to the entrance of the bunker now guarded by a pair of grim-faced Guardsmen. Like Nathan, Putnam lacked the strong bond between Brian McIntire that the others in their small circle had. Their homes, their families, their friends and neighbors had not been endangered in the same manner that the others they were with had been. And both Nathan and Terrance Putnam were professional combat arms officers, men who had spent their entire adult lives conditioning themselves and their minds to deal with the unthinkable with unflinching logic that was as cold and impersonal as their questions and responses were. So while the others in this impromptu gathering struggled to come to terms with this horror and sort out their emotions, Putnam got right to the heart of the issue at hand. "So what are we looking at? Is there a connection between a bioterrorist plot and that little shit in there?"

Lanston nodded. "We're hoping he'll help us sort that out."

Like Putnam, Nathan concentrated on the practical issues they faced. "How do we go about 'encouraging' him to talk. As far as we know he's innocent."

"Innocent men don't run like that," Hough countered.

"That may be true in Virginia where the people are used to living under the rule of law," Nathan pointed out to the amazement of everyone gathered about.

Still reeling from everything that had happened in the last twenty-four hours, Alex Faucher stared at his company commander. "Are you defending him?"

Taken aback by his first sergeant's rebuke, it took Nathan a moment to reply. "Not at all, First Sergeant. It's just that the Palestinians have been conditioned to fear people like us. They've been living in a region torn by conflict for so long that it would be natural for him to assume the worse."

Unable to contain his rage and forgetting who he was speaking to, Faucher planted his fists on his hips and spun around to confront Nathan. "Well excuse me, Captain, if I don't get all choked up and teary-eyed over Syed's unfortunate childhood."

Sensing that things were getting way out of hand, Lanston grabbed Faucher's arm and jerked him away. "At ease, First Sergeant! Captain Dixon wasn't trying to defend the Palestinian."

Faucher glared at Lanston for a moment before pulling back, both physically and emotionally.

Anxious to do what he could to defuse the situation, Putnam sought to get back to the matter at hand. "Who's going to question him?"

Relieved that an unpleasant confrontation was avoided, Reed took up Putnam's question. "We were talking about that while waiting for you guys to return. While the CDC thinks we're in the clear vis-à-vis an outbreak, they want to be one hundred percent sure. While they've told us we can dispense with the protective clothing and such, just to be sure the camp-wide quarantine remains in effect until further notice. This means that it will be some time before an interrogation team from division can be brought in."

Russ Hough looked over at Lanston. "We don't need anyone from the outside to handle that. Let me be the first to offer my considerable experience."

"I was considering that," Lanston admitted, "but I'm not sure I want to do that. First off, there's something to what Nathan tried to point out to us."

Still smarting from what he took as a reprimand, Faucher stared at Lanston but said nothing.

"We don't really know these people," Lanston continued, ignoring Faucher as he responded to Russ Hough. "Your experience with our homegrown thugs may not do us any good."

Hough shrugged. "Well, Colonel, I'm ready to give it a shot."

Sensing that his commanding officer was seeking input, Nathan looked around at the small gathering. "What about our Israeli translator?"

Nathan's response puzzled Jeff Reed. "Granted, he speaks the language and knows a hell of a lot more about the Palestinians than all of us combined, but what makes you think a former yeshiva student can do a better job interrogating the Palestinian than a Virginia state trooper?"

Rolling his eyes, Nathan scoffed at Reed's naiveté. "Oh, please. Do you really think he's actually a yeshiva student? Who handled recruitment of our Israeli translators? The Israelis. You do the math."

Reed thought about it for a moment, then nodded. "I see your point. Is he in the camp?"

"He was with B Company at the checkpoint and returned with them when the order to pull everyone in was issued," Hough replied. "So I imagine that he's still here."

"Well then," Hough concluded when no one made any effort to argue down Nathan's suggestion, "let's find out what the Talmud says about interrogating suspects."

Avner Navon didn't do the actual interrogation. After a halfhearted effort to feign ignorance, he finally admitted that he was in fact working for the Israeli government. Though he didn't admit that his contacts were Mossad, he didn't need to, especially after he offered to contact people he knew who were quite good "at that sort of thing."

None of Avner's "friends" seemed to have any qualms about breaking the quarantine and entering Camp Lee. Brought to Camp Lee aboard a helicopter provided by the Israeli Army, the three experts wasted no time getting to it. The only thing they asked was that no Americans be present during their interrogation. "Our methods," the senior Israeli explained to Lanston, "are a bit different than what your people may be used to." They even asked that the pair of guards stationed at the entrance of the bunker be removed. Uneasy with this, Lanston insisted that they remain, but agreed to the Israeli's request that they wear earplugs while the interrogation was being conducted.

It was just after dawn when the trio of Israeli specialists accompanied by Avner emerged from the bunker and headed for the battalion ops center where Lanston, Hough, Nathan, Putnam, Reed, and Faucher had adjourned to await the results. Since Jack Horne and Matt Garver had spent so much more time with the Palestinian during the preceding forty-eight hours, they had been called to the battalion command post to see if they could add anything to what the Israelis found out when they delivered their report to Lanston.

Upon entering the room the senior Israeli rep dispensed with the usual social niceties as he seized an unoccupied chair and sat on it backward facing the circle of anxious Americans. With the briefest of preambles he launched into his briefing. "My name is Levy, Matan Levy. The man you have here is a member of the PLA, the Palestinian Liberation Army. It is an organization that emerged in the past year as one of the more radical terrorist organizations, a group whose sole purpose in life is to make sure that the peace accord your government has worked so hard to cobble together does not succeed."

As he spoke the Americans listening could not miss the cynical tone the Israeli used when mentioning the word "peace." "We think your man was personally recruited by a character named Hammed Kamel."

Having spent years dealing with this sort of situation while serving as a state trooper, Russ Hough found he could not keep himself from interrogating the interrogators. "You think? Or you know?"

Stunned by being questioned in this manner, Levy gave Hough a hard look, one which the state trooper turned ops officer returned without batting an eye. Coming to the realization that he was up against a man that was every bit as self-assured and determined as he was, Levy relented. "Hammed Kamel took over management of the experimental farm just east of here in the fall of 2003. At first no one paid much attention to this. Since we saw no change in the day-to-day operations of the experimental farm, it was decided to keep an eye on him using the same people and techniques we were already using to monitor the farm's activities. That was how we learned that your Palestinian, the one who calls himself Syed, paid a visit to the experimental farm on the hill just to the east of here every morning before reporting for duty as a translator for you. About a week ago they began to give him bags of oranges to pass out to your soldiers. The little shit swears they were meant to be nothing more than gifts, a ploy meant to endear him to you. The man who gave him those orders was Kamel."

Impatiently Hough twisted about in his seat. "What's so important about this Kamel character?" Hough pressed.

While it was quite childish of him given the circumstances that caused him to be here and what he had just learned, Levy couldn't help but be pleased that he had managed to irritate the American. Making no effort to conceal a hint of a smirk, Levy went on to explain. "It is important, my friend, because Hammed Kamel might very well be a man who used to go by the name of Hassan Fadyl, a viral biologist who once taught at the University of Baghdad. He also did some interesting research for Saddam Hussein's biological warfare program."

This single sentence, delivered in such a casual matter-of-fact manner, destroyed any hope the assembled Americans had been holding on to that Brian McIntire's death was nothing more than an unfortunate incident, a single chance event as far as the Virginians were concerned.

Ignoring his hosts' stunned expressions the Israeli pressed on. "We knew Fadyl survived the war in 2003, that he managed to flee Iraq just before it fell to the Americans. We just didn't know where. Just as your CIA had difficulty sorting out where all of Saddam's top people went, our efforts to track Fadyl and others like him were frustrated by a web of security that puts our efforts to protect some of my nation's special projects to shame. It was rumored that Hammed Kamel and Fadyl might be one in the same, but there was never any evidence to connect the two. That is," Levy added after a brief pause, "until now."

Stopping a moment to take a cup of coffee offered by one of Russ Hough's assistant ops officers, Levy went on to detail what he had learned from his interrogation of Syed and information he was privy to that the Americans around him knew nothing about. "I now believe that

Hammed Kamel and Hassan Fadyl are in fact one in the same based on what your Palestinian told me and what happened to your man who died in Germany. It all makes sense. The biological agent, a strain of the Marburg fever, is exactly the same thing Fadyl was working on in Iraq." As he paused to take a sip of his coffee, the Israeli watched the faces of the Americans out of the corner of his eyes. The stunned expressions on their faces were no different than the one he and his fellow Israelis had affected not more than an hour before when they discovered the true identity of the man who had been running the experimental farm for years under their very noses.

"If that is true," the senior Israeli continued, "we cannot discount the very real possibility that he is responsible for the death of your man."

Reed shook his head. "Then that means that farm up there isn't a farm at all."

The Israeli shrugged. "Perhaps. You could be right about that, but I don't think so."

For the first time, Hough detected a hint of doubt in Levy's voice. "You're not sure, are you?"

"I've been working this region since before the Europeans took over the old farm that was there. Together with my friends we kept tabs on what was going on up there as it was converted into a research facility," Levy explained. "I have personally been through every one of the buildings in that compound myself posing as a visiting scientist. They don't have the proper equipment or sufficient space to conduct the sort of work that I have been told is necessary to develop a weapon like the one that killed your people. There's got to be another facility, someplace we don't know about where Kamel is doing his weapons research."

Jack Horne, who had been listening to all of this, cleared his throat in an effort to gain the Israeli's attention. When the Mossad officer looked over at him, Horne started to speak, but then stopped as he took a moment to glance over at Lanston as if seeking permission to speak. Sensing what was afoot Lanston waved him on. "Jack, if you have something to add, this is the time to do it. That's why you're here."

"Mr. Levy," he stated as he began once more to cautiously address the Israeli, "what about the subterranean chambers beneath the old castle, the ones that run from the northeastern keep all the way to the sally port in the southern wall? Why couldn't this Kamel fellow use them to do his work?"

Dumbfounded, the Israeli took a moment to look at Horne before answering. "There is nothing under that castle. And the castle's sally port was part of the northern wall. It was buried when the northeastern keep collapsed. Everyone who knows anything about the history of that place knows this."

"No," Horne countered without a hint of doubt. "I understand that's what everyone thinks, but it just isn't so."

Sensing that there was something important going on here, Lanston raised his hand. "Jack, I'm afraid you've lost us. Back up some and tell me how it is that you know so much about a place you've never visited?"

Russ Hough nodded. "Yes, please. And do pray tell us how it is you know more than a man whose job it is to know everything there is about everyone and everything that goes on there?"

For the next few minutes everyone in the small circle listened as Jack Horne told them about a professor he had taken some courses from who was an expert in medieval fortifications. "His name is Dr. Theodore Kinkade. If you ever met him you would swear that he was the last living Templar knight."

"That's all very interesting," Levy sneered, "but unimportant at the moment."

Ignoring the Israeli's incredulity, Horne continued. "His claim to fame was that he carried out the most extensive work on the very castle that sits over on the hill to our east before the Intifada and other troubles put an end to that sort of thing. Shortly after we arrived here I sent him an e-mail and told him where we were in the hope that his knowledge of the area might be of benefit to us. During our exchange of e-mails, in his excitement he told me all about the place and the work he carried out there. He was even kind enough to share his private notes and diagrams of the castle with me, information that he has never published hoping that one day he would be free to return and finish the work he had started. One of the more interesting items he revealed to me during that exchange was the fact that there are a series of chambers under the castle itself."

The Mossad agent was unimpressed. "We know about your professor and the work he did here. But I am afraid he is wrong about the castle. In eight hundred years no one has ever found any subterranean chambers."

More confident now, Horne straightened up in his chair. "That's because they didn't know where to look. Kinkade was something of a fanatic when it came to doing research. He wasted no effort when it came to tracking down information about a subject he was researching. In his preliminary workup on the castle he stumbled upon the story of a German officer, a Major von Ostermann, who served as an advisor to the Turks during World War One here in Palestine. Apparently he was quite an amateur archaeologist, a man who spent more time collecting rare manuscripts on the castles of the region than he did advising the Turks. Kinkade located Ostermann's private collection during one of his sabbaticals in Europe the year before he made his first trip to the castle. It seems one of them was written by the Muslim general who laid siege to the castle. Kinkade spent months translating it himself. In the process of doing so he came across what he believed was the only full description of the place that survived the siege."

"This professor of yours, does he mention where Kamel's lab is?" the Israeli asked, making no effort to hide the sarcasm he felt at having his knowledge questioned in this way by a young American officer.

Though it was becoming more and more difficult to do so, Horne ignored the Israeli's snide remarks. "The notes Kinkade sent me mentioned that when he started his research, he was surprised to discover that everyone was under the impression that the sally port was part of the northern wall. He believes archaeologists who came here centuries after the event left the site with that impression because none of them could find a sally port. He thinks they assumed it was buried when the northern wall and the northeastern keep collapsed when the castle fell to the Muslim attackers. But according to the description in Ostermann's manuscript that's flat-out wrong. It's actually located in the southern wall, right where that farm compound is. He also learned that no one knew about the underground chambers, which made sense since the French knight who built this castle wanted to keep their existence a secret. It seems that when he was in the process of building the place he stumbled upon a network of caves quite by accident, caves that even the locals who were here at the time knew nothing about. He realized the value of this find right off and decided to turn those caves into a vast underground storage complex where the castle's garrison could maintain the vast quantities of supplies they would need to hold them over during a siege. It also gave the French knights who occupied the castle a handy place to keep their stock of wine safe from the ravages of the summer heat."

"How did the Muslim general find out about these underground chambers? And why did he keep knowledge of this a secret after the fall of the castle?" Hough asked in an effort to keep Levy from irritating Horne any more than he already had.

"It seems one of the Christian knights was captured during an attack against their besiegers launched from the castle through the sally port. He told the Muslims about the underground chambers while he was being interrogated." Pausing, Horne looked over at Levy. "I can only guess he gave in since the Muslims used techniques that I imagine some folks still find popular."

Sensing the growing tension between the two, it was now Lanston's turn to clear his throat in an effort to get everyone's attention. "Jack," he stated in the sort of voice that conveyed to him and everyone else in the small circle that he would not tolerate any more of the petty bickering that had been going on, "keep your eye on the ball."

Horne took a moment to regroup as he and Levy glared at each other. "Upon discovering that there were underground chambers, the Muslim general ordered his men to dig a tunnel into the side of the hill in an effort to break into them."

Suddenly Putnam began to smile. "Let me guess. They broke into the wine cellar."

"Bingo! The story that was spread in the aftermath of the siege told of how the defenders were suddenly overwhelmed and put to the sword by the warriors of God who sprang from the earth like flowers in the spring."

"Nice touch," Putnam snickered, "but I don't think that chronicler would get a passing grade in Major Benton's class on military writing back at Benning."

"That bit of romantic drivel could be key," Nathan exclaimed. "If what Lieutenant Horne says is true and Kinkade is right, no one knows about this tunnel."

"So as far as we know," Horne replied, "only Kinkade and a couple of assistants who were with him on the dig know the true story. It seems Kinkade found the tunnel's entrance, or what he thought was the entrance."

Lanston leaned back in his seat and raised his right hand, signaling Horne to hold his thoughts as he turned to face Levy. "The Palestinian, do you think you can find out if he knows anything about this tunnel or the underground chambers?"

For the first time Levy cracked a smile. "I believe you Americans have a quaint little saying that pretty well sums up his condition."

"Which is?"

"I am afraid he will never play the violin again."

Despite the fact that Syed now seemed to have been the agent of Brian McIntire's death, the Israeli's statement sent a chill down the backs of every American in the room. When he saw their expressions, the Israeli sighed as he turned to leave. As they left the ops center, he turned to one of his assistants. "They are still new to this game," he stated in Hebrew.

His companion agreed. "They will learn, they will learn."

Arlington, Virginia

Trailed by a brigadier general to his right and a colonel carrying a collection of folders, maps, and files on his left Scott Dixon burst into Henry Jones's outer office. Jones's executive officer jumped to his feet as Dixon flew past his desk. "General Jones is expecting you." Scott paid the executive officer no heed as he stormed into the Chief of Staff's office. As the colonel passed into the room, he closed the door behind him.

Jones, bent over his desk listening to someone on the phone, pointed to a small conference table that occupied one side of his office. Only when he was finished, or more correctly the other person on the other end of the phone was, did Jones hang up the receiver and turn to Dixon and his two assistants who were busy laying out their briefing material on the table. "Talk fast. The Sec Def is expecting me to be in his office in fifteen minutes with viable options he can take to the President."

"Do you want to hear all of them or just the U.S. only options?"

Jones grunted. "That was the State Department on the phone. For now Israel is taking a wait and see attitude."

"What are they waiting for?"

"Us. They're waiting to see what we do about this. Now, speaking of that, what are we going to do, Scott?"

Without having to be told the colonel tossed aside all the draft plans he had brought with them requiring active Israeli participation or support. When he was ready he turned to Dixon. "Which one first, General?"

"Let's start small and go from there."

Unable to sit, Henry Jones paced back and forth behind the seat he usually took at the head of the table as the colonel launched into his presentations. "This first option entails a reconnaissance in force using forces on hand within the area of operation."

Jones stopped. "That would be the Virginians."

"Yes sir. Third Battalion of the 176th from Camp Lee to be exact."

Instinctively he looked over at Scott. He didn't need to ask him if that was the unit his son was with. He already knew that. What he wasn't sure of was if his Guardsmen could carry out an operation as sensitive as this one would be. With a nod, he signaled to the colonel to continue as he once more took up his pacing.

"The purpose of the mission is limited to confirming or denying the information the Mossad provided us concerning the presence of PLA facilities. In a nutshell a company-sized force would go through the wire, or the fence along the eastern boundary of the security zone. Once on the other side they would establish a perimeter around the castle where the biowarfare lab is supposed to be located. If it is there, we would then have the option of either using forces on hand to go into the castle to confirm or deny or isolate the site until other forces, such as Delta or a Marine force recon, can arrive and execute a discreet inspection of the target."

"The upside," Scott pointed out, "is that we can initiate this option on very short notice using forces on hand."

"And the downside?"

Scott's two assistants exchanged nervous glances. Being

professional soldiers with over forty-five years of service between them, they had discussed the wisdom of relying on National Guard soldiers for this sort of mission as they had been working up the options they were now laying out. Each had wondered if their boss, Scott Dixon, would make mention of their concerns to Jones.

Sensing the pronounced pause, Jones again stopped and looked at Scott, then his two planning officers. "Never mind. I think I can figure that one out on my own." Resuming his pacing, he waved his right hand in the air. "Continue."

One by one Scott's people outlined the plans they had thrown together. When they were finished and he had no more questions for them, Jones thanked the brigadier and the colonel and asked them to step outside and wait for him there. Alone with Scott, he returned to his desk where he plopped down in his seat as if exhausted by the burden he was shouldering. Jones slowly rotated his seat away from Scott until he was facing the wall behind his desk. "Scott," he stated in a low, almost mournful voice, "I'm going to ask you to do something that I am not sure I could do myself." Pausing, he brought his chair around until he was facing Dixon who was standing in the center of the room watching, listening, waiting. "I'm going to recommend that we go in as soon as possible with the recon force using the 3rd Battalion of the 176th Infantry. If the Joint Chiefs, the Sec Def, and the President buy off on this, I want you to find a way of making sure that the company that goes in is the one your son is commanding. I don't care how you do that, I don't care who you piss off. Just do it. Is that clear?"

Scott understood exactly what Jones was saying. He wondered if he would have been as hesitant as he was at the moment if they had been talking about someone else's son. Hell, he thought to himself as he listened, he'd spent a lifetime ordering and leading other people's sons into battle. When he became aware that Jones had finished and was waiting for him to respond, Scott found it took far more effort to respond as he was expected to than he had anticipated. "Yes sir. I understand completely."

Jones felt the need to say something, not as the Chief of Staff of the Army but as one of Scott's oldest friends. But like him, Jones found himself unable to find the words that fit this most unusual and very awkward situation. So like Scott, he relied on prescribed military protocol to keep him from having to betray his personal feelings.

Coming to his feet, Jones drew in a deep breath as he subconsciously tugged at the hem of his uniform blouse. "Okay, Scott. That's all. I'll call you as soon as a decision has been made. Until then, have your people draft the necessary orders for my signature."

With little more than a nod, Scott pivoted about and headed back to his own office where he would set in motion a sequence of events that would, if his commander in chief gave the word, place his son in harm's way.

CHAPTER 24

Camp Lee

Charles Lanston had an office, a true luxury in the cramped confines of Camp Lee. Unlike the majority of the men belonging to 3rd Battalion of the 176th Infantry, this provided him with a place he could retreat to and be alone if he chose to. It was a sanctuary he avoided whenever he had the opportunity to do so for nothing important happened there, at least not as far as he was concerned. He viewed his office as little more than a black hole, one that daily sucked in every scrap of trivial paperwork Army regulations required the battalion commander review, respond to, or sign. It was the only place in the entire camp that reminded him of his civilian job, one he enjoyed but one that his time with the National Guard was meant to provide him relief from. Had he wanted to do nothing more than shuffle papers about from one stack to another he would have stayed in Bedlow, Virginia.

The battalion operations center was another story. There was always someone there doing something that was related to his battalion's real-world mission. No matter what time of day or night, when the only people awake were those prowling about in the security zone on routine patrols or standing watch over the camp's two gates, the ops center was fully functional and manned by personnel who were doing what they had been trained to do. At times this duty could be quite boring and downright tedious. But even the most inane spot report from a mounted patrol stumbling about in the dark seeking intruders who were not there trumped sitting alone in his office responding to insipid correspondence generated by staff officers whose value was measured by the volume of paperwork they produced. So when someone needed to find their battalion commander, the first place they checked was not his office but the ops center.

Few assigned to man the operations center shared the joy of having their battalion commander in their midst around the clock with the same relish that he derived from being there. Even in an organization that treated their superiors with a casualness that appalled active Army types like Nathan Dixon and Terrance Putnam, every member of Lanston's battalion still appreciated the fact that when they were wearing their BDUs, he was a lieutenant colonel and they his underlings. The easygoing attitude and laxness that makes the graveyard shift in the ops center a duty less onerous could not be enjoyed when the "Old Man" was constantly hanging out in the corner, chatting with the people on duty, holding impromptu meetings, or conducting business that should have been done elsewhere. Efforts by the staff of the ops center to surreptitiously encourage him to vacate the premises were ignored. It was after all Lanston's battalion, making this "his" operations center.

There was an upside to having Lanston within easy reach, especially when planning for a complex operation was under way. Russ Hough in particular found having his commanding officer within arm's reach at times like this handy. Crucial decisions concerning a plan he was pulling together could be obtained as issues cropped up, making it easier for Hough's battle staff to crank out the final product in a timely manner. And never was Lanston's command presence more appreciated than when the order from brigade came directing the 3rd Battalion of the 176th to conduct a reconnaissance of the suspected PLA biowarfare lab.

The mission itself was a simple one, one that was an intriguing part of every infantry battalion's mission essential task list. Every rifle squad, platoon, and company within the battalion practiced their respective patrolling techniques at least once during their annual training cycle. It was the object of the patrol, coupled with unusually detailed coordinating instructions passed down through the chain of command, that gave Charles Lanston and Russ Hough pause.

The idea that his men would be violating an international boundary established by a multinational accord to confirm or deny the presence of a facility capable of producing a weapon of mass destruction filled Lanston with trepidation. Follow-on reports concerning Brian McIntire's death only served to heighten his concern. The specter that more of his men might soon share McIntire's fate if things did not go well only added to apprehensions that grew as the operation his battalion was committed to slowly morphed from plan to reality. He made no effort to hide this, going out of his way to tell everyone involved that the whole thing terrified him. "I can't imagine any sane man not being scared shitless by the prospect of kicking in a door and finding a room full of vats overflowing with bugs designed to wipe out every man, woman, and child in the U.S. So as you pull this operation together," he cautioned his battle staff after presenting his initial planning guidance, "make damned sure you do it right, 'cause I don't think we're going to get a second chance if we screw this one up."

As horrific as the object of the exercise was, that proved to be far easier for him to accept than some of the coordinating instructions the commander of the 3rd Battalion of the 176th Infantry found himself saddled with. While Russ Hough's people were running about coordinating with other staff officers and crafting the battalion operations order, he sat in Lanston's favorite corner of the ops center doing his best to point out to his commanding officer that they would have picked Nathan Dixon to lead the patrol even if the operations order they had been handed had not directed it.

"Chuck, it makes sense," he repeated over and over again. "Dixon is a proven commodity, an officer who has spent his entire adult life preparing himself for this sort of thing. None of our other company commanders have seen combat. Nathan has."

Lanston grunted. "There has to be a first time for everyone, doesn't there?"

Hough rebuffed this flimsy defense by presenting his good friend and battalion commander with his alternatives. "Okay, if not Dixon and his company then who? Cliff Stanifford? He may be a crackerjack accountant, the best in the county, but he's been in command for what, three months? He's never even had a chance to take his company to the field for a weekend drill. And despite the high retention rates Frank Barrett has been able to maintain and his company's performance during their last annual general inspection, he isn't a field soldier and you know it. He was given the company for no other reason than to strengthen the administrative mess Bill Kinsley left behind. How many times have you told me in private that he's gone as soon as he's racked up enough command time?"

Folding his arms tightly across his chest, Lanston scowled. "I know, Russ, I know. Everything you say makes sense. But damn it, why in the hell did they have to put it in writing? It's nothing more than another example of the low opinion they have of the National Guard."

Hough understood that "they" meant the regular Army. Determined to help his commanding officer get over the bitterness he felt at the manner with which Nathan Dixon had been selected to lead the pending operation, Hough continued to argue on behalf of the very system that irked him as much as it did Lanston. "You know, Chuck, I think the people who directed us to put Dixon in command of this had such a good idea that I'm going to recommend that we send Putnam out there with him."

Lanston glared at Hough. "Do you know what will happen if we do that? It will only reinforce the low opinion every regular Army officer has in regards to our officers. When they teach leadership and tactics at Fort Benning, some asshole instructor will use this operation as an example of how to use Guard troops."

Softening his tone, Hough leaned forward and laid his hand on Lanston's knee. When their eyes met, Lanston could tell that the man he had hand-picked to be his ops officer was as serious as he had ever seen him. "Chuck, would you rather we do it with our own people, officers who don't have the experience in this sort of thing, and have Benning use this as an example of how not to do things?"

Turning his head away for a moment, Lanston let his anger subside before he looked back at Hough. "Russ, I know you're right. You and those people in Washington are dead right. But damn it, that doesn't mean I have to like it."

Realizing that he had won and that this would be the last time anyone would openly debate the issue, Hough leaned back and forced a smile. "I guess that's why you get paid the big bucks and get a fancy office all your own."

"No," Lanston countered as he stood up and prepared to wander over to where Hough's minions were busy working on the operations order. "The reason I'm the battalion commander is because I'm the only one dumb enough to eat every shit sandwich they hand me and go back to them with a smile from ear to ear chanting thank you, sir, may I have another."

Decked out in full battle kit and toting a rifle that he had borrowed from one of his supply clerks, Terrance Putnam rushed into the tent that served as the A Company orderly room. He found Nathan was seated at a small folding table putting the finishing touches on his company operations order, flanked by Alex Faucher and Jack Horne. All of them had draped their flak vests and load-bearing equipment over the backs of their chairs. Only Jack Horne had taken the time to apply an intricate patter of camouflage paint to his face, giving him an ominous, unworldly appearance. Putnam grinned as he approached them. "Hey, First Sergeant, are you goin' out with us too?" Unable to contain the excitement he felt at being given a role in the operation, Putnam's salutation proved to be far too cheery for either the occasion or the situation at hand.

The expression that greeted this remark warned the battalion supply officer that Faucher was not at all pleased about seeing him. Looking up from the map he had been working on, Nathan sensed the tension between the two. "The first sergeant will be leading the breaching force at the eastern fence. Once the main body of the company is through, he'll keep it open as well as establishing a casualty collection point there, just in case we need it."

"I see," Putnam replied as he pulled up a chair across the table from Nathan and joined them. "What about your XO?"

"Since he used to run the battalion's mortar platoon I'm putting him in charge of the mortar section which will set up in the ditch next to the road just inside the Palestinian zone. From there they'll be able to provide us with indirect fire support if necessary as well as block any reinforcement that might come streaming down the north-south road that runs along the eastern fence. During our egress, they'll also provide direct and indirect covering fire if we're pursued."

"He's over at your shop," Faucher stated in an accusatory tone, "trying to straighten out our ammo draw. Seems even at a time like this paperwork still wags the dog."

Taking his eyes off Faucher, Putnam chose to ignore Faucher's swipe at the procedures that he adhered to when it came to issuing ammunition and supplies and instead looked down at the map that Nathan was working on. He had already plotted out his company's routes to their objective, blocking positions around, and checkpoints that would be used for coordinating his platoons. "Okay, so where does that put me?"

"You'll be going with Second Lieutenant Teeple's third

platoon. Initially you'll lead us through the wire. Once across the north-south road you will continue to press on into the orchard and up the hill. When you reach this point here, you'll deploy your platoon along the eastern edge of the orchard to cover the castle's main gate and support the rest of the company by fire if needed."

As he listened to this, Faucher could not help but grimace when he heard Nathan refer to the third platoon as if it were Putnam's.

After taking a moment to study the map, Putnam looked up at Nathan. "Sounds simple enough. What's this Teeple like?"

"He's a good officer," Faucher stated bluntly. "He's young and may not be the sharpest tack in the box, but you can depend on him."

Faucher was no different than his battalion commander. He understood the logic behind using the two most experienced combat officers in the battalion to lead this patrol but shared Lanston's ingrained resentment every time their skill and competence was placed in doubt by regular Army officers like Putnam. Even now, when he was on the cusp of the most important military operation of his life, he could not contain the bitterness he felt over this affront. For as long as any of the officers in Company A stayed with the Guard, they would always be haunted by the belief that when their military moment of truth came they were found wanting and incapable of doing what their peacetime superiors had charged them with.

Nathan suspected that there was more going on below the surface than any of his subordinates let or. He could tell. He knew how men going into battle behaved. He had listened to their banter and their nervous boasts. He had watched them as they made their separate peace with their God, scribbled hasty notes to loved ones, or sought a last moment of solitude to reflect upon what they would soon be asked to do. While much of this was in evidence throughout his company, he also took note of the manner with which they returned his gaze, the expressions some of the men wore as he passed through the company area and the way their conversations stilled as he approached. Whether it was resentment, distrust, or simply a form of prebattle jitters was hard to gauge. What he was certain of was that he could not let their feelings and concerns, real and imaginary, interfere with what they were about to do. He had to maintain his focus on the mission at hand and keep them from forgetting what was at stake.

Ignoring the unspoken discord that was still obvious to all, Nathan continued to lay out the plan in a crisp, businesslike manner. "Once the third platoon is set, the first platoon will swing around your right. Their objective is to surround the farm compound that has been built within the castle's outer bailey."

Putnam looked up. "Its what?"

Horne answered before Nathan could say a word. "The courtyard that lies between the outer wall and the castle's main wall."

"Oh, I see."

Nathan paused to explain. "Lieutenant Horne's professor has been most helpful, providing us with everything he has on the place." Terrance Putnam reached across the table and took several of the hand-drawn sketches of the castle Jack Horne offered up like a kid turning in a school project he was proud of. Putnam took a moment to familiarize himself with them before nodding to Nathan to continue.

"Access into the castle from the farm compound is achieved through the postern, or sally port, located in the southern wall. That leads to the inner bailey. From everything Israeli military intelligence has given us there's nothing in the farm compound itself that is of interest to us. Of course, their information could be wrong. And there is a chance that they may not be sharing everything with us in an effort to protect their own sources. Be that as it may, they seem to think the experimental farm is nothing more than a gatehouse and a facade, one that serves as a security checkpoint as well as providing cover for the coming and going of the people working in the biowarfare lab that is located somewhere in the castle itself."

"If it is there," Putnam added dryly as he inspected the photos.

Horne looked over at Putnam. "If it is there, you won't see it in any of the photos. It would be tucked away someplace under the castle, in the underground chambers that the Arabs broke into using the tunnel they dug during the siege."

"It's the task of Horne's second platoon," Nathan explained, "to circle around the castle to the eastern wall and find the entrance to that tunnel, the one Kinkade found and hid when he finished here. If it's there, our next task will be to see if there's a way to worm our way into the caverns unseen and undetected."

"Then what?" Putnam asked, looking up from the photos he held.

A frown clouded Nathan's face. "We go in, look around, and back out, covering our tracks as we go. Once we've returned to Camp Lee we report what we found. If the biowarfare lab is there and the folks back in D.C. decide to take it out, a special ops team will be brought in to do the deed."

"What do you think? Delta or the Rangers?"

Disheartened by this aspect of the plan, Nathan stood up. The instrument he had in his hand with which to perform this mission was an imperfect one, a collection of men snatched from civilian life and thrown into a situation that his superiors suspected they could not handle on their own. He had been with the unit long enough to know there was some truth to this. They were not a fully trained and cohesive military force. They lacked many of the advanced skills that this sort of operation would require. But neither were they as inept as he had once suspected them of being. In many ways they were no different than any active Army unit he had ever served with. As a whole they had many of the same faults and weaknesses found in any rifle company in the Army, either active or Guard. But what he thought of them now did not matter. Somewhere within his chain of command a decision had been made that his company wasn't good enough to deal with the task of securing the biowarfare lab on their own.

Perhaps they were right. Perhaps his company wasn't good enough. Of course, it didn't matter one way or the other who was right. His people wouldn't be afforded the opportunity to prove themselves, so dwelling on the issue was moot. And that, he thought as he threw the marking pen he had been using down on the table, was that. "Does it make a difference, Terry?" he finally admitted. "The only thing that matters at the moment is that it isn't going to be us."

No one who heard Nathan's comment quite knew how to take this last comment, nor did he expand upon it before turning away from the table and walking away. Each man—Putnam, Faucher, and Horne—was left to interpret it based upon their own predilection, none of which did anything to heal the resentment that the manner with which this operation had come to them had already unearthed.

In the rush of events following their unexpected isolation in the southeastern bastion and their efforts to prepare for the company-sized recon, no one had taken the time to inventory and pack up Brian McIntire's equipment and personal belongings. Throughout their scramble to get themselves ready, both physically and mentally, McIntire's neatly made cot and carefully stowed gear served to remind Jack Horne's third squad just what this mission was all about. The image of the empty cot amid the chaos of their personal preparation for the pending mission had a psychological impact on the men of McIntire's squad that no one, in all their haste, had factored into the carefully crafted operations orders drawn up at battalion, company, and platoon level.

Every man in the third squad found themselves looking over their shoulder, back toward McIntire's empty cot, as Ollie Rendell briefed them on their mission. In the process, the sorrow, the anguish, and the shock that had overwhelmed each man when he had been told that their good friend and neighbor was dead slowly evolved into something else, something more powerful: anger. No one spoke of this, for no one had to. Each man could sense the rage that was slowly building up within themselves and their companions, a rage that enflamed a desire, a need to strike back, to extract revenge on the faceless scum that had taken one of their companions from them and had endangered their families.

While some gripped their weapons and others slowly, methodically, fed round after round into magazines, they listened as Ollie Rendell laid out Nathan's plan in detail. None found any fault in how they would approach the castle. All silently embraced with enthusiasm the prominent role their platoon would play. The only part that they collectively found fault with was what they would do if and when they uncovered the biowarfare lab. Like their company commander, the Guardsmen of Ollie Rendell's third squad resented that they would not be allowed to strike a killing blow, that the task of extracting revenge would be left to others. Unlike Nathan, every man gathered about Ollie Rendell secretly pledged to himself that if the opportunity presented itself, Brian McIntire's death would be avenged that night.

CHAPTER 25

East Boundary Fence, the Security Zone

In an effort to maintain the appearance that nothing unusual was afoot Lanston had his B Company take over the task of conducting the roving patrols in the security zone from Company A. This left Nathan's company free to prepare for the recon in force while maintaining the outward appearance that life in Camp Lee had returned to normal.

Keeping up a veneer of calm was no easy feat for American forces in the Middle East. In addition to keeping the perpetrators of the biological attack in the dark as to the effectiveness of their efforts, the Army needed to fend off questions being raised by journalists in the area. Until they had answers for their questions and the National Security Council had been afforded an opportunity to determine what they were dealing with and craft an appropriate response, all information concerning the attack and initial responses was classified top secret. The unusual flurry of activity that followed the deaths of Brian McIntire and his fellow traveling companions that could not be hidden from the press was explained away by public affairs officers as little more than part of an unscheduled exercise, a test of the entire command's alert procedures. Few of the journalists bought this story. Sensing that something was up, they took steps to seek out the truth of the matter just as Nathan and his command were setting out to do.

There were those who were waiting for this small army of correspondents to pull away the cloak of secrecy that the American military was hiding the deaths of the four soldiers under. Lacking a reliable and comprehensive intelligence network of his own, Hammed Kamel depended upon the world's press to track the progress of his attack. He suspected the statements released to the journalists by spokesmen for the American military were false, but lacking any independent means of confirming them and with no sign of mysterious outbreaks bubbling up anywhere, Hammed faced a serious dilemma.

To address some of his concerns, Hammed assembled his principal assistants. After summarizing what he did know, he opened the discussion by pointing out that any number of things could be going on. The most obvious cause of a failure, if indeed they had failed, might have been due to the pathogen they had selected. Perhaps, he ventured, they had erred in selecting the orange as a medium with which to deliver their weapon. The virus could have died or been rendered harmless before the fruit was consumed. One of his chief assistants pointed out that maybe it had yet to be consumed, that the soldier selected to carry the package back to his hometown was waiting to share it with them. A lab tech who frequently traveled between the Middle East and the United States even suggested that the oranges might never had survived the trip, pointing out that they could very well have been taken away during a routine customs inspection. "For all we know," he stated glumly, "they are sitting in the bottom of a trash bin at some airport, harmlessly rotting away."

None of this idle speculation proved to be of any help to Hammed. He had to make a decision as to what he and his people would do. For all he knew his efforts had somehow been compromised. Just how that happened and whether or not the Americans could trace the source of the virus to its true point of origin was moot. Any compromise was a threat to his efforts, one that could not be ignored. Being a cautious man, Hammed therefore decided to play it safe. Rather than waste time mulling over idle speculation, he decided to give his first full-scale test of what some of his people were calling "Marburg Plus" a little more time to blossom. He therefore ended the meeting by announcing that until they had measurable results in hand, he would temporarily suspend their work at the subterranean lab. "We have all been working hard. Take two weeks off. Go home. Relax, rest up, and enjoy some of your newfound fortunes. By then the results of our little experiment should be in. When we return we will analyze them, make whatever corrections we need, and continue our work."

He did not tell any of his subordinates that he would spend his "vacation" in Damascus, securing additional funding for his work as well as tapping into their intelligence network. Nor did he bother to inform his technical staff of the special instructions he issued to his security chief after he had dismissed them. Just in case something did go terribly wrong, Hammed told him to be ready for anything. "As soon as they have departed, prepare the entire complex for destruction. If the Americans come, you must make sure that nothing is left behind, nothing."

When evening fell and the appointed hour came, the lead elements of Company A began to slip out through Camp Lee's own version of a sally port and make its way east on foot. To mask this maneuver a covey of Humvees made a great show of wandering about in the darkness well south of Camp Lee. The evening watch at the base of the castle duly took note of the show this mounted patrol was putting on. After reporting to his superiors that a mounted patrol had departed Camp Lee, the PLA sentinels continued to track its progress, ignoring the real threat that was coming their way.

Leading off this unseen menace was the breaching team led by Alex Faucher and made up of one squad taken from Keith Stone's first platoon. They made for a spot in the fence that Stone had discovered several days previously during the course of one of his daily inspections of the fence. It was a natural blind spot, dead ground that could not be observed by anyone on either side of the border unless they were within a few meters of the fence itself. Stone had made note of it in his patrol reports, stating that it was the ideal spot through which to infiltrate. Now he and the entire company would find out if he had been right.

The initial breaching was little more than a small hole big enough for a person to wiggle through. One at a time six men slipped under the first chainlink fence, tumbled into the antivehicle ditch that lay on the other side, and scurried up the sloping incline to the second chainlink fence. Again only a small hole was cut. This time only four men went forward while the other two remained at the new breach, ready to widen it if all was clear or cover the retreat of their companions if they ran into trouble. When the four Guardsmen reached the north-south road they established a listening post. After ensuring that no one had seen them and that follow-on forces would be free to cross the road at this point without fear of being observed from the castle that now loomed above them, they passed word back that all was clear. Only then did Faucher and the men at the second fence begin to widen the gaps.

Standing back a bit from all this activity, Nathan nervously watched. Like a river-crossing operation the breaching of an obstacle left a unit vulnerable. Behind him his three platoons lay in the open with only the night to cloak them. While his first sergeant's breaching party widened the gap, the remainder of the company was susceptible to detection from listening posts or observation posts manned by hostile personnel as well as casual traffic that regularly traveled up and down the road that ran parallel to the second fence. At this stage of the operation it wouldn't take much to screw things up. A careless act by a soldier in one of the platoons waiting to go forward or a member of the breaching party spotted by an innocent passerby could compromise their mission before it even cleared the fence.

Inactivity during an operation like this breeds fear in

those who have little to do but wait. Lying on the ground, seemingly alone and exposed, leaves a soldier's mind free to conjure up all sorts of unseen dangers and demons lurking out there in the darkness. So Faucher's pronouncement that all was set came as a welcomed relief to everyone waiting to press forward. Action is the best cure for the dread that can cripple a man in combat as completely as a bullet.

First through the widened breach was Gordon Grello and his mortar teams. Together with a pair of machine guns and soldiers armed with AT-4 antitank rockets they rushed forward to establish a blocking position along the north-south road. From there they would keep the company's escape route open and provide covering fire during the company's egress with mortar fire if the situation so dictated. Standing to one side of the first breach was Nathan Dixon. Across from him on the opposite side was Alex Faucher. Both men watched as Grello's people quickly passed through the gapping hole in the wire.

All did not go smoothly. Every now and then someone burdened with a heavy weapon or hauling ammo boxes snagged on a piece of the fence. Caught unaware, the soldier's hasty advance was brought to a screeching halt. Those behind him, hell-bent on clearing the obstacle as quickly as they could, inevitably plowed into the rear of the snarled soldier, resulting in a confusion of flailing arms and a flurry of muttered oaths and exclamations. Whenever this occurred Nathan and Faucher would quickly intervene, commanding the men as loud as they dared to shut up while freeing the man who had been caught by the stray ends of the chainlink fence.

There was a slight pause after the last of Grello's detachment had cleared and before Terrance Putnam emerged from the darkness with the third platoon. Stepping aside, he motioned for Allen Teeple and his men to continue through. "I'll catch up," he whispered to the anxious platoon leader.

Drawing up next to Nathan, he watched the Guardsmen he was taking forward for a moment. "So far, so good."

Keeping an eye on his men as they went past him while standing by to intervene should one of them stumble or get caught up in the fence, Nathan wasn't quite as upbeat. "We're not even clear of the wire yet," he reminded his fellow captain.

"Be that as it may, I think we're looking good. Now, if you'll excuse me." Without waiting for Nathan to respond, Putnam stuck his hand in front of one of Teeple's men, ducked through the fence in front of him, and began to work his way back to the head of the platoon column.

Across the way, Faucher had heard the exchange. He found himself agreeing with both points the pair of regular Army officers had expressed. Things were going well. He knew these men. He knew everything there was worth knowing about them in a way that neither of the captains could ever hope to. He could read their mood, gauge just how motivated they were, and tell by their expressions what they were thinking. Some of the men passing before him belonged to his fire company. He had already seen them in action and knew he could trust them. In fact, the only man he had any questions about at that moment was the one who had been appointed to lead them. He suspected that he and his beloved company were in good hands. But he could not know for sure. Like the castle that loomed over them all, Nathan Dixon was still something of a mystery.

For the second platoon the march across the security zone came to an abrupt halt some one hundred meters short of the fence. In the briefing Jack Horne had told them they would occupy an attack position within the security zone before crossing the wire into the Palestinian area. In his mind Paul Sucher had imagined that they would hunker down in something like a ditch or behind a rise of some sort when that time came. Much to his bewilderment, they were in the open when Ollie Rendell passed the word to go to ground and wait.

He was not alone. To his left Sam Rainey stood hunched over, seeking a spot near at hand that offered even a modicum of cover. Being more practical Rendell had dropped prone without hesitation the moment Jack Horne had signaled them to do so. Expecting his men to have followed suit, he was perturbed when he looked back over his shoulder and saw several of his people still standing, looking about for cover. "Down," he hissed. "Get down and stay down!"

Though he was still apprehensive about having to plop down in the middle of nowhere with nothing to hide behind, Sucher complied. Left with nothing to do until Jack Horne gave the order to move forward again, he picked himself up on his elbows as high as he dared and began looking around while nervously fidgeting with his rifle. Through the night-vision goggles pressed against his face he could clearly see the gap in the fence ahead. Like everything else in his field of vision the two figures standing on either side of the gap in it appeared green, unworldly apparitions generated by an electronic process that collected the slightest hint of ambient light and magnified it a thousand times over. The end result created a world of green images that were displayed on a tiny screen before his eyes. Like all American soldiers Sucher took the technological marvels that turned night into day for granted. They were little more than a tool of the trade, an instrument that made an already lethal predator even more deadly.

From where he had gone to ground, Jack Horne could see everything that was going on at the gap in the fence as well as the platoon to his immediate front. He saw the last of Keith Stone's first platoon disappear through the gap and drop into the antivehicle ditch on the other side, making the call by his commanding officer to move his platoon forward all but unnecessary. Coming to his feet, Horne looked behind him. "Second Platoon, in single file, move out."

Horne's hushed voice carried through the still night air, eliciting an immediate response from men ready to get on with the task at hand. From his post at the fence, Nathan Dixon watched as thirty phantoms rose up from the ground and began to move toward him. Anxious to escape the exposed position he and Faucher had occupied for far too long, Nathan fought back the urge to grab the radio hand mike from his RTO's hand to order Horne to pick up the pace. They would get here soon enough, he kept telling himself in an effort to calm a nervousness that seemed to redouble with every passing minute he remained standing at the fence. All was going well so far. But this, he reminded himself as he turned toward the east and studied the dark outline of the castle on the hill above, was just the beginning, the first move in a game of chess where all of the opponent's pieces and all his moves were hidden from sight.

During his briefing to his platoon back at Camp Lee Jack Horne all but skipped over the next phase of the operation, summing it up with a single sentence: "We will proceed forward to the far edge of the orchard in column and pass to the left of the third platoon." The movement he described had seemed simple enough back at Camp Lee. Performing this rudimentary task proved to be an altogether different matter.

When they were sure it was clear to do so, Ollie Rendell's squad sprinted across the road in line, covering the last few meters of open ground on the other side and into the orchard without pause or hesitation. The forward momentum from this initial burst allowed them to ascend the first twenty or so meters of the hill without problem. It did not last long. The steepness of the hill quickly slowed their rate of advance to a trot, then a walk, and finally a crawl.

Within minutes the stillness of the night was filled with the sound of men huffing and puffing as they toiled under burdens that most were still unaccustomed to.

Because of the threat they would be facing once they reached the castle each man in Jack Horne's platoon wore chemical protective suits designed to shield the wearer from chemical and biological agents. The price the wearer paid for this protection was additional weight and a garment that kept the body's heat from escaping, heat that quickly began to build under the weight of the equipment each man carried up that hill. The body armor they wore over the chemical warfare suit only added to the problem. With the front and rear small-arms protective plates inserted the armor alone weighed close to seventeen pounds. Hanging from this vest and strapped about each soldier's waist was a collection of mission-essential items. This included more than six pounds of small-arms ammo in thirty-round magazines, four M-67 fragmentation grenades weighing a little over one pound each, a pair of one-quart canteens totaling close to five pounds, a protective mask in a carrier strapped to the right thigh that added two pounds, and an assortment of other items such as field dressings and compass. All of this was topped off by a three-pound Kevlar helmet with two-pound AN-PVS-7B night-vision goggles hanging off it.

Soldiers carrying an M-16A2 rifle up that hill considered themselves lucky. That weapon, with one fully loaded thirty-round magazine locked in place, weighed just under nine pounds. Sam Rainey's M-249 squad automatic weapon alone was fifteen pounds. To make it an effective weapon, he needed to haul a pair of the two hundred-round boxes of 5.56mm four-in-one linked ammo adding an additional seven pounds each. In addition to their rifles Don Olkowski and Daniel Travers were each issued one fifteen-pound AT-4 antitank rocket launcher that they carried slung over their backs. Most pitiful of all was Ron Weir, Nathan Dixon's radioman. Not only did he have to carry his own equipment, weapon, and the radio, he had to keep up with his spry young commanding officer and go wherever he went, which for a company commander was just about everywhere.

By the midpoint, everyone was doubled over, huffing and puffing like a steam locomotive assaulting the front range of the Rocky Mountains. Most men removed their night-vision goggles during the climb in order to allow the rivets of sweat to run freely down their faces. Pausing to catch his breath, Jack Horne looked about at his platoon. His men were becoming strung-out and scattered as each man took on the hill at his own pace. Gulping down a breath of air, Horne called out as loud as he dared. "Keep up, keep together."

Behind him his squad leaders heard the call over their own labored breaths and did their best to comply. Ollie Rendell looked over his right shoulder as he passed the word back along to his squad. "Keep up with me. Keep going."

Under ordinary circumstances Paul Sucher would have responded with a snide remark. But even he realized that this was no ordinary night, that the stakes they were playing for this night were about as high as they could be, life and death. Ignoring the sharp pain that cut into his side like a hot knife Sucher bowed his head, sucked down as much air as he could, and pressed on. Like every man in the third squad, the image of Brian McIntire's vacant cot blinded him to all the pain and suffering their advance up the hill was inflicting upon them.

At first Terrance Putnam had been disappointed that he was going to be saddled with little more than providing a base of fire for the advance of the rest of the company. Upon completing their climb, he hung back and watched Allen Teeple deploy his platoon. Fishing his canteen out of its cover, Putnam began to reassess his feelings on the matter as he slowly unscrewed the cap and took a sip. Though he would have died before admitting this to anyone else, he now found himself more than content with his assigned mission.

From out of the darkness of the orchard Nathan Dixon, trailed by Ron Weir, came up to Putnam. "How's your deployment going?"

As he returned his canteen in its cover fastened to his flak vest, Putnam looked about before answering. "They're doing fine, Nate. We should be set any moment."

As if on cue, from somewhere off to the right, Allen Teeple approached the pair of captains. Pausing, he looked first at Putnam, then Dixon, and back at Putnam as if trying to figure out which officer to report to. Finally, he turned to Putnam, the man who was in charge of this position. "We're set. There's an OP located in the southwestern tower with at least two men."

"Heavy weapons?" Nathan asked.

"Can't tell. Gregg D'Angello is over there. He said he just saw two heads above the parapet. There could be more, but we don't know."

Nathan looked over to Putnam. "Keep an eye on them. At the first sign of trouble, take them out."

"Roger that."

Turning, Nathan reached out with his right hand. Without having to be told, Ron Weir handed him the radio hand mike. "Alpha One Six, this is Alpha Six. Three Six is set. Move out."

Even as they heard Keith Stone acknowledge his order over the radio, Nathan could hear Stone's men resuming their advance behind him as they shifted over to the right. Standing there motionless, Nathan imagined he could hear every footfall, every labored breath, every clank as unsecured gear banged against something else. He fought the urge to call over the radio and order Stone to caution his men to keep the noise down. He knew to have done so would only have slowed things down and added an unnecessary flurry of whispered orders to the cacophony of muted sounds and noises that men stumbling about in the dark inevitably generate.

Equally concerned, Terrance Putnam moved closer to the edge of the orchard and peered off in the direction of the southwestern tower. "I hope those people up there are as deaf as they are blind."

Nathan grunted. "Just in case they're not, Putt, get over there and be ready to put some serious lovin' on them if they become a problem."

"Wilco, good buddy." With that, his fellow captain took off to comply, followed quickly by the third platoon's nominal platoon leader. By the time they had disappeared down the line, Stone's men were gone. In their place, Nathan could hear Horne's platoon as it closed on his position. Having caught his breath and anxious to get on with their mission, he turned to Weir. "Let's go."

Still struggling to recover from his own labors, Ron Weir rolled his eyes and took off at a trot in an effort to catch up to his company commander. Oblivious to the danger that was but a stone's throw away, only one thought kept rolling around in Weir's head as he struggled to keep up. "It's going to be a long, long night."

CHAPTER **26**

The Castle

The cover provided by the fruit trees that had been planted on the side of the once barren hill provided just enough concealment to allay the fears of even the most anxious man in Jack Horne's platoon as they circled around the northern wall of the castle. Only one man picking his way forward through the orchard felt particularly vulnerable. Avner Navon knew it was wrong for him to be there. He felt it in his heart. To "volunteer" to become a translator with the Americans was one thing. But to join them on a foray into Palestinian territory was quite another. As affable as these Americans could be, he didn't think much of them as soldiers. Their movement up the hill didn't do anything to ease his concerns on that issue. Despite their sophisticated equipment and an abundance of weaponry, he suspected they were not up to the task at hand. Their ceaseless puffing and groaning as well as the difficulty they seemed to have keeping up with their company commander only served to reinforce that view. Had he been afforded the opportunity, he would have opted out of this adventure.

Unfortunately, the man who led the Mossad counterintelligence officers he had summoned on behalf of the Americans made it clear to him that he was to accompany the Americans if and when they took action against the castle. The Mossad agent had stressed the importance of knowing exactly what the Americans found at the castle in real time so their government could prepare the Israeli people for any fallout that the American actions might precipitate. "You speak Arabic," he told Avner before leaving. "Go to them, convince them that they cannot do without your services if they make a foray into the Palestinian zone." Dutifully, when word began to seep out of the battalion's ops center that this was exactly what the Americans were preparing to do, Avner did as he had been told.

Despite being in fair condition, the burden of scaling the hill under the weight of unfamiliar equipment was taking its toll on him. His reserve unit was mechanized infantry, a unit that prided itself in the fact that the greatest distance they ever walked while on duty was when they went from the motor pool to the mess hall. He was not used to participating in operations that demanded the agility of a mountain goat and the stamina of a bull.

His physical discomfort paled in comparison to his concerns over what would become of him if, for whatever reason, he was captured by the Palestinians. The Americans he imagined would have a better than fair chance. Holding on to them for propaganda purposes would be a real coup for the PLA. But he was an Israeli, a Jew decked out in an American uniform leading them into Palestinian territory. Avner had little doubt that he would not survive very long or if he did the PLA would make what his Mossad companions had done to Syed seem like child's play.

Avner was doing his best to keep up with the man in front of him when that soldier suddenly stopped, crouched down, and turned toward him. Placing his hand on Avner's shoulder, the American leaned forward and whispered in his ear. "They want you up front."

Pausing, Avner took a moment to gather up his courage before making his way forward past the long file of American soldiers who had dropped down onto one knee. He paid no attention to their tight, tense expressions or the manner with which they clutched their rifles. He had seen this all before. It didn't make any difference whether the man was Israeli or American, Christian or Jew. The fear, the apprehension, the anticipation one felt when going into harm's way was no different.

The going was not easy. Ascending the hill had been difficult, a task that had required brute force and determination. Cutting across its slopes was something entirely different, more of a balancing act. Avner slowly stumbled forward, doing his best to keep from toppling over. Every time he put his right foot forward it hit much sooner than his inner ear told him it should while his left foot seemed to fall away in what seemed to be a vain search for solid ground on the downhill side. Rather than taking full strides, the only solution was to take tiny half steps. Even then he found it necessary to grab the nearest tree or soldier as he pressed forward in an effort to keep himself from teetering over and rolling back down the hill.

At the head of the column he came to a small knot of men gathered about in a tight group before a vertical outcropping of rocks. There was a small clearing in front of the outcropping. Drawing up just outside this gathering, he made his arrival known. Ollie Rendell, who was also hovering just behind one of the figures that was part of the inner circle, looked over at him before leaning over and whispering. "If Jack is right, this is the tunnel entrance."

Avner straightened up in order to peer over the heads of the men before him and see what Rendell was talking about. Though it was dark, from where he stood he didn't see anything that even remotely looked like an opening. A little closer to the pile of loose rocks Nathan was having the same problem. Kneeling on the ground next to him and doubled over like a devout Muslim praying, Jack Horne was studying a hand-drawn diagram using a tiny penlight with a blue-green filter. Only when he was sure did Horne flick the light off, straighten up, and stare at the outcropping before him. "This is it. It's got to be."

Nathan murmured, "It better be." Looking about, he

caught sight of Ollie Rendell. Pointing at him, then at the pile of rocks, he motioned Rendell forward. "Start moving them, but take it easy."

Making his way forward, Rendell studied the tumbled mass of rocks before doing anything. When he was ready, he fixed his eyes on one, took it in both hands, and lifted it away. Bringing it up to his right shoulder, he handed it to the man behind him. "Pass them back. Do not throw them. Lay them on the ground. We don't want to start a rock slide that'll wake the neighbors."

Moving aside, Avner eased himself back on his haunches and watched as the American sergeant carefully lifted one rock at a time from the tumbled mass before him and passed it on. Down the line the rocks went, one by one until it reached Barry Lasner, the last man in Rendell's squad. Doing as he had been told Lasner slung his rifle over his shoulder so that he would have full use of both hands. When handed a rock, he carefully placed it on the ground next to him. In no time he had created a small semicircular wall off to his left. When the height of this wall appeared to be getting a bit too precarious, Lasner scooted over to his right a little and continued to widen the circle of rocks by starting another row.

After five minutes of this a rock Rendell was reaching for suddenly fell away. Tumbling forward into a freshly exposed hollow, the loose rock rolled deeper into a dark void beyond, creating an echo that resounded through the night air as it tumbled down a shaft that seemed to go on forever. To a man everyone in Jack Horne's platoon froze in place. Those who had not been passing rocks back tightened their grips on their rifles as they nervously looked about waiting for a response to the unexpected din. All around Nathan could hear the sound of safeties on weapons being flipped off. "Steady," he whispered. "Steady." Only when he was sure that the dislodged rock had not caused a stir inside the castle above did Nathan give Rendell the go ahead to continue on. When he did, the former deputy sheriff redoubled the care he took when removing a rock from the shrinking pile before him.

When there was a hole big enough for him to fit his head into, Rendell stopped, crawled forward, and peered into the pitch-black tunnel beyond. After slowly backing out, he turned to Nathan and his platoon leader. "It's blacker than a witch's heart."

Horne smiled. "That's good. It means they're not using it."

Rendell looked back at the newly opened hole. "Or it means no one's home."

Nathan already suspected otherwise. The presence of a two-man OP in the southwestern tower meant that there was someone in the castle. Whether or not they were protecting an elaborate underground biological warfare lab or were nothing more than a pair of local yokels charged by the head of the neighborhood terrorist cell to keep an eye on Camp Lee was impossible to tell. At the moment, using this tunnel to gain access to the castle, if in fact they could do so, was the only viable option available to Nathan to find out one way or the other. "Okay, keep digging." Without a word, Ollie Rendell went back to work as before. Only when the hole was big enough for a fully equipped soldier to pass through without any trouble did Nathan order him to stop.

Now came the hard part for Nathan. Instinctively he wanted to go first, to lead the way and see what was really in there. Had he been a platoon leader that is exactly what he would have done. But he was a company commander now, an officer responsible for controlling and coordinating the actions of over one hundred men scattered about in five different locations on the hill and at the foot of it. Going into the tunnel would reduce his span of control to himself and the men behind him. The task of going forward into the castle would have to be delegated to Jack Horne's platoon. They had talked about this when he had been giving his operations order back at Camp Lee. That had been his stated intention, one that Nathan had not, until this moment, decided whether or not he would hold to. Taking a moment, he weighed the matter one last time before concluding that he really had no choice. Turning to Horne, he motioned the young officer forward.

There was no hint of hesitation on Jack Horne's part. Like a child set loose on Christmas morning to see what wonders awaited him under the tree, the Virginia schoolteacher snapped his night-vision goggles in place and signaled Ollie Rendell to start sending his men in behind him as soon as he entered the tunnel.

Within the first few meters all ambient light disappeared, momentarily rendering Horne's night-vision goggles useless. To compensate for this the young officer switched on the small IR illuminator that was built into their goggles. This illuminator was in effect a flashlight, but one that emitted a beam that operated in the infrared region of the light spectrum, making it invisible to the naked eye but easily detected by the sensors of Horne's night vision's monocular eyepiece. While this did help, it was limited, forcing him to focus his full attention straight ahead or down at the uneven floor, making it necessary for him to hold his rifle by its grip in his right hand while running the fingers of his left along the rough-hewn ceiling above. This permitted him to gauge the ceiling's height as he advanced through the tunnel, permitting him to know beforehand when he needed to bend over to avoid hitting his head on a protruding rock. Behind him Jerry Slatery followed suit.

At the entrance Nathan watched as Ollie Rendell's men disappeared into the dark void. Sucher went in after Slatery, followed by Rainey who was toting the squad automatic weapon. Rendell was next. At this point, Nathan turned to Avner. "Go." Though caught off guard by this, he was a soldier who knew an order when he heard one and how to follow it. Rising up off the ground, the Israeli slid into line in front of Don Olkowski and went into the tunnel after Rendell.

When he saw Barry Lasner go by, Nathan reached out behind him with his right hand. Dutifully Ron Weir slapped the radio hand mike in it. To simplify matters for Company A, battalion had decided to use Nathan's company radio net to control the operation. The normal battalion command net was left to handle the routine patrols that continued on as part of the overall deception plan. Keying the mike, Nathan reported their progress.

Within the battalion ops center at Camp Lee Captain Ken Oliver, a home builder by trade and the battalion assistant ops officer when in uniform, acknowledged Nathan's report. When it was complete Oliver glanced over toward the corner where Russ Hough and Lanston were sitting, sipping coffee as they maintained their anxious vigil. "Russ, do you have anything for Company A?"

Hough simply shook his head. The matter was out of his hands. Nathan's report led him to believe that it was out of his hands as well. Success or failure now rested entirely upon the judgment and tactical skill of Second Lieutenant Jack Horne and a squad of National Guardsmen who were, at that very moment, inching their way along an eight-hundred-year-old tunnel five kilometers from where he was sipping coffee. This sense of helplessness caused Hough to squirm in his seat. "No. I've got nothing. Relay that report to brigade. I'm sure they're eager to hear how things are going."

Throughout this exchange Lanston said nothing. What was there to say? Things out there were unfolding as planned. The men he had selected to lead his fellow Virginians were doing what they were supposed to do, leaving him nothing to do but sit there with his ops officer sipping coffee and praying that this night would pass without incident.

Having just barely survived the climb up the hill, Jack Horne was grateful that the Mamelukes who had dug the tunnel some eight hundred years before had not found it necessary to use much of a downward slope in order to reach the castle. The same steep slopes that had been so daunting to Horne's platoon during their approach march permitted the Mamelukes to bore almost straight ahead until they reached a point that their chief engineer determined placed them under the castle's northern wall. From there a discernible upward pitch told Jack Horne that their goal was at hand.

This realization elicited a noticeable change in his attitude. Suddenly all the excitement and childish anticipation that he had experienced upon discovering the tunnel vanished. In its place a growing sense of apprehension began to well up as he began to realize that success or failure of the entire mission now rested squarely upon what happened in the next few minutes and how he responded to it. These thoughts caused him to slow his already cautious advance to a crawl. Bringing his left hand down, Horne grasped the forward hand guard of his rifle and crouched even lower until he was almost doubled over.

Every sense was peaked as he cautiously pressed on. In the close confines of the tunnel the sound of loose dirt and small stones being ground underfoot was almost deafening. The still air and stale dry smell of the ancient excavation mingled with the pungent odor sweat-laced with fear. Even the eerie green images his eyes beheld conspired against him as his subconscious mind involuntarily elicited memories of scenes from old horror movies he had once found so amusing.

Inch by inch he went on. The incline became more noticeable. His efforts to measure the total distance they had gone was frustrated by a riot of thoughts that filled his mind and kept him from maintaining his focus. Was he losing it? Was this what fear was really like? A loss of one's ability to think clearly, to maintain one's mental discipline? Would he have the strength of character to overcome this confusion when the time came?

Then, before he realized it he was there. Stopping, Jack Horne took a moment to look to his left and right to make sure that the tunnel didn't suddenly veer off to one side or the other. Only when he was satisfied that he had in fact reached the end did he cover the remaining distance toward the pile of rubble before him. Standing upright, he lowered his rifle while reaching out with his left hand to touch the loose rocks before him as if he needed to confirm that his eyes were not lying. Only when he was sure did he take the small hand mike from the strap it was hanging on and key it. "Alpha Six, this is Two Six. We're at the end of the tunnel, over."

As he waited for an acknowledgment to his report Horne began to study the rubble. In many ways it resembled the pile of rocks that had covered the entrance, a jumble of stones and rocks that measured anywhere from six to nine inches in diameter. Only upon closer examination did he notice some of the stones appeared to have a discernible shape to them, one that suggested that they were not natural but had been worked. After slinging his rifle over his shoulder, he reached out, took hold of one of them in both hands, and picked it up.

He was studying the stone when he suddenly became aware that there was someone next to him. "Are we there?"

Ollie Rendell's question caught the young officer completely off guard. Startled, he spun about to see who it was, dropping the stone he had been holding in the process. In a way fortune favored him as the stone slammed onto the floor between his feet. The impact of it on solid rock shattered the stillness of the cave, sending echoes reverberating down its length. Startled, everyone stacked up behind Horne and Rendell brought their weapon up to the ready, preparing to meet any response that the sudden report of stone on stone elicited.

At the far end of the tunnel the sharp report that put Rendell's men on guard emerged as nothing more than a thud that was barely audible. It was loud enough however to catch Nathan's attention. Concerned, he repeated his call on the radio for a status report, one that Jack Horne's tactical radio never received.

Within the ops center at Camp Lee this second call for an update from Horne put both Hough and Lanston on notice that his first had not been answered. Even more unnerving was Nathan's tone, one that told them just how anxious he was becoming. Sensing that something was not going right out there but unable to guess what was wrong, Hough and Lanston looked at each other but said nothing. If things were really getting out of hand they were confident that Nathan would tell them as soon as practical. He was, after all, a professional. Besides, at the moment both men appreciated the sad fact that there wasn't a thing either of them could do to help. Their role for the moment was limited to monitoring Company A's progress, sipping coffee, and waiting.

Waiting patiently for the situation to clarify itself did not strike Nathan as an option, at least not one that he was comfortable with. Sensing his company commander's concern, Weir leaned over. "Our signal might not be reaching them."

Already suspecting that this was the case and having waited for what seemed to be an eternity without getting any sort of response from Horne, Nathan turned to Matt Garver, the most senior second platoon NCO present. "I'm going in," he announced to the platoon sergeant.

Garver had been listening to what had been going on and suspected that sooner or later Nathan would do something like this. "Sir, I don't think that's a good idea."

In the darkness Nathan could just make out Garver's expression, one that left no doubt that the professional truck driver was as concerned about their situation as he was. "Let me go in," he volunteered. "I'll find out what's going on. I'll take a runner in with me and send him back once we find our what's up with the radios."

Nathan wavered. Garver's logic was impeccable. If the tunnel rendered radios useless, going in himself would effectively decapitate his company. With Gordon Grello unable to exercise effective command and control of the company from where he was, Nathan saw that he had no choice. "Okay, Sergeant Garver. But be careful. At the first hint of trouble, double-time back here."

"Roger that, sir." Standing up, Garver looked about until he spotted someone he could depend on as a runner. "Zuke, on me."

Not having been privy to his platoon sergeant's conversation with Nathan, PFC Sean Zukanovic left his spot on the perimeter surrounding the tunnel entrance and trotted over to Matt Garver. "What's up, Matt?"

Knowing how much the satellite dish installer hated working inside, Garver grinned. "We're going spelunking."

"We're what?"

"Just follow me."

Under ordinary circumstances Nathan would have enjoyed the exchange between Garver and Zukanovic, just the sort of humor that he himself often relied upon to lighten things up when the situation was getting tense. At the moment he was far too keyed up, uneasy with the manner with which the situation was developing, to enjoy such a flippant repartee. Perhaps, he found himself thinking as he watched the two Guardsmen disappear into the tunnel, his responsibilities as a company commander rendered that sort of thing frivolous. Maybe he was simply maturing as a leader. Or, he grimly thought to himself, it could be he was getting old and becoming more like his father, a man who was as lighthearted as a Lutheran minister.

Be that as it may, Nathan mused as he looked about at the remaining Guardsmen scattered about in a semicircle throughout the orchard, there's nothing I can do but hold here and wait, something that he was not very good at.

At the other end of the tunnel it quickly became clear to Jack Horne that his mishap hadn't betrayed their presence.

Taking a moment to collect his wits, he began to breathe normally once more. When he was ready, he glanced over at Rendell. "Okay, Ollie. Let's get to work."

After slinging his weapon across his back, Rendell turned to Slatery, the next man in line. "Pass the word, we're digging again. Tell the last man to be careful where he puts the rocks. Don't block our exit."

Slowly this message made its way from man to man, followed by the first stone. This process had just gotten started when Matt Garver and Sean Zukanovic came upon Barry Lasner. Looking up from his toils Lasner wasn't surprised to see Garver. Like everyone else in second platoon he was used to turning around and finding his platoon sergeant standing there, watching them. With a nonchalance that was oddly out of place, Lasner nodded toward the front of the line. "Jack is up front."

Satisfied that there were no major problems, Garver turned to Zukanovic. "Go back and tell the Old man we've found third squad and that everything's okay in here." As Zukanovic took off to carry this message back to his anxious company commander Garver pressed on toward the front, squeezing past the line of men, taking care as he went to keep from disturbing the rhythm that they had settled into as one stone at a time was passed from hand to hand. When he found his platoon leader Garver hung back a bit waiting until Horne turned and took note of him. "Jack, is your radio working?"

Confused by the question and Garver's presence, Horne ceased his labors and stepped back away from the pile of rocks. "It should be." Lifting the small mike from its strap on his combat vest, Horne keyed the mike. "Alpha Six, this Alpha Two Six, over." He waited several seconds for a response from either Weir, who was constantly monitoring the company net, or his commanding officer. When neither answered Horne checked to make sure his radio was still on before repeating his call. "Alpha Six, this Alpha Two Six, over."

In the darkness of the tunnel, illuminated only by the pencil-thin beams of light emitted by their night-vision goggles, Ollie Rendell's men stood by as they watched and listened to their platoon leader's efforts to reach the outside. They suspected that this was a problem no one had counted on. Just how serious a snag it was was difficult for them to gauge. To determine this those who could kept an eye on their platoon leader and platoon sergeant, waiting to see how they dealt with it.

When he was sure his efforts were for naught, Horne looked up at Garver. "Negative contact."

Garver grunted. "Ron suspected as much. The signal is being attenuated. It's sort of like trying to use a cell phone while driving through a highway tunnel."

"Okay, but where does that leave us, Matt? Do we go on? Do we go back? Or do we wait for the Old Man to sort this out?"

Garver turned to the closest man at hand. Grabbing Jerry Slatery by the sleeve he pulled him closer. "Go back and tell the Old Man we can't communicate by radio. Tell him we think we've reached the entrance to the castle's underground chambers but our way is blocked just like the tunnel entrance was. Tell him that we're clearing it. Clear?"

Slatery nodded. "Got it."

"Now go. And come back with an answer one way or the other as quickly as you can."

When Slatery was gone Garver turned to Horne. "Why don't you take a break, Jack, and let me in there."

Horne demurred. "I'm okay. I'm just getting the hang of this."

"Hey, you're forgetting who's the platoon leader and who's the sergeant. Now, if you don't mind, *sir*, this looks like NCO work to me."

Appreciating his platoon sergeant's efforts to arrest the gloom that had descended upon Rendell's men by using humor and a bit of theatrics, Horne stepped back. "Have at it, *Sergeant* Garver."

Quickly the line of Guardsmen fell back into their rhythm, slowly reducing the pile before them. This continued in silence as one stone at a time was passed down the line from one man to the next. The close quarters they were working in, the stillness of the tunnel's stale air, and the burden of their equipment left them all sweating profusely, soaking every stitch of clothing that their climb up the hill had not already saturated. Only when Matt Garver detected what he thought was a hint of light coming through the pile from the other side did he pause. Most of Rendell's squad took this opportunity to take a drink of water. Standing off to one side Jack Horne guessed the reason for the halt and moved up next to Garver, who had already removed his night-vision goggles and was in the process of leaning forward in order to peer into the tiny opening he had uncovered.

"Well?" Horne whispered in his ear.

Backing away, Garver moved next to Horne until his lips were but an inch from his lieutenant's ear. "Can't see anything. But there is definitely light coming from the other side. Do we keep going? Or do we send word back and wait for further orders?"

Stepping away from his platoon sergeant, Horne looked toward the small shaft of light that was seeping into the tunnel and thought for a moment. Their stated mission was to confirm or deny the presence of a biowarfare lab. In his mind he could make a case that light coming from underground chambers of a medieval castle that no one was supposed to know existed was ample evidence that something suspicious was evident. The question the young platoon leader found himself wrestling with at that moment was whether or not this was the sort of conclusive evidence the decision makers back in Washington would find convincing. He imagined that those people, having been burnt one too many times by faulty or inconclusive information, would demand something more tangible, evidence that was so solid and irrefutable that even the most ardent opponent of the current administration could not ignore.

Standing on the threshold of the lab where the biological agent that had killed Brian McIntire had been developed and doing nothing but sending another runner back for new orders from his commanding officer was something more than Horne could deal with. Unnerved by the situation he found himself in, he looked back down the tunnel where his men were lined up, resting as they waited for him to make a decision. He knew what they wanted. He had seen it in their faces as they had prepared for this mission. He heard it in the way his NCOs drove them on as they made their way across the security zone, through the wire, and up the hill. They wanted the sort of biblical justice that this land was noted for. He suspected each and every one of the men there with him personally wanted to take an eye from the people who had deprived them of Brian McIntire's. He knew that's what he wanted. While allowing them the pleasure of engaging in that sort of personal vendetta was definitely out of the question, Jack Horne concluded that the least he could do was to make sure that they left this place with the sort of evidence that would ensure someone else would be set loose to finish that end of the bargain for them.

Deciding that he already had all the authority he needed to continue on and secure that evidence, Horne made up his mind. Turning to Garver, he issued his orders. "We're going in. Pass the word back that we're breaking through." He was going to add a warning for everyone to be extra quiet, but saw no point in doing so. They knew what was at stake.

Word that the second platoon had confirmed the existence of the castle's underground chambers galvanized everyone who was listening in on Company A's command net. Both Alex Faucher and Gordon Grello went about rousing men whose inactivity had left them on the verge of succumbing to sleep. Realizing that something was actually going to happen, the battalion medics with Faucher gathered up their equipment as they readied themselves to go forward if and when the call came. Grello's mortar teams set up in the antivehicle ditch stood by their weapons with the first round in hand, waiting for the order to hang it over the muzzle of their mortar tube and let it fly on preregistered targets. Up one the hill Terrance Putnam made his way from one end of his line to the other, making sure that each and every man was awake, alert, and covering his assigned sector. To his south Keith Stone was doing the same with the two squads watching the farm compound. "Heads up, they're in," Stone whispered as he moved among his fellow Virginians. "Stand by."

Back at the battalion ops center Russ Hough and Charles Lanston finally abandoned their corner as they moved over to the situation map. Hough himself relayed the news the runners had passed on to Nathan confirming that they had found the underground chambers up to brigade, a call that set into motion a chain reaction that resonated across the eastern Mediterranean. Aboard the carrier USS *Regan* F-18 strike aircraft that had been locked and loaded were catapulted into the night sky. An Air Force AC-130 loitering in a holding pattern over international waters turned east and made its way into Israeli air space. At a NATO airfield in Turkey a company of Rangers with little to do but lounge around in a secluded hangar as they waited were ordered to fall in for final combat inspections while out on the runway crews of UH-60s equipped with extra fuel tanks hanging from their stubby wings ran through their preflight checklists and brought their aircrafts to life. Above them all an E-3 Sentinel stood by, ready to orchestrate and coordinate a swift telling blow against a threat only a handful of their countrymen were aware of.

And in Arlington, Virginia, an aide-de-camp knocked on the door of his general before opening it a crack and sticking his head around the corner. Looking up from the busywork he had been using to keep his mind off the operation that was unfolding on the other side of the world, Scott Dixon knew before his aide told him that his son was once more headed into harm's way.

Back on the hillside, shrouded in darkness, Nathan waited for Horne to emerge from the tunnel with the news that the tunnel did in fact empty out in the underground chambers they were looking for, blissfully ignorant of the fact that Horne had made the decision to press on into those chambers.

Deep inside the hill Jack Horne and Matt Garver were oblivious to all of this. Even if they had been aware of the effect their discovery was having on the world out there and the new orders that were making their way to them they had no time to dwell on it. Like the men behind them who were taking the stones they were passing back, Horne's and Garver's full attention was fixed on the dwindling pile that separated them from the chambers beyond. Stone by stone the gap grew bigger and bigger. The light that was now flooding into the tunnel through it allowed them to remove their night-vision goggles and continue on with their efforts unhindered by them. Every now and then Horne would stop to peer into the chamber beyond, listening for any hint of activity from beyond. Only when he was sure that it was safe to do so did he pick up where he left off, carefully choosing the next stone before lifting away and passing it on. When he was sure that the hole was big enough to accommodate a fully equipped soldier he stopped and turned toward Garver.

Sensing that the moment had arrived, Garver eased forward next to his platoon leader, slowly peeking up over the remaining pile of stones. To his surprise he found himself looking at something that reminded him of the rear of a metal storage cabinet. Just to make sure of this he reached out and touched it. Confused, he glanced over at Horne. "Well?"

"That," the young officer whispered, "is definitely not a twelfth-century artifact."

"Could it be something the archaeologists left behind?"

"I hardly think so." Taking great care, he backed away from the gap. Garver followed. Moving away from the pile of stones they had been working on, Horne motioned to Garver and Rendell to gather around him. "The way I see it we have no choice," he stated bluntly in hushed tones as all three leaned forward until their helmets touched. He didn't bother to tell them about the doubts he had previously entertained concerning his decision to go on. As far as he was concerned, going back now was no longer an option. In his mind, they were committed. "We have to go in there and see what's there."

Neither Garver nor Rendell said a word. They only exchanged glances as Horne laid out his plan. "Matt, you'll hold here at the gap with the bulk of the squad." Pausing, he looked over Garver's shoulder to see who was near at hand. "Ollie, you Sucher, and Rainey will follow me in."

"What are we looking for once we're in?" Rendell asked hesitantly.

His question was a good one, one which Horne didn't have an answer for. "I don't mean to be flippant," he finally admitted, "but I'll know it when I see it."

Sensing that they were out of their depths, Matt Garver was on the verge of suggesting that they hold where they were and send a runner back to their commanding officer. Horne didn't give him an opportunity to voice his opinion. Anxious to get this over with one way or the other, the young Guard officer stood up. "Ollie, let's go."

Again the two NCOs nervously eyed each other, both waiting for the other to raise an objection. But neither did. Jack Horne was their platoon leader, a man whom they respected and had, by joining and remaining in the National Guard, sworn an oath to follow. To violate either of those trusts now given their circumstances was unconscionable and dangerous. Placing his hand on Rendell's shoulder, Matt Garver closed his eyes and gave his friend a quick nod.

Understanding, Ollie Rendell forced a hint of a smile before turning away to organize his squad. As he was doing so, Garver grabbed Horne's sleeve to get his attention. "Perhaps you should take the Israeli. You can't read Arabic. He can."

"Good idea. Go get him and tell him what we're up to."

When Garver turned away, Horne eased himself back toward the gap, studying the cabinet before him, trying to gauge how best to move it so they could squeeze by, and steeling himself for what he was about to do. He even found time to recite the prayer Alan Shepard muttered as he waited to be launched into space. "Dear Lord. Don't let me screw this up."

CHAPTER **27**

The Castle

Every trivial screech and groan the metal storage cabinet made as it scraped along the stone floor set chills down Jack Horne's back, causing him to stop pushing it away from the hole, wait, and listen. Stacked up behind him Ollie Rendell, Paul Sucher, Sam Rainey, and Avner held their collective breaths as well, ready to follow their platoon leader forward through the breach or flee back down the tunnel to safety. That call rested squarely on Horne. It was his burden to bear. It was one he had unknowingly taken on the day he accepted his commission as an officer in the Virginia National Guard. Back then he hadn't given much thought to what that commitment really entailed. It wasn't until this moment that he appreciated just how heavy the golden bar of a second lieutenant could be. The fate of the men crouching in the dark tunnel behind him rested in his hands. The success or failure of their mission also hinged upon what he did or failed to do. This dual responsibility, men and mission, is the crux of the dilemma every combat arms officer faces at a moment like this. To go forth and execute his assigned duties requires that he place the soldiers that have been entrusted to his care into harm's way. He must be willing and ready to sacrifice any or all of them in order to achieve a goal that has been handed down to him by his superiors. Every decision he made in the next few minutes, including the simplest one such as just how far he needed to push the cabinet before him away from the passage, carried with it consequences that he did not have time to contemplate.

Wiping away the sweat streaming down his face, Horne once more put his shoulder up against the cabinet and leaned into it ever so carefully. Only when he figured that there was enough room to squeeze by it did he turned to Rendell and the others. "Get ready, boys. Here we go." Behind him the Guardsmen selected to go in behind him screwed up their courage, tightened their grips on their weapons, and waited their turn.

Slowly, cautiously, Horne made his way over the last of the stones that had concealed the passage from the tunnel and into the vault. Standing up in the narrow space behind the storage cabinet and the wall he eased his head around the corner. They had definitely made their way into the castle's underground chambers. The cut of the stones used to line the walls he was able to see as well as the barrel ceiling above all conformed to what Kinkade had described in his notes. What did not fit were the modern overhead light fixtures linked in series by exposed steel conduit. Nor did the assortment of cardboard boxes and wooden crates that filled the vault he was in match anything that one would expect to find in an abandoned medieval castle. They were definitely onto something, Horne concluded. But what?

Pulling his head back he took a moment as he tried to figure out just how far they would need to go in order to confirm that this was in fact a biowarfare lab. To him boxes with Arabic scrawl that he could not read were not conclusive evidence. He could ask the Israeli with them to come forward and translate the writing on the boxes, but that would do them no good later. They needed to bring back something that was so irrefutable that even a panty-waisted congressional liberal could not ignore. Resting the back of his helmet against the cabinet, Horne closed his eyes and took a deep breath. When he opened them, he found himself staring into Rendell's eyes. Poised within the passage leading into the chamber, the leader of his third squad was waiting to see what his platoon leader would do next.

Ollie Rendell understood what Horne was thinking. Like

his platoon leader he was torn between a compelling desire
to back away now while they could do so without detection
and an urge to press on until they found something that
would fulfill their mission's primary goal. Were it not for
the haunting image of an empty cot back in his squad's
tent, Rendell would have reached out, grabbed his platoon
leader's flak vest, and pulled him back into the tunnel.

Having decided that they were committed, Horne turned
away from Rendell as he prepared to leave the relative
safety of the storage cabinet. After making sure that the
vault he was in was empty, he slowly stepped out into the
room. With his rifle held at the ready, he made his way
along the side wall off to his right, hugging it as best he
could. The low, curved barrel ceiling as well as the boxes
that were scattered about on the floor made this difficult.
Behind him Ollie Rendell emerged from the passage,
moved around the cabinet, and paused as soon as he was in
a position from which he could cover his platoon leader.
One by one the men selected to go with him reluctantly
inched their way forward, watching and listening to everything that was going on up ahead.

The vault Horne found himself in was small, the size of
a modest bedroom measuring some ten feet by twelve. It
opened into a well-lit corridor opposite the wall he had
come through. Like the vault he was in the corridor had a
barrel ceiling, but one which was considerably higher. On
the opposite side of the corridor was another vault, a mirror image of the one they had broken into. None of this
came as a surprise to Horne. All was as Kinkade's notes
had described. All told there were two dozen vaults or storage chambers exactly like the one he was in facing each
other on either side of a main corridor. At one end there
was a large room, just under the castle's kitchen. At the
other a narrow passage leading up to the postern located in
the castle's southern wall. After getting his bearings,
Horne guessed that the passage to the kitchen was at the
end of the main corridor to his right. That would put the

exit leading to the postern, the one leading to the farm compound, somewhere down the corridor on the left. It was also clear to him that this particular vault was being used for nothing more than storage. Though he could be wrong, he suspected that the evidence he would need was in one of the other vaults. To confirm this one way or the other, he would need the Israeli to help him find the sort of documentation he suspected the folks in Washington were looking for.

Using hand and arm signals Horne motioned to Rendell to take up a position along the wall across from him. While Rendell was well on his way to doing this Horne gestured for Sucher to move over next to him as soon as he peeked out from behind the cabinet. That made Rainey, toting the squad automatic weapon or SAW, the next man out. When Rainey appeared, Horne signaled him to join him. If it became necessary, all Rainey would need to do in order to engage reinforcements coming down from the farm compound was drop down prone and scoot forward a bit into the main corridor.

The last man to emerge from behind the cabinet was Avner. He was not at all thrilled about being here. But he complied. Though this was an American operation and the attack that had prompted it had been directed against them, this lab was but a few kilometers from the borders of his nation, an easy walk that would take a healthy man less than an hour. He didn't need much imagination to appreciate that whatever the PLA was producing down here, much of it would find its way across that narrow strip of land.

When everyone was where he wanted them, Horne looked across the vault at Rendell. With his right hand he signaled as best he could that he was going to venture out into the corridor and search some of the other vaults. Rendell knew why his platoon leader was doing this. He understood the logic. That did nothing, however, to alleviate a dread that multiplied as they moved deeper into the underground complex.

Once more it was up to Horne to make the next move. Tapping Avner on the shoulder, Horne used his index finger to indicate that he was to follow. Then, with his back pressed against the wall, he slipped out into the corridor, around the corner, and into the next vault to the right. In all his life the Virginia schoolteacher had never experienced a more terrifying moment. Snapping his head about as he went Jack Horne scanned the room as he clutched his rifle at the ready should he happen to find anyone in it.

Though fortune continued to smile upon him he felt little relief as he continued to move swiftly and silently into the new vault. Unlike the one he had just left, this one was set up as an office. A desk with a computer monitor was butted up against the back wall. Next to him, along the same wall he was sliding along, was a table with a printer and several open boxes filled with files. Across the way was a massive stainless-steel refrigerator, the sort one would expect to see in the kitchen of a restaurant. This had to be it, he told himself. There had to be something in here that they could use as evidence.

Avner was also quick to appreciate this fact as soon as he joined Horne in the room. Without needing to be told he· flew by the American officer and began to leaf through the open boxes of files. When Horne was sure that they were safe for the moment he joined the search by making for the desk where he started pulling out drawers, searching for computer disks. Each time he came across one he took it and stuffed it in the cargo pockets of his pants before going on. Only belatedly did he notice that the handwritten labels on them were in German as well as Arabic. After riffling through the last drawer, he turned toward the refrigerator. He was tempted to open the door, to see what was inside it. He suspected he already knew. He also suspected that taking anything from it would be akin to pulling the pin of a grenade before stuffing it down the front of his trousers. Sensing that they had pressed their luck as far as they dared, he turned to Avner. "Well?"

The Israeli looked up from the box of files he had been inspecting and nodded. "More than enough," he whispered.

"Okay, let's . . ."

The sound of boots shuffling along the stone floor of the corridor suddenly filled the room. Ever so slowly, ever so carefully, Horne came about, faced the open end of the vault, and stared out into the corridor, easing his rifle up to the ready as he did so. To his horror he saw a Palestinian with an AK-47 slung under his shoulder moving into view from his right, slowly backing down the corridor toward the passage leading up to the farm compound. The man's full attention was focused on a spool he held in one hand while paying out a twin strand of wire from it as he shuffled his way down the corridor with his other. What he was doing did not matter. All that was important at the moment was that both he and Avner remain absolutely still.

In the next vault over Ollie Rendell had caught sight of the Palestinian backing up toward him before his platoon leader had. Having no means of warning him, Rendell found the only thing he could do was to bring his rifle up to his shoulder and train it on the man. The idea of dispatching the Palestinian with his knife crossed his mind as he watched the man draw nearer, tracking him in his sight as he did so. Rendell wondered if he could actually take out the Palestinian without stirring up a hornets' nest. In the end the deputy sheriff discarded the idea as being foolish. He was no commando. He was just a part-time soldier who was beginning to appreciate that he was out of his depth.

In the corridor the Palestinian continued on, oblivious to the danger all around him. Moving nothing but the eyes in his head, Horne watched the man pass on by. He could feel the beads of sweat as they rolled down off his forehead, over his brows, and into his eyes, burning them as it gathered about under his lower lid before continuing on across his cheeks. Horne found the terror that gripped him slowly fade as a deep-seated anger began to well up within him, an anger that came from being tormented like this. The urge to kill the man and put an end to his own anguish became acute, almost compelling.

Beside him Avner also shared a burning desire to strike out, to kill the Palestinian. The man he was watching was his enemy, an armed terrorist who wouldn't give a second thought to using the rifle slung over his shoulder to kill Israeli citizens. In Israeli's unending war with them it was rare for a soldier like Avner to actually see an armed foe this close. To pass up an opportunity to kill one was nothing less than a sin.

The Palestinian was well past the vault where Horne and Avner were and moving along in front of the one where the rest of the Americans were when the sound of another pair of boots moving down the corridor began to echo throughout the underground chambers. Unlike the shuffling of the Palestinian with the spool of wire, this new threat was coming on fast and with a purpose. By the time Jack Horne was able to ascertain that this new threat was headed their way, coming from the same direction that the Palestinian with the wire had come, the man was there, rounding the corner into the vault he was standing in. Stunned, the second Palestinian dropped the box he had been carrying in both hands and began to fumble about for the AK that was dangling from his right shoulder.

Jack Horne didn't need to assess the situation he now faced. There was but one solution to this problem, one correct answer. With an ease that belied his civilian background, the young Guard officer brought his rifle to bear, flipping its safety off as he did so before wrapping his index finger about the trigger. With his target no more than six feet away there was no need to bring his rifle up to his shoulder and take careful aim. Point and shoot was all that was required.

The Palestinian with the spool of wire never did understand what was going on. He saw his companion drop the box of explosives he was carrying and caught a sudden movement out of the corner of his eyes before he felt a searing pain like the sting of a bee pierce his back. That was all it took to end his life.

The fading echoes of gunshots reverberating off stone walls throughout the underground labyrinth left everyone stunned. Through the passage Ollie Rendell's men had opened and down the tunnel the Mamelukes had dug eight hundred years before the sharp crack of gunfire rippled, diminishing in volume but losing none of its distinct signature or significance.

Out in the orchard Nathan heard the faint echoes of small-arms fire. Seizing the hand mike from Weir, he mashed down the push to talk button. "All stations this net, all stations this net. Two Six is in contact. Execute suppressive fire now."

In the antivehicle ditch Gordon Grello didn't bother to reply. He thrust his arms forward as he pointed to his mortar teams. "Fire!"

Along the edge of the orchard facing the northern wall the Guardsmen with Terrance Putnam who had been eyeing the Palestinians in the castle's southwestern wall opened fire as soon as the Army captain with them gave permission to do so. While it was hard to tell if the first volley of small-arms fire took all of them out, no one had any doubt that the 40mm grenade lobbed up into the tower by a grenadier belonging to Allen Teeple's third platoon finished the job.

Within the ops center of Camp Lee, Hough took up a hand mike attached to a radio on the battalion net and ordered those units that had been standing by to move out. The roving patrol that had been wandering about the security zone in an effort to draw attention away from Nathan's platoon abandoned its deception mission and made for the beach where Alex Faucher waited. A quick response force standing by to reinforce Company A that had been mounted up and ready to roll charged through the gates of

Camp Lee as soon as the opening was wide enough for the lead Hummer to squeeze through. In the skies above, the crew of the AC-130 disengaged the safeties of their weapons as their pilot turned the nose of the lumbering aircraft toward the medieval castle that was, once more, the scene of a desperate battle.

Standing in the middle of the room he and Avner had searched, Jack Horne stared at the dead man at his feet. He had actually done that, he found himself thinking. He had killed a man. He found this all very strange, very, very strange. He wasn't a warrior. He was a teacher who had a reputation as being a pushover. He was a father who did not believe in spanking his own children. He wasn't a killer. It had been the right thing to do, he told himself. It was the only thing he could have done. But . . .

Avner had no trouble sorting out what was going on and responding appropriately. Seizing the box he had been leafing through, he pushed past Horne, into the corridor and back into the storage vault where the passage was. Within that passage Matt Garver also had no trouble responding to the situation that now faced his platoon. With all his might he gave the storage cabinet that still blocked direct access to the vault beyond out of the way, uncovering the breach that connected it to the tunnel. Glancing about the room, he took in the situation as best he could, stepping aside to allow Avner, burdened with the box of files, to duck back into the tunnel.

To his left he saw Ollie Rendell, pointing his weapon down the main corridor. In the corridor itself he saw the body of a Palestinian dressed in faded fatigues sprawled across the floor. What he didn't see was his platoon leader. "Ollie? Where's Jack?"

Rendell had been watching and waiting for his platoon leader to emerge from the vault he had gone into to search.

Only after Garver called out did the squad leader become concerned. "Jack? Are you okay?"

The sound of his name finally sliced through the mental fog that had momentarily left him all but paralyzed. Without another thought, Jack Horne stepped over the body before him, into the corridor. He was in the process of turning away and sprinting for the open passage Garver had cleared when the image of something to his right caused him to arrest his flight, spin about, and face back down the corridor once more.

To his horror Jack Horne saw another figure emerge from one of the other vaults farther down the corridor. Bringing his rifle up, Horne prepared to meet this new threat, a new danger to the safety of his men and the success of his mission. Were it not for the sudden realization that this new fair-skinned and blond-haired apparition was wearing a white lab tech's coat, Horne would have fired. He had no way of knowing that this new apparition was an unfortunate soul who had been selected by Kamel to remain behind to monitor experiments that were in progress. It was the incongruity of what he was seeing that stayed his hand, something keeping the Virginia schoolteacher from doing what he needed to do.

Behind him Ollie Rendell was confused and angered by his platoon leader's hesitation. Instinctively he knew that the man in the white coat was far more dangerous than either of the armed Palestinians had been. The Palestinians could only kill the Virginians who were physically there. The man in the white coat, armed with the armies of microorganisms that he and his coworkers were breeding, had the potential of striking down every man, woman, and child in Bedlow. Unable to fire because Horne was blocking his line of sight, the best Rendell could do was to plead with his platoon leader to act. "Jack, kill the bastard."

For a moment nothing seemed real to Horne. It was as if he were watching himself from a safe distance, as if the man with the rifle standing in the middle of the corridor were someone else. Horne didn't feel himself bring that rifle up to his shoulder. He didn't feel the coolness of the plastic stock against his cheek as he sighted down the barrel. He didn't feel the recoil of his weapon as it slammed into his shoulder after each shot. He saw all of this, he saw the effects his rounds had as they tore through the lab tech's coat, staining the crisp white material red. He watched unmoved as the lab tech tumbled over backward and onto the floor. Dumbfounded by what he had just done, Horne stood rooted to the spot. This time he paid for his hesitation.

Sam Rainey saw the new threat coming but could do little to save his platoon leader from it. The door at the far end of the corridor that led up to the farm compound above was thrown open, but only partially and in a manner that kept Rainey from seeing who was on the other side. Bringing his light machine gun up to his shoulder he flipped the safety off, bellowing out a warning as he did so. "Jack! Behind you!"

A volley of automatic fire erupted from the unseen assailants hidden by the steel door at the far end of the corridor, hitting Horne before he had a chance to react to Rainey's warning. Stunned by the sudden hail of 7.62mm slugs, the young officer dropped to his knees and toppled over facedown onto the stone floor. Hoping for the best Rainey began to return the fire, spraying the partially open door with a steady stream of fire. In a dazzling shower of sparks his rounds peppered the steel door but did nothing to stop the Palestinian security guards on the other side from firing another burst as Horne tried to push himself up off the floor.

Across from him Ollie Rendell saw his platoon leader go down and watched as Rainey cut loose with his machine gun. Peering around the corner in the direction of the door he quickly realized that Rainey's fire was having no effect. Seeing no other choice, he slung his own weapon over his shoulder, drew a grenade from its pouch on his combat vest.

Rainey saw what his squad leader was up to. He continued to fire until Rendell gave him a nod, his signal to Rainey to cease fire and allow him to sprint into the corridor and down to the door.

Luck was with the former deputy sheriff. The same angle of the door that had kept Rainey from getting a clear shot now protected Rendell as he raced toward it. As he drew near Rendell pulled the pin and let the arming spoon fly free. He held the live grenade until he was but a meter from the doorway and sure that he could not miss. Only then did Rendell toss it through the narrow opening. At the same time he reached out with his left hand, grabbed the door, and pushed it closed. His forward momentum was arrested when it slammed shut. Using his body, he kept the door closed until the muffled detonation of his grenade on the other side reverberated through the steel, bouncing him back and away from it. Only when he was satisfied that he had put an end to that threat did Rendell slide the bolt shut, push himself away from the door, and head back up the corridor.

Neither Matt Garver nor Paul Sucher had remained idle during all of this. Even before he heard the grenade detonate Sucher abandoned his post, dashing out into the corridor to Horne. Garver had planned to wait for Rendell to finish, but joined Sucher when he saw him take off. They both reached their platoon leader just as the grenade exploded.

Outside the tunnel entrance the company command net was alive with a flood of breathless reports. Keith Stone, facing the farm compound at the postern in the southern wall of the castle, alternated between informing Nathan that his men were taking fire from it and calling in corrections to Gordon Grello's mortar teams. Terrance Putnam cut in when he could to inform Nathan that additional

Palestinian fighters had taken up positions along the battlements on the western wall but were being held at bay by Allen Teeple's third platoon. At the breach through the wire Alex Faucher announced the arrival of the Humvees belonging to the roving patrol. And from Camp Lee, Russ Hough called to let Nathan know that the AC-130 gunship was on station.

Ignoring as best he could his mounting concerns with what was going on at the other end of the tunnel, Nathan turned to deal with those situations over which he had control. As soon as he heard that the AC-130 was available he knew right where its awesome firepower needed to go. Grabbing the radio from Ron Weir, he mashed the push-to-talk button. "Blue Three, this is Alpha Six. I need the gunship to support my Three Six along the southern wall. Target is the farm compound, over."

Hough acknowledged with a crisp "Wilco," as he turned to watch the Air Force liaison officer next to him relay Nathan's request. Overhead the lumbering AC-130 Specter gunship came around and took up position. Only when its pilot was confident that they were properly aligned to engage the designated target did he give the order to fire.

On the ground a momentary pause took hold as both Guardsmen and Palestinians in and around the castle ceased what they were doing. With awed silence they watched as the night sky was torn apart by streams of 20mm rounds slicing their way through the darkness from the heavens above it like an endless ribbon of fire. All were dumbstruck by the dazzling display of firepower they were witnessing, all but those Palestinians who had the misfortune of being on the receiving end of it. Even the men in Stone's platoon, watching the farm compound disappear in a hail of explosions from a safe distance, found themselves overwhelmed and more than a bit frightened by the wrath that the unseen aircraft was raining down before their very eyes. It is a sight few live to tell about. It is an experience even fewer who are on the receiving end survive.

At the tunnel entrance Nathan was listening to the radio while watching the gunship hammer the farm compound when Avner Navon suddenly emerged. Panting as he stumbled forward into the open, he clutched the box of files he had brought out with him for dear life. Nathan knew in an instant that they had succeeded. Grabbing Sean Zukanovic, he pointed to the Israeli. "Give him a hand."

The Guardsman tried to comply with this order by reaching out to seize the box from the exhausted Israeli. Avner, oblivious to anything but hanging on to his prize and still frenzied by his mad dash back down the tunnel, refused to let go. Bewildered, Zukanovic was all but knocked aside as the Israeli reservist continued to put as much distance as possible between himself and the tunnel he had just escaped from. Confused, the Guardsman turned to Nathan. When he saw the state the Israeli was in as he flew by him, Nathan yelled out to Zukanovic. "Stay with him. Grab someone else and get him to escort him down the hill."

He had no sooner uttered these words when Barry Lasner emerged from the tunnel. Turning toward him, Nathan reached out and took Lasner by the arm. "What the hell's going on?"

Sweating, breathing rapidly, and disoriented by his sudden return from the underworld, Lasner looked around for a moment before answering. "Jack's been hit," he finally blurted out. "They got Jack."

Lasner's words hit Nathan and all who heard them like a sharp punch to their stomachs, a numbing blow that stunned them. "How bad? Is he alive?"

Dropping down on his knees and bowing his head, Lasner did his best to respond as he gulped down mouthfuls of air. "He's alive . . . Matt's . . . Matt's got him. He's . . . right . . . right behind me."

Again Nathan took the hand mike from Weir to relay word across the company net.

* * *

At the breach in the fence Alex Faucher heard his commanding officer's report. Without having to give it any thought he turned to William Carney, the senior medic with him. "Jack Horne has been hit. Grab your stuff and let's go." Though the plan had been for the medics with the platoons to stabilize their wounded and then bring them down the hill to the collection point at the fence, Carney didn't bat an eye when Faucher ordered him to follow. Tapping another medic on the shoulder the three men gathered up gear and a stretcher before they took off at a dead run. Passing the mortar teams in the antivehicle ditch who were still busy firing away at the farm compound, Faucher and the medics didn't pause until they reached the road. They were about to cross when Faucher became aware of a vehicle somewhere off in the distance moving toward them at speed. Stopping, he threw his arm out to arrest the mad dash of the medics accompanying him while glancing down the road. As he listened he could clearly make out the sound of a truck's engine racing along through the night. Yet despite the clear line of sight he had down the narrow dirt road, he didn't see a hint of headlights. "Back into the ditch."

Carney was confused until he began to hear the noise Faucher was keying in on. In their mission briefing they had all been warned about the possibility of reinforcements coming in from a village to the north of the castle that intelligence suspected had strong ties to the PLA. Like his first sergeant, the senior medic guessed that this was exactly what they were hearing. Doing as he had been told, the senior medic backed away from the road, watching as Faucher turned to one of the men assigned to cover the road. "Give me that AT-4."

The man Faucher was speaking to handed over the lightweight multipurpose weapon, better known as a LAW, to his first sergeant. Based on a Swedish design, the AT-4 replaced the Vietnam era M-72 LAW as the Army's primary single-shot antitank weapon. Easing himself back up onto the shoulder of the road Faucher cradled the weapon in his arms as he waited for the approaching vehicle to come into sight.

In Faucher's opinion the chances that the vehicle barreling down on them was being driven by some hapless Palestinian who just happened to be tooling down this stretch of road in the middle of the night were just about nil. Between the mortar fire and the hellfire that the AC-130 was raining down on the farm compound the man driving the truck would have to be deaf and blind not to appreciate that something terrible was going on. This left Faucher convinced that the vehicle was the PLA's equivalent to his own battalion's ready response force.

When he finally caught sight of the blacked-out truck rounding a bend some two hundred meters from where he was sitting without slowing, the former fireman decided then and there that he had been right. Standing up, he calmly walked into the middle of the road, brought the AT-4 up to his shoulder, and took careful aim as if he did this sort of thing every day. By then the truck was but one hundred meters away from him. Satisfied with his aim, Faucher mashed down on the lever that served as a trigger and let the 84mm rocket fly.

The driver of the truck had no idea he was in danger until he was suddenly and unexpectedly blinded by a brilliant flash. By the time he realized what was happening, it was too late to do anything before the rocket slammed into the grill of his truck. The jet stream of molten metal formed by the warhead's shaped charge cut through the engine block of his truck like a hot knife through butter, severing fuel lines and igniting the engine oil.

Up ahead Faucher remained standing in the middle of the road, watching the truck career madly to the left and right before it rolled over onto its side. A dozen or so men who had been riding in its open cargo bay were sent flying through the air like rag dolls. From their positions in the ditch the Guardsmen Grello had stationed at the road as security opened fire on these hapless figures even as they rolled and tumbled about on the road, killing them before they could recover and make a nuisance of themselves. Only when he was sure that the situation was well in hand did Faucher call out to Carney who had been watching all of this from the ditch. Above the chatter of small-arms fire the company first sergeant yelled out to the medic in a voice that was shockingly calm and collected. "Okay, we can go now."

Warned by Nathan that the Israeli was headed his way with an escort Terrance Putnam greeted Avner. By then the adrenaline rush that had propelled him nonstop to this point was beginning to wear thin. Sensing that it was finally safe to do so, Avner dropped down on the ground behind the line of Guardsmen facing the castle's western wall as he took a moment to collect his wits and catch his breath. Despite his exhaustion he refused to relinquish the box of documents he was carrying. Not wanting to antagonize the frazzled Israeli and having more than enough to do already, Terrance Putnam let him be, though he made sure the two men Nathan had sent along stayed with him.

Several minutes went by before Nathan himself showed up at Putnam's position. He was accompanied by Ollie Rendell's squad. Like Avner before them they took refuge just down the slope of the hill behind their fellow Guardsmen. Paul Sucher and Gene Klauss, who had taken over carrying Jack Horne from Matt Garver, laid him on the ground so that the medic who had initially treated him at the entrance of the tunnel could check his work and prepare him for the trip down to the collection point. The bleeding from a wound in his right arm and another that had pierced his inner thigh of his left leg had slowed but not stopped, something that concerned the medic. He was about to recommend to Nathan that they call down the hill and ask for additional assistance when Alex Faucher and Bill Carney showed up.

After pausing a few seconds to watch the three medics set to work on Jack Horne, Nathan, Putnam, Faucher, and Rendell moved off to one side to assess their situation and determine what they needed to do next. By now all return fire from the farm compound had ceased, allowing Nathan to call for the mortars to lift their barrage and request that the AC-130 cease fire. The silence that followed was stunning, plunging the entire hill into an eerie stillness that was almost as unnerving as the firefight had been. When the two officers and two NCOs spoke they did so in low, hushed tones.

The first order of business was to determine just how much of a threat remained. No one was willing to venture a guess as to how many PLA fighters were still alive in the castle. Both Nathan and Putnam assumed that some had survived. "From what Lieutenant Horne said during the mission briefing," Nathan concluded, "those chambers could hold a lot of people."

Rendell had a different take on this. Having been down there he was fairly confident that none had survived his squad's brief foray into them. "I barred the steel door myself. And while Matt and Paul were dragging Jack out of the corridor I stood watch over them. From where I was I didn't see or hear a thing."

Nathan thought about this a moment. "Be that as it may, we can't take any chances. Until there's a thorough search of that place from top to bottom and everything in between we must assume that a threat still exists."

There was a pause as everyone nervously glanced at the man next to him, waiting for what they suspected would come next. Not having been directly involved in any of the fighting himself Putnam took on the task of asking the obvious. "Well, does that mean we go in?"

Nathan had been considering this option, weighing the pros and cons of doing so. His orders had allowed him a

large measure of discretion on this matter if contact with a
hostile force was made. Looking into the eyes of each of
the men around him, he tried to discern their thoughts
while reflecting upon his own. None of the men with him
made this easy. All returned his stare with a grimness that
hid all traces of emotion, one that communicated a willingness to carry out whatever task they were handed.

Still unsure of what to do, Nathan looked away, scanning the firing line along the edge of the orchard. When he
was ready he drew in a deep breath and began to deliver his
decision while staring through the rows of trees at the castle beyond. "We've accomplished our primary mission," he
announced firmly. "We have the evidence that we were sent
to secure. All the rat holes leading in and out are plugged,
making it impossible for anyone that is still in there to escape. The rest of the hill is secured, the situation is stable,
and help is on the way." Turning back to face the small
clutch of men gathered about him, Nathan stared directly
at Faucher, forcing himself to muster up a hint of a smile as
he did so. "This company has performed brilliantly. No
one could have asked for better. We'll hold our current positions and let the Rangers mop up when they get here."

Had his company commander made a statement such as
that as little as twenty-four hours prior Alex Faucher would
have taken great offense. He would have seen Nathan's decision as a slight, an indication that he had no confidence in
the Guardsmen he commanded. But things had changed.
He had changed. Faucher was also more than satisfied with
what his people had done. And like Nathan, he was ready
to hold what they had, count his blessings, and leave the
rest of the mission to the professionals.

Having made his decision, Nathan issued his orders.
Leaving Bill Carney and his medics to deal with Horne's
evacuation, Nathan instructed Faucher to remain on the hill
with Allen Teeple's third platoon. This freed up Terrance
Putnam, whom he sent around to where Matt Garver and
the balance of second platoon stood watch over the tunnel

entrance. Ollie Rendell and his squad were sent down the hill to escort the Israeli with the box of files as well as a handful of computer disks that had spilled out of Jack Horne's pockets while the medics had been working on him to link up with the waiting Humvees. Once they were back at Camp Lee, Rendell would be able to report in person to the battalion commander and fill him in on what he had seen within the underground chambers. Nathan announced that he would head over to where Keith Stone's first platoon maintained its vigilance around the farm compound to assess the situation there himself. When he was sure everyone understood their assigned tasks, he cautioned them to be alert, keep their people on their toes, and stay on the radio. He wanted to add some sort of witty saying or provide them with some suitable advice. But at the moment, he felt such words were unnecessary. His people knew what was expected of them. "Okay," he finally stated. "Make it so."

With that, the impromptu meeting on the hillside broke up as the four men scattered to carry out their assigned tasks.

CHAPTER 28

Arlington, Virginia

Taking a break from the round-robin of meetings he had been ducking in and out of all afternoon, Scott Dixon made for his private office. Ignoring the calls of his secretary and executive officer as he strolled by them he closed the door to his office behind him. This was his way of informing his personal staff that he did not want to be disturbed. Taking the hint, Dixon's staff settled back into their seats to wait until their boss was ready to deal with the next wave of panicked phone calls and emerging crisis.

Taking his time, Scott removed his blouse, draped it over the back of a chair at the small conference table, and loosened his tie before settling down in his seat. Propping his feet up unto his desk, he picked up the phone and paged his secretary. "Okay, Sarah, you can put that call I asked for through now."

As he waited for his call to weave its way through the dedicated military links, he took up a TV remote and pressed the on button, followed by the mute. The monitor across the room sprang to life, displaying a panel of grim-faced "experts" who were babbling nonstop as they stumbled over each other in an effort to present their own thoughts and speculations on what the news from the Middle East would mean to the nation and the world as a whole. Scott already knew how the predawn assault in the Palestinian area would affect national policy. He'd spent a fair portion of the morning overseeing the drafting of the Army's portion of that policy. Later, when he had the time to do so and needed a good laugh he would listen to what the Washington pundits and television talking heads had to say on the subject, wondering what they would have been saying if the true reasons for the raid had been leaked to them.

The decision to keep a lid on the true magnitude of the bullet the nation had collectively dodged troubled Scott. As the Israeli government had done several weeks before, those who decided such things in America opted to withhold the truth about the four deaths in Germany that had prompted the raid as well as what the Virginians had actually found during it. Scott understood the reasons behind this policy. By keeping the American people ignorant of the dangers that threatened them it kept the stock market from crashing, the consumers consuming, and the current administration in office. Just how wise this approach would prove if the truth did become known was hard to gauge, a concern that Scott was thankful he would not have to deal with. At the moment, he had a more pressing concern that required his full attention.

When the phone rang on his desk, Scott reached out and grabbed the receiver. "Well, cowboy. How's it hanging?"

In a tent some nine thousand miles away Nathan Dixon sat on a folding chair behind a rickety field desk in his stocking feet with nothing on but a T-shirt and his BDU pants. The sound of his father's voice brought a smile to his face. "I'm doing fine. A wee bit tired and in desperate need of a shower but otherwise all present and accounted for."

Now it was Scott's turn to smile. "Your mom will be glad to hear that."

"No doubt," Nathan reflected, recalling how she had always fretted whenever she knew that his father was involved in a major operation. "Tell Mom that she has nothing to worry about, that our little foray was a piece of cake."

Scott chuckled. "Yeah, right. I'm afraid that she's been there too many times before to believe that. Besides, you'll have a chance to tell her all about it yourself in a few weeks."

A frown darkened Nathan's face. "Oh, no. Don't tell me she's gotten herself another news gig and is coming over here to cover the story for herself."

"No, no, G.I. You're coming back here."

"Oh?"

Pleased to be the bearer of good news, Scott found he was unable to toy with Nathan as much as he had wanted to. "You're going to be getting your dream assignment."

Wanting to make sure that he clearly understood his father, Nathan sat up and cleared his throat. "Excuse me?"

"The first batch of Guard officers who were sent off for some additional training will be headed your way in two weeks to replace you wretched regular Army types. As of this morning, your name is on the top of the list to be pulled out and reassigned."

His father's announcement didn't elicit the sort of joy that he had once thought it would. Taking a moment, Nathan looked around the tent that served as his orderly room. It was filled with Guardsmen dressed in much the same way as he was. At his own desk, Alex Faucher was busy filling out a morning report to reflect the company's change in personnel status. Across the desk from him Ron Weir was using part of it to lay out pieces of his rifle as he cleaned them one by one. Seated on the floor in the corner the company medic was going through his medical bag, taking stock of what he needed to replace. In the center of the tent Gordon Grello was seated on a folding chair no different than Nathan's, busily composing an e-mail to his wife on a laptop computer balanced on his lap. This collection of men were more than members of his company. While it could be argued that they were not the best soldiers who had ever shouldered a musket, they were his. And that in turn meant he was part of their world, one that transcended the traditional bonds that are normally associated with military units.

On the other end of the line, Scott took Nathan's silence as a sign that he was overwhelmed by the joyous news.

This pleased the aging general. His son was a man now, all grown up and well on his way to staking out a name for himself in a profession that both men loved with a passion few understood. His ability to look out for the welfare of his son and do something for him was diminishing with each passing year. The idea that he had played a part in helping his son achieve a long sought after dream made Scott's day. Satisfied at hearing his son's voice and passing his news on, Scott decided this was a good place to bring their little chat to an end. "Well, Nate, duty calls. I'm sure you've got some loose ends on your end that are crying out for your attention as well."

Clearing his throat, Nathan took a moment to fight back an unexpected pang of regret. "Yeah, I do. Thanks for calling, Dad. And remember to tell Mom I said hello."

"Will do, son. Take care."

Finished, Scott hung up the phone. He looked across his clean, solid oak desk at the picture of his son. A smile lit his face until the phone on his desk rang. Taking a moment, he removed his feet from the desk as he allowed his normal "General Dixon" expression to reassert itself before picking up the receiver. On the other end his secretary informed him that his briefing of the Joint Chiefs had been moved up an hour. "Okay, Sarah, pass the word on to all those involved. Sound boots and saddles."

On the other side of the world Nathan remained seated at his desk for several minutes staring at the phone. He wanted to call Christina, to let her know that he was all right. He had no doubt that she would already know that. Still, neither of them would rest easy until each heard the other's voice. He had held off calling her, not because of the hour of the day back in the States, but rather because of her feelings concerning personal calls during normal duty hours. She felt embarrassed by Nathan's habit of peppering his conversation with sexually charged innuendos and suggestive language. She preferred to have him wait to call her when he was in the field until she was home and free to parry his crassness with her own brand of wit and adult charm.

His father's call had changed his mind. He was about to reach out and take up the receiver when his first sergeant rose up from his desk, looked across the room at him, and called out. "Hey, Captain. I hear they're fixing us a special breakfast over at the mess tent. Let's say you, me, and this motley collection here wander over there and see how it's coming along, sort of a recon in force of our own?"

Pulling his hand away from the phone, Nathan looked around the room at the eager faces that had turned toward him. With a wink, he returned his first sergeant's grin. "Alex, that's the best idea I've heard all morning. Why hell, I'll even pick up the tab."

Faucher grinned. "Good, 'cause we were sort of counting on that."

Turning, Faucher called out in his best first sergeant's voice. "You people have thirty seconds to wrap up whatever you're doin' and fall in for chow." No one had to be told twice.

EPILOGUE

Bedlow, Virginia

Not long after the trumpets faded and the last of the yellow ribbons had been taken down, Paul Sucher found himself driving down Bedlow's main street in the middle of the day. He was in no particular hurry to get to the new job his construction company was sending him to. Slowing his truck as he neared the small park in front of the city hall, he noticed several men gathered at the base of the memorial honoring the town's fallen sons. Pulling over to the curb, Sucher climbed out of his truck and crossed the street to join them.

Even from behind he knew who each of the men standing there were. Alex Faucher was wearing his dark blue windbreaker embossed with the name of the town's fire department. As he was on duty, Ollie Rendell was decked out in his brown and tan deputy sheriff's uniform. Between them, leaning on a cane he had not yet managed to ween himself off of, stood Jack Horne. All were standing there in silence, shoulder to shoulder staring at the new plaque that the town fathers had added to the memorial. Even after he had joined them no one spoke, no one turned to greet him. All stood lost in their own thoughts.

Eventually, Alex Faucher spoke up. "My father was already an old man when I was born. He didn't seem to have many friends, at least none that I ever met. He pretty much stayed to himself. The only reason he bothered coming to town was to visit here. I came with him whenever I could. He never told me why we were here. And I never thought to ask him. I just held his hand as he stood before the names of those who died in 1944, staring at them as if he were listening to some distant voices that I could not hear."

Paul Sucher slowly shook his head. "My granddad did the same thing every week after church. I always thought the old man was touched."

Lapsing back into silence, the four Guardsmen looked down at Brian McIntire's name, tacked onto the bottom of the long roll of names, each representing one of Bedlow's sons, men who had left behind everything they knew in order to serve a country they loved even more than life itself. "Well," Ollie Rendell finally stated dryly, "now it's our turn."

When each man was ready, he bowed his head before turning away to return to lives that would forever be marred by the brief yet violent interruption that their dedication to their community and way of life had visited upon them. Though none of them said it aloud, each shared the same thought before departing. "I'll see you next week, Brian. Till then, take care."

Mexico City, Mexico

The customs agent was taking his time going through the visitor's luggage. Ignoring the box of computer disks with handwritten labels in both German and Arabic, he chose instead to pick up the bag of oranges he had come across in the visitor's briefcase. Waving it before the foreigner, he did his best to sound official. "I am afraid that I must confiscate these. We do not allow fruit to be brought into the country like this."

Prepared for this the traveler reached into his pocket, pulled out a wad of American bills, and began to pull a fifty off the roll. "I had brought them along to eat during the flight. But I fell asleep before I was able to. I would appreciate it if you allowed me to keep them. They are very, very special to me."

While he thought the man was a fool to make a fuss over fruit that he could easily replace for a fraction of the amount he was offering him, the customs agent shrugged. Smiling, he placed his hand over the money the visitor had discreetly placed on the counter between them. "I think you will find that we are a friendly country, señor. Friendly and most accommodating."

Hammed Kamel returned the Mexican's smile as he carefully replaced the bag of oranges in his briefcase and began to gather up his belongings. "I appreciate your understanding." With that settled, he reclaimed the rest of his luggage and thanked the customs agent once more before disappearing into the crowded terminal.